CRODOR THE ANCIENT

CRODOR THE ANCIENT

The Elementalists
Book 2

Ephie & Celia Risho

CRODOR THE ANCIENT
The Elementalists, Book 2
Copyright © 2021 Ephie & Celia Risho

For more information: info@theelementalists.net

Cover Illustration © Stephan Martiniere
Developmental Editing/Line Editing: Ann Castro, AnnCastro Studio
Inside illustrations, maps, dragon symbol: Olena Bushana
Book & cover layout: Ephie Risho
Fonts used in book: Desire Pro; Minion Pro

Bozeman, Montana
ISBN (paperback): 978-1-7349741-3-3
ISBN (EPUB): 978-1-7349741-4-0
ISBN (hardcover) : 978-1-7349741-5-7
Library of Congress Control Number: 2021907377

First Edition

10 9 8 7 6 5 4 3 2 1

Dedication

Dedicated to explorers everywhere.
May you resist the temptation to ever stop discovering.

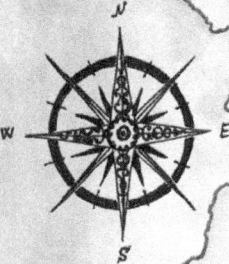

Seabrook
Sanford
Mira
Lorcaster
(elves)
Sage's Lookout
Goblins
Ballmore
Hamilton
Nocea
(elves)
Kindlemere
(dwarves)

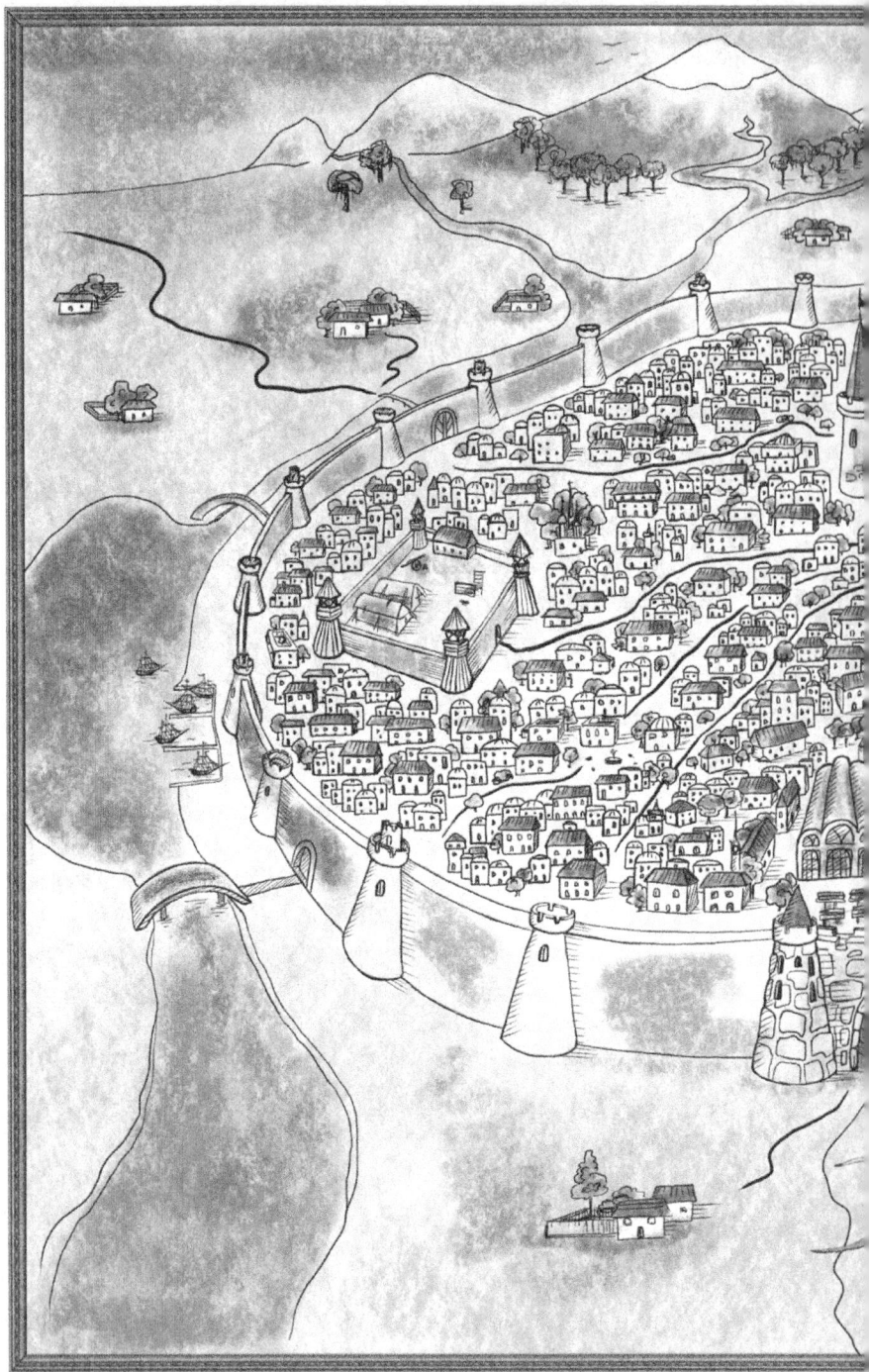

LUGO

CONTENTS

Chapter 1

An Army of Goblins

THE WIND RUSHED through Amber's hair, whipping it about wildly and stinging her eyes to tears. Far below, the dense forest whizzed by as the massive golden-red phoenix carefully flapped its wings, keeping her from falling off.

As they approached taller mountains, she used a single hand to tuck her hair into her black-and-bright-yellow striped wool hat. She briefly thought of Flurry, her pixie friend, who'd laughed at the hat a month ago before disappearing with all the other pixies near her hometown. Her brow furrowed. Would the pixies feel safe enough to come back now that she'd helped get rid of the fire danger from the phoenix?

Villages and towns appeared small no matter how large they actually were. She saw some specks that looked like they could be children playing with a dog and she smiled. It reminded her of the children she'd just parted with in her hometown of Seabrook.

A gigantic mountain loomed on her right amidst plains and smaller hills—and just beyond it, a city with incredible stone walls and a castle with turrets. A huge river ran from the mountain down past the city and widened to a small lake filled with the sails of different types of ships.

Even from that great height, the city was impressive. That must be Lugo, she thought.

They circled the city once. Even as dots in the distance, the sheer number of people was overwhelming. How do they all live together like that? Do they all get along?

She pointed the phoenix toward Sage's mountain. Some dark shapes were moving in the plains to Amber's right, so she patted the phoenix's right side and turned to investigate.

The phoenix kept its wings spread, catching a warm air current. Amber patted him twice with both hands, and the bird dropped lower, giving her a better look.

Goblins! Five of them traveling together, focused, moving toward a nearby town. Where are they coming from? she wondered and turned eastward.

Other small groups came into view, traveling similarly. There was a clear pattern: they were all coming from a valley in the great mountains to the east. So she continued on.

The terrain changed from plains to foothills, and then to smaller mountains covered with trees. When the landscape turned into dense forest, it was hard to spot much, except for a large road that passed through the valley. Once in a while she would see a small group of three to eight creatures like the ones she'd seen traveling the road.

Curious and afraid of what she might find, she kept flying. She passed steep, snowcapped mountains, then somewhat shorter ones. Soon after the terrain turned back into foothills.

As the trees thinned, she noticed a much larger group of moving shapes in an open area. She double-patted the phoenix again to fly lower.

Close to a hundred goblins were moving together slowly over the plains, toward the main road through the mountains. They had portable canopies over their heads to protect them from the sun.

Amber dipped even lower to get a closer look. The ugly green creatures were pushing large carts and appeared well organized compared to the goblins she'd seen before. Six much-taller goblins spread out among them, looking more menacing and powerful—and not as stupid-looking.

One of the taller goblins saw her and shouted something. A goblin grabbed a crossbow, pointed it at her, and let a bolt loose. The phoenix abruptly dodged it, causing Amber to feel like she was going to fall. Her heart stuck in her throat. She gripped the bird tightly and kicked it with her two feet.

The phoenix flapped its wings and rose up, with more bolts flying after them.

That was close! I can't get that low again. And what are those tall goblin-creatures? Not normal goblins, that's for sure.

She felt dread, realizing how difficult it would be to take on this massive group of goblins compared to the smaller ones they'd encountered before.

As the phoenix rose higher and higher, Amber's heart sank lower. There were even more dark moving forms in the distance. She urged the phoenix to head toward them, dreading what she might see.

It can't be. There can't be that many goblins.

Goblins followed by more goblins, and then more again. There didn't seem to be an end.

Thousands, Amber thought. There are thousands.

She did some math in her head: If there were around a hundred in that first group, then this group was about fifty times that size. Five thousand! And not just goblins. The tall, menacing goblin-creatures were spread throughout—but even worse, what she at first thought were large structures turned out to be two enormous giants.

She circled far above, not wanting to get too close. The ogre-like green giants stood at least five times higher than the tall goblins. Easily forty feet tall.

Immediately she started to calculate how far the creatures were from people: Depending on how fast a large number like this could travel . . . in a few days they could pass through the valley and reach the first villages. Nobody would survive. Then they could head for Lugo—even a city of that size wouldn't stand a chance.

Three dark-gray creatures rose from the mob and flapped toward her. From her height, they were hard to make out. But they were larger than imps and definitely heading her way. Gargoyles, perhaps?

She didn't want to wait around to find out. Lowering her head, she turned back toward the north.

As she passed over the thick forest of the mountainous countryside, she continued to see even more goblins—all traveling in smaller groups, less than five.

Then it hit her: These aren't just some random goblins. They're scouts.

Fifteen minutes later she saw the tall mountain with Sage's glass lookout tower. She circled around, waving to the people inside the tower as the phoenix let out a loud screech, then landed gracefully. Amber dismounted and motioned for the others to come over.

Theo and Basil climbed down the tower's ladder and approached the phoenix.

"You look like you just swallowed a live fish," Theo said happily. "Did Blazey do a flip for you too? That's what made *my* stomach turn." The phoenix came up to Theo, and he patted it gently. He and the phoenix had become instant best friends, thanks to Theo's elemental power of connecting with animals.

"No." Amber's face was pale. "Unfortunately, nothing so fun. It's a goblin army. And it's huge. Probably five thousand, plus giants and large-looking goblins who are leading them."

"Hobgoblins." Basil swallowed grimly. "Must be. They're taller and smarter—and usually lead goblins. I read about them in one of Sage's books just this morning."

"Yes, that sounds right. And they're sending scouts out across the land. It looks like they're heading toward our cities. I don't know how fast they're traveling, but as soon as that army decides to head out, they could get to Lugo in a week."

Basil squinted into the distance. "That sounds awful. And if they do head to Lugo, could it withstand an army that big?"

"No way." Theo furrowed his brow. "I've heard that Lugo has a big army, but a troop of five thousand goblins is huge. If they're planning on attacking our cities, they could destroy all of Arendon by midsummer."

They looked at each other seriously. Amber's throat tightened. "Why are they doing this?"

Theo scrunched his nose. "Do you think it has anything to do with that other wizard burning the villages down the coast?"

"All of this activity is marked on Sage's map," Basil said. "Even the goblins. Although I doubt Sage knew there were this many. But that means there's got to be a connection somehow. Amber, the phoenix could have burned down your town and others along the coast. This is the same. These goblins aren't gathering for fun. They're obviously up to no good."

Amber took a deep breath. "I was feeling so proud of saving my village. And now this. This . . . is impossible. Three young elementalists aren't going to do much."

They stood in silence for a moment, then Basil said, "We have to warn them at least. I know that won't do much to save them. I don't know. Come on, Theo. *You* come up with a plan. Sage isn't around to help this time."

A few weeks before, the old wizard had sent them on a quest to free the phoenix from the evil spell it was under. Not only had they freed the phoenix, the evil wizard who'd been controlling it was killed in the process. They had returned to the tower with his scepter hoping Sage could use it somehow—or tell them what to do with it. But after a couple of days, the friendly wizard was still missing, and the scepter sat useless, as did they.

Theo sighed. "We could certainly use another powerful ally, something bigger than Blazey perhaps."

Basil raised his eyebrows. "You mean you're considering my idea of finding that dragon and breaking the spell on it? According to Sage's map, it's way south of here."

Theo shrugged. "That's . . . not exactly what I was thinking. But . . . it's the only idea so far. Let's think on it a minute."

Basil scratched his head, then turned to Amber. "Well, how did it go with your folks? Were they happy to see you?"

Amber brightened. "You should've seen their faces when I showed up on Blazey! Everyone was hiding when I landed in the middle of the street. But when they realized it was me, my dad almost fell down in shock!"

Basil and Theo laughed, then Amber grew quiet. "They said it's been more of the same. I guess before we broke the spell on Blazey, he had returned and burnt down a building—but only one. The pixies are, of course, long gone . . . no sign of them at all. And more goblins have been spotted nearby, so everyone's scared to leave the village. But having the phoenix threat gone made people happy."

She gazed into the distance a moment. "My dad was really proud. After hugging me, he looked into my eyes and said, 'I always knew you would do great things, but this is really something.'"

"And I said, 'If you think *that's* something, watch this!' I tossed some seeds on the ground and made them grow into little plants. Then I had one of them make a beautiful white flower, which I plucked and handed to him."

Theo beamed at her. "That's awesome! What did he do?"

Her face lit up. "Well, his eyes got huge, like this. And his mouth was wide open. And after I handed him the flower, he actually staggered a bit!"

Theo laughed so hard, he snorted loudly—and that got them laughing even more.

Still smiling, Amber twirled a strand of hair in thought. "It's amazing to think that it was barely over a month ago when I left Seabrook, and how much we've changed."

"More has changed than us." Theo gazed into the distance toward the goblin army. "If I were playing Castles right now, I'd say we're down to three soldiers against a full enemy lineup. We might be able to find some help in Lugo, but there's no way that will be enough. I hate to say it, Basil, but your harebrained scheme to find that big red dragon might be the best idea we've tossed around so far."

"Of course." Basil smiled smugly. "You should take my advice more often."

Theo snickered. "Like your idea to ride Blazey onto the waves? But I'll give you this one."

They climbed up the lookout tower and checked the maps. The goblin army was southeast from them—and from Sage's markings, the dragon was far south, somewhere in the Eerie Mountains. Lugo, on the other hand, was due west, far out of the way.

As they looked at the plan more seriously, Amber wrung her hands. "This is impossible. Do either of you seriously think we can stop an army like that?"

"I agree." Theo pulled on the sleeve of his elegant white shirt. "Definitely not possible. Think about it. We know there are wizards behind this. If they could enchant all sorts of creatures to do their bidding and gather goblins, they're powerful. Too powerful for us to stop them."

Jaw set, Basil locked his palms onto the table and stared at his friends. "We can't just let that army trample the cities and villages. We have to at least warn them. We may not be able to stop it, but we can do something. Nobody else freed Blazey from the spell. We did it. And killed an evil wizard in the process. Don't give up before we've tried."

Silence rang in the room. Amber spoke first. "Yes, Basil. We'll do something. But the phoenix seems pretty small now, compared to this. Can anything we do make any difference?"

"I don't know," Basil said. "But we have to try."

Theo took a deep breath. "What are the next steps?"

Basil pointed out the window. "My vote is we warn Lugo and other villages on the way about the goblins, then head as fast as we can to find that dragon and see if we can break the spell on it. Who knows if it will help us like the phoenix has— but at least it won't work *with* the goblins!"

He brushed a long curl of hair out of his eyes and put his fists on his hips. "It's not a great plan, but it's a start. We could get to Lugo by tomorrow if we leave now.

Theo gazed out the window with pursed lips. "I don't think it'll stop the army. But warning everyone is a start. Amber? What do you think?"

Amber stood, looking at their horses tied to the trees in the shade below. "Searching for some random dragon feels like a long shot. But it's something. Better than staying here waiting for Sage."

The views from the enormous windows of Sage's lookout were magnificent. But as they gazed at the rocky mountains and plains beyond, they all began to think of the challenges ahead. They couldn't see the huge army without a telescope, but they knew their time was short. With or without Sage's help, they needed to act quickly.

Chapter 2

Merciless Smoke

THE THREE HORSES KICKED UP ROCKS and brushed against branches as they slowly traversed down the steep incline of Sage's lookout mountain.

Amber led the way on her golden horse and patted its neck. "We've been together six years now, Buttercup. I'll bet you never thought you'd be on an adventure like this!"

As they traveled, she continued to practice her newfound elemental powers over plants and trees.

Sage had said they needed to practice their gifts so they could grow in strength and skill—and he'd also said that they might be among those mentioned in an old prophecy about countering evil magical plans. Even though he hadn't shared the prophecy with them, they felt the urgency to improve quickly.

She mentally positioned herself among the trees and plants around her, feeling the deep resiliency of the shrubs growing out of sheer cliffs and the stability of the larger trees—giant firs and spruces—climbing up to the skies. With some of the smaller plants, she sensed more than just their roots, perceiving even the world around them.

She detected an animal hunting a smaller one in the bushes nearby. A fox and a squirrel perhaps. She wasn't entirely sure how she knew that, but somehow the plants gave her the feeling—so she chose to trust the impressions.

Amber also felt comfortable guiding the tree branches out of their way to create a natural path, so she went first. The trees and underbrush could be thick and impassible at first sight, but by the time Amber reached them, they'd parted and formed a perfect path for her and her companions.

Using her powers like that took a toll on her energy, whereas sensing things seemed to come easily. At one point, Amber practiced closing the branches back to their prior state after she and her friends had passed through. Not that she was worried about being followed—she just wanted to see how much she could do at once. She grew weary multitasking, though, and stopped after a few minutes.

One thing at a time, she thought—until I'm better at it.

An hour into their journey, the mountain grew less steep and their pace quickened.

Theo called out, "I found a deer!"

"Shall I hunt it?" Basil eagerly pulled the bow off his shoulder.

Theo furrowed his eyebrows. "No, I want to ask it the best way down."

Basil sighed. "We haven't eaten well in days."

"True." Theo paused. "But getting there quickly is more important. This deep-forest path is going slow."

Amber smirked. "I can make you a delicious salad later."

Basil put his bow back over his shoulder. "Yeah, yeah. No disrespect, but can you make something substantial? Can you find potatoes out here?"

Amber shook her head. "No, but if we get to the first village soon, they'll probably have something for us."

The idea of real food spurred them on, and they followed the deer down a perfect deer-path, winding down the mountain on stable ground and avoiding the more-steep sections as well as the thickest brush. As they walked through the thicker forest, the phoenix flew back and forth above them.

All at once, Amber sensed creatures trampling the brush a few hundred yards to their left.

"Theo!" she called. "Do you sense creatures that way?"

He frowned and stared intently into the forest. "I think it's goblins. Blazey!" He mentally reached out to the phoenix. "Ok, Blazey is on his way. We'll find out soon enough."

They stood their horses silently and listened. There was a loud commotion in the distance—shouts and the clashing of metal. Then there was silence again. The three turned their horses in the direction of the noises.

Before long, they came upon the scene. There were four charred, dead goblins on the ground with the phoenix sitting nearby, watching them closely.

Nothing interesting stood out on the goblins, besides the fact that one had a pocket telescope of reasonable quality, which Basil picked up.

Amber examined the medallion around the neck of a goblin, then stood. "This was a search party. I saw groups like this fanned out from the army for a hundred miles."

Theo kicked the leg of one. "Well, if they were searching for something, they certainly found it! Not what they wanted to find, I bet." He grinned.

Amber couldn't help but smile back. If it weren't for Theo, she'd have been a lot more repulsed by the goblins.

"It certainly is nice having Blazey here." Basil walked over and patted the phoenix on the neck. "Not that I think we couldn't have handled these ugly guys."

As they mounted their horses and continued on their way, Blazey flew above them and disappeared again.

Basil turned to Amber. "Do you remember where the first village is?"

"Not exactly. I don't think it's too much farther, though. And I think . . ." She looked up at the sky. "Yes, we're still going in the right direction. Hey!" She turned back to Basil. "Why don't you climb one of these trees and use that spyglass?"

"Sure!" Basil dismounted and quickly scaled the tree with little effort, like it was second nature.

At first the branches were perfectly placed, but then the going became slower as he looked for strong branches that would get him above the tree line. Amber blinked tree-bark dust from her eyes as she peered up at him, then asked the tree to lower branches as well as lift the ones he was on.

Basil called down, "Thanks!" He sped to the top and stuck his head above the tree into the sunlight. "There's smoke! Toward the southeast."

He climbed down quickly. "If that's the village, it's on fire. There's a lot of smoke. It's not far from here. Let's go!"

The three climbed back onto their horses and galloped through the forest. Tree branches whipped at them, but Amber found the quickest path of least resistance. After ten minutes, they smelled a whiff of smoke.

"This is bad." Theo frowned. "This is really bad."

They rode until the smoke grew thick. It stung their eyes and stuck in their throats. Amber covered her face with her shirt, and Theo coughed.

"I got this one." Basil held his hands out and concentrated. A light breeze picked up, lifting the smoke in their area above the trees. In a few moments, a perfect non-smoky path led them straight toward the fire's source.

They continued more slowly, with Amber parting tree branches and Basil continuing to drive smoke out of the way. They wound through the trees to a large clearing completely obscured by smoke.

Basil breathed deeply and lifted his arms. The smoke swirled as it rose, dissipating slowly up into the atmosphere. A gentle breeze joined the swirl, blowing a wide path and revealing the charred remains of a house, still smoking and hot.

"Oh no!" Amber kicked Buttercup forward.

Fire still smoldered on some of the larger logs. There were no signs of household items, just a pile of black ash.

"Can you put the fires out, Basil?" Amber asked.

He focused, but the fire started getting bigger.

"No, Basil," Amber said. "Air makes fire grow. You need to take the air *away* from the fire to make it go out."

"Oh yeah." Basil's eyes darted sheepishly. "I knew that." He focused again. The smoldering embers on the logs immediately went out, and the three dismounted and approached the ruins. Most of the house was completely burnt to the ground, but they could make out the remains of a table, a mostly intact stone fireplace, and some odds and ends.

"Oh!" Theo sounded upset.

The others ran over quickly. A woman's body lay beneath one of the fallen logs. Her body was scorched and black.

Amber gasped and turned away, choking back tears. "We have to do something! Basil, can't you do something?"

Basil frowned, looking at the dead woman. He stood frozen, hands clenched.

Theo gestured to the wall of smoke surrounding them. "Basil! Wake up! You've got to lift this smoke and put out all the fires! What if there are people still in there!"

Basil gritted his teeth and raised his hands, running toward the wall of smoke. A huge gust of wind rolled in with him, clearing a path and dissipating some of the smoke.

"Come on!" Basil yelled, his eyes ablaze. He stood with legs apart, as if reaching from one direction and pushing to another. The wind picked up and whipped the smoke into a whirlwind, lifting it higher. The ruins around them became more visible—but dozens continued to smoke and flame.

As the air became breathable, the trio approached the next charred home, still on fire. Basil pushed the air away from it, extinguishing the fire. They quickly scanned the building for bodies or any other clue, then continued on their way.

They walked past another building burned to the ground, and then another. Every building they came across was completely destroyed.

It took them an hour of walking through the village before the smoke and fires were completely put out. The three travelers sat exhausted, covered in soot and dirt. They had found eighteen houses, all destroyed, and ten dead bodies, including one goblin.

"These people shouldn't have died." Amber shook her head sadly, wiping her hair out of her face and smudging black soot across her forehead. "We should have flown here on Blazey and warned them."

"But we didn't think to leave our horses," Basil said. "We didn't realize how bad it was. We can't blame ourselves."

"He's right." Theo patted her on the shoulder. "We're doing the best we can."

"But those goblins are still on the loose." Amber's eyes flared, and she smacked her palm. "There were eighteen houses, which means fifty or sixty people who survived are being chased by goblins right now."

Basil fidgeted with his sword hilt. "You're right, Amber. And we *can* do something about that. Theo, call Blazey over."

Theo nodded. "Right." He put his fingers up to his temples and closed his eyes. They stood in silence for a moment, then heard the phoenix's call. It slowly flapped its enormous wings, stirring up ashes everywhere as it landed next to them.

Amber and Theo shielded their eyes from the flying ash debris while Basil walked directly into it, controlling the air to swirl around him as he approached the phoenix. "I'm going. I can make the winds go in our favor, and I'm the best fighter."

"Be safe." Amber called. "We'll come as quickly as we can."

Basil nodded, then mounted the phoenix and kicked his heels. The phoenix instantly rose, and the winds picked up, sending the two of them flying toward the west.

Amber grabbed the reins of Basil's black horse and they galloped off in the same direction.

As they reached the plains, Amber kept an eye on the ground, following the tracks of the dozens of feet that recently had traveled before them. She guessed around fifty or so people and about a dozen goblins. But with so many tracks—including those of some horses—it was hard to tell.

They rode as fast as their horses would allow. After an hour, the horses grew tired, so they walked them for a bit to help the animals regain their strength.

Amber stared ahead with a fury in her eyes.

"How far out do you think they are?" Theo squinted.

"Not far now." Amber eyed the tracks again and looked back out into the distance.

Theo sighed. "That was hard—seeing those dead people."

Amber blinked back tears. "That could have been my village. Or yours, Theo. This is just the beginning. There are what, a dozen goblins? There's a whole army coming. They're not messing around. And we have magic. We need to do our part to save them."

"We are, right?" Theo fumbled with his blackened shirt sleeve.

"It's not enough. Obviously." She kicked Buttercup, and the beautiful horse sped into a gallop again.

It was only ten minutes of riding hard when they saw the shapes of people in the distance. Amber leaned in. "Come on, Buttercup!" They galloped faster until she could determine what they were up against.

About forty people were gathered behind Basil, the phoenix, and a few other men with pitch forks. There were ten to twelve goblins hiding behind rocks with crossbows, peeking and sending bolts every once in a while. They were split into two main groups, attacking the villagers from different angles.

After Amber and Theo slowed their horses, she noticed two bolts sticking out of the phoenix's scales. Poor Blazey! She stopped and calmed her horse. "Let's bring in some trouble!"

She focused on the tall grasses around the goblins, which thickened and wound up their legs. The goblins yelled and hacked at the growing grasses with their swords. Basil saw the distraction and dashed toward them with his sword drawn.

Three large hawks swooped in, and the goblins swung their swords wildly as the large birds clawed at their faces. The two with crossbows shot and missed. The goblins were so busy dealing with the entwining grasses and attacking hawks, they didn't notice Basil rushing toward them.

He swung his glowing sword and took out one goblin instantly. Two goblins drew their swords, and Basil stepped back. Even with attacking grasses and hawks against them, the goblins had a tactical advantage with large rocks they could hide behind. The two with crossbows loaded new bolts.

On the other side of the battle, Blazey charged in with flames emanating from his entire body and engulfed two goblins before they could react. A large hobgoblin with an arm shield, a long sword, and a crossbow ran toward the phoenix.

The hobgoblin blocked Blazey's attack and thrust with his long sword, stabbing into the phoenix's side. Blazey shrieked and stepped back, then breathed fire toward the hobgoblin.

The hobgoblin ducked and rolled, evading most of the fire blast, then aimed its crossbow and fired into the phoenix's neck. Blazey shrieked again and clawed at the short arrow. The fields all around them caught on fire and began to spread.

Amber pulled off her bow and drew an arrow in one fluid movement, releasing it toward the quick-moving hobgoblin. The arrow landed solidly into its side. The creature yelled and turned, spotting Amber. Its eyes, filled with hate, pierced through her.

It slowly raised its arm, pointed, then snarled. Even though she was forty yards away, Amber felt a chill run down her spine.

Seeing the tide turn, the three men with pitchforks ran toward Basil, who continued to swing wildly, keeping the goblins behind the rocks.

While Blazey tried pulling the bolt out of his neck, the hobgoblin and two other goblins ran in. The phoenix leaped back and spit fire. The hobgoblin shouted something in its guttural language and moved so the phoenix was between it and Amber.

Amber focused on making the grass grow thick around the goblins and drew another arrow aimed at the hobgoblin—but Blazey was in the way. He reared up, lifting his wings to flap and blow back the goblins, then blew fire again.

One of the goblins was directly in the path of the fire and exploded into flames. The hobgoblin took the opportunity to attack, its sword slightly penetrating the phoenix's chest.

Blazey had had enough. His scales shimmered brightly and began to look like molten lava. One of his claws raked the arm of the hobgoblin as it attacked again with its sword.

Amber continued to aim an arrow, waiting for an open moment.

Then suddenly Blazey earned his namesake and exploded. A burst of fire engulfed the area, burning everything within twenty feet. A deep-red fire, blue at its core. No goblin could live through that.

Remaining calm, Amber shifted her attention from the phoenix to Basil. On the other side of the battle, the three men with pitchforks were just joining him behind a large rock. One goblin was separated from the group, swatting and yelling at swooping hawks out in the field. Four others squatted behind the large rocks, waiting for an open opportunity.

She drew an arrow and shot through the tall grass into a goblin, dropping it. Another one whipped toward her, took aim with its crossbow, and let a bolt fly.

"Aaah!" She tried to dodge, but the bolt landed in her left shoulder and she fell off Buttercup.

Theo drew his bow and squinted, but the distance and tall grass were too difficult for him. His eyes darted around, looking for ideas, then he focused back on the hawks. Were there other animals nearby?

Basil yelled at the men. "As one! Hold your pitchforks out together!" The men gathered near each other and pointed their pitchforks as a group, taking a step together toward the goblins.

The goblins snarled and tried attacking the pitchforks with their swords, but when one man would drop back, the other two fighters would be there jabbing forward.

A small whirlwind formed, blowing straight into the goblins. The grass whacked them in their arms and faces.

With the goblins distracted, Basil climbed the rocks and leaped. His sword sank into the chest of the nearest goblin, and it fell to the ground.

He wrenched his sword free and blocked a blow from another one just in time. But one of them let a crossbow bolt loose into Basil's side at short range. The bolt sank in halfway, and he cried out, grabbing it with his free hand.

Thankfully, one of the men with pitchforks took a risk and climbed over the rocks, stabbing the goblin. The creature dropped instantly, leaving only one goblin standing.

The last goblin swung its sword toward Basil, who parried with his sword weakly, stumbling back as he held his side with his other hand. The goblin attacked again and again, driving Basil back.

Amber's shoulder was in tremendous pain, but she gritted her teeth and stood to help. Her bow was strewn somewhere in the tall grass, so she focused on the grass around the goblin's feet, trying to see if she could hold it in place.

The grass entwined up the goblin's legs, but the creature kicked free easily.

Amber paused her attack, suddenly remembering a time when her older sister, Kirsten, had showed her how to use grass to make a rope, saying that anything can be made stronger in a braid. An image flashed of them braiding a grass rope and using it to swing across a creek.

Amber got to it—her powers working quicker than ever. All along the goblin's feet, the grasses braided themselves. They entwined quickly and with incredible strength, then wrapped themselves up and around the goblin's legs.

The goblin gurgled and looked down. This time it couldn't kick its feet free—it had to use a sword. As soon as it started swinging its sword at the grass, Basil leaped forward with his sword, and the goblin dropped to the ground.

No more goblins were visible, and the field was still.

Amber scrambled for her bow and arrows, notching one at the ready. She wavered a moment, her shoulder screaming in pain, but she held firm and scanned the area. Had they taken down all the goblins?

The field remained quiet, with fires starting to pick up and goblins lying all over.

Suddenly there was a whistling sound as a bolt went flying through the air and grazed Basil's neck. He screamed and fell to the ground.

Amber quickly searched where the bolt had come from. There! A goblin was ducking behind a rock. Without a thought, she released the arrow. It landed straight and true, dropping the goblin instantly.

There was an eerie silence. Everyone breathed heavily and looked around. Goblin bodies were everywhere. Basil, Amber, and three villagers had serious injuries. The fields were on fire and spreading dangerously. One last goblin ran around in the field ducking from hawks that pecked at its head.

She pulled the bow back and let an arrow fly. The goblin gurgled and dropped to the ground.

"Basil!" Amber lowered her bow and notched another arrow but didn't pull the string back. Her shoulder screamed in protest.

One of the villagers ran over and helped Basil to his feet. Theo nervously kicked his horse over to Basil and dismounted. The flames grew higher and spread into the plains.

"Basil, we need you to put out the fire." Theo quickly joined the villager and put his healing ring on Basil's neck, glancing around furtively at the goblins lying around them.

With Theo and the villager helping, Basil struggled over to the fire and clenched his fist, removing the air from it. It died down quickly, and he slumped to the ground. Theo peered at the scrape along Basil's neck from the crossbow bolt. Thankfully, it hadn't fully penetrated and was healing quickly with the power of the enchanted ring.

Then he saw the bolt sticking from Basil's side. "Oh no!"

He began putting the ring on it but withdrew his hand nervously. The bolt would have to come out first. He looked at the villager with pleading eyes, seeing him for the first time. The older man was wrinkled and friendly looking, with a charred light-brown beard. "Please. Can you pull it?"

The man nodded and pursed his lips, putting one hand on the bolt and one on Basil's body.

He gave a small tug and Basil groaned. "No. No. No."

The man looked Basil in the eyes. "You'll be alright. Take a deep breath with me."

The two breathed deeply together, and the man yanked.

"Ow!" Basil howled and held his side. Theo quickly put his hand on it, and Basil winced.

Amber slowly walked toward Theo, holding her bow loosely. There were rocks to hide behind all over the land, and she kept imagining one last goblin waiting for the right moment. Her left shoulder throbbed, and she felt like dropping the bow with every step. She glanced at the shoulder with a grimace. The enchanted protective cape from Sage had shifted in the battle, otherwise the bolt would have bounced off.

As Basil's face regained some color and Blazey's fires completely dimmed, she considered their situation. With the exception of Theo, they'd all taken significant injuries. The phoenix rose out of the ashes, looking uninjured and fresh. She watched it, wishing she could feel that renewed so easily.

Since leaving her home, she'd encountered goblins, trolls, a phoenix, and even a powerful wizard, but this conflict had resulted in the worst damage. These goblins were better trained—and with that hobgoblin and the crossbows, they were difficult even for Blazey.

She pictured the army she'd seen earlier that morning. Was the whole army full of well-trained goblins? She frowned. Was there *anything* that could counter a force that strong?

She felt a sudden, intense desire to go back home to her normal life.

What am I doing out here? I'm just a child.

Theo walked up to Amber and put his hand on her shoulder. "I'm going to pull the bolt out. Are you ready?"

She nodded and gritted her teeth.

"Ok, here goes!" He yanked. and the bolt slid out of her shoulder quickly.

"Aaaah!" She dug her fingernails into her palms.

He placed his hand over the wound and focused his energy on healing. The wound instantly closed up, and Amber relaxed, feeling a warm tingling sensation.

After a few minutes, Theo lifted his hand. "I'm going to heal the others now. I'll come back and give you more time when I know nobody is going to die."

She nodded and moved her arm around. It wasn't perfect. She could tell it had been injured, but it was amazing how much better she felt. A large hole in her clothing revealed a small scar, as if the injury had happened months earlier.

Moving her arm again, she closed her eyes, sensing the grasses moving in the gentle breeze. Did the grasses behind any rocks complain that goblins were hiding there? It felt safe and she relaxed, mind racing.

We need to make some decisions fast. All villages are in danger, but we can't warn them all ourselves. We need to get to Lugo as soon as possible.

There's no time to lose!

Chapter 3

A Tiny Bit of Advice

AS SOON AS BASIL AND AMBER WERE BETTER, they joined the village leaders to discuss their situation, while Theo healed other injured villagers.

After Basil and Amber explained about the nearby army and numerous goblin parties roaming the countryside, it quickly became clear that they should all make their way to Lugo immediately.

The villagers agreed that the three youths should go ahead of them to ride faster and warn the city as soon as possible. Now that they had some weapons from the goblins, they felt more confident—especially with the crossbows.

An old man with gray hair and a rugged, strong spirit gathered them before they mounted their horses. He lined them up and stood before each one, looking into their eyes purposefully. Then he stepped back and squinted. "You youngsters are important. We'd have died without you. Your powers are impressive, but your spirits are even more so. You didn't have to save us, but you did. You risked your lives."

Theo fidgeted with the strap to his splotchy horse, Butterfly, and glanced at Basil who glanced back and frowned.

The man sighed deeply, then continued. "We just lost a lot of our dear friends and family. This has been a hard day, and I don't think our lives will improve for a long time. People like me will probably have a difficult life till the end of our days. I don't have a home, I have a smaller family, and I have no idea what to do next. But now I have hope."

He pointed at each of them, one at a time. "Sometimes it's easy to lose track of folks like us. But we're important. More than you can imagine. Whatever happens to you next, remember us and remember what you're fighting for."

Amber blinked away tears and looked down. Her mind raced with what-if scenarios. What if they'd flown Blazey right from the start, to search ahead? They'd have seen the goblins and been able to do something about it before they burned down the village. What if they'd left two hours earlier? What if they hadn't waited around for Sage those last few days? How many more people were going to die? Did this man really have his hope in the right people—a bunch of youths from small villages themselves?

She looked around at the villagers gathering belongings and preparing for their journey to the city. Twice before, her townspeople had faced burning by the phoenix but were still mostly intact. These people had lost everything, yet had the spark of life in their eyes.

She suddenly felt very young and unqualified for these people to put their hope in her. A mere month earlier she'd been a regular villager like them. She glanced at Theo and Basil.

Basil stared at the villagers with a solemn expression, his face blackened with ash. He turned back to the older man. "You have my word—we will do our best to help."

Theo fiddled with his ring and stared down. Basil looked over and elbowed him with a smirk. "Come on, Theo. We got this. I'm sure the army at Lugo knows what to do with goblins and giants . . . and all-powerful evil wizards."

Theo shook his head. "A dragon sure would help right about now."

The three friends mounted their horses and galloped across the plains. Blazey took to the skies and flew above them, immediately becoming a dot in the distance. They couldn't carry on a conversation over the noise and speed of the galloping horses, so they became lost in their thoughts and observed details in the countryside.

The landscape was like nothing any of them had seen before. The wide-open spaces and tall grasses made it appear flat, yet there were slightly rolling hills and gullies and occasional large rocks bulging upward in odd places.

They stopped for dinner by a creek since it was getting late. Sitting around a small fire, Theo took a hearty bite of old, dried meat and sighed. "Should we ride through the night?"

"I don't know." Basil squinted at the sun setting directly where they were headed. "How much farther is it?"

Theo shook his head wearily. "You must know, Amber. You were just riding Blazey this morning over the city."

Amber felt her eyes drooping and stared at the fire. "I don't know. These fields all look the same from up there. But there are goblins everywhere now. And they like the night more than the day. If we press on, we might run into some."

"I can ride Blazey and find out," Basil offered. Theo and Amber nodded their heads, so Basil put on a warmer jacket and walked over to Blazey.

The phoenix lowered his head for Basil to climb on, and the two of them disappeared into the sunset.

The two stared at the speck disappearing into the distance. Finally, Theo broke the silence. "I wonder what the words of that prophecy are and how we can find out what it is."

"Yeah." Amber twirled her hair absentmindedly. "I wish I could put more faith in it. Sage didn't seem entirely convinced it was about us. It sure would help to know more. Wouldn't it be amazing if it *is* about us? That would make me feel ... I don't know ... more important, anyway. Like maybe we can actually make a difference here."

"Exactly." Theo poked the fire with a long stick. "I keep thinking—what if it turns out we're just a few lucky kids who happened to meet each other randomly? Or was it really fate that brought us together? Is there something going on outside of us that's keeping us safe? Because I'll tell you what ... " He looked at her shoulder where the shirt was torn open from the bolt. "It's pretty amazing we're all still alive."

"True." She watched some embers throb and fade, then blew on them so they grew bright again.

Theo sighed. "This adventuring stuff scares me every time we run into trouble. When I was little, my dog just up and disappeared one day. I cried for months. I don't know what I'd do if I lost you or Basil."

Amber looked him in the eyes, then back down at the fire. "For me, I guess I just don't think about it. I'm the youngest in the family, and always felt kind of alone—like I always had to take care of myself. This is the closest I've ever been to anyone, actually. You guys are the best."

Theo gave a wry smile and fluffed up his collar. "Well, if you must say so, I do think I'm pretty swell myself."

She laughed. "That prophecy . . . Didn't Sage mention it included *all* the elemental powers? There are six, right? Does that mean there are more people we need to connect with?"

"Hmm." Theo scratched his head. "That's an interesting question. I'll bet there are lots of books and scrolls in Lugo. Maybe we can learn more there. Did Sage say anything about when the prophecy was given?"

"No. But he did say it was old. I wonder if it was before or after the Wizard War two hundred years ago. I got the impression it was after."

"That would help us pinpoint where to look." Theo sighed. "Otherwise it's like looking for a needle in a haystack. We'll never find anything."

Amber glanced up and noticed stars. "Riding in this won't be safe. There are so many unexpected dips and rocks, we'd probably hurt ourselves anyway."

"True." Theo looked up, just as they heard a familiar screech in the distance. He concentrated, letting Blazey know their exact whereabouts. Half a minute later, the large phoenix came flapping from above and landed gracefully in the grass nearby.

Basil leaped off. "It's not terribly far, but I'm thinking we should try for it in the morning. I had a thought to fly in on Blazey, but then I wondered if they'd shoot us out of the sky—with all the stuff going on. So, I'm thinking we should just walk in together. There's a big road only an hour's ride from here that leads right to it. We'll make much better time once we get off this rough countryside."

Amber and Theo agreed, then they rolled out their beds for the night.

Amber lay her head down thankfully, gazing up at the dark sky. "The stars look exactly the same as they do in my hometown, but there's more here with the wider view. I've never seen some of these constellations before."

"Oh yeah." Theo perked up. "Look over there." He pointed toward the horizon. "Those are all new to me too. How much more is out there that we've never seen before?"

They watched the stars quietly for a while, thinking of prophecies and the sheer enormity of undiscovered things.

✳ ✳ ✳

Amber awoke with a start and looked around. Something didn't feel right. She stood up. The day was just beginning—the first light peeking over the distant hills.

Basil and Blazey were still lying asleep, but Theo was missing. She walked over to Buttercup and mounted her to get a better view. Theo was nowhere to be seen. A strange pit formed in her stomach. What if Theo was hurt or gone? She took a breath to calm herself.

Wild grasses covered the landscape around them, with the occasional tree in the distance. She closed her eyes—what could she sense from the grasses? All at once she felt Theo's presence, crawling through the grass.

What's he doing? She shrugged her shoulders. Probably not a big deal. She went back to the camp to pack up and prepare some breakfast. By the time Basil was awake and packing, Theo came back with a large grin and his hand behind his back.

"What's up?" Basil turned to him from his saddlebags. "You look like you're hiding something."

Theo moved from foot to foot excitedly. "Yep." He pulled his hand out to reveal a tiny pixie, her wings sparkling in the new sun. She was a cute little fairy, with large brown eyes and long blonde hair. Her tiny outfit—a mix of browns and yellows—looked perfectly tailored yet practical, with a tiny sword on her side.

"Hey! How'd you find her?" Amber asked.

"My powers don't work with pixies. But she was riding a sparrow over our camp this morning, and I got a sense from the bird."

"Riding a sparrow?" She looked at the pixie curiously. "Why weren't you flying?"

The tiny pixie spoke in a high-pitched voice. "We pixies of the plains have long distances we like to go, and our wings would get tired quickly. You're probably more familiar with our relatives in the forest."

Amber nodded. "Yes, that's right. I've never seen a pixie flying on a bird."

"Until now." The tiny pixie proudly put her hands on her hips. With her sword she looked almost as if she might appear daunting to someone or some thing. But to what, Amber was uncertain.

"Her name is Lila," Theo said. "And she has news for us."

"Yes, I do." The cute pixie folded her arms. "We've had a lot of visitors these last few weeks. You're only some of them." She looked at them smugly.

"What kind of visitors?" Amber asked.

"Yes, it's very interesting, isn't it?" Lila looked proud.

Amber remembered her techniques talking to the pixies in her hometown. You have to make them feel special, she thought. Make them feel like they're doing you a tremendous service.

She cleared her throat. "You pixies have all the best knowledge. Even back in my home village, we always appreciate when the pixies share their understanding with us."

Lila grinned happily. "Well, well. That's not a surprise."

After pausing to ensure she had everyone's full attention, the pixie unfolded her arms and began gesturing grandly. "There have been less humans and lots more goblins than we've seen in a long time. But that's not all." She paused dramatically. "Not long ago, there was a griffin through these parts—and after that, a dragon!"

She waited as if expecting a response, to which Amber said, "Oh my."

Lila continued. "Yes, a dragon is back! It's a large red dragon, and it was around here only two days ago."

"Really?" Amber cocked her head and looked at Theo who was nodding emphatically. "What do you know about it?"

"Well, we think it's Crodor the Ancient. He has a great lair in the Eerie Mountains and hasn't been seen in these parts for over twenty years."

"Do tell." Amber was now truly interested. "Do you have any idea why he's come back? Or all of the creatures, for that matter."

"Oh, yes. Our people know why." She looked at them and folded her arms proudly, waiting.

"Um . . ." Amber stammered. "Your people are very impressive, with all your knowledge. Can you tell us? We'd be ever-grateful to you."

Lila bowed. "Of course. It would be my pleasure." They eagerly leaned in closer.

"We pixies know that one hundred and seventy-nine years ago there was a time just like this where all the creatures of the world were stirred against the civilized people— humans, elves, and dwarves alike. The troubles began with powerful spells by some evil wizards."

She hunched forward and tried to look mysterious, which was hard for such a harmless, cute pixie. "Back in those days, the wizards were searching for the Great Stone Tower. And we think that's what they're looking for again!"

"Where is this Great Stone Tower?" Amber asked.

"I can't tell you that, of course! No one but our people can know. I'm certain our secret is what saved us last time!"

"Of course." Amber looked down, disappointed. "It must be by the great sea."

"No," Lila said. "I won't fall for that! I'm not going to tell you where—but I will tell you this." She looked at them carefully. "We pixies have a lot to lose if the evil creatures win the day. We need to turn Crodor back to our side, like before. We can tell he's under an enchantment."

"That's what we thought! Good to know. That means the amulet will work. Is he a friendly dragon?"

Lila laughed. "No dragon is friendly. But Crodor can be reasoned with, which is more than most."

Basil cleared his throat. "If you can give us any other information about him, that would be helpful."

"Well . . ." Lila turned her head slightly. "We know he lives in a giant cave and the hole can be seen from above, not from the side. He also has a gigantic treasure. Oh, and one more thing. He likes peanut butter."

"What's that?"

"I don't know. But that's how the story goes."

Amber turned to Theo and Basil who shrugged.

"Anything else?" Amber asked.

"It's enough. Time to go." Lila let out a high-pitched whistle. A sparrow came fluttering from seemingly nowhere and landed on Theo's hand, next to her. "Good luck!" She mounted and flew off, quickly disappearing from sight.

"What a stroke of luck!" Basil grinned at Theo.

"Yeah!" Theo wiped his hands and went for the last biscuit by the fire. "Finding that pixie was really helpful. I felt it in my sleep—that sparrow circling overhead. Seemed like it wanted me to find her."

"I imagine *all* living creatures want us to stop this evil from happening." Amber gazed into the distance.

Theo grew thoughtful too. "Yes. All of creation—and all the elements."

✳ ✳ ✳

They were packed up and riding their horses in no time. As soon as they made it to the road, the going went much more quickly. Within two hours, they started seeing farms and people.

Blazey was flying above them. But as they got nearer, Theo called him down to walk next to them, so there would be no doubt he was with them. As soon as the giant phoenix was on the ground, people scattered and fled. But the three didn't want to waste time stopping to explain to every person they came across.

A large river came into view to their left, with a wide variety of ships from large to small coming and going toward the distant city. Some of the ship designs looked familiar to Amber, like the large sailing vessels she'd seen growing up in a sea town. But others looked exotic, with dozens of oars, ornate prows with figures on them, and colorful sails.

Lugo's gates and turrets became visible in the distance, with a small lake and an enormous snowcapped mountain far behind the city. As they got nearer, the city's massive size awed them. White flags with a red-and-gold griffin emblem flew at the top of every tower; the walls were a solid forty feet high.

Before they arrived at the gate, a large group of soldiers on horses rode to meet them. The trio slowed their horses to a walk, making sure Blazey drew in his wings to look less menacing.

The soldiers wore chain-mail armor and helmets—and carried long swords at their sides. They wore white tabards, each having a single red-and-gold griffin emblem on its center. Their horses—twenty-four in all—were large breeds with armor of their own. One rider in the front carried a pole with a triangular flag at the top. It was white with the same picture of a griffin. The helmets had grates, so the youths could make out some of the faces but not much.

The riders slowed down, then the man in front took off his helmet. He had a long brown mustache that dangled far past his chin on either side. "What is your business here?" He spoke with authority as if he was used to being listened to immediately.

Theo gulped and couldn't say a word. Amber felt at a loss—there was so much they could say. But what should they say first?

Basil held his hands out. "We come bearing urgent news of a large goblin army approaching."

The man looked at the three of them, not once looking at the phoenix. "How large?" He twirled the right side of his long mustache. "And how close is it?"

"Should we talk about this here?" Basil gestured awkwardly to the other people in the vicinity who were starting to gather around in interest.

The man nodded and Basil went on. "We saw five thousand goblins, along with two large giants. Judging by the small groups of scouts and the hundred-strong group they sent ahead, we think they're heading this way. Once they start moving, it'll probably be one or two weeks before they arrive."

"And you know this because?"

"We rode our friend here and were able to see them from far above."

"I see." He turned to the man next to him and exchanged a few words quietly, then turned back to Basil. "You will come with us. And you may bring the phoenix—as long as it's safe?"

Theo whispered to Basil, "Safe? Blazey is anything but safe."

Basil smirked and nodded to the man.

The soldier gave them a piercing stare. "You're about to meet the most dangerous man in all of Arendon. I hope, for your sake, you're prepared."

Theo gulped. The soldiers turned, and the trio followed them through the large city gates.

Chapter 4

Fortress of the Queen

RYDER SLOWLY WALKED his splotchy horse Rocky along the well-beaten road toward Hamilton. He'd spent a day in Ballmore, the small city just after the mountain pass beyond Lugo. From the scattered reports he'd received, there was more goblin activity just outside the mountains, a little way north of Hamilton. When he mentioned he was heading to Hamilton, news spread quickly and many people passed him letters for loved ones, hoping they were still there.

The poor village of Hamilton had been mostly evacuated because of the numerous goblins showing up in larger and larger numbers. He hoped some people had held out, so he could find one last safe haven before venturing to the evil center of activity.

What was even more interesting than the goblin activity was learning that the ancient fortress used by the evil wizards two hundred years earlier was located a mere four miles away.

He had a moment of indecision—should he walk Rocky slowly to be ready for attacks or gallop as fast as possible? Galloping would potentially run straight into danger. But in his experience, when he rode fast, he could pass danger quickly without giving adversaries enough time to react.

Instinctively, he kicked his horse forward to a run. Better to get to Hamilton in one day and get to safety, then strategize his next plan. As the countryside passed by quickly, he thought through his next steps.

From what the quirky scholar Chandler had said, goblins didn't come out of their homes without a reason—so wizards were probably behind their new activity somehow, just as Amber had guessed. Chandler was holed up in Lugo trying to learn more. And he had seemed pretty excited that Ryder was taking the risk to do exploration on the ground.

Ryder was intent to work hard, learn some things, and stay alive in the process.

First thing: Make it safely to Hamilton and get some rest, then head to the place Chandler had marked on a map as the possible location of the evil wizards' fortress. That is, if it was still there. And perhaps spy on some goblins and see what they were up to—without getting killed.

He galloped across the rocky countryside, keeping a vigilant eye in every direction possible. The biggest mountains were behind him to his left, but the terrain still rolled up and down. And there were scattered trees and bushes all around, creating many places a goblin could hide or simply be out of view.

As expected, in the distance he saw five large squat-looking figures walking down the road. Goblins. Definitely goblins. He mentally calculated how far they were and his speed, then kicked Rocky forward faster. He grew close enough for them to pull out their swords and start ranting, at which point he lifted his hand, then clenched his fist and brought it down. The earth rippled underneath them, sending them sprawling to the left and to the right.

The goblins grunted as they tripped over themselves, landing in the trees and bushes near the road. He galloped past them, keeping an eye out for any other threats. He was far past them before they had time to react. Let's just hope it's always this easy, he thought.

He rode quickly and saw more goblins further ahead to his left, but quite a ways from the road. They spotted him—but far too late to do anything about it. He flew past a small sign with the words *HAMILTON 5 MILES*.

The next half hour passed by stressfully. Five more times he spotted goblins, although none as close as the first ones. The occasional farm along the way was deserted, and two were burned.

In the distance, the stone walls of Hamilton beckoned. The gate was up, which he hoped meant there were people safely inside. He grew close enough to see someone on the wall watching him. Before he got there, the large metal gates opened from the inside, just enough to let him pass through.

The gates closed behind him, and he breathed a sigh of relief. Safe again. For now. Half a dozen men looked at him curiously. One older man with a patchy beard recognized him and walked closer. "You bringin' mail—or news?"

"A bit of both. Although that's not why I'm here." Ryder patted Rocky as he dismounted and nodded at the man. "As far as the news, nothing pleasant. Goblins are everywhere. I saw seven groups of them between here and Ballmore."

One of the men spat on the ground and grumbled. "See, Greg? We should've left when we had the chance, with Jimmy."

"How many are still here?" Ryder peered down the empty, quiet streets. It was a small town, about the size of Seabrook where he grew up, but he still expected to see a few people.

"Not many." The old man gazed into the distance. "Goblins started showin' up two months ago. Just kept comin'. Farmers came here first, but as the buggers kept comin', people started leavin' here too. Don't think everyone made it to Ballmore. Now it's hard to decide—stay here and risk them attackin' the whole town or face 'em out there on the road. I'd say there are maybe a hundred or so still here. Definitely less than two hundred."

He looked at Ryder curiously. "And why you out here by yo'self, if you're not here primarily to deliver the mail?"

"I'm on a mission to learn more about what's going on. If we can find out why the goblins are crawling the whole countryside, maybe we can do something about it."

The old man nodded and pulled on his gray-and-black beard. "We'll put you up in my niece's house. They were some of the first to leave. You comin' back through after you check out the goblins? I'm sure there will be a lot of mail people'll want you to deliver to Ballmore."

"I don't know. Maybe not. Better get it to me in the morning before I leave. Do you know where the goblins are coming from?"

The old man scratched his beard. "No, but they're definitely from the mountains up north. The Ancares. You can see the mountains from here, in the distance." He squinted and pointed. "Just a few miles." He turned back with raised eyebrows. "Are you plannin' on goin' into their home? That seems likely to kill ya."

"Doubtful." Ryder shrugged his shoulders. "I'll play it safe. I'd like to stay alive."

"Good. Good." The old man walked Ryder to a small house down the street where he could also feed and quarter Rocky. Tomorrow would hopefully be a day of learning many things.

$$* * *$$

Ryder found a deer trail through the sparse forest and plains, then walked Rocky on foot, keeping alert eyes on the countryside. Every once in a while, he'd stop and put his hands on the ground, feeling the tremors of the goblins. At one point he guessed there were five out of sight to his left, and another eight or so in front of him. He took a route in between and continued toward the mountains.

Every few minutes he'd stop again to feel the earth, and although the going was slow, he safely made it to denser woods and the foothills of the mountains. The closer he got, the more intense the tremors grew—as if there weren't just a handful of goblins but hundreds gathered in one spot. He walked more cautiously, keeping the activity far to his right.

He made it to the mountain and figured he'd passed the busiest of the goblins. But he couldn't see through the thick trees, so he hiked up, looking for a vantage point to see them. After a few minutes, he came upon a clearing with rocks. He tramped up and around, then looked through an opening in the trees to view the valley below with a small spyglass.

His heart sank. There weren't hundreds of goblins—there were thousands. The goblins had canopies set up as far as he could see, and all were busy. Some were building weapons

while most were training in military techniques under taller hobgoblins. The shorter, dumber goblins were practicing crossbows, swords, and battle formations. Some were also were building large catapult-looking weapons.

The goblins were preparing for war.

He instantly did some calculations. They seemed to be at a size and preparedness level able to leave any day. And if the smaller goblins were scouts preparing the way, they were most likely headed to Ballmore, then Lugo. His mind raced. Should he rush back to Lugo immediately to warn them? Or should he continue to search for the old wizard fortress?

He watched the goblins, then decided he would explore the fortress first. The more information he could bring, the better. He unrolled the map Chandler had made him. He was right near the mountain where they thought the goblins lived, and the fortress was probably two mountains away. He'd have to keep his pace slow, checking the ground often, but he imagined he could get there in less than an hour.

He set off through the woods. No other goblins were around the entire way, which confirmed his theory that the others he'd seen were scouts for the human cities. They weren't heading into the deeper mountains at all.

Instead of going around the next mountain, he hiked to the top for a view. His heart sank for the second time that day. The fortress on the next mountain was absolutely occupied—and it was enormous. He pulled out his spyglass to see more detail.

Six white spires rose behind a massive white wall that looked perfectly crafted from his vantage point. The roofs of the spires were pointed and red, and the wall had turrets all around, with many safe lookout points.

Even from a mountain away, he could tell the castle was busy. People and creatures of some sort or another walked along the turrets. Behind the walls appeared to be a courtyard, some smaller buildings, and then the formidable castle.

Ryder had never seen anything like it, and he was tempted to panic. He took a calming breath and considered his options. The pure existence of the castle was good to know. Realizing that, he pulled out his map and drew a little castle on the mountain where it actually existed, close to where Chandler had guessed it would be.

Part of him wanted to find out about their plans—were they the cause of these goblins and other creatures coming out, as Amber thought?

But there was also something more. Real wizards . . . they were people like him. Nobody else he'd ever met had understood him. What if he could learn more about why he had powers and even how to use them better?

He walked Rocky down the mountain, continuing to pause every few minutes to feel the ground. The forest felt oddly normal, with such an amazing castle nearby. But then he remembered it had been there at least two hundred years, so of course the forest would grow up around it.

He reached the bottom of the valley between them and walked slowly, listening intently. He was searching for a good place to leave Rocky when the rustling of a moving creature sounded in the branches above him. He turned quickly to see a dark shape flying out of the tree, then he lost sight of it.

What was that? Too big to be a bird. Have I been discovered? Maybe I should just leave.

But he couldn't. He felt drawn to the castle more than ever, so close. He tied Rocky to a tree and approached the fortress. The tall red gates were shaped like a giant archway, blocking any view of what could be inside. Humans—as well as elves and other creatures—walked along the top of the wall. Some were dark and nasty looking with wings. Probably gargoyles, he guessed. Others were short, green, and ugly like goblins, only much skinnier.

He patted the short sword at his side to reassure himself, not that it would do him much good if he was discovered. Best idea would be to not be seen at all. He stayed hidden in some bushes and watched the castle, then carefully walked through the woods to the backside.

Since the castle was built into a mountain, the back of it was higher than the front. Ryder looked for another entrance but to no avail. Then he had an idea. He put his hands on the ground and sensed the earth, how it was shaped, how it formed into the castle above him. He began to get a mental picture of the walls and how the earth formed around them. And then he sensed what he was looking for—a tunnel under the ground that led into the castle.

He closed his eyes and breathed deeply. The tunnel went far below the earth, far beneath his very location. He walked through the woods slowly, making sure to stay out of view from the inhabitants on the wall.

Further into the valley, he wandered till he arrived at a rocky area and found what must be the opening. It was blocked by a large rock. He put his hand on it—he could have moved it with his power but figured there must be a way to open it. The rock was enormous, covering up a small lever hidden between two smaller rocks next to it. He reached his hand in, pulled it, and the rock released, opening to the tunnel behind.

Placing his hand on the tunnel wall, he sensed whether there were other living creatures inside. Silence. No tremors. Ryder stepped into the tunnel. He'd gone five minutes and lost nearly all light when he realized how foolish he was to travel underground without light. He closed his eyes. Somehow that was easier. He could sense the entire tunnel, every rock he could trip on and even which way would lead to the castle.

Twenty-five minutes in, he came to a bend and saw light in the distance. The tunnel split, then came to a T, where he turned left to follow the light. Voices sounded in the distance.

The light illuminated ancient runes inscribed along the walls of the tunnel. They had an other-worldly feeling to them, and he felt like he recognized them somehow. A chill ran down his spine. He ran his fingers along the grooves of the etchings as he continued slowly.

On his right he saw the source of light. A large tapestry hung over a narrow doorway with a small rip right at eye level.

Muffled voices came from the room, and he looked through the hole. Inside the spacious room, a cold-looking woman all in white stood talking to a friendly looking, brown-skinned man with a trimmed black beard, red cape, and a smart black-leather outfit. He looked as if he'd just been traveling. Both of them had small smooth sticks in their belts.

Ryder's heart skipped a beat. Wands! Wizards! He dared not move and slowed his breathing carefully, straining to hear their conversation.

The white woman with long flowing clothing spoke again: "What I'm asking you, Caster, is to try to use your imagination. If Lucio is truly gone, we'll need to get that scepter back. Who could have it? You've been with him closely these last months—what is your best guess?"

The man pursed his lips and shook his head. "It had to be a powerful wizard. The spell was obviously lifted from the phoenix—it killed both Lucio and his hippogriff. His wand was ruined in the flames and the scepter was taken."

"Where is the phoenix now?"

"I have no idea. It hasn't been back to its cave at all."

"I can't tell you how important it is that we keep to our plan. With Lucio gone, we'll need another element . . . and without the scepter, we'll need another way of leading the army." She sighed. "How are the pixies coming along? I need some good news."

"Excellent. They're half gone and headed south down the coast. It's obvious they're heading to the tower. And I have another idea which might help." He raised his eyebrows a couple times and smiled.

"Good. Good. You stay focused on them. Our army is nearly ready to attack. I've been told two weeks. What do you think about that timing?"

"Two weeks?" He shrugged. "I *might* be able to find the tower by then. But without Lucio and his scepter, that army will be harder to control. Are you sure you'll be able to get them to work together?"

She nodded, looking regal in her finely tailored outfit and thin white crown. "Most definitely. I have my means as well. You must remember. Some days I wonder what exactly you've learned from me these last years."

He smiled happily. "Oh. You know. All sorts of things."

She stared at him icily, and her eyes flashed black. "That will be all. And now, I have someone else I need to talk to."

"You bet, your majesty." He bowed and stood next to her patiently.

Ryder watched curiously as the woman pulled out her wand. "Illuminado!" She smiled and stared straight at him. His eyes grew wide, and he pulled back. She spoke soothingly. "No need to be afraid. I know you're here. We saw you this morning. Please, come in."

Ryder stood in shock. His feet felt glued to the ground as she strode over and lifted the tapestry, beckoning him to step into the room. He stared at her in panic. *This is the day I die.*

But then he took a step, and she didn't kill him. In fact, she smiled at him.

"I am Laticia, Queen of Westerlye, soon to be queen of all. And you are?"

"Um ... Ryder. I'm ... um ... just a normal person."

"Hardly." She smiled gently. "I see you have power, Ryder. Earth, I would guess. After all, how else would you have found our little secret passageway? That's quite a useful gift. I'm certain our elementalist mage with earth power could teach you many things to use it more skillfully. It takes years to master the elements."

Ryder stammered. "Wha— um ... Elementalist?"

"Why, yes. You see? You've had no one to teach you all these years—*imagine* what you could do if someone gave you a proper education! The elemental powers are your birthright. They're the best type of magic—requiring no wands, spells, or any outside magic."

"Yes. That sounds right." Ryder pulled on his jacket sleeve nervously. He glanced from Laticia to Caster and back again. "So ... you're not going to kill me?"

"Kill you? What a waste that would be. Why, you could be so helpful to our cause."

"Huh?" Ryder pivoted from foot to foot awkwardly.

"I would love to give you something as a token to show that I'm genuine." She went to a nearby cabinet, pulled a small blue stone from a drawer and put her hand out. When Ryder looked at it hesitantly, she gestured for him to take it. "This is an enchanted stone. The holder of this stone has deeper courage and insight. I think you'll find it quite helpful indeed."

He stood for a moment staring at it as she held it out. She continued, "I assume you came here seeking insight? The power in this stone will sharpen your senses so that you may discern the most difficult of situations. Consider it a token of trust—you see we have nothing to hide. Besides, deeper insight will only help your cause."

Ryder took the stone. It was smooth to the touch, and instantly he felt more confident—and more aware.

He suddenly noticed a dozen other details about the room he hadn't noticed before. Caster had dirty boots, as if he'd just been walking outside and also looked like he'd been riding—but not a horse. There were two other humans in the room standing by a door, and there was another smaller door to the side. There were eight tapestries in the room, each one with tremendous detail depicting elaborate scenes with creatures and magic. He was curious if they told one story or each told a separate story.

With his new boldness, he stared into the queen's eyes. "What are you doing with that big goblin army?"

"Ah, yes. A necessary evil for us to bring about times of greater peace and prosperity. You can't cook eggs unless you break them, as they say. The same is true of our wretched civilization. Let me ask you, Ryder, if you could have limitless power, what would you want?"

He thought for a moment. "What kind of power? Magic?" The queen nodded. He shifted his feet. "I'd try to get rid of suffering."

"Good. Good. Because in the state of things today, people are miserable, of course. Well, Ryder, what would you think if I told you we have a plan that would let you do that?"

"What do you mean?"

"We are on the cusp of releasing an incredible amount of power, and you could have a part in that. If you do, you could impact this entire world in whatever way you desire. Imagine the possibilities! You could help others, and at the same time, why not have some more comforts for yourself?"

"But—that army looks like it will take over the entire land."

"Possibly. But only for a time. It's not as if any of us wants *goblins* running things!" Caster laughed, and the queen smiled cheerfully. "Heavens, no. Let's call it a diversion. Goblins are wonderfully expendable. So different from wizards like us." She gestured to Caster and Ryder with open hands.

"What would you want me to do?"

"Simple. Join our team and begin learning how to use your powers better than ever."

Ryder paused for a moment in thought. She's right. I don't know anything about my powers. And what if she's telling the truth? What if I could become a powerful wizard like them? I could do far more for the world.

"What would be the first step?"

"Ah, whatever you'd like. You could help Caster find the pixie tower, perhaps. Or I could team you up with Mik to learn how to use your earth powers. What would you prefer?"

"I . . . I don't know." He fingered the stone, then put it in his pocket.

Although the idea of growing his elemental power was appealing, and the idea of gaining even more magical power was certainly enticing, Ryder felt deep down it would be a mistake. Too good to be true. It couldn't be true. They were releasing goblins on the world. There was no way that could be good. He needed to get back to Chandler and get more information. He needed to find Amber.

He stared at her, and the realization struck him. *If I say no, she might kill me. I need an answer that will convince her to let me go.* Clearing his throat, he said, "It's tempting. But I want time to think it through. Would it be ok if I consider my options?"

"Of course!" She smiled. "But do be aware, you don't want to be on the other side of our army, so do try to make a decision quickly."

Caster walked over and patted his shoulder. "I took a while to decide as well. You'll come around. Anyway, let me show you around the castle! You may as well leave through the front door." The wizard was cheerful and bright.

Ryder stood in shock and dumbly followed Caster through the castle. He couldn't believe he was still alive, let alone invited to join their forces. How could he even have considered it? They were doing evil things! Caster led him through a few hallways into the courtyard. A green elf stood at the gate watching. At Caster's signal, the elf gestured to two large men who opened the doors.

Ryder walked alone into the forest toward his horse in a complete daze. What had just happened? He needed to get back to Lugo. And fast. The army was going to be on the move in two weeks, and all their worries about wizards was true. Lugo would need help, and Ryder wasn't going to hide his powers any longer.

If he truly wanted to stop suffering, he could do it by helping people here and now. There was no time to lose.

Chapter 5

The Prophecy

SEEING THE SPRAWLING CITY OF LUGO from above on the back of Blazey had impressed Amber—but seeing it up close was even more amazing. The walls were massive and strong, designed for war. The stones looked aged, some seemed hundreds of years old, enormous, and weathered.

People were everywhere. Everyone had a place to go and was going there quickly. Amber tried looking people in the eyes, but most ignored her and continued on their way. Many were so wrapped up getting where they were going, they didn't even realize there was a giant phoenix walking down the street next to them.

One young man was making his way so urgently that he walked right into Blazey! He stood back and said, "Hey! Watch where you're going—" Then he realized what he was looking at. His eyes bulged, and he grabbed his hat and ran off in the other direction screaming. Amber, Theo, and Basil laughed.

And all the people were different from each other—not like in any of their towns where almost everyone had the same skin tone and dressed similarly. In a matter of seconds, they walked past a dark man with a long mustache wearing bright ornate reds and oranges and then past a pale, blonde woman wearing a stylish brown outfit with yellow frills.

Dozens more, all so different from each other, tightly packed the wide street. Most of them wore far more colorful clothing than those living in the other towns the youths had been to. It was as if each person was trying to outshine the person next to them.

The sides of the street were heavily lined with shaded stalls where people sold things. Shouting came from many of the stalls as people bargained for better prices.

And the smells! Exotic spices, animals, unusual perfumes, and horse manure. It was enough to make them grow dizzy trying to take it all in.

The youths rode their horses along with the soldiers escorting them in the front and back. From the higher vantage point, they could better see the types of items offered in the vendor stalls: jewelry, food, clothing, household items, and basic necessities.

There were some eccentric items they couldn't recognize—a big bronze pot with tubes coming out of it, a small spinning top that sparkled, and even a man with a glowing orb shouting that he was selling magical items.

The animals surprised them the most. There were the usual type of animals for sale like in their small villages—chickens, rabbits, dogs, and cats. But there also were snakes, turtles, lizards, and other wild animals. Even small dragon-looking creatures were being sold with a sign that read *APPROACH SLOWLY.*

After navigating a maze of crowded streets, the number of people started to thin out, replaced with more soldiers. Amber realized they weren't heading for the castle in the center of the city as she'd imagined—they were headed for a nearby building that seemed to be military related.

They strode through a set of large gates and past a sizable wall into what appeared to be a military training ground. Soldiers were running through drills and practicing with wooden swords. Basil watched them closely as he walked past.

When they arrived at a smaller building, the man who they'd spoken to earlier turned to them. "I'm afraid it'd be best if you leave the phoenix outside."

"Ok." Theo patted Blazey on the neck and mentally communicated that he should stay. "Would it be ok if we let him fly and get out of the city?"

"Let's wait on that. We wouldn't want it to get shot at," the soldier said sympathetically.

Theo sighed and gave another pat. The large creature sat down, causing a few people to look over nervously as the group walked inside.

A regal-looking man with gray hair and a mustache looked up from the table where he was sitting, gesturing for them to come in. He wore an elegant silver breastplate with an emblem—and had a scar running down his left cheek, from the temple down to his jawbone. It looked distinctive more than ugly, like a medal for bravery.

"Captain." He nodded, then turned to the three youths. "And these are?"

The man spoke respectfully and quickly. "General, these children claim to have seen an army of goblins headed this way. They also showed up at our gates with a phoenix."

"Indeed?" The General looked the children over. His face seemed to be in a permanent frown. "Well? Tell me more."

All three began to talk at once.

"There are evil wizards controlling the creatures—"

"Goblins are coming in the thousands—"

"We were flying our phoenix over the countryside—"

The General interrupted. "One at a time!"

The three looked at each other. Basil nodded and began speaking. "As I was saying, we've learned that there are wizards controlling all sorts of creatures with a powerful spell, and we think there might be more than one wizard. We broke the spell on the phoenix that we brought with us, using a counter-spell from our wizard friend, Sage. Then we flew over the countryside to see what's going on around the land."

Basil paused. The General nodded, and he continued. "Well, we've come across lots of goblins and even some trolls, but then we saw an army—about two weeks away from here— and they could be headed straight this way, judging by the smaller groups they keep sending out in this direction. We think there are around five thousand goblins and hobgoblins and two very large giants."

The General frowned and spoke sternly. "Five thousand! That's a big number. We have less than a thousand soldiers at Lugo. Are you sure about the number?" His eyes pierced Basil as he continued to frown. He spoke without moving his top lip and had an accent that sounded as if he were holding pebbles under his tongue.

"Um . . ." Basil opened his mouth awkwardly, then turned to Amber with raised eyebrows.

She stammered. "Uh . . . well . . . that is . . . it's definitely more than a thousand. Yes. I mean, no. I don't know if it's five thousand. But it's a lot. A lot. I mean . . . I saw a hundred or so, and it was so much bigger than that."

The General's gaze seemed stern and angry. She looked down. "Sorry." She didn't know why she apologized, but she wanted him to stop looking at her.

"What do you have to do with wizards? You say you got help from a wizard named Sage. What's your connection to him?"

"Ah, yes. W-w-well . . ." Basil looked down, fidgeting with his hands. "You see, all three of us were eager to learn why the goblins and other creatures have been coming back, and so we struck out to find Sage."

"You struck out? Where?"

"He was in the mountains east of here. Hard to find without an enchanted stone."

"Enchanted stone? So, three youths somehow decide to find a wizard in dangerous mountains with magical help. And you ran into goblins and trolls. Anything else?"

"Yes, sir. Of course, the phoenix. And a wizard who nearly killed us."

The General almost laughed. "I see. You must be wizards yourselves?"

Basil choked a little. How did this man seem to get to the point so quickly? "Um . . ." He looked back at Theo and Amber, who nodded approvingly. "Yes, sir. Sort of. That is, we have elemental powers."

"I see." The General leaned back slightly and tapped his fingers together in thought. "Forgive my lack of knowledge. We have some magic in a city of this size, but wizards are a scarcity these days. Explain these elemental powers—compared to these other wizards you seem to be spending so much time with."

"Elemental powers. They give us control over the elements. In our case, wind, animals, and plants." He pointed at each of them as he spoke.

"Ah-ha!" The General narrowed his eyes and pointed at Basil. "And you're coming here to help us fight these goblins with your powers."

"Um . . . actually . . . no. Not exactly."

"No?" He stood and smacked his fist into his other hand. "You obviously have great power if you can defeat a mighty wizard. Why would you choose to not help us when we clearly need all the help we can get?" His eyes flared angrily. Amber and Theo tried disappearing, shrinking down and looking at their feet.

Basil lowered his head, then lifted his gaze. "It's not like that, sir. We *do* want to help. We do. We heard from Sage that there's a dragon south of here, so we wondered if we could break the spell on it—like we did with the phoenix. Don't you think a dragon would be a helpful ally?"

The General stared at him with icy eyes.

Basil withered slightly. "Unless, of course, you have a better idea . . . sir."

The General paused, then began chuckling. All three youths visibly relaxed. "A dragon. Yes, some folks in these parts have seen a red dragon in recent weeks. And a few days ago, we heard of a red dragon that attacked a village to the south. I know which one you speak of."

He sighed. "Thank you for bringing this news to us. I can see you've been through a lot to bring me this information. I'm afraid our city isn't designed to withstand an army of that magnitude, even if it were only the goblins. Adding giants and wizards and who knows what else will make this a difficult challenge indeed. A dragon would be a welcome ally."

He gazed at each youth in thought. "We've been preparing. I was wondering if some news would come my way, with all the goblins being spotted. But I didn't expect to hear this. There must be two or three goblin kingdoms gathered together to make an army of that size."

He stared at Basil with narrowed eyes. "I assume you three have quite the powers. But if what you say is true, speed will be of the essence. You must return as quickly as possible, with or without a dragon."

"Yes, we'll do that." Basil nodded so much it looked like his head might fall off.

The General slowly pointed at each one of them in turn. "What can I do to help you? There must be something the Commander General of the largest army in all of Arendon can do to help three powerful elementalists."

Basil looked at Amber and Theo.

"Yeah." Theo fidgeted with his sleeves and looked down. "I'd like some better equipment. I feel like I keep scavenging off the goblins."

Basil suddenly lit up. "I could use a long sword for horse attacks . . . and maybe someone to show me how to use it differently than my short sword."

Amber got excited. "I'd like to find some information, like from a library historian. And I'd like to see if we can get something called peanut butter."

The General gave a slight smile, erasing his permanent frown for a moment, then snapped his fingers. "Stephen! Take care of these children and all they ask for. And then meet me in the planning room."

Within no time, Basil was in the courtyard learning proper attack techniques for using a long sword while riding a horse, and Theo was taking lessons on using a crossbow.

Amber was escorted down the street to a large library. The building had enormous pillars and looked to be built of marble covered with inscriptions. A wide set of stairs led to the main doors. She walked in and gasped—there were thousands of books and scrolls lining every wall on both floors and many more bookcases besides. How would she ever find the precise information she needed in such a place?

Her guide led her to a plump man sitting in the back. "Help Amber find whatever she needs, by order of the General."

The pudgy man looked up with droopy eyes and spoke with a lack of enthusiasm. "Of course." Amber frowned—this didn't seem hopeful.

Just then there was a loud *smack* from the back of the library, like a book dropping. "Amber?"

Her eyes darted around in confusion. Who in Lugo could possibly know her? Then from in between lines of books strode Chandler. "Amber! How delightful to see you!" His fancy white shirt was crumpled, as if he'd been sleeping in it.

Amber brightened. "Chandler! What are *you* doing here?"

"Looking for information, of course! And I've learned a mountain's worth! What are you doing here?"

"Oh! I'm so happy to see you!" She felt a warm glow and looked around at the massive walls of books hopefully. "I'm sure you can help. But first, we have a lot to catch up on!"

✳ ✳ ✳

The next hour was full of stories—Amber was excited to tell Chandler how they'd found Sage the wizard, how they discovered they had powers, how they encountered and broke the enchantment on the phoenix, and then how they battled the evil wizard with the scepter.

Chandler asked dozens of questions at every turn of the story, digging deeply into every little detail. When it was his turn to talk, he went into lecture mode. At first, he explained some of his learnings in the library.

When he mentioned Ryder, Amber instantly perked up. "Ryder came here with you?"

"Yes, yes. As I said. He talked to some pixies who sent him searching for information, and now he's off searching for the possible fortress of the wizards—we found out where it used to be during the Wizard War, and he was eager to see if it's still occupied."

Amber picked up a history book Chandler had been pointing at and leafed through the pages. "Maybe we should learn more about the Wizard War? It keeps coming up, and I feel like we have more questions than ever about it. What sorts of things happened? How did it end, specifically?"

She gained some energy. "And there's more I want to know. What's this prophecy Sage mentioned, which might be about us? Can we find it in one of these books? Who gave it and when?"

Chandler nodded. "It's good to come with questions—it's much easier to find answers if you know what you're looking for. Is there anyone in particular we care about in the Wizard War?"

Amber's eyes lit up. "Oh yeah! Not that it matters to figuring all of this out, but apparently I'm related to someone named Majestic Rose. If you come across that name, let me know."

"Can do!" Chandler gave her a thumbs-up with a grin and turned to the book in front of him with excitement.

They spent the next two hours going through books that explained the history of the Wizard War. The books went into great detail about the rise of the creatures, the gathering of an army, and the attacks on all peaceful, civilized folks. Humans, elves, and dwarves had all banded together to attack the goblins on the great plains of Almeda.

Amber twirled a strand of hair in thought. "Chandler, I can't help but wonder if history is repeating itself. It's like this exact same thing happened over a hundred and sixty years ago."

"Well." He shook his head proudly and adjusted his glasses, back in his lecture mode. "That is a common thing, you know. History doesn't just tell us about things in the past. It points us to what people and nations are prone to do and helps us understand many things in the present. For example, the General would do well to pay close attention to how battles have been lost and won. Every tactic, large and small, could help in making decisions at the time of battle."

He ruffled his shirt and gazed out a stained-glass window. "I assume he has tactical advisors, but I may be willing to lend a hand if he reaches out."

Amber snorted quietly, then hid her smile. "How would the General know about you? Have you ever met him?"

"Me? No. No." Chandler shook his head and sat quietly for a moment.

"Well . . ." Amber cocked her head. "If I talk to him again, I'll let him know about you."

"Of course you will, dear." Chandler smiled smugly and Amber tried hard not to roll her eyes.

There was a lot of information about the Wizard War, but it was slow reading, and there didn't seem to be any specific information that felt relevant. Amber looked out the window and sighed. Was she wasting her time when there was such a rush?

There was one interesting thing Chandler found, not about the Wizard War but possibly about the prophecy. There were ancient prophecies that seemed old and crusted. But there was an elf wizard named Darius mentioned during the time of the Wizard War who apparently gave a number of prophecies, including one that was described as "a great and ominous prediction." The book didn't go into details, but it was the closest clue they'd found.

Chandler loved the task of finding information and pored over a stack of books without rest. Amber looked up from a book, rubbed her eyes, and watched him. She had been feeling frustrated at the lack of answers but was encouraged seeing his excitement. She realized he wasn't reading word for word, like she was. He was quickly flipping pages, as if reading them all at a glance.

"How do you do that?" she asked him.

"Do what?" He continued reading without looking up.

"Read so quickly."

"Ah." He paused and smiled at Amber. "I don't actually read all the words—I just skim."

"What's that?"

"It's like looking around a room quickly to get a sense of what's going on without actually looking anyone in the eye. In a second or two, you can know about how many people are there and what they're up to. It doesn't take long."

"But . . ." She frowned. "That's people. These are words. How do you do that with words?"

Chandler shrugged. "Well, I guess it takes practice, but it's the same thing. You have to get past reading all the words— just look at the page as a whole and get a sense of it. If it doesn't apply, then you can move to the next page. Once you get used to it, you can look at a whole book in a matter of minutes."

"Huh." She turned back to her book and tried to skim but found it hard to stop reading the words. She found herself frowning.

Chandler watched her for a minute. "Try forcing yourself to turn a page after a few seconds, even if you haven't read it. That'll help."

She nodded and turned back to her book. After a few pages, she realized she was starting to do it! She didn't know exactly what the words were, but she had the basic idea. She smiled and flipped pages as quickly as possible. Much faster!

Unfortunately though, her excitement and newfound skills didn't help them uncover any specifics on the prophecy. She did go through a dozen books with potential, far more than she'd have thought she could just earlier that morning.

Then Chandler shouted, "I've found her!"

The other people in the library looked up with scowls, and Chandler shrunk his shoulders. "Sorry. Too loud." He tiptoed over to Amber holding a large leather-bound book and set it down quietly. He opened it halfway through with a grin. "Look! Majestic Rose!"

Amber's jaw dropped. "She was involved in the Wizard War?"

Chandler smiled at her triumphantly. "She was a wizard! A part of the war? According to this she was one of the critical people involved in ending it! And you're related to her?"

"I guess it makes sense." Amber shook her head. "Sage said I probably have wizards in my heritage, in order to have elemental powers. He also talked as if he knew her. Do you think Sage is that old?"

"Who knows with wizards." Chandler shrugged. "But look here." He pointed at a small drawing. "This is her emblem. Do you recognize it?"

"Yes!" Amber lifted the small silver pendant from under her shirt.

Chandler pushed his glasses up and peered at it closely. "A sun with a face. Perfect match. Let's see . . . what can we learn from it . . . nine wavy rays coming from it. I wonder if that number has any significance. Do you know anything about it?"

"Not really . . . my mom said it's supposed to give me luck. But who knows if she knew what it really does."

"That should be useful." He chuckled, then paused. "Well, my understanding of mana is incomplete. And maybe something worth researching while we're at it. There seem to be different kinds of magical influences out there. For example, there are those we call wizards, like Sage. And there are elementalists, like you. There are creatures, like pixies, who are all born with some level of mana in their core. And then there are enchanted objects, possibly your little pendant there."

He looked up thoughtfully. "From what I've gathered from other books, wizards tend to be good at spells in one area only—so if a wizard is good at attack spells, they usually don't do well at defensive spells or enchanting things. It's mostly a mystery to me, honestly. But what I can determine about your relative here is that she was able to fly and control light. See here—"

He pointed at the next page. "She used bright flashes of light to blind the army . . . and the opposing wizards. They were fighting without seeing where they were aiming. She seems pretty critical to the success of her side."

"Wow!" Amber shook her head. "What else?"

"Well, to be honest, it's hard to tell whether one side was good and one was bad. When I read about those days, it feels like a dark time for humanity. Whatever they were fighting about, things definitely quieted down after the war, so one can hope she was on the good side, if there was one."

Amber scrunched up her face. "Gosh. I hope my relative was on the good side. Can I read it for myself?"

Chandler passed her the book. As she read, she felt pride and also wondered about her own life. Was she going to play an important role? She was already doing far more than she'd ever imagined. If she really was one of the people in the prophecy, what did that mean?

"But what's this?" Amber felt a rough edge close to the binding. "A page is missing."

Chandler pushed his glasses up his nose and peered at it. "Veeery interesting. Interesting indeed! What was on that page—and who would want it?"

They were puzzled, but without more ideas, they went back to their individual searches. After such a grand discovery, going back to her book felt like a waste of time. She glanced at the late afternoon light coming through the beautiful stained-glass window. "Maybe it's time for a break?"

He nodded and stretched. They met up with Basil and Theo for dinner back at the military grounds and told them what they'd learned. Theo was excited. "That's great! It can take weeks of research to find that kind of information. You learned a lot about the Wizard War, some stuff about your relative, and you have a possible name and date for the prophecy. We'll find it for sure now. I'll help you tomorrow."

Amber perked up. Theo was much more of a book-loving person than she was. She'd read only a handful of books her whole life to date, whereas Theo grew up with books and a library in his small town of Sanford. With Theo and Chandler both helping, they were bound to find something else useful.

✳ ✳ ✳

The next day, the three walked to the library at the crack of dawn. Much like Amber had the day before, Theo looked around in awe at the sheer magnitude of information in the building. They picked up where they'd left off the day before and skimmed dozens of books. Over the course of a few hours, the stack of books was piled high.

Finally, Chandler shut his book. "Time for a break. It's good to rest your eyes and regain some perspective. This is tiring work."

They stood and stretched. Amber felt exhausted, and they hadn't been moving at all! Theo saw the look in her eyes. "It can be even more tiring exercising your brain than your body!"

She nodded in agreement. They joined Basil for lunch.

After telling him how they hadn't found anything, Theo asked, "How's it going with you, Basil?"

"Great!" He grinned, baring his teeth. "I'm learning some techniques I've never seen before. The long sword is an amazing weapon. I might even switch to it in general." He patted the well-built sword with a wide hilt sitting by his side. "Although it doesn't have magic powers like my little guy."

"You got that right." Theo stared at the sword admiringly. "But you'll never be able to have good attacks on a horse with a little sword, so I think you're doing the right thing."

"Me too. I had a real breakthrough today when I looked at sword-fighting from a different angle. There are the swords and the connections, but there's also all the space in between, how you hold your body and place yourself against your opponent. That's actually even more important than the fighting itself."

"That's it!" Amber said.

Theo, Basil, and Chandler looked at her quizzically.

"We're looking at the moment of the war—but not the spaces in between."

"Ah!" Chandler leaned back and fussed with his glasses. "Interesting..."

After lunch the three hurried back to the library to do more research, but this time they looked at different books. Ones on magic, elves, goblins, pixies, dragons, everything they could think of that had to do with the things they were encountering.

At first, it slowed their research way down. Skimming books on history that weren't relevant seemed a lot faster than trying to find a gem of information on a book about pixies. After an hour, Theo called out, "I've found something!"

Chandler and Amber rushed over, and Theo pointed at the book excitedly. "According to this, the pixies have a spot they look at as the source of their mana. It's kind of like their headquarters. It sounds an awful lot like our pixie friend's Great Stone Tower."

He pointed at the page repeatedly. "It says here that no human has ever reported where the mana source is—the pixies keep it secret. But they think the spot is potentially far to the west of here in some tall mountains, by the coast. Nobody has ever found the exact spot, because the pixies disguise it with their magic."

"Aha!" Chandler beamed. "I knew there were mana sources. And pixies hiding them explains why it's only remained a theory all these years."

"The coast?" Amber cocked her head. "In Seabrook the mountains aren't big. Where do the mountains get tall?"

Chandler pulled out a nearby map and pointed. "Tall is a relative term, unfortunately. It could be that it was right under your nose all these years. Many hundreds of miles south are the Mountains of Cush, which seems like a worthy spot to search."

"But that's by the Great Sea. Lila said it wasn't there . . ." Amber trailed off.

Theo grinned at her. "Exactly!"

She studied the map. "Nice find! Let's keep digging."

Amber was impressed with some of the knowledge she was gaining about dragons. They had an entire civilization apart from other creatures. She found herself slowing down and reading word for word, fascinated at the details and wondering if any of the information she was learning would help them with Crodor the Ancient. Across the Great Sea there were apparently places where hundreds of dragons lived together. In her part of the world, they were much scarcer.

Chandler suddenly shouted. "I've found it!"

He stood with a lopsided smile, holding up a book. Amber tried making out words but couldn't. "What language is that?"

"Oh, this is elvish." Chandler looked smug and proud of himself. "It's a book on elf lore from the last few hundred years. And I think I may have your prophecy. Let me try writing it down in a way that makes sense for us."

He pored over the book, then squiggled on a piece of parchment, then back again. Amber and Theo held their breaths. Was this it?

Finally, he held up the paper and shook it slightly. "I believe this is the prophecy you've been looking for."

Amber and Theo sat spellbound, waiting for him to continue. Could they really have found it after all this time?

Chapter 6

Trouble in the Woods

CHANDLER CLEARED HIS THROAT and lifted the paper proudly. "The prophecy is from Darius the elf, one hundred and eighty years ago. It's titled 'Prophecy of the Green.'

This is how it goes . . ."

The world will face a great darkness
For ages and ages to come,
And those who would stop it
Must pay a dear price,
Till we reach the time of the One.

The scepters must all join together
At the great mana tower of old.
The stars will align

And the ancient spell cast
To bring about power untold.

But six in their youth will arise—
Elements all harmonize,
Releasing the Serpent,
And gaining the Green,
Till the One takes the path of the Wise.

"Does this seem like what you were looking for?" Chandler asked.

"Definitely," Amber said. "But it's awfully vague about a lot of stuff. I can see why Sage wasn't fully convinced it's us. But I can also see why he thought it might be. It doesn't really say what the evil side is going to do here. But it does seem like we're on track looking for the Great Stone Tower—that's probably the same thing as the great mana tower in the prophecy. I bet the wizards are trying to find it. But why they're working with goblins to destroy everyone still is a mystery."

"This has to be it." Theo took the paper and read it again. "I really think we're onto something here. Do you think 'elements all harmonize' is referring to people like us, with elemental powers?"

"Yeah." Amber nodded. "That would make sense. Otherwise, why would Sage have been talking about that? But then . . . there are only three of us . . . and six elements, right?"

"Right." Theo pointed at the paper. "Also, I wonder about the Serpent, could that be the dragon? And what's the stars aligning part? And of course, the Green and the path of the Wise. Lots of questions still."

"True. But it's enough for now. The General is right—we'd better get back on track to finding that dragon!"

"Agreed."

Chandler looked excited, as if he'd just conquered some evil beasts. "I'll keep digging! Next time you come back through, we'll know even more!"

After putting countless books and scrolls away and then making a copy of the prophecy to take with them, they decided it was too late in the day to set off. So Amber and Theo decided to make the most of their time and do some training on the military grounds. They could leave in the morning.

When they showed up, Basil was thrusting his sword with his foot planted, mimicking an older man who was slowly doing movements with the same kind of sword. They watched as the older man peacefully and gracefully pivoted, raised the sword, then brought it to his side, pivoted again, lifted one leg, then stepped back, sword raised. Every step, Basil followed and mimicked perfectly.

They walked past him toward the shooting range where Theo picked up a crossbow and greeted the brown-haired man. "Hi, Jim. I'm back to get some more practice in."

"Sounds good." The slender man handed Theo a dozen crossbow bolts. Theo picked up one of the short, stocky arrows and loaded it into the crossbow, then aimed carefully at the targets fifty yards away.

"Hold your left hand under the stock." Jim came behind Theo and moved Theo's left hand up a few inches. "There. Now close your left eye. Good. And straighten your right arm more. Perfect. Ok, now focus on the front sight, not the target. Don't worry if the target gets blurry, you can double-check."

"Okay," Theo said. "Ready."

"Take a breath and hold it. Now fire."

Theo let the bolt loose, and it flew toward the target. Not a perfect bullseye, but a decent shot.

"Good. Let's try again. And this time, I know you're holding your breath, but try to be relaxed."

Amber watched in fascination. Although the crossbow seemed powerful, she was happy with her bow. She couldn't imagine switching. She left Theo and walked over to an area with various weapons covering the wall.

There were hundreds: short swords in a dozen different styles and varieties, long spears with different types of weapons at the top, like a chain and blade or a spear with three points. Most of them were familiar—swords, knives, axes, bows, spears. But there were some odd ones she'd never seen before, like small throwing weapons that looked like stars, double-bladed short weapons, and a staff with a blade that could pop out at the end.

A voice from behind startled her. "Which do you fancy most?"

She jumped and turned to see a blond-haired man with a short, scratchy beard, dressed all in black.

"Um, I don't know." She tried to act calm. How had he snuck up on her like that?

"Everyone is drawn to something more than another." The man trailed his finger along a worn-looking mace. "I for one love the spear. I can use it as a staff or throw it if necessary. Never failed me yet. But you don't strike me as a spear person."

She shrugged. "I can use the bow. I've done it all my life."

"Ah, of course. But what about in close combat? What do you use then?"

"Well . . . I have a knife?"

The man shook his head. "I think you might be ready to try your hand at something a bit more advanced."

Amber nodded. "Like what?"

The man looked at the wall for a minute, then pointed to

a long dagger with less of a blade than the others. "This is called a stiletto. It's often used by assassins, because it pierces leather and even metal armor better than a normal blade—and it's lighter and easier to use. But it is only used for full piercing, not for slashing, like a normal dagger."

He took it off the wall, lightly bouncing it in his hands. "Perfect balance." He abruptly leaped forward with his right leg and stabbed it forward into the air. "Deadly in an instant."

Standing up straight, he handed it to Amber. "You'll need training. It's not the same as a sword. You need to get in close and have a clean shot. It's not good for blocking. I'd suggest a stiletto in your preferred hand, and a short sword or dagger in your other—for blocking and slashing."

Amber nodded, watching him attentively.

"Have you got a dagger?"

Amber reached to her side and pulled out her fishing knife. The man held out his hand and she gave it to him. He glanced at it with a frown. "You'll want better than this. Cheap iron—and old. Also, too short to be any good in a battle."

Amber shrugged. The man turned back to the wall and took a long dagger off the wall, a bit shorter than Basil's short sword. He pulled it out of its sheath and held the blade up to his eye, looking at it carefully, then tossed it up and down a few times. "This is perfect for you. Here." He tossed the long dagger to Amber, who caught it deftly by the hilt.

She was amazed. She would have thought it would be much heavier. It felt graceful and fluid in her hand. She swung it around a few times. Although it was a twelve-inch blade, much longer than her old knife, it felt lighter and easier to wield. The hilt was wide with two knobs, one on each side, ornately curved upward, presumably for blocking other blade attacks. She grinned.

The next three hours were spent training with the man, learning how to use the stiletto and long dagger in combination. He was a good teacher, introducing different weapon attacks against her, from swords to spears to axes. Although the techniques were all new to Amber, she did feel confident she could use them against a goblin if she had to.

By the time she'd gone to bed that night, she marveled at how much they'd accomplished in just two days. The next morning, they set off with saddle bags filled with food, a decent map of the mountain region where they were headed, a copy of the prophecy, and a little extra confidence from their training. Basil was now wearing leather armor, and something about the way he carried himself seemed more confident and capable.

The General greeted them before they left. "I hope you remember the great urgency of your mission. And thank you for pointing us to the goblin army. We've sent scouts to monitor them. I also have these."

He gestured to a woman in chain mail standing next to him holding a leather bag. "Two jars of peanut butter."

"Oh, thank you." Amber had completely forgotten about it. She took the bag and looked inside. "Can I try some?"

"It's up to you."

She took a jar, untwisted the lid and dipped her finger in. The flavor—she'd never had anything like it before. Her eyes widened as the peanut butter glued to the roof of her mouth. "Derishush!"

Basil saw her face and brightened. "Hey, I want to try too!" He and Theo each tried a dab. Basil's eyes glistened. "My new favorite food."

Amber chuckled and put the lid back on. "Ok. Enough! Let's leave the rest for the dragon."

"Ah . . ." The General nodded with a frown. "I was wondering why you requested it."

"One more thing," Amber said, putting the jars in her saddle bag. "There's a man named Chandler in the library who might be able to lend some insight when it comes to history and battle tactics. He's offering his services, if you'd like."

The General raised his eyebrows. "Indeed. We'll make sure to reach out. And now, please do hurry back. Even if you do bring a dragon as an ally, I fear it may not be enough. All you can do to help will be well received."

They nodded somberly, then mounted and followed six soldiers, who parted a path through the city crowds. They passed through the gates and waved back.

Theo patted the phoenix on the neck. "Ok, Blazey, you can open your wings now."

The giant bird stretched his wings out, startling a few of the other travelers on the road. It had been a wonderful time for the three friends the last two days but not the phoenix. Blazey had stayed to the side, keeping himself as small as possible to prevent disturbing others or causing a scene.

They traveled the road for an hour, then took a fork in the road toward the south, headed toward the mountains in the distance. Nobody was on the road anymore, and they wondered if goblins had come through already.

It was still a bright, beautiful day when they came upon trees and a light forest. The mountains were still a ways off, but the terrain was starting to change. The road remained wide and solid, though, so the going was quick.

Finally, they came to another fork in the road that wasn't as obvious. They stopped and looked at the map. The main road wound to the left, but the smaller path to the south appeared to be the way they should go. The forest was much denser, although they still felt the bright sun on their faces. As the path grew narrower, so did the amount of sun. The possibility of enemies around any corner filled their minds with uncertainty.

Amber strained her senses with the plants and trees to ensure nothing could sneak up on them. Over the last weeks, the more she pushed, the further she felt she could sense. What seemed like an impossible distance of two hundred yards was now easy, and five hundred yards now felt like a stretch.

They traveled this way for a few good hours, then suddenly Theo stopped and held out his hand. "Wait!"

Basil and Amber obeyed and watched him silently. Theo listened for a moment, then called, "Someone's in trouble! This way!" He pointed directly into the forest. Amber rode straight into the middle of the trees, parting the branches in front of her as she galloped.

Basil and Theo followed close behind. Within a few minutes, they heard commotion in the distance.

"It's over to the right!" Theo called. "And just ahead!"

Amber galloped into a small clearing to see four goblins and a hobgoblin who had cornered a small elf girl with pale-blue skin and deep-blue hair. She was against a big rock, holding out a small slender sword.

Amber quickly caused the trees around the elf to lower their branches, blocking out the goblins. She galloped into the area and the goblins turned as one toward her. She stopped and a plant barrier grew out of the ground between them.

With long sword drawn, Basil galloped past Amber, leaping over the growing brambles and headed toward the first goblin. "Ha!" he yelled.

He deflected the goblin's meager attack easily and planted his sword into its chest in one fluid motion, then pulled it out and moved on to the next. Amber marveled, Basil's training the last two days had obviously paid off!

Theo stopped his horse next to Amber and pulled out his crossbow, taking aim and firing into the next goblin. Not a perfect shot, but the goblin dropped to the ground.

Basil took down the next goblin as well. But the tall hobgoblin easily blocked him. Basil rode past, then turned his horse around in the small clearing.

Amber focused on tightening a ring of branches around the remaining goblins, giving them little room to attack but also making it harder to attack them.

"Hold on!" Theo called as he reloaded his crossbow. "I won't get in another shot if you block them out completely."

"Right." She created an opening to the goblins for Theo, while thickening the other parts of the wall. She amazed herself at how fast she was causing the trees to move and shift. Somehow the adrenaline from the battle was giving her extra speed and intensity.

Theo took another shot, dropping another goblin, but the hobgoblin hacked at the branches and broke through toward Basil, who had just turned around.

The hobgoblin swung hard, and it was all Basil could do to block without getting hit. He tried thrusting, but the hobgoblin easily blocked. That's when Basil realized he couldn't use all his new training from atop the horse.

He slipped off, stepping back with sword raised. The ugly green hobgoblin snarled and stared at him icily. Then it attacked relentlessly, its curved sword clanging down with great strength over and over. Basil blocked every time, barely able to divert the strong blows, let alone counterattack.

Theo reloaded and shot the last standing goblin stuck in the wooden prison, but not enough to drop it. Amber pivoted her attention to Basil, who was barely keeping up with the hobgoblin's strength. Roots sprung up out of the ground in front of the hobgoblin.

The hobgoblin charged forward and stumbled on a root. Basil seized the opportunity and thrust. The added length of the long sword did the trick. The sword pierced the creature's armor, causing it to stumble back further.

Basil jumped forward and finished it off, in the same moment that Theo sent a final bolt into the last standing goblin.

As many times before, the three waited, breathing heavily and watching for more movement. Had they really taken out those goblins so quickly? They were obviously improving in their skills as well as their teamwork.

They heard a "Caaaw!" above them and realized Blazey had tried to fly into the fray but with the cramped space and speedy battle, it had been impossible to get in to help.

Amber suddenly thought of the elf, and with an extra push of effort caused the protective branches to open up.

The elf stepped out and looked down at the dead goblins, then at the three humans. She paused, breathing heavily. "Thank you." The words came out in a lilting singsong-ish way, and her accent sounded exotic.

Amber dismounted and walked over. "My name's Amber. This is Basil." She pointed at him, as he wiped the goblin blood off his long sword. "And Theo." He was fumbling his crossbow back into its holster on his horse's side. "What's your name?"

"Mizu." The elf spoke quickly and with very little emotion.

Amber was inspired by how Mizu held herself with such agility and confidence. She stood about half a foot shorter than Amber and wore a tight-fitting elegant blue outfit and a cloak. She was beautiful, with hair that was a striking blue, like the dark sky at dusk, and her eyes had a blue sparkle as if in direct sunlight. Her eyes were shaped like almonds, narrower yet larger than human eyes. Her ears were long and pointy, rising a good five inches through her long blue hair.

Theo looked up at the elf and took a loud breath, eyes wide.

Amber had never seen an elf before and realized she was staring. "Um, are you okay?"

Mizu nodded. "Thanks to you, I am indeed. But not so much my Lorien."

"Lorien?"

Mizu frowned, then suddenly dashed out of the clearing into the trees. Amber followed close behind. Within moments they came upon two goblins dead on the ground with throwing knives sticking out of them, and a large black cat lying next to them, motionless with a large gash down its front.

Mizu ran to the cat—a good forty-pound creature—and hugged it. "Oh Lorien! I'm so, so sorry!"

Amber's mind raced. "Theo! Come quickly!"

Theo came dashing through the woods and saw the scene, then approached the large cat. "May I?"

Mizu looked up and nodded, moving over a little bit. Theo placed his hand with the magical ring over the sword wound running down the cat's neck and chest. The wound began closing up, but was it fast enough?

They all watched silently as the cat lay still, then suddenly gave a big gasp and began breathing ruggedly.

"Lorien!" Mizu's eyes sparkled. "You've survived!" She turned to Theo happily. He smiled sheepishly and his cheeks turned a slight shade of red. As the wound closed, the cat breathed more and more regularly. After two minutes, it opened its eyes. It saw Theo, licked his hand, and began purring.

Theo smiled. "He's going to be okay!"

Mizu beamed and hugged the large cat.

Amber straightened her bow and weapons. "What are you doing out here by yourself? It's dangerous."

Mizu looked up. "I might ask you a similar thing."

Amber instantly answered, "We're going after the dragon that's been coming through these parts to see if we can break the spell on it."

Mizu cocked her head. "Interesting."

"Why's that?"

"I, as well, am heading to find a dragon."

Silence hovered in the air. Theo and Amber waited for her to say more, but she sat petting her cat, as if she'd said all she had to say.

Finally, Theo asked, "Why?"

The elf looked up from her cat as if surprised by the question. "At the eve of spring, a magical spell enchanted many creatures—hippogriffs, gnomes, even Lorien here. All were deeply impacted. We found them angry, violent sorts, not like their normal selves. Our mages broke the spell, of course, on all the ones we found. But we know the spell reached hundreds of miles—the goblins woke from mountain homes, emerged to daylight nonetheless, those evil ones, and more. My people do live long compared to human folk like you, yet none of us has seen a spell quite like it. And so it was the council chose to send some elves to seek advice—five elves with different strengths sent to seek the wisest creatures. The role they passed to me, you see, was due to my grandfather's friendship with an aged red dragon, an ancient great beast, who helped us with difficult questions long ago."

"Ah," Theo and Amber said together.

Mizu patted the large cat absentmindedly. "I am forever grateful. Perhaps I could have handled some, but no, not seven goblins, much less the tall one. I am glad to be alive. And more, with Lorien."

Amber's eyes brightened. "Yes! So glad we came when we did! Without a moment to spare!"

"Indeed it was. Such perfect timing. Almost as if by destiny." Her eyes turned thoughtful, and she cocked her head. "Your powers. You control the plants?"

"I do." Amber nodded. "It has helped a lot these last few weeks."

Mizu pursed her lips, then turned to Theo. "And you. I see you heal. But something tells me there is more. Have you any other gifts?"

"Well, I guess there's this." Lorien instantly stood up and sat next to him, allowing Theo to put his hand on his head.

Mizu stood fluidly and watched with a cocked head. "I see. Connection to animals—even, I dare say, better than us elves!"

Theo smiled back shyly. "I guess so."

The elf pursed her lips. "More and more surprises."

Amber stared at Theo a moment curiously. He fumbled with his shirt sleeve a moment, then looked up at the elf with a shrug.

At that moment, Blazey came walking through the trees over to them. The phoenix poked its large head through the bushes and looked at them quizzically. Mizu jumped up and reached for her slender sword.

Theo leaped in between them and held out his hand. "And this is Blazey. We saved him from the evil spell only a few weeks ago."

Mizu approached the phoenix slowly and reached out to touch his large beak. Blazey stepped forward and nuzzled her.

Amber smiled and gestured them to walk back to the clearing. "Come on."

Mizu stood and followed. "This third companion of yours, Basil, does he have powers as well?"

"Yes," Amber said. "His power is with air. This is all new for us. We didn't even know about our powers till recently."

"Have you been friends a long, long time?"

"Basil and Theo have. But I'm from a different village, by the sea. I just met them less than two months ago. But we're best friends—we've been through a lot together."

"Of course you are. That much is clear. Enchanted items, powers, and skills, enough to kill five goblins. Not to mention friends with this great phoenix. You obviously work well together."

"Yes. Exactly." Amber paused, appreciating how Mizu seemed so observant.

"And your power with plants—they listen to you quickly."

"Yes, I'm getting faster."

"Does it not drain your energy?"

"Yes. Yes." Amber looked at the elf with interest. "It does. But I've found that I'm able to do more—and do it faster—than even a week ago."

"I see. I see. Your power is strong." Mizu looked at her with understanding.

They approached Basil, who was crouched next to the hobgoblin. He waved them over. "This one here has a different medallion. We haven't seen this one before. And look at this." He held up a rough map rolled in a small leather tube.

Basil spread out the map. "This proves it! Look."

The writing on it was in a different language and seemed crude. The map was simplistic, with little triangles for mountains, rough lines for roads, dots for human dwellings, and larger dots with words next to them.

"Look here—I obviously can't read the words, but I think these larger dots with words are where they're from. There's one in the Ancares Mountains. And here—if I'm right—they have five cities on the map. So that must mean there are five different goblin kingdoms. Looks like one of them is located in these mountains we're in now. I bet that's where these are from."

"Basil." Amber gave him a dirty look. "You seem awfully happy to find out there are goblins living nearby."

"Well, no, not exactly." Basil paused. "I don't think they're actually *that* close. I figure we're here, and Crodor lives a bit south of us, here, and the goblins are much further east. See?"

"If that's true, then what are they doing all the way out here?" Theo frowned. "Do you think they're part of the larger army that's gathering?"

"That doesn't really make sense," Amber said. "The army was over there in the plains." She pointed to the right side of the map. "That's close to the Ancares, and the groups I saw seemed like they were sending scouts toward Lugo. These ones here must be doing something else or going somewhere else."

"Perhaps they were just wandering about." Mizu peered at the map over Basil's shoulder.

Basil looked at her. "Who are you?"

"Mizu." She gave a slight bow. "Thank you, sir, for rescuing me."

Basil scratched his head releasing a long curl of hair, and Amber noticed that the dark brown curls were looking longer and curlier than a month earlier when she'd first met him. She wondered what *she* looked like, with all their travel and nights sleeping in the countryside.

"Where are you from?" Basil asked.

"Lorcaster," Mizu said. "Do you have knowledge of the elven cities?"

Basil shook his head. Mizu glanced at Amber and Theo, who also shook their heads.

"My home is far away from here, in the great, great forests to the east, up here, just north of the Ancares Mountains." She pointed at the map to a spot in the mountains, north of the goblin dot. "And where do you call home? Amber said she's from a village by the sea."

"Yes," Basil said. "Theo and I are from Sanford, a small town not too far from Amber's. Looks like we're all a long way from home."

Mizu nodded. "Indeed, we are."

Amber gazed at the elf curiously. She felt like she had an affinity to Mizu somehow—as if she knew her from somewhere but couldn't place it.

After they finished gathering their belongings and surveying the area, Basil gathered them in. "We're heading south. Are you going to join us, Mizu?"

Mizu nodded. "Thank you, yes. Most surely. We all are searching for the same old dragon. I do believe it was no accident, running into you."

"Then it's settled." Basil kicked a goblin and walked toward Storm. "Let's get a move on. There's no time to lose. That goblin army could be a week away from Lugo at this point. Amber, get us back on track. I'm going to take Blazey up for a better view."

Amber nodded. Finding the dragon was going to be difficult. Having Mizu seemed like a bonus, but it didn't make the task any less daunting.

Chapter 7

The Pixie Trap

CASTER EYED THE DWARF SUSPICIOUSLY. He slowly tapped his wand in his other hand, his red cape billowing in the wind for a moment before it relaxed against his elegant but practical black outfit. Craning his neck, he pursed his lips and looked at a peculiar flat-topped orange-and-yellow mushroom.

Finally, he turned back to the dwarf. "Attracts pixies, you say?"

"Aye." The weathered dwarf wiped his hands on his dirty-brown apron and picked it up. "Ye must be planting it in the middle o' the forest, and they'll start comin'. They won't even know why." He chuckled.

"And there are no spells? No need to say an enchanting word?"

"Nay. Us dwarves don't be doing that type of magic. Just plant it in thick soil next to some moss, and it'll get to work within the day. You'll see."

The handsome wizard pulled a sack of coins off his side and handed the dwarf a single gold coin.

The dwarf's eyes twinkled, then he frowned. "I not be havin' change for ye."

"No need." Caster waved his hand dismissively, then held his palm out. The dwarf gently placed the mushroom into it, watching the young man's face cautiously.

The dwarf held his breath. The wizard carefully wrapped the mushroom into a piece of cloth, then gave a friendly, relaxed smile that put the dwarf at ease. "Well then. I bid you goodbye. If this works as you promised, it will be worth its weight in gold. We'll see."

He gazed to the north, to the great sea just beyond the walls of the dwarf city. He whistled, and a hippogriff came trotting from a side building. The dwarf eyed it cautiously, but the wizard ignored him as he leaped onto the flying horse-eagle and gently placed the mushroom into a side bag. Then he gave a slight kick, and the creature opened its enormous wings and soared into the sky, over the great sea.

As the wizard flew for the next few hours, he reflected on his great fortune. It had been a long journey finding that dwarf. The dwarven city of Luxorio was far from home, a full day's journey over the sea, past many other lands. He'd caught wind that dwarves might have this ability from some closer to home, but it seemed the stuff of legend.

Still, wouldn't the White Queen be thrilled with his new plan? It would all prove worthwhile. He'd pick up right where he left off.

It was nearly dusk when he saw the familiar coastline of Arendon ahead, with the old-growth forests and enormous trees reaching far into the sky. Not enough cities around to chop them all down, he thought. Not like where I grew up.

He turned and flew down the coast. The imps would be about twenty miles further, and with them, dozens of pixies on the run. He could tell the hippogriff was getting weary—her flapping grew slower and her breathing rough. He cast a quick spell to boost her energy. Couldn't have her slowing down now, not this close. Then he chuckled and cast the same spell on himself. Why not? He laughed out loud as he felt strength and stamina return.

Magic was so great. It really did make his life easier. And thanks to the White Queen, he'd learned twice as many spells in the last three years than he'd known his whole life. Now to return the favor and help her find those pixies and their magical tower.

He slowed as he neared a craggy section of the coastline and landed in a clearing. He dismounted and called out, "Reconicio!" Then he smelled the flowers in the gentle breeze and glanced over at them. They were bright purple and pink and stood out vibrantly in the setting sun. How nice.

The first imp arrived.

The wizard lifted his wand and mind-spoke: *How many pixies are in the area?*

A bunch. More maybe.

Darn imps. So stupid they couldn't count. *Well, is it less than ten?*

The imp paused. *Less than ten. Yes. Yes.*

Well, it was a start. Two other imps arrived. They all had pixies on the run. Excellent. He gingerly pulled out the mushroom in its protective cloth from the side bag and looked it over. Still intact. He trooped into the woods till it grew dark, then lifted his wand and said, "Lumino."

The forest brightened a good twenty yards around him in every direction, enough to see details of trees. It was a gentle light—not casting dark shadows but giving the forest a peaceful feeling. He found a nice mossy area that felt quiet and protected. This would be the spot.

He planted the mushroom and stepped back. What had the dwarf said? It wouldn't work immediately. A good opportunity to sleep for the night.

He lifted his wand. "Alark." Instantly, he felt perfectly tuned in to all things coming and going from the area. He sensed a squirrel looking for a chestnut. With a furrowed brow, he focused—just pixies. Don't alert me for anything but pixies.

He smiled pleasantly as he felt the power of the spell tune to his desires, then turned to the three imps: *When the pixies come into the clearing, make sure you don't kill them all. I want you to save me one.*

The imps chorused together: *Save me one.*

He shook his head. Stupid imps. It was amazing how effective they were at catching those crafty pixies. He found a comfortable spot to lie down and extinguished the light.

✳ ✳ ✳

Flurry awoke with a start. She blinked and looked through bleary eyes at her friend Wix shaking her gently. His friendly smile put her at ease.

He mind-spoke: The imps have left. Time to go.

She looked around, confused. It was still dark. Pixies could see well in the dark but not as well as during the day. The night was the imps' world more than theirs, most definitely. Still, the elders had decided.

A regal-looking elder she'd only met two weeks earlier mind-spoke to all present: *We will split up into two groups. I'll lead one, and Fantifa will lead the other.* She gestured to the other elder who hovered next to her. *The first group to reach the Great Stone Tower will be able to save the other with its magic. Now remember, as soon as we leave our ring the imps will know where we are, so traveling fast is critical.*

She gestured to the ring of mushrooms surrounding them. *Since the imps can find us when we fly, we suggest a big burst of speed all together, then stopping all together. No flitting about. We make a straight line. However, we can't go straight to the tower, or they might figure it out. So my group will go inland first. The second will go to the coast and make their way down from there. Any questions?*

The clearing was silent. All the pixies were dirty and tired. They hadn't come across any new pixies in the last couple of weeks, which was discouraging. But they also hadn't lost any more to the dangerous imps either.

Flurry had a bad feeling about splitting up, but who was she to suggest a different plan to her elders? She was only fourteen. As the groups were chosen, she made sure she stuck with Wix. He was the only friend she had left through all the events over the last months. First, the burning of their home. Then the persistent attacks from imps and evil wizards. What did they want with the simple, harmless pixies, anyway?

The elder Fantifa spoke to Flurry's group. "Our group is heading back to the coast, then down to the tower. It's a longer journey than the other group, so we'll need to be focused and prepared. Let's fly for an hour, then rest our wings. If anyone spots an imp in the area, alert us all right away, so we can stop flying."

The eleven other pixies surrounding her fidgeted nervously. Would they really be able to fly that long without being noticed? It felt so risky. Fantifa mind-spoke: *We'll be going so fast we won't have scouts. We stick together, no matter what. Understood? We leave at once.*

She hovered, then turned and zoomed through the trees, the other pixies fast on her trail. They sped through the old growth forest at an unbelievable speed. After ten minutes, Flurry's wings were already tired. She'd definitely need a rest soon. An hour? Would she be able to make it?

But she had no choice. They sped past bushes, over a creek, continuing on and on. After forty minutes the elder stopped, landing on a tree branch. The other eleven pixies all flitted onto the branch and rested, breathing heavily. She counted them quickly. *We're all here. We need a rest.*

Nobody spoke or disagreed. They were already exhausted, sleeping in random places, always on the run. The long sprint just added to it.

After a few minutes, Fantifa pointed to Wix and two others: *Scout the area.*

The three pixies obediently fluttered upward and disappeared in three different directions. Flurry's heart dropped. Not Wix! Why were they always splitting up dangerously? They should be sticking together.

A few minutes later, the sound of heavy footsteps approached. They waited nervously on the safety of the branch. Normally pixies were friends with any forest creature and able to get away from danger. Imps really were one of the few things that could harm them. Still, with her entire tribe scattered and chased by the imps, it was hard to be calm.

Her face brightened when she saw Wix riding happily on the head of a beautiful white unicorn. He mind-spoke so all could hear: *Our friend here says he'll give us a ride, at least to the coast. No more flying needed.*

The pixies gave little cheers. Flurry smiled at Wix. His abilities with animals were excellent, better than most pixies. He probably didn't even use a charm spell.

The mood on the unicorn was happy. Unicorns would never be caught by an evil wizard. They were too crafty, and their powers with illusions were unmatched. The pixies felt safe and relaxed for the first time since their last mushroom ring.

Flurry smiled at Wix. Nice work, finding this unicorn.

He could tell we needed the help. Wix shrugged. He can tell the whole forest is thrown off without the pixies. He wants us back as much as any of us do.

He patted the unicorn. "This way, friend."

The unicorn hesitated, then went slightly to the left. Flurry felt comfort with the slight change. She wasn't sure how she knew, but it felt like it was going to lead them to a perfect place of safety. Perhaps a large fairy ring.

The day brightened and the forest felt calm, peaceful. A few pixies had dozed off. Flurry felt like dozing as well. May as well get sleep now, when she could.

"Hmm. Interesting." Wix peered at the nearby trees.

"What is it?" Flurry blinked and cleared her groggy thoughts.

"See here. Look at the bark. Someone wrote here not too long ago."

He stopped the unicorn, and they all peered at the tree. The beetles had written warnings using the pixie's intricate squiggle language. Humans would look at it and think the beetle eating out the bark was simply going about it in a random beautiful pattern, winding around and creating interlocking swirls. But the pixies could read the message as clear as day: "It's a trap."

But *what* exactly was a trap? The message was fresh. They sat there for a moment, then Fantifa, as the elder among them, decided. "I can sense a fairy ring not far from here. Let's head there for safety. Whatever trap is laid, we have a unicorn to help us. Wix, would you please explain to him our troubles and make sure he understands we'll need his help?"

Wix nodded and spoke in low tones into the unicorn's ears. The ears twitched and the unicorn gave a little mumbling breath. Wix gave the thumbs-up sign, and they continued on their path. Soon they could all sense it. Yes, definitely a fairy ring coming up. Just the thought of it gave them all encouragement. They would have all relaxed fully if not for the warning they'd just read.

The smell of the great sea wafted on the next breeze. They weren't far now.

Suddenly, the forest erupted into action. Three imps came flying out of the trees and headed straight toward them. Pixies darted in all directions.

Wix mind-shouted: *Come back!*

But it was too late. Only Flurry and two others were still on the unicorn with him, and the imps darted after the flying pixies with shrieks of glee. Flurry's heart dropped.

The unicorn's horn glowed slightly, then they all completely disappeared. Flurry looked down at her invisible arms. It was an unusual, eerie feeling, to know she was there— the four of them were there on a unicorn and yet not visible at all.

The unicorn slowly walked across the clearing, causing the grasses and brush to remove his tracks as he passed. The painful sound of imps catching pixies filled the forest.

Then, there was silence.

A moment later a human dressed all in black with a red cape walked into the clearing with a smile. "Oh. I know you're here somewhere. You're a unicorn! I've read about you. Are you working with the pixies? I have a few spells up my sleeve that might find you. Let's see . . . Ventus!"

A gust of wind blew through, lifting branches and leaves off the ground and causing the unicorn to sway slightly.

"Nope. Not enough. I know. Disrupto!"

A nearby rock exploded, sending shards in the area where the unicorn had been. A few nicked his backside, and he tensed. They felt heat come from the unicorn, and then a second, identical unicorn carrying pixies appeared on the other side of the clearing and dashed into the woods.

"Ah ha!" The wizard raced after the illusion, leaving them alone for the moment.

Now what? Flurry asked urgently.

Wix scanned the trees. *There's a bird. I'll ask it what's going on.* He mumbled something and the small sparrow fluttered down to them, landing awkwardly on the invisible unicorn. Wix spoke with the bird for a moment, then mindspoke to the other three pixies: *It thinks the mushroom there is causing us to think there's a fairy ring. We need to destroy it. And get out of here.*

He mumbled to the unicorn, who casually strode over to the mushroom and squashed it fully with one well-planted hoof. Then they casually strolled out of the clearing and headed south, down the coast. Wix convinced the unicorn to carry them another half hour before parting.

When they were on their own again, Wix whistled into the air and made an odd gurgle-sounding call. Dozens of beetles appeared. "Go find any pixies you can. Send them messages in the bark to come here. We'll wait."

He turned to Flurry and the other two young pixies. He was now the oldest, at seventeen. No more elders to tell them what to do. They would be making their own decisions, from now on.

Flurry gazed at her friend. "You did great back there."

Wix smiled gently. "Thanks. Just doing my part."

"I've never seen you use your gifts with animals like that." Flurry smoothed her filthy white-and-blue outfit. "That was incredible."

"Well, usually the elders are telling me what to do." Wix gave her a little smile.

Flurry gazed at him curiously. "Yes. That's true. Maybe things will be different now that there are no elders with us. Do you think this smaller group of us can make it to the Great Stone Tower?"

"Perhaps." Wix sighed wearily and patted her back. "Yes. Yes, we will. Two days. We'll wait for two days, then keep heading to the tower. With or without elders. We'll find it. And we'll turn the tide in our favor."

Chapter 8

The First Cave

"TELL US MORE ABOUT THE ELF PEOPLE." Amber rode through the woods keeping a watchful eye—with Mizu situated behind her on Buttercup. Lorien loped alongside them.

"We're not all blue. To answer your question, Theo." Mizu had a firm but light grip around Amber's waist.

Theo blushed as he rode next to them. "Hey, how was I supposed to know?"

"I suppose."

Amber wondered again about Mizu's accent. Not only did the elf speak in a singsong way, she elongated certain vowels and didn't pronounce some consonants fully.

"Most forest elves from my people are brown or green. But we come in all colors. A lot of elves mirror the colors of their environment. I happen to be pretty well acquainted with water, so maybe that's why I'm blue."

"Interesting." Theo fell behind them to dodge a large tree, then pulled up next to them again. "And you said there are elves all over the world?"

"I imagine so." Mizu shrugged. "I've been to two other locations with elves. One group lives in a city in these mountains, beyond the dragon. The other group lives by the sea—but I visited them a long time ago. I'd love to go back now that I'm older."

"I *see*," Theo said smirking. Amber giggled.

"What's funny?" Mizu asked.

"I made a pun. Don't elves have humor with words?"

"Oh, I don't know." Mizu thought a moment. "Maybe it's because this is not my home tongue. We elves speak a different language—and for us, yes, we do have humor with words."

Amber lifted her hand to ask a branch to move out of the path. "How far away is your home?"

The elf whispered to herself, counting in her native tongue. "It took me twelve days to get to this point. It's a great distance on foot."

"What's it like?"

"Elves live in old forests where the trees are giant. Our homes and other buildings are in the trees. Sometimes we allow outsiders—special ones—to come see them." She looked at Theo carefully. "Perhaps one day you may be able to see them for yourselves."

Theo blushed and turned away. "That would be wonderful. Is it like a city? Are there many of you?"

"It's a city to us." Mizu peered into the distance in thought. "But not a large one. There are elves who live in much larger cities in different parts of the world. So I've been told."

It was starting to get dark, and Basil called from behind. "We need to set up camp. I'll ride Blazey ahead to find a good spot." He whistled and the phoenix landed next to him. He leaped from Storm onto Blazey and instantly took to the sky. Amber watched him navigate the branches with ease. He was getting quite good at riding the phoenix.

He returned a few minutes later. A clearing next to a creek was only ten minutes away on foot. At the creek, the group unloaded their horses and gave them water, then built a fire and laid out their blankets.

Mizu stood. "I'm going to scout the area to make sure it's completely safe."

Theo scrunched his face. "In the dark?"

"Of course." She stood proudly. "We elves see well in the dark—not with regular eyesight, but we see the heat and shapes of living things when there is little light."

Amber's eyes widened. "You mean, you can see the heat from bodies, like a slightly glowing light?"

"Yes."

Theo turned to Amber curiously. "What is it?"

"Well, that's what it was like for me back in the cave a few weeks ago. The one the trolls were in."

"Oh yeah."

Mizu watched nonchalantly. "Maybe you have some elf blood in you. It's not unheard of. Back in the last Great War, when all the humans and elves were working together against the great evil, there were some elves who left our people and stayed among the humans."

"My parents never mentioned anything to me. The only thing I know about my family and the Great War is that I'm related to a woman named Majestic Rose. But why don't I look anything like an elf?"

"I don't understand why certain traits are passed on while others aren't. But your special gifts with plants are the most common power among elves. It wouldn't surprise me at all."

Basil chimed in, "Hey, Theo. Remember that story of the half-elf we read back home. What was it—Lantau and the Ravens."

"Oh yeah!" Theo's face lit up. "That's right. Was that based on a true story?"

"I think so. Yeah." Basil chewed on a piece of dried jerky as he reclined next to the fire. "If I recall, he was a few generations removed, but the elf in him made him quicker and more in tune with nature."

"Hmm . . . Makes sense." Theo pursed his lips and glanced over at Mizu in thought, then quickly back to Basil when he saw her looking at him. "Thanks for the reminder."

Amber had a lot to think about, but the conversation shifted to their plans for the next day. The first of the mountains needed to be crossed. They hoped the mountain they had to find would be easy to spot—especially because Mizu told them Crodor's mountain was quite rocky with less trees and a huge cliff on one face.

In the morning, they made their way slowly up the first mountain. There wasn't a trail, so Amber used her powers to clear away deer paths to find better footing. Even with that, the going was slow. The trees were packed tightly together, forcing the group to travel single file along the path.

Blazey circled above, but the trees didn't allow a good view of the sky.

After a few hours, Theo called out, "Hey, everyone. We've got a problem."

"What is it?" Basil looked at him concerned.

"It's Blazey. He's getting tired. He can't see us, and there's nowhere to land. Just big trees."

They sat on their horses for a few moments, hoping for an idea.

"Theo," Basil finally said, "maybe you should ride him and see if there's a good place to land ahead—or see if you can find the dragon's mountain."

"How will I get on Blazey's back? There's nowhere for him to land." Theo wrung his hands.

Basil smiled wryly. "You'll have to climb a tree."

Theo looked up at the towering trunks and gulped. "Amber, you'll help, right?"

"Of course." She dismounted and scanned the area. "This tree over here is great. The branches will make you a ladder."

He nodded reluctantly, and Basil patted him on the back. "I'll climb up with you and help. I can make the air more stable for you to jump on Blazey. You go fly him around, and I'll stay up the tree with a cape to wave when I see you come back."

Theo sighed and started climbing. With Amber's help the tree was indeed easy to climb—even in the higher branches—so Theo was at the top in short order.

Basil swung up on a branch next to him. "Ok. Tell Blazey to hover next to us. When you're ready, I'll make the air lift you a bit like we planned."

"Ugh." Theo shook his head and looked below, then called out. "Amber, can you raise my branch a bit more?"

The branch slowly lifted above the tree, along with another branch for him to hold on to. Blazey hovered nearby as Theo took a few deep breaths, then leaped. His heart pushed into his throat when he thought he hadn't jumped far enough. But sure enough, a gust of wind lifted him an extra foot, and he landed on the huge bird.

"I made it!" He tightly grabbed the phoenix and adjusted himself. "Ok. There's forest as far as the eyes can see—and mountains everywhere. I'll fly south and look for a craggy mountain with less trees."

Blazey flapped and lifted higher, then soared over the trees. The forests all looked alike. He glanced around in a panic. Would he find Basil again?

He turned and circled back. Basil saw him coming and waved a cape. Theo flew back to him and hovered. "It all looks the same!" he called. "If I go too far, I might not find you again."

Basil shouted back. "Try going a bit farther anyway. See what's past the next mountain, then come back. I'll ask Amber to make this tree taller in the meantime. We'll make sure it stands above the others, so you can find it more easily."

Theo nodded and flew off again. He glanced back a few times but couldn't see Basil in the tree that was supposedly taller than the rest. He just had to trust that he'd be able to find them again. He wouldn't go too far.

It was a beautiful day, and if not for their circumstances, he might have enjoyed riding Blazey. But as soon as he got close enough to the first mountain and saw identical ones beyond it, he turned back and scoured the landscape for signs of Basil.

Blazey was slowing down. "Are you getting tired, Blazey?" Theo concentrated. The phoenix seemed capable of flying longer but hadn't rested since early that morning and was doing less flapping, more soaring. With nowhere to land for miles in every direction, Theo wondered if Blazey would be able to continue.

They circled the forest a few times, then spotted Basil in a much larger tree in the distance. They flew in and hovered nearby. Amber had crafted the top of the tree to have a giant branch so Blazey could partially land. The phoenix tried landing, but the tree wobbled, and the giant bird lifted off again.

"Wait!" Theo called. "Let me off first!" Eyes wide, he grasped at the tree. Basil grabbed his hand and pulled him down, just as the phoenix moved up and away.

They climbed down together to meet with Amber and Mizu. Theo's eyes were downcast.

"What is it, Theo? No luck finding the dragon's mountain?" Amber tried to look into his eyes.

"No. It's not that. I didn't find it. There are mountains and trees, and they just keep going. I'm afraid Blazey can't take it. He needs to land. He's getting tired."

"Oh no!" Amber frowned and gazed above the tree.

"That's not good." Basil scratched his head. "There were no rocks or clearings?"

"Nothing." Theo sullenly stared at the ground.

"Well . . ." Basil patted his shoulder. "Let's not make this worse than it already is. Tell Blazey he can go home."

"Are you sure?" Theo's eyes started tearing up.

Basil looked at Amber, who nodded reluctantly. "Yeah. We're sure. He's already done plenty."

Theo had a lump in his throat that made it hard to swallow. He looked up with tears in his eyes. "Ok. Blazey, you can go home now."

There was a piercing call from far above them, and Theo smiled. "He got the message. Who knows? Maybe we'll see him again someday." He stared at the upper branches of the trees, as if he could actually see the phoenix flying back to its home.

"Sure." Basil smiled gently. "You never know."

$$* * *$$

They traveled in silence for a couple of hours, winding around the next mountain. Basil climbed another tree after a while and had the same impression: trees followed by more trees. They continued around the first mountain and journeyed partway up a second mountain, with Basil climbing a tree every hour or so. After a full day, they set up camp under the large, dense trees.

The next day they continued in the same vein, traveling slowly through trees with Amber parting the underbrush and Basil periodically climbing a tree with her help.

Midafternoon, Basil called from the top of a tree. "That mountain over there is much rockier! There might be caves."

They crossed the mountain they were on and traveled up the craggy mountain. The horses' hooves clambered over loose rocks slowly.

Basil frowned. "This is going to be much harder to find a cave without being able to fly overhead. In fact, it's probably impossible."

"Don't be discouraged." Mizu gracefully hopped two rocks and stood next to Basil. "My people have found Crodor many times. If our drawings of the mountain are accurate, it pinpoints exactly where the cave is. I think we can find him if we find the right mountain."

They ate some lunch, then continued on. At one point, Theo stopped everyone. "Wait! There are creatures ahead!"

Everyone quieted and listened.

"What kind?" Basil strained his ears but couldn't hear anything.

"I have no idea. Like nothing I've encountered yet. But they seem larger than most of the wildlife we've come across. I think they're up in some caves over that ridge." He pointed to their right.

"Should we investigate?" Basil asked.

Theo shrugged. "Hard to say."

They looked at each other awkwardly. Finally Amber said, "They might be able to give us a clue about where Crodor lives, don't you think?"

Theo nodded. "Yes, if they're friendly."

They proceeded slowly toward the ridge. Basil drew his enchanted short sword that glowed when it neared creatures under the evil spell. So far, it remained pale.

Basil gestured to his sword. "That's a good sign, isn't it?"

Theo gulped. Something didn't seem right. He couldn't put his finger on it, but he walked slower and slower as they approached the edge of the large rocks.

They rounded the ridge and saw the caves below them. All was quiet. They watched and waited.

"Can you feel anything else, Theo?" Amber asked.

"No. I just keep sensing the same thing—they're not like the regular creatures we've been seeing in the forest. It's hard to say . . . but I think they're inside the cave."

Basil looked at his sword, still pale. "Ok, well, there's no use sitting up here." He started clambering down toward the cave entrance. Amber pulled the amulet out of her saddle bag, then followed at a short distance. Theo and Mizu stayed up above with the animals.

Basil reached the entrance and drew his long sword, switching his short sword to his left hand. "Hello!" His voice echoed down the cave for a moment, then all was silent.

Suddenly a giant creature with spindly legs flew out of the cave toward Basil as huge pincers reached toward his head. Basil quickly spun and swiped upward with his long sword, slicing through its belly. When it dropped to the ground, they got a better look.

It was like a gigantic ant, with a body the size of a wolf and six gangly legs. They stared at it a moment, and Basil touched it with his foot.

There was a sudden cry from above. "Run!"

Basil and Amber looked up at Theo, whose eyes were wide with horror, and he yelled again. "Run! As fast as you can! They're coming!"

Basil and Amber turned and ran down the mountain. Amber heard hundreds of clicking feet. She turned to get a look and saw dozens and dozens of huge ant creatures spilling out of the cave entrance after them.

She slipped and scraped her leg, then kept running.

The two ran faster and faster down the mountain face, the ants gaining on them every second. Amber glanced all around for trees or any kind of plant growth. Anything to help. But the entire mountain seemed to be rocks, large and small. She leaped off a boulder, an ant scurrying just behind in pursuit. Basil leaped from boulder to boulder in front of her, finding a path with sure footing.

Suddenly, Basil stopped and drew his swords. "It's a cliff!" He turned and charged toward the ants. Amber took a few more steps as she slowed and saw the long drop below. The cliff was hundreds of feet high. It was too dizzying to look down. She turned and drew her stiletto and dagger. Basil had already killed another ant as dozens more approached.

Amber sliced into an ant as it leaped toward her and then another. The dead ants dropped to the ground instantly, piling up. Basil killed them quickly and continued dodging, moving away down the ridge of the cliff face.

Before Amber knew it, three ants had climbed toward her at once, and she couldn't slice into them all. One of them sliced her leg and body with its large pincers.

"Aaah!" Amber yelled, staggering back and stabbing.

But the ants kept coming toward her, causing her to step back again. She dropped a third one, but three more ants took its place, crawling toward her, then another one clamped its pincers onto her leg.

She stumbled and the pincers released—but she now was on the edge of the cliff, with close to a dozen more ants clambering after her.

As she tried to stand her ground, an ant leaped onto her body and two more grabbed her arms. She plummeted off the cliff to the ground below.

Time slowed to a crawl. She marveled as every moment of her life played in her mind—from childhood watching her dad go off to the fishing boats to the moment where she took her first fishing trip with him on the Great Sea and to the time the phoenix burned their farm and she set off on this adventure.

I wonder if this is how I die.

She watched in fascination as the three ants slowly free-fell beside her.

She suddenly felt perceptive and thoughtful: After all these great adventures, I die by some insects. I guess I'm not one of the people from the prophecy after all. And I won't be able to help my family, even with all my powers.

Oh, yes, my powers.

Amber looked below her. It felt like an hour had passed since she'd fallen off the cliff, but it had only been seconds. Her heart leaped happily . . . below her was thick forest.

She reached out with her mind and asked the trees to catch her. The branches of the tallest trees acted like gentle hands and cushioned her fall, then dropped her to the ones below, and the ones below those, like many strong arms. The last branches lowered her to the ground with hardly a scratch.

Unfortunately, the three ants seemed to be able to land in the trees easily as well and were soon scrambling after her. She turned around dizzily. She'd dropped her dagger in the fall but still had her stiletto. She lunged as she'd been taught, dropping one ant to the ground—the other one leaped on to her back and scratched across it.

Thankfully, her magical protective cape prevented her from any injury, but she still winced at the force of the attack. She flung it off her back and stabbed it, then turned to face the last ant. Despite an injured leg, it picked itself off the ground and scrambled toward her, then leaped with its pincers open. Amber stepped to the left and lunged her right hand forward, piercing it in the neck.

As the last ant fell to the ground, she stood for a moment before collapsing into a heap. She was utterly exhausted and had multiple injuries—with Theo nowhere in sight. With adrenaline coursing through her veins, she wasn't even sure what was injured, but she could see that her left leg was bleeding. She felt like she'd been battered all over.

Not only were the trees too dense to see the sky, but she had no way of getting back up that enormous cliff.

As her heart slowed its beating, she looked around at the dark forest.

There weren't a lot of options, at first glance.

She could try walking around to find another way up. But would the others just stay there with the ant creatures? Probably not . . . too dangerous. Where would they go? Probably they'd keep going to find Crodor and hope that she'd do the same.

She felt an urgency and stood, but her body instantly complained. She tried lifting her arm. It felt five times heavier. Exhaustion settled in. The already-dark forest was growing darker by the minute, and she felt anxiety tighten her throat. There wasn't going to be an easy solution.

She was lost and tired, with none of her equipment. For the first time in her life, Amber felt completely alone.

Chapter 9

An Impossible Search

BASIL WAS STILL IN SHOCK from seeing Amber fall off the enormous cliff. But he had no time for that yet.

He turned and scrambled down the rocky mountainside. More than thirty enormous ants scuttled after him. He spun with both swords out and slashed an ant in half with his long sword, then leaped onto a boulder for a better vantage point.

Ants clambered up the boulder after him, but he held them off with his swords, piercing and slashing with all his might. After slicing three of them into pieces, the long sword felt heavy and slow, the wrong weapon for the job. The ants just kept coming.

Two crawled up the back side of the boulder, up his legs and penetrated his back.

"Aaargh!" Basil whipped around, twirling a gust of air that blew the ants off his body and slowed the approaching ones.

He dropped his long sword, sheathed his short sword, and lifted his hands. A whirlwind formed. In his anger and adrenaline, it grew quickly till it was a small tornado. The ants scattered in every direction, running away from it.

He directed the wind toward the oncoming ants, which swallowed them up, hurling the ants into the funnel as it lifted and twirled into the sky.

A few ants clambered around and continued to head toward him. He kept the tornado going while causing huge gusts of wind to sweep the stragglers toward the wind funnel. They were swallowed up with the others and twirled about in the upper reaches of the tornado.

With his hands raised, he took a step up the mountain back toward the cave and gave a slight pushing motion. He stepped further, focusing, focusing, and straining ever so slightly.

Faster now, he leaped up boulders till he saw the cave in the distance. As he sent the tornado toward it, weariness began to seep in. Just one more minute—the cave entrance couldn't be far now.

There! Dozens of ants scurried around in confusion, some poking their heads out and then retreating quickly when they saw the approaching tornado. With a shout of triumph he slammed all the force of the wind into the cave.

The giant ants flew down toward the opening. Some were squished by the impact, others caught themselves and scrambled back inside. Some rocks broke free and blocked part of the entrance. The remaining ants scurried and disappeared inside the cave.

Basil watched the cave entrance for a moment, then ran back down the mountain to where he'd seen Amber fall.

The entire edge of the cliff looked more or less the same. It was a sheer drop and a huge height—five hundred feet or more, ending in a dense canopy of ancient trees. The ground was completely obscured by all the trees.

Basil furrowed his brow angrily. Why did I wait so long to use my powers! Stupid! Just pulled out my swords as usual.

His heart beat wildly. Could she have possibly survived a fall that big? At least there are trees.

He cupped his hands over his mouth and shouted. "Amber! Can you hear me? Amber!"

The wind whistled through his hair. Was that a faint response? He couldn't be sure. "Amber!" he called again as loudly as possible.

It was almost not audible, but he faintly heard "Here!"

His heart skipped a beat and he breathed raggedly. "We're coming for you!" he shouted.

He stared down at the enormous trees far below, stomach in knots. The cliff looked impossible to climb, even for someone with his abilities. He scratched his head in thought. She had survived. But was she ok?

Rocks clattered on the slope behind him and he turned. Theo and Mizu were climbing down with Lorien, leaving the three horses above, on more solid ground.

Theo had a look of panic. "Where is she?"

Basil's eyes darted and he shook his head. "She fell off the cliff with all those ants on her. She survived. I heard her down there, but it's too hard to hear anything specific."

Theo and Mizu peered over the cliff. The elf frowned, and Theo put his hand on his cheek and shook his head. "Can you climb down?"

"No." Basil turned, walking briskly to where he'd dropped his long sword. He came back and peered down the huge cliff with a frown. "There's no way. Our best chance of finding her is to try to go around."

"Wait! Let me see if I can sense any animals." Theo shook his head up and down. "I think at least one ant fell with her. Over there." He pointed to the left. "It's still alive, barely. We'll have to hurry! She might be seriously injured."

"Yes." Basil turned and began to jog.

"Wait!" Theo called after him. "You're just going to leave? Aren't you going to try something?"

Basil turned with fire in his eyes. "Like what?"

"You just created a huge tornado. Like that evil wizard. Remember how he used his powers to fly? What if you can do that?"

"I literally just figured out how to make a tornado that big, and now you think I'm going to try flying down a cliff?"

"No. I guess not. But . . . going around could take all day."

"Do you have a better idea?" Basil watched his friend, then softened. "If only I'd tried that tornado two minutes earlier. Stupid, useless swords against a hundred ants. Don't know what I was thinking."

"Hey, you were under pressure. It's not your fault." Theo put his hand on Basil's shoulder.

Basil stood silently for a moment, lost in thought. Mizu broke the silence. "If we think to find her today, we must be leaving now."

They turned and dashed back to the horses.

Mizu rode Amber's horse, and the three turned back the way they'd come, heading down the mountain toward the base. The horses struggled with the rocky terrain but soon they were in more of a wooded area.

Thankfully, they had the trail Amber had made from when they'd come up, otherwise it would have been grueling with such dense brush. Even so, the horses had to go single file, with branches and rocks constantly blocking their path. They slowly made their way down the mountain as the sun set.

"We need to make camp." Basil scanned the area. "I don't see any good areas around here. And now that there are trees, it's getting harder to see in this low light."

"I could try to find her." Mizu sat on Buttercup calmly. "I can see in the dark, if you recall."

"That's right." Basil frowned in thought. "But I don't like the idea. I don't want us to split up any more than we already have. This forest is so dense it's almost impossible to find someone. It'll be hard to enough to find Amber with no tracks to lead us to her. We'll basically be guessing. Let's find a place to sleep and figure it out in the morning. Sorry, Theo."

Theo looked upset but nodded. They went down a little further till they came to a section that was flatter. Bushes were everywhere, and once again they missed Amber's ability to ask the plants to move. They cleared a space to sleep using their swords and settled in for the night.

✳ ✳ ✳

The next morning, they continued on their slow journey through the thick undergrowth. Theo stopped at one point and a small brown-and-yellow bird landed on his outstretched arm. "Have you seen a human around here?"

The bird cocked its head, then flew off.

"Any luck?" Basil watched the bird disappear into the trees.

"No. Nothing unusual around here. Let's keep going where we think she fell."

They continued along the mountain until they came to the cliff. "This must be it." Basil led the way along the base into the much taller, old-growth trees. The horses had a much easier time walking through the taller trees, with less underbrush to slow them down. "Can you try asking another animal?"

Theo paused, and a chipmunk approached from a nearby bush. It looked nervously at the large black cat nearby, but Lorien sat calmly licking his paw. "Have you seen a human around here?"

The chipmunk chattered briefly in a high-pitched squeak, then dashed off. Theo looked puzzled.

"What is it?" Basil stared at him nervously.

"Well. I don't think it saw a human. But I think there are other things in this forest that are pretty large."

Mizu craned her neck watching the chipmunk dash into some bushes. "We should spread out. We may be losing time."

"I already said, I don't want us to split up." Basil turned to her angrily.

"Our search is much too slow. What if she's hurt? She'll need the healing ring."

"No! This forest is too thick! We're practically lost ourselves." Basil put his fists on his hips. "I say we stick together."

Mizu's eyes flashed. "I am an elf. This is my life. I know thick forests, just like this. Plus I can hear from far away. I'll find her faster on my own, and then come back to you."

"Are you listening?" Wind whipped around Basil as he spoke. "We've already lost Amber. We can't lose anyone else."

Mizu deftly leaped up to a tree branch and looked down, her blue hair dangling past her shoulders. "You humans are so petty. You do not understand what elves can do."

Small branches and leaves whipped past Basil's face as his eyes flashed. "No. *You* don't understand. What makes you elves so superior? Do you have no common sense?"

Mizu stared at Basil coldly. "Have you no heart?"

"Ahem!" Theo stood between them with his arms raised. "Let's calm down a minute, you two."

Basil took a deep breath, and the wind died down around him.

"Listen. You're both right." Theo turned back and forth between them as he spoke. "Mizu, he doesn't want to lose you too. Also, there *is* strength in numbers. I think Basil's got a point. That chipmunk seemed to think there are lots of dangerous things out here. And you're also right, Mizu. We don't know what you're capable of. Yet. So why don't you tell us? Maybe we can work together."

Theo and Basil stood watching her expectantly. She sat with pursed lips for a moment, then stood. "We elves are at home in forests, and I could travel these more quickly by myself. But I will honor your desire to stay together for now. Though first, allow me here to climb this tree to see if I can view the cliffs more clearly. Perhaps we'll spot the section where she fell."

Basil nodded, and Mizu dashed up the tree as if it were flat ground. Even the larger spaces between branches were easy for her—her short frame leaped up with an enviable ease. She disappeared from view higher up and was gone for a few minutes, then appeared next to them from another direction.

Basil and Theo jumped in surprise. She'd come down from a totally different tree. Mizu shook her head. "The cliff is this way, far along. Let's hurry then and hasten toward our friend."

They continued slowly, looking everywhere for signs of Amber. Every once in a while, Mizu would leave Buttercup behind and dash up into a tree. She'd return a minute or two later and point in the direction for them to go.

They continued for a couple of hours like that, with Mizu climbing trees and Theo asking woodland animals questions. They paused near the cliffs to let their horses rest.

"It must be somewhere in this vicinity," Mizu said.

The next few hours were spent laboriously searching the base of the cliff for any sign of Amber or the ants. They fanned out and swept the entire area where she might have fallen. The going was slow and painful, because they all felt the urgency of finding her.

It started getting dark early in the covered forest, so they set up camp again, hoping for better luck the next day. They searched most of the next day, still going slowly. Did Amber survive at all? Were they even on the right track?

Mizu caught a rabbit for dinner that night, which was welcomed by Basil, but Theo looked at it and swallowed hard. "I can't eat that."

"Why not?" Basil asked, inhaling the delicious smell as he cooked it over the fire.

"I . . . I just can't. I don't think I can ever eat another living animal. Ever."

Basil stared at him curiously, then his eyes brightened. "Oh, I see. Because of your power."

"Yeah. I . . . it just doesn't seem right."

"Well . . ." Basil scratched his curly head. "What will you eat?"

"Nuts. Fruits. Vegetables. I don't know. I've heard there are people who do that. I don't think I'll starve."

"Well, you might out here." Basil looked around. "But we can look extra careful to see if there's anything edible."

"There is plenty to eat without killing creatures," Mizu said, turning the rabbit over the flames. "I will help you find some food as soon as I'm done cooking this."

"Thanks, Mizu." Theo looked relieved. He gave her a smile and her eyes softened toward him.

Basil watched him curiously. Would his connection with the air cause him to change in a major way as well?

Theo stretched. "I think there might be some wolves or other large creatures around here. Maybe. I just sensed from a rabbit in that bush over there that there's something large. A large creature of some sort that seems scary. Trying to figure out what—it's hard to tell. Rabbits aren't that smart."

Basil let out a little laugh. "No. I guess not." Then he sighed. With Amber gone, they'd been so serious the last day. It felt good to smile for a moment.

Theo's eyes grew wide. "Basil! It's a troll!"

Basil instantly drew his two swords and spun around. The short sword was faintly glowing. Theo pulled his crossbow out of its holster and put a bolt onto it. Mizu drew two throwing knives, while Lorien instinctively lurked into a bush and peered out.

They waited silently and watched the forest. Loud rumbling footsteps pierced the silence of the woods, coming from the cliffs. They shifted their focus and waited as it drew near.

Thump. Thump. Thump.

Theo's mind flashed to the last time trolls had attacked them. Their weapons couldn't do a single bit of damage, and they'd ended up running for their lives, lost in caverns.

Trolls were huge, strong, fierce, and with impenetrable skin. And this one was headed straight toward them.

Chapter 10

Survival Skills

PANIC RACED THROUGH AMBER'S BODY. How could she possibly survive alone in the forest with serious injuries? Weariness and pain throbbed everywhere. The giant trees loomed above, daring her to think of the huge distance separating her from her friends.

She shook her head. Survive. I need to focus to survive.

Taking a deep breath, she looked down at her battered body. The wound on her leg from the ant's pincer had torn the pant on her left leg, and the gash was bleeding. It throbbed and pulsed in pain, and she wondered if it was at risk for infection.

Using her fishing knife, she ripped off a strip of her shirt and wrapped it around the wound. If only Theo was here, she thought, wincing as the shirt touched the open gash. She wondered what they were doing. It had been hard to make out specific words, but it sounded like Basil had shouted they would keep going. She'd have to do the same.

She looked at the three giant ants. What other dangers lurked in the dark woods? Her eyes darted around at the shadows. Every nook felt full of possible enemies. She frowned. Without her dagger, she felt weak and unprotected. Time was precious, but still, the dagger was worth searching for.

She glanced all around the area. No glint of metal anywhere. Frantic, she got down on hands and knees feeling through the leaves. Nowhere. The dagger was gone, and she was practically defenseless.

She stood, then crouched back down. It had to be somewhere. The dagger took on new meaning. It was her lifeline—her sign that things would work out in the end. She searched for half an hour. About to give up, with dirty, raw fingers, she suddenly saw a glint under some leaves.

She grasped the dagger with a deep breath of relief. A proper weapon. She wasn't defenseless, at least.

Now what? She ran through the order of priorities her father had drilled into her head time and again.

First, safety. She'd done that—bandaged her wound and found her dagger. Next, shelter. And then food and water. She tried using her powers to feel out the forest for a stream. Nothing. No help at all.

She needed a direction. She closed her eyes in thought. They'd been heading southeast. Which way was that?

She looked at the trees for moss. Where she lived, moss always grew on the north side of trees, because there was less sunlight on that side. It was an easy way to tell the direction if the sun or stars weren't visible. But to her disappointment, the trees seemed to have moss on all sides. She checked tree after tree to no avail and looked for other possible clues.

Which way had she run from the ants? She replayed the events in her mind, then walked over to the base of the cliff. The rocks were crumbling and loose, with a sheer cliff disappearing into the trees above. Impossible to climb. She gazed at the cliff disappearing past the trees. Following it might work out—or it might not. There was no way of knowing without a better sense of the land.

She sighed deeply and looked up. The only sure way to know was to climb a tree and take a look. Her body ached from head to toe, and she was favoring her right leg. The wound on her left was throbbing, and blood was staining the makeshift bandage she'd tied around it.

Her older brother Patrick suddenly came to her mind. Right now, he'd be scoffing at her. Calling her some name or other. Squirt. That was one of his nicknames for her. She'd already proven him wrong by freeing Blazey—proven she was up to big challenges.

The pain in her leg ached. Patrick would have told her only a young, thoughtless girl would fall off a cliff. He never seemed to get injured. He'd give her a lecture about being smart and preventing issues before they arise. Would he have approached the ants at all?

She laughed out loud. Maybe he wouldn't have gotten hurt by the giant ants, but would Patrick have survived all the things she had? She'd fought with goblins and hobgoblins! Encountered a powerful wizard and come out ahead. They'd dealt with trolls and a phoenix. She was a powerful elementalist and an adventurer.

Meanwhile Patrick was staying warm at home. And here she was out in the woods on an adventure.

Alone.

She imagined her mom tucking her into bed. That would sure be nice right about now.

A single tear rolled down her cheek.

She blinked it away and focused on the tree next to her. Taking a deep breath, she mentally asked the tree to lower its branches to her. Exhausted, she sat on the branch and asked it to lift her to the next. Due to her fatigue, she figured out a system to lower branches to step on while also providing others for holding on. It was like walking up a moving staircase.

She struggled to the top of the tree and looked out. The sun was setting. She sighed in relief. Of course, the direction was obvious above the trees.

With the sun setting to her right, southeast was directly toward the mountain behind the cliff. She had no choice but to go around. She considered both directions—the right side seemed as good as the left, so she lowered herself down and began walking.

It grew darker with every step, and she felt more and more tired. She kept thinking about what to do to stay alive. Setting up camp seemed like the wisest idea. She looked through her small side bag. The amulet was there, which made her laugh. Not very useful. Next to it was her flint and steel. She could have a warm fire, at least.

But the lack of water was concerning. She was feeling more and more thirsty. She imagined her water on Buttercup's back and her heart skipped a beat. What if the horses couldn't outrun the ant creatures on that crumbly mountain? Did they survive? Did Basil figure out a way to deal with the ants?

She shook her head and clenched her jaw. No, I'm not going to worry. Basil called to me, so they're ok. Everything is going to be ok. I just fell off a cliff and survived! She tried to sense water again, but there were only trees and underbrush.

Was that a movement to her left? She strained her senses. More than one thing. Squirrels? Probably larger. She kept walking. The woods crawled with imaginary creatures. No friendly flits of light from pixies. Something else was out there, and it was dangerous.

Or was that her imagination? Maybe she just needed to think of other things. She thought of her mom's gentle eyes. If she were home, her mom would tuck her in, rub her feet and sing a song.

She hummed a familiar melody. Her pace quickened and she began singing out loud.

> The road has called with tales to tell,
> And so, we rise and bid farewell.
> Our path is long but sure, my friend,
> And leads to where there is no end.

> The day's a gift, with song so sweet,
> The traveling song will guide our feet.
> And when one day we meet again,
> New stories shall we share, my friend.

The song gave her strength, and she sang it over and over as she went.

Even with her powers, the underbrush was constantly in her way. She had to be careful not to trip or scrape into branches. Her energy was draining, especially as she limped, so she decided to only use her powers when necessary.

The cliff wound in and out, and the going was slow. The forest grew dark so that she could barely see. She peered into the bushes. Where to set up camp?

Mizu suddenly came to mind. The elf was perfectly comfortable walking in the dark forest. She did have perfect elf vision, but maybe it wouldn't be so bad for Amber. Regardless, it didn't feel safe to stop in a random place after the giant ants. Plus, she was so thirsty.

She closed her eyes, then opened them and focused. Yes! Trees and plants were slightly visible even in the dark. That combined with her ability to sense the living plants around her made her more confident in the pitch dark than she would've imagined possible.

And … if a dangerous creature did come, at least she she'd probably see it first. Not amazing, but that certainly helped. The forest was starting to feel less scary. She walked confidently into the dark, especially when she recalled how a mere two months earlier she'd have been stumbling and inching along.

It was still slow going, though, and Amber knew she needed to find a place to rest soon. Her leg throbbed and she looked down. The bandage was full of blood. It had looked shallow, but what if it was deep after all? At home her mother would have pulled out a needle and thread to stitch it up. Was there something to stop blood without a needle?

She ran through different kinds of injuries and ways to heal them she'd seen. Bandages and splints and herbal concoctions. She knew *some* healing remedies with plants, but not very many. And the plants were different here—some she recognized, but there were many new ones as well. Would her powers with plants help? Could she find out if a plant had healing properties more than another?

She kept walking, then paused suddenly. Was that a creek up ahead? She reached out with her powers. Yes. A small creek. So small she almost missed it. There were many smaller plants following a dense trail, from the cliff face through the forest till she couldn't sense any more. Definitely a water source of some sort.

She walked toward it, gaining even more confidence. It wasn't big, probably no fish, but it would do. She heard it burbling quietly and quickened her pace. She parted the bushes and leaned, smelling it.

It didn't smell of algae, and she didn't sense any plant danger, so she cupped her hands, filling them with water, and took a sip. The water was crisp and tasted fresh. She drank and drank, feeling energy return to her whole body.

A few feet away, a small plant with wide leaves caught her attention. She sensed that it could help her wound and staunch the blood flow. She sliced off some leaves, mushed them together, and removed the bandage on her leg. Unable to see the wound in the dark, she smothered it with the leaves, then ripped another piece of cloth off her shirt and wrapped it around.

Just then, a glimpse of movement caught her eye in the branches above. She whipped her head and squinted. A small creature hid behind the trunk—she could see the heat emanating from it. It was just a glimpse, but she thought it was about two feet tall. A racoon? Or some other creature . . .

She tried to stay calm and peered through the dark woods. Another scurry of movement in the distance. Not a racoon. Something on two feet, short and almost human looking. Would she be able to rest at all?

Amber drew her dagger and stiletto and watched the forest for a few minutes. A few more flits of movement. They came closer—at least five, maybe more. She ignored them to see what they'd do.

The thought of battling yet more creatures sagged her shoulders. The creatures approached closer till they were twenty feet away on all sides. Her heat vision wasn't ideal for making out details. One thing was for sure—they weren't racoons! Seven little furry men approached from all sides, with long racoon-like noses. They didn't wear clothing but had items she couldn't make out. Bags and tools, possibly weapons.

She stood still. What would they do? Could she battle them with her little blades?

A moment passed and one of them let out a quiet, high-pitched gurgle. They all approached her cautiously. Amber continued to stand still, estimating how she'd deal with an attack. She strained her senses again—would a nearby plant help?

A thornbush! A mere ten feet from her, nestled next to the tiny creek. It began to snake along the ground toward her, then set down roots in a ring all around her, crawling up quickly to form a wall.

The creatures paused their advance as the thornbush created a dome around Amber, then thickened, tightening every gap, growing many inches thick. She grew the walls till she could no longer see any trace of them, then she sat down and closed her eyes, sensing her body.

Would it be safe to sleep? Would the creatures get through the large thorns? Would the wound get worse? Little clicks and clacks of the creatures poking the base of the dome sounded, then it went silent. After a moment, the gash on her leg stopped pulsing in pain and she sighed. She wrapped her protective cloak around her body, pulled the hood over her head, curled up into a ball, and fell instantly asleep.

✳ ✳ ✳

For being so tired, Amber slept poorly. At first, her dreams involved giant ants racing toward her and falling off cliffs onto rocks below with no trees to catch her. They were followed by little furry men who poked her uncomfortably. But then her dreams shifted to trees. Most of the trees in the area were sleepy giants, getting their rest for the next hundred years. But some were awake.

One of them had a face made out of its knobby bark. "It's nice to see one of your kind in these parts. It's been a long time." It spoke in a deep and friendly voice.

"What do you mean *one of your kind*? What kind is that?" Amber felt calm and curious.

"The ones who can speak to us."

"But I'm dreaming. Why can't I speak to you during the day?"

"I don't know. Some of your people do. You seem young. Perhaps one day you will."

"What do people like me usually talk to you about?"

"Oh, a great many things. We trees have much wisdom over the years, you can imagine."

"Do you speak to each other?"

"Oh, yes. Well, not the sleeping ones. But many of us do."

"Can you help? I'm lost. And I'm trying to find the dragon who lives somewhere around here."

"Ah, yes. The dragon. He lives two mountains from here. Not far at all. He's burned some trees over the years, but overall he's quite friendly."

"Can you show me the way during the day?"

"That depends on you."

Amber thought for a moment. She knew she was dreaming and hoped she'd remember the conversation when she awoke.

142

"I have many wounds. Are there plants here that can help heal them?"

"Oh, yes. Definitely."

"Which ones?"

"You'll have to ask them. Your kind have done things with plants I wouldn't have imagined possible."

Amber smiled. She didn't want the moment to end but could feel the forest around her coming to life. Birds chirped nearby, and she knew she'd wake up soon. She grasped for more time with the ancient tree. "Tell me a story about my people."

"Hmm. Long ago, way before I was around, your kind worked with the trees not too far from here and decided to live together. Your people sustained the trees, and we trees, in turn, offered your people a place to live."

Amber couldn't imagine a place like that, however much she tried. She wanted to ask more but felt herself waking up. Sadly, she stopped trying to hold onto sleep and opened her eyes.

The thorn dome was still intact above her, and she asked it to untangle itself and move out of the way. She stood and stretched.

The creek was now visible, a tiny little rivulet meandering through moss, with shrubs and bushes lining it. She examined it more closely. It was so small there was no chance of fish. As if on cue her stomach gave a little gurgle.

Next up, check the wound. The bandage had no blood on it, which was a good sign. She removed the strip of cloth and the salve of leaves she'd made before falling asleep. It wasn't terribly deep, thankfully, but deep enough to bleed again if left untreated. She sensed the plant she'd found would help with keeping the blood from flowing but not necessarily help with healing. She added some more and rewrapped the cloth on it.

What plants could help heal it? She thought about what the old tree had said and mentally reached out to the area: *Can any of you plants help heal me?* She listened carefully, then laughed out loud. What? Did she expect an answer?

She limped down the creek scanning the different plants. One with small leaves and yellow flowers looked hopeful. She focused on it. Instead of asking it, she envisioned it in use with a person. Is this something you swallow? Or something you put on a wound? All at once she had a strong sense and she knew— this plant could help with healing by removing infections. She took some leaves and put them in her pouch.

Encouraged, she continued focusing on different plants, one at a time. Down the creek a ways, there were some other plants that helped with stomach pains, some that helped with dizziness, and some to help sleep at night. She got a sense of each one and relied on her powers to envision them in use. She gathered some leaves from each. Better to be prepared.

A tall willow tree beckoned, and she focused for a minute, then realized it wasn't the leaves that were interesting but the bark. She had the sense that she could soak the bark and drink it to relieve her pain.

She walked past a mushroom, then turned back and focused. This would help her relax. She picked it and smelled the pores underneath, instantly relieving some of the stress she'd been feeling. She felt strangely happy and made a mental note to get more if she found them.

Further along, a tall leafy plant entwined with a shorter, stubby one. This could be used as a glue. She was silent for a moment, considering. Would it hurt if she used it on her wound?

It seemed safe, so Amber decided to try. She sat down and made salves with some of the different plants, adding water and grinding them with a rock.

Carefully she unwrapped the bandages and lifted her pant leg. The wound wasn't bleeding but had signs of possible infection.

She carefully rinsed out the bloodier of the cloths and wiped around the wound. Then she gingerly applied the different salves and wrapped the dry bandage around the wound. She rolled her pant leg down and stood up.

It felt much better already. She tried putting pressure on her foot. The bandage held. Would it heal if she walked?

Amber took a gentle step, then another. She could walk, but would have to go slowly. She used her powers to climb another tree. Rockier mountains were in the distance to the south. The tree had said two mountains away. Maybe that was it?

She hobbled downstream and thought of all the people she missed. Her parents and friends from Seabrook came to mind, but she was more concerned for Theo, Basil, and Mizu. Were they ok? Then she thought of the General and the people of Lugo. Were the goblins on their way there? And where was Sage in all of this? The urgency of their situation sunk in again, but she couldn't speed her pace.

After a while the trees thinned out as the terrain grew rockier, bringing in glimpses of sky. She smiled and kept on, then realized there was a bigger creek ahead, judging by the types of plants she sensed. Her stomach growled, and she quickened her pace.

The creek was wider than the last one, enough that she couldn't leap across. There had to be fish. She walked over and peered in. No fish visible, so she walked downstream, then paused. A natural root vegetable was growing in a patch on an embankment. She pulled one out. They looked like long, narrow purple potatoes. She washed one off and took a nibble. Edible, but needed to be cooked.

She made a small fire and roasted some of them. They tasted incredible. And the fire—it was the first warmth she'd had all day, and warmed deep into her soul. She leaned back on a rock, with the sun on her face, and ate three of them.

Energy returned to her weary body and she stood again on wobbly feet, then continued downstream. The ground was rocky with only scattered trees and some plants along the side of the creek. Down the mountain to her left she thought she spied a pool. Carefully watching for rocks and roots, she hobbled along the creek scanning for fish.

The pool turned out to be much larger than she'd expected and was fed by two different creeks, the large one Amber had been following and also a much smaller one across the pool. The far side of the glistening water seemed somehow odd . . . it was steaming as if hot. She scanned the pool for fish. Seeing none, she decided to cross and explore the steaming side.

She walked back upstream and asked a tree to extend its roots across the creek, making a solid bridge. After crossing the bride, she went back downstream to explore the steaming creek.

This side of the pool had moss and algae covering the rocks inside, and a strong smell that at first seemed stinky. She leaned over and felt the water.

Her eyes widened and she smiled. It was warm—a wonderful temperature. A natural bath!

She removed her cloak, then her outer clothing, and carefully put her foot into the hot water where the small creek emptied into the pool. It was pure pleasure to her aching body, and she lowered herself all the way into the hot spring.

Amber sighed with relief, wondering how it was possible to have hot water out here in the wild. Her aches and pains began to diminish, and she closed her eyes, completely relaxed.

The worries of the last two days slipped away. She dipped her head in, then pulled it out just enough to listen. The wind blew gently on her face and whistled slightly between some rocks. The two different creeks bubbled happily. Her body fully relaxed, and she started to dose off.

Suddenly a thump sounded nearby followed by the crunching of grass from footsteps. Without moving, she opened her eyes and glanced around.

There, standing next to her—a mere twenty feet away— stood a large, menacing creature with huge wings. Amber's mind scrambled to figure out what it was.

The back half of the creature was a light brown fur, like an enormous lion, with a long tail that swept back and forth, and its rear legs ended in ferocious-looking claws. But its head and front half were like a gigantic brown eagle, complete with clawed front feet, feathers, a curved yellow beak, and eyes that darted around. It obviously had just landed, since it was folding in its massive wings.

Her mind raced. Don't move! What is it? If you know what it is, you can figure out what to do. What would Mr. Thompson say? He'd say frame the question another way. Ok. Ok. What's the question?

The creature looked around, then started walking slowly toward the pool.

Ok, it has the head of an eagle and the body of a lion. What creatures are like that? I know this. Ah, yes! A griffin! It's a griffin! Ok. What do I know about griffins? Not much. I don't think they're known to be friendly or unfriendly in the wild. But I'm pretty sure I've heard stories about people riding them. So that would be a good sign. But what does this one want?

Amber waited and watched as it approached the pool. From its movements, it obviously hadn't noticed her yet and looked as if it was going to step into the water.

Her heart raced. Can I make myself less visible? She slowly inched down under the water till only her eyes were showing. The griffin stepped into the water, then waded in deeper and deeper.

She tried not to panic . . . it could notice her at any instant. She forced herself not to make any sudden movements, even though every last part of her wanted to flee. Her luxurious bath suddenly felt like a dangerous trap.

Could her powers help? Her mind raced, but it was hard to imagine a way to get out of the situation alive. Could this be the end?

Chapter 11

Ancient Allies

AS RYDER APPROACHED the army barracks of Lugo, he prepared his speech. They needed to know about the approaching army—and the wizards.

He was surprised at all the commotion. Large numbers of soldiers were training in various fight tactics, massive catapults and other war machines were being built, and numerous military personnel were hustling in every direction throughout the area.

Ryder turned to one of the gate guards. "I have important information for whoever's in charge."

The guard nodded, then gestured to the other guards and walked Ryder inside. They strode past ten soldiers practicing lunges with spears and into a square building with another soldier just inside. "Someone's here to see the captain."

The second soldier looked Ryder up and down. "What's this about, then?"

"I've found a giant goblin army, and they're almost prepared to attack. I have many more details I can share."

The soldier nodded, seemingly not surprised. They must already know somehow, Ryder thought.

He was told to wait for a few minutes before being taken into a chamber where five men were steeped in discussion. A tall man—with a long light-brown mustache elegantly reaching past his jaw—motioned to him. His armor was like the others, but everything about him appeared more regal. His helmet, which sat on the table, had tall ruffles; golden tassels adorned his shoulders.

Ryder gushed. "I saw a goblin army and spoke with the wizards behind it. There are thousands of goblins and even giants and other creatures. The wizards said they're beginning their attack on human cities in one or two weeks. Right now, they're just past Ballmore, a few hours north of Hamilton."

The man raised his eyebrows and examined Ryder for a moment. "How do you know all this?"

"I crept into their camp and watched the army, then I infiltrated their castle. There are wizards—all sorts—and they're headed here!" He stared at the man. He'd expected more of a response and some quick answers, but the man looked almost dazed, unable to say anything.

"I'll have to introduce you to the General. Follow me." They walked through the building and past many more men training. Some were shooting at targets using crossbows or bows. Others were practicing swordplay while others worked with spears.

The General was busy, so it took nearly an hour before Ryder finally stood before him. It was clear this man was in charge—from the bold griffin painted on his breastplate to his gray hair to the regal scar down the left side of his face. He held himself with confidence; an air of control surrounded him.

"Speak," he said, coldly peering into Ryder's eyes. Three other men stood at the table, watching.

Ryder faltered for a moment, but then quickly repeated what he knew.

The General asked for more details here and there, and then eyed Ryder up and down. "You're a courier? Where do you hail from?"

"I'm from Seabrook, originally."

"Really? Are you familiar with Amber?"

Ryder was taken aback. "Yes! How do you know Amber?"

"She came here with two boys and a phoenix earlier this week. They were the ones who told us a goblin army was amassing."

Ryder beamed. "So they were successful breaking the spell on the phoenix! I *knew* she could do it."

The General nodded slightly. "They have an amulet the wizard Sage gave them, which can break the enchanting spell. They've gone off in search of a great red dragon in the Eerie Mountains to see if they can free it and convince it to help our cause." He sighed deeply. "They are a formidable trio with their powers, but even so . . ."

"Powers?" Ryder cocked his head.

"Yes, Amber with plants, Basil with air, and Theo with animals. Is this news to you?"

Ryder nodded slowly. "I also have powers. Over earth. But since meeting these wizards, I have to tell you that they have a strong army—and many powers of their own, far greater than mine."

The General pursed his lips in thought. "Powers . . . we haven't heard of anyone having powers in our kingdom for over a hundred years, and suddenly you . . . elementalists . . . are popping up everywhere. Very curious. I will add this to my planning. Can you do anything to strengthen our city walls in the weaker spots and help create a trench to surround the city?"

Ryder nodded strongly and the General continued. "Good. These will be important defenses. But first I have another thought. A courier with special powers . . ." He paused for effect and cleared the table, revealing a map. He pointed south of Arendon. "We have ancient allies far from here who owe us a great debt. If you rode quickly, I believe you could be there in less than two days. And if you pass them a sealed scroll with my insignia, I believe they will come just as quickly."

"Who are they?"

"Zylin monks. They live at the top of an incredible pinnacle hundreds of miles south of here. It's a long and difficult journey that would take a normal person a week to get there. But something tells me you could do it faster."

"Yes, I can ride fast. I've heard of couriers who can make a long trip like that quickly if they bring multiple horses and switch between them regularly. I'd want two more horses in excellent shape, saddled and ready to go."

"Consider it done." The General waved to another man in the room, who immediately disappeared. "I'll ensure you have enough provisions and anything else you require. And the sealed scroll. You must leave at once."

✳ ✳ ✳

The journey south went more smoothly than Ryder could have hoped. He did spot a couple different groups of goblins in the distance in the first few hours. But that was the end of any dangers. At that point, it became purely a matter of navigating the road and making sure he was headed in the right direction.

Four hours into his journey, he'd switched horses three times and had gone farther than he'd ever gone before in such a short period of time. And faster too—estimating close to twenty-five miles an hour. Since the horses seemed to be doing well with the hourly switching routine, he figured he could keep up the pace.

He finally stopped to rest the horses next to a creek and pulled out the map the General had given him. He figured he was about halfway to the monks' home. The General hadn't said much, except that Ryder's earth powers may be a huge help with the incredibly tall, steep pinnacle they lived on.

After a brief rest, he continued his journey at the same fast pace and rode past dusk. It felt too dangerous to ride in the pitch dark without knowing the terrain, so he camped for the night.

The next morning, he set out at first light and covered the last forty miles quickly, coming through the wide plains and toward mountains that reached far into the sky. The height of the tallest mountain was unnerving.

He squinted at the mountain, looking for a clue. It had to be the right mountain—it fit the description perfectly: a red rocky base and a gray-brown summit, jutting impossibly into the sky, unlike any mountain he'd seen.

But there was no visible way up. How did the monks go up and down? There had to be a road of some sort. He'd have to circle the entire mountain.

What if he didn't find a road? What if he had to go straight up? Could the monks really live on that tremendous peak?

He rode toward the base, hoping to find a clue. Having to circle the entire mountain meant losing hours—maybe even days—looking for a way up.

He almost began but then thought of the White Queen's gift that was in his pocket. Curious, he reached in and held the smooth white stone.

Instantly, he noticed something he hadn't before. A barely visible line circled the mountain perfectly—a thin bit of slightly darker earth that barely stood out. It spiraled all the way to the peak and at times disappeared. It clearly wasn't natural. He tracked it back to the base of the mountain and figured out that he wasn't far from the starting point.

Ryder marveled. *That stone really does work. Why would the White Queen give it to me if she really is evil? Maybe their final motives aren't bad, as she insisted.*

Regardless, its power was undeniable. Ryder put it carefully back in his pocket, a precious treasure.

As he rode toward the base of the mountain, thoughts flooded his mind. How could he think about the wizards in a good light? Of course the White Queen was evil. Or at least doing evil acts. She'd gathered a huge goblin army intent on killing people. He wondered about her offer to him, to gain enough power to end suffering. *That* was certainly an interesting idea. But not at the expense of killing people—of course.

He lowered his body to ride faster. Sure enough, he realized that an overgrown dirt road cut through the grasses, not too far from his vantage point. He veered to his right and followed the road to the mountain base. It cut around the rocks and hugged the mountain steadily.

The road started out ten feet wide, big enough for riding with two horses, side-by-side. But other times, the road narrowed. The higher he rose, the more he found himself using his earth powers to ensure the road was solid. It was grueling and tiresome to constantly check the road ahead.

An hour into his ascent, he'd circled the mountain once. And although his vantage point gazed down on the valley from a great height, the peak reached far above. He'd have to go faster if he wanted to get there before dark—but carefully, not pushing the horses too much. There was no water source, and he needed them all to make it.

Two hours later, he stopped and gazed at the plains far below. It was an incredible view, yet he was only halfway up. After a quick rest, he continued until reaching a nearly impassible section. The road was all but gone, destroyed by a landslide. A small path hugged the mountain, enough to pass on with the horses one at a time.

Ryder went first on one of the horses from Lugo. Suddenly, the earth crumbled. The horse whinnied and fell, and Ryder plummeted down the steep mountain right behind it.

An impossible drop.

He and the horse plunged down, scraping their bodies along the rocks as they tumbled to the rocky death trap far below. A bump to the arm, the back, the head. His body was getting battered.

He felt dizzy. How much longer before he blacked out? His mind could barely form a thought.

Enough!

He willed the earth to help.

And suddenly he stopped his descent. He wasn't on a ledge or a rock, but the earth held him. He didn't slip further, even though he was at such an incredible steep angle. He was held on like glue.

The earth rippled, lifting him up. He rode the mounding earth, rising up and up, like a wave on the ocean.

Although tired, dizzy, and bruised, he willed the earth to lift him back to the path. He found himself on solid ground again and looked around with dazed eyes. He'd survived.

He took a deep breath and held his hand out. It shook slightly. He waited till he calmed enough to have a sure hand, and rubbed his head where he got a big bruise. Brushing himself off, he looked down the cliff, then back at the road. The earth grew and strengthened, reinforcing the road so that it was stronger and wider.

A few minutes later, the road was in better shape than it had ever been before. He gazed down the edge again but couldn't see the horse anywhere. Calming himself another moment, he mounted another horse and continued up the trail.

As he got higher, the traversal around the mountain took less and less time, but the wind blew more fiercely. Looking down at the land below was unnerving.

Near the top the road disappeared into a cave entrance. Without a pause he entered the cave, using his powers to gauge the level of safety. At times he cleared rocks that might have tripped his horses, but all in all it was a well-built tunnel.

The next corner plunged him into utter darkness. He had only a small oil lantern, not designed for this kind of travel. It would have to suffice. His eyes adjusted to the light—seeing twenty feet in front.

The tunnel continued much as the road had, circling the mountain before turning into stairs. Ryder dismounted and carefully walked the horses up, constantly scanning for loose or unsafe steps. One step was crumbled, and he magically strengthened it to ensure the horses would be safe.

After half an hour, the lamp flickered. Did he have enough

oil? How far was the tunnel? He picked up his pace slightly, then sensed an end to the stairs ahead. He pushed forward and saw a slight beam of light. The end!

The stairs soon turned back into a smooth path, and the tunnel continued toward the daylight. He extinguished the lamp and urged the horses till they emerged into the open. The air was crisp and thin, a bit chilly, almost like winter. The terrain was mostly tall grasses, with the occasional shrub among loose rocks.

An unkept road led through a grand archway made of enormous brick pillars and a dark beam of wood that curved upwards on the ends. Beyond that sat an enormous castle-like complex. It rose inspiringly into the air with nine towers and sheer walls that dangerously hugged the side of the mountain.

Along the road, exotic statues and rock pillars stood out at seemingly random intervals. The statues were all unique, mostly with animal heads and the bodies of humans. At every point, the view was breathtaking, with the incredible building ahead, the unusual statues, and the heart-stopping height to the world below.

Ryder breathed deeply through his nose and took in rich herbal scent. He wanted to soak it all in, but he remembered the urgency of his situation and mounted one of the horses, riding toward the giant buildings. The tall rock walls had two impressive wooden doors, which were slightly open. He walked inside and looked around for people.

No movements anywhere.

The courtyard was spacious, with small buildings and a stable toward the back. He led his horses in and breathed a sigh of relief. There were five donkeys and six horses with hay and water. People were here. He shut the gate, then walked down the hall, holding the General's sealed letter.

"Hello? Is anybody here?" He wandered through halls and back onto streets in between buildings. "Hello?"

Small homes lined the streets, and a large building rose ahead. He opened its heavy, plain door. The inside was simple, yet somehow elegant. The wood was a rich, polished red. Even the floor seemed shiny and well kept, without a single scuff. Walking across it with his dirty boots felt instantly wrong.

He wondered if he should take his boots off, then looked back at the doorway to see a simple rack filled with hundreds of sandals and shoes as well as another nearly empty rack with a handful of indoor slippers of varying size, mostly much smaller than Ryder's feet. He trusted his instincts and removed his boots, putting on the largest pair of comfortable slippers before he continued inside.

A faint hum echoed through the halls, so he followed the sound past two rooms, which led to a large, open area filled with hundreds of men, women, and children sitting cross-legged with their eyes closed, humming.

He awkwardly stood in the doorway, watching and waiting. Even with the great urgency he'd been under, he felt himself relaxing. The minutes passed, then one middle-aged man at the back gently stood and slowly walked up to Ryder. He quietly gestured to follow him and walked out of the room and down the main hallway.

He wore a brown flowing robe with a wide yellow sash, all made of a smooth material that made no noise when he walked. He was clean-shaven and much shorter than Ryder, almost by a full head.

When they'd gone enough distance from the room to not distract the others, the man spoke. "Greetings. You've come during a time of group meditation. You're welcome to join us. We'll be done within an hour."

"I have an urgent message from the General of Lugo." Ryder held up the sealed letter. "There's an enormous goblin army coming to attack the city."

The man's eyes widened. "Goblins?"

Ryder watched him curiously. It was as if the man was waking from a dream. "Yes. And giants and other creatures. They're led by a group of wizards and coming to attack in less than two weeks. The General sent me here for help."

He looked around, wondering what possible help these meditative monks could give.

✳ ✳ ✳

Ryder gazed into the monk's eyes carefully, trying to figure out which one he was. Not only were they all dressed in the same type of yellow-sashed brown robe, they were all clean-shaven with dark hair and similar features: wide noses and cheeks and narrow eyes. Even though some were taller, some fatter, and some with other obvious traits, their similarities were confusing. He'd spent the last hour and a half mostly wondering who was who.

A monk named Pax quietly walked over, and all eyes turned to him. Ryder guessed he was a leader of sorts, although he couldn't discern if there was a true hierarchy of leadership among them. Much like the others, Pax was shorter than Ryder by half a head and had a serene peace in his narrow brown eyes.

Pax held the General's letter and tapped it with his hands in thought. He spoke slowly and carefully. "Your motives, Ryder. Before I read this letter, tell us why you're here."

Ryder's eyes darted between the different monks. "I've told you, it's an enormous army of thousands of goblins. What more do you need to know?"

"Yes. Yes. Goblin army. I'm sure the people of Lugo are eager for our help. But you. What motivates *you*?" He cocked his head slowly and pointed at Ryder's chest.

Ryder's gaze turned up in thought. Is there something I need to say to convince them? What are they looking for? "I'm . . . just wanting to stop a war."

The monk shook his head. "Of course. That's the surface layer. Let's go to the next layer down. And perhaps we'll go to the layer below that as well."

Ryder felt impatience well up within him. We're in a great rush! Can't they see that? Why are they asking about *me*, when the General's letter is right there?

He took a breath, trying to calm his thoughts. "I . . . I have power over the earth. Magic. I've never understood it, and I've kept it secret my whole life. It feels like now is the time to let the world know, and to get better at it. To use the power to help people, not just myself."

"Hmm." Pax wrinkled his brow. "That's good. Another layer down. Let's go one more layer down before we open the letter. Why are you here, Ryder?"

As Ryder stood in exasperation, the monk held his hands out, palms up. "If the words aren't coming, there is another way. Give me your hands."

Ryder put his hands out. The monk's hands were firm but gentle as he grasped Ryder's wrists. Pax's thumbs found Ryder's veins on both hands, and he lowered his head down, feeling the pulse and listening. They stood like that quietly for a minute, and then another. The twelve other monks stood surrounding them, watching in patient silence.

The minutes felt like hours. Ryder's mind raced, thinking of what possible thing the monk might discover. Can they read my mind? Can they sense things about me? What *are* my deeper motivations? If I were pure, would they have opened the letter already? Is it because I've been alone with my thoughts for so many years now? Have I become selfish?

Maybe I'm doing this for myself, more than the city. To grow more in my power. The White Queen certainly had me interested. Why is that? But these monks wouldn't want to know that, would they? What is he waiting for? Maybe I should just calm down. He took a breath and felt himself relax. If the monk waited all day, there wasn't much Ryder could do about it anyway.

Pax lifted his head and gazed into Ryder's eyes with a smile. "Well then. Let's read that letter."

He stepped back and broke the seal, then unrolled it and scanned it quickly. "We'll leave today. Nine of us. I will select the group myself."

Ryder raised his eyebrows curiously. How can nine monks be a big help against thousands of goblins? As if reading his mind, Pax continued, "Your trip will be worthwhile. All who join will be masters at Ra. Our ancient ways have great power against mindless evil."

"Ra? What's that? Is it magic?"

"In a sense, but probably not what you think. We do use the ether, but not to cast spells. We are peaceful people, and much like all aspects of our life, we work alongside the unseen world." When Ryder kept looking at him skeptically, the monk said, "Observe. Throw a rock at me."

Ryder found a small pebble nearby and threw it. Pax gracefully stepped to the side, lifted one hand and gestured with his other hand below. The rock swerved, looped around him, and flew back toward Ryder gently. He caught it and smiled. "Well then, let's get going."

In less than two hours, five men, four women, and Ryder waved goodbye and headed out the gates, each atop a single horse. At the archway before the tunnel, the monks dismounted and turned back to their home, kneeling and lowering their heads in silence.

Ryder stood watching them, the wind whistling through his hair and the horses shuffling. Something about their quiet peace was intriguing and desirable. Yet it also felt too slow. How long does it take to master their ways? And does it mean slowing down everything? Do I have the patience for that?

They were soon traveling down the tunnel stairs, carefully and quickly. The monk in the lead went into a trance, then moved her body in a graceful motion and suddenly the tunnel was lit up. Ryder couldn't see any light source, but they now could see all the way down the tunnel as clear as day, so they made it through the tunnel quickly.

It was late in the day, but downhill was faster than up, and they made good progress down the road. The monks were generally quiet and traveled single file for the most part, so there wasn't much conversation. However, when they got to the section of road that Ryder had fixed that morning, Pax rode up next to him.

"Is that your handiwork?"

"Yes."

Pax gazed at him for a moment with a curious expression. "Thank you."

"Just curious," Ryder said. "Why do you live high up, on top of this mountain?"

"That's an ancient question . . . Tops of mountains can be holy places. Do you live near mountains?"

"Yes. I grew up next to the sea, but there were mountains not too far. Although nothing this enormous."

"Have you ever noticed that on the top of some mountains you have a richer spiritual experience? A deeper connection to all things good? It's common for people to build temples or shrines at the tops of mountains."

"Is there more mana there or something? I've heard about the idea of mana epicenters."

"Not exactly. There are indeed centers of mana in this world, but they are obscured from us humans, protected by pixies for thousands of years so that we don't make the same mistakes we made long ago and abuse their power."

"Oh! Maybe that's what the wizards are trying to do."

"What do you mean? What wizards?"

"The wizards gathering this army of goblins and other creatures together. They're also chasing and killing the pixies. Maybe they're hoping the pixies will reveal their source of mana."

Pax looked thoughtful, gazing into the distance. "This army they're gathering, do you have any idea why?"

"No," Ryder shook his head. "They tried to convince me to join them. They said it would lead to great power, and it was just a means to an end."

"Indeed." Pax gave a slight smile to Ryder. "It always is, isn't it?" He urged his horse forward, and they traveled down the road in silence till they arrived at the base. By then it was dusk, and they set up camp for the night.

After eating a simple bread-and-cheese meal around the campfire, Ryder watched in fascination as the nine monks stood in a circle and moved their bodies in unison, ever so slowly, as if in hand-to-hand combat. They all lifted their right knees as one, then spread their legs and pivoted, holding their arms gracefully out, almost like weapons.

They continued as one for a good half hour, then stood silently for a moment before ending their trance-like state and returning to the fire. Ryder considered the power they wielded—calm, slow, patient—so different than what he felt inside himself.

He tossed a rock at Pax, who grinned, then twirled, causing the rock to spin around himself and up into the air.

Ryder chuckled. "What other magic can you do besides change the course of rocks and light up tunnels?"

"Oh, a great many things, indeed. It takes many years to master Ra, but when you do, you have full insight into all your surroundings. Nothing is a surprise. And we are also . . . friendly . . . with the ether. We can ask it to help us move faster, to protect us, even to heal."

"Anything useful for attacks?"

Pax frowned. "That's not the natural order. We practice self-defense—using the other's power against them. No Zylin monk will ever attack another living being unless absolutely necessary."

"So you're peaceful, your powers take a lifetime to learn, and you practice them by your slow movement stuff. It's pretty different than the other kinds of magic I've seen."

Pax gave a slight laugh. "Quite different, indeed. I think you'll find we can be quite helpful against mere goblins, my dear Ryder."

"Oh, I'm sure you will. I just hope we get there in time."

As they went to bed that night, Ryder's mind turned over. These monks had amazing power, but so did the White Queen. Her powers were immediate, strong, and obvious. But the monks' slowness seemed strong in its own way. Which would prove stronger in a clash?

There's something about this realm of magic I still don't get, he mused. It seems like there are many different approaches and ways to use it. So many mysteries to unravel. He just might have to join Chandler in the library again and read a book or two. Or have another conversation with an experienced wizard, like Sage . . .

Or even the White Queen, perhaps. That would help him learn faster. Much faster.

Chapter 12

Encounter at the Springs

AMBER'S MIND RACED as the griffin waded deeper into the pool, then fully submerged itself, the top of its incredible eagle's head disappearing.

This is my chance! I could try to get away right now.

But she couldn't run very fast with her leg wound—and she needed her boots either way. Would her powers help? And what if the griffin was enchanted? Could she get the amulet around its neck somehow?

She looked over to where her clothing and pouch lay. The amulet seemed to beckon to her. If the griffin was enchanted, that would be the best plan. Break the spell first, just in case.

Rising out of the water, she stepped toward her clothing. Thankfully, the griffin remained under the water, which gave her time to pull the chain and amulet out of the pouch.

Now how can I get it around its head?

She took a deep breath and scanned the water. The griffin wasn't too far away, lying at the base of the deepest part of the pool. She mentally calculated where it would raise its head out of the water and whether she could leap that far. She shook her head. Way too far.

She looked around, then noticed a small tree not too far away. Maybe she could make it stretch its branches far enough. Reaching out with her powers, she caused the tiny branches to spread over the pool. They grew further out, entwining themselves for strength. But it didn't seem like they'd be able to hold themselves up for a great distance.

Amber let them gently touch the water and continue to grow across. Gliding along the water, the branches looked like they'd get only halfway.

There were some grasses near her feet. She placed the amulet chain around them and encouraged them to take it toward the center of the pool. The grasses met up with the branches, so she focused again, causing them to work together to open the chain and form it into a circle where she thought the griffin would raise its head.

Then she waited.

It seemed as if time stopped. She focused on making the chain's opening as wide as possible, then slowly reached down and grabbed her cape, tying it around her neck.

All at once the griffin lifted its head out of the water, barely missing the center of the circle. The amulet's chain got caught in a ruffle of feathers and dangled precariously. The griffin spotted Amber and let out a loud shriek.

"CAAAAAW!"

Amber's eyes grew wide as the griffin splashed out of the water wildly, an angry fire in its eyes, bent on attacking her.

She turned and ran toward the nearest trees thirty yards away, the griffin hot on her heels.

"Aaaaawk!" The griffin crashed after her a little clumsily at first as it stepped on loose rocks, then picked up speed.

The trees lowered their branches like arms, welcoming her. She made it to the branches, swept into the air as others lowered beneath her—the griffin only a few feet behind.

It clawed at the tree limbs and climbed up the first ones. Wildly cracking through more branches, it clambered upward, heading toward her with fierce red eyes.

Amber panicked. I'm not fast enough with my powers to stop it!

It splintered through the next branches and lifted itself another yard closer, just out of reach—nearly snatching her foot. Amber edged up higher and drew all her inner strength to thicken the branches.

It has to be under the spell, Amber thought, then scanned the ground for the amulet.

There! At the base of the tree. It had fallen off the griffin.

The enormous bird-lion clawed higher, just out of reach. The nearby branches grew thicker. They wrapped around, creating a thick cage. The griffin grew more furious as it went, but all its anger couldn't help as the tree bound the creature more tightly.

It inched up a little more, within reach of Amber's left foot, and her heart beat wildly. Letting out an angry squawk, it clawed to no avail, held in a prison of branches.

Some crawling buds grew around the amulet and soon sprung into a young tree, lifting the amulet higher till the higher branches received it. The branches slowly twined upward and carefully draped the amulet around the neck of the struggling beast.

Instantly the thrashing stopped, and the red glow left its eyes. It blinked and looked around as if confused. When it saw Amber, its eyes grew wide, and it squawked but sounded much friendlier.

Amber released her breath, and the branches broke their hold, letting the griffin drop gently to the ground.

The two watched each other for a moment, then the griffin relaxed and pulled its wings in tight. Amber sighed with relief. Her injured leg throbbed—she'd have to look at it again. But now wasn't the time.

She climbed down and stood before the large beast. Neither of them moved. She slowly extended her hand.

"Hi. I'm Amber. You were under a spell, but the amulet I put around your neck helped you."

She wasn't sure if the griffin understood anything she said, but it seemed to relax more as she talked. "I'm lost in the woods and trying to find my friends. We're on a quest to find the old dragon named Crodor. I need to find my friends. Are you a friendly griffin?"

The griffin took one step toward her. She tried not to cringe, keeping her hand out as she continued talking calmly so it would approach. "You see, we've been working with a great wizard named Sage who's been helping us with an evil enchantment on all kinds of creatures, like you. And we think the dragon is under the spell as well. Like you were, before I put that amulet around your neck."

The griffin came up and smelled her hand, then slowly walked around her, taking intermittent sniffs. She took a deep breath and stayed still. The griffin snuffled her a few times from behind, then continued circling till it stood two feet from her, peering into her eyes.

Its eyes had enormous brown pupils, and the feathers were various browns and whites, weaving a beautiful natural pattern down to its claws. Its enormous front claws were a crusty pale yellow, with incredibly sharp-looking talons. At the rear, it had oversized lion's paws with dark-brown claws. The area where the eagle ended and the lion began looked surprisingly natural, with feathers shifting to a slightly lighter orange-brown fur. It had a smell like a wet dog . . . somewhat repulsive but natural.

She reached out her hand slightly toward its pale curved beak, and when it didn't flinch, she slowly stepped toward it, then touched it ever so gently with her fingers. The griffin kept its head stable, watching her calmly, so she stepped forward a little more and placed her whole hand on its beak.

As the creature remained calm, she breathed in relief and smiled. "You see? We can be friends after all." It looked as if it expected something of her. *Maybe it expects me to walk around it?* She carefully stepped to the side and walked around the creature a little at a time, keeping her hand lightly touching it, much as it did to her.

On closer inspection, not only did the feathers make overall patterns with dark and light browns, each feather had its individual pattern, which gave it a lush, full look. There was a scar on the griffin's right side where some of the fur never grew back. Its rear paws were massive, and its tail had a dark-brown tuft of hair on the end of it.

The tail swatted her gently as she walked past. While the feathers were dry, the fur was still wet from the water. The griffin kept its wings completely folded in along its back, and she marveled at how tightly they fit onto the body, as if they weren't even there.

When she had completed the walk around the griffin, they looked at each other face-to-face again. "Could I take back the amulet around your neck?" Amber pointed to the necklace.

The griffin stood calmly, so she reached and gently lifted the chain off its neck. When her arms were as high as they would go, the griffin lowered its head so she could pull it off more easily.

"Now I'm gonna get some clothes on!" She backed toward her clothing, keeping her face toward the griffin the entire time. As she walked, she continued talking calmly, a string of sound to fill the air more than giving any meaning. She kept an eye on the griffin while she looked at her wound.

The creature stayed calm and walked over to her, watching curiously.

The gash from the ant was bleeding again, and she quickly made more salve and rebandaged it. Dressed with her weapons strapped on, she turned to the griffin, who was watching her patiently.

"Now, here's a question for you. Would you be willing to give me a ride somewhere?"

The griffin didn't react, so she walked over to it and motioned as if she would climb on. The griffin lowered its front half, making it easier for her.

It's done this before, she thought. She grabbed some tufts of fur and feathers. The area where the fur and feathers came together was worn down, like a horse that wore a saddle. Yes, it has been ridden before.

She settled in with one leg on each side. Definitely a lot wider creature than Blazey. Although she felt like she could grip the feathers, she felt less of a hold overall. Thanks to its width, she didn't think she'd slide off. She'd make sure to hold on tight.

But how should she tell it where to go?

She didn't have time to figure it out. With a slight crouch, the griffin spread its wings and suddenly leaped, soaring gracefully into the sky. She felt the familiar exhilaration of leaving the ground quickly while simultaneously seeing a fantastic view of the surrounding land.

Oh yes . . . and then there was the wind.

Her eyes filled with tears, and she squinted, tempted to lift a hand to wipe her eyes. She focused on keeping her intense grip. With a few flaps, the griffin was already nearing the top of the mountain and then crested it majestically. There were mountains as far as she could see in every direction.

The griffin took two more flaps, before it soared toward a large mountain next to them.

I need to keep track of where I am! Amber suddenly panicked. Which direction are we going?

Without looking around too much, she could tell they were heading southwest—somewhat similar to the direction she had been headed but not entirely. Was that Mount Eerie, where Crodor lived? It certainly was very rocky and craggy, with very few trees. But there were others very similar around it, so it was hard to know.

The griffin continued to coast toward the mountain, giving an occasional flap. It approached a central spot on the mount, which was rocky and full of cliffs. It circled to the left and headed toward a flat, grassy clearing with a cave entrance. The griffin gracefully lifted its wings, slightly to slow itself, then with barely a sound landed in the center of the clearing.

It lowered its head and Amber slid off. She landed on her feet but limped a little to take the pressure off her injured leg. She straightened her clothing and checked to make sure her weapons and pouch were all intact.

There were signs of people everywhere—fences and posts, a trailhead, and a sign. She walked over to the sign, but it was in a language she didn't recognize. The letters were completely different—far from the elf letters she'd seen with the prophecy but unlike anything she'd seen before: thick, diamond-like shapes repeating themselves.

The griffin walked into the cave. Not knowing what else to do, she walked after it.

The cave entrance was large enough to fit two or three griffins side by side. Inside, a wide hallway disappeared into the darkness. It looked as if it was manmade, perfectly shaped. After a short distance, it opened into a vast cavern. Highly crafted slits ran up and down through the walls to let in just enough light to see, as well as to keep the room's air fresh without letting in rain or snow.

Wall sconces with strange-looking unlit torches hung from the cave walls every ten feet. Three other griffins lay on a large bed of hay, over to the back. To Amber's right were two large tables with chairs; to her left were seven large saddles hanging on some racks. There were also three smaller exits toward the back that went further into the mountain.

When the other griffins saw Amber and the first griffin, they instantly stood and cawed. The sound echoed painfully in the chamber, and Amber covered her ears. They approached with lowered front bodies and narrow eyes, making a sort of growling sound, as if they were ready to attack. They looked at Amber with great animosity, eyes glowing red. The hair and feathers on their backs were ruffled, like a cat about to pounce.

Her heart fluttered. *They're enchanted! We've walked right into a trap.*

Amber's griffin lowered itself and made the same growling noise toward them.

They slowed a moment, then continued to approach angrily, piercing her with furious eyes.

Her mind raced as she glanced around for options: One griffin I was able to handle. But how can I get the amulet around the necks of three angry, enchanted griffins in the middle of a cave with no trees in sight?

Chapter 13

Captured

LOUD FOOTSTEPS THUMPED through the woods, bringing dread into the hearts of Theo, Basil, and Mizu. Theo looked around wildly for ideas. Mizu balanced her throwing knives at the ready while her large black cat bristled next to her. Basil stood poised, gripping his swords.

In his left hand, his short sword glowed a fierce orange. Only his enchanted short sword would be able to do any serious damage. Or maybe he could open a wound with the short sword, then try to plunge the long sword in? He continued to think of possible strategies. A tornado would be helpful—but could he create one big enough to pick up a troll?

And could they really handle a troll? The last time they'd taken on trolls they had been asleep. Even a sword that was enchanted to cut through anything would have to be used properly to be able to do any real damage.

The creature suddenly crashed into the clearing, causing the horses to jump and neigh. The sun wasn't directly shining on it, but even in the scattered light, they saw it in all its fearsome detail.

A good twelve feet high, its huge, muscular body had a much larger top torso than bottom. It looked like it was made of rocks, gray and earthy colored, with moss and even small seedlings growing out of random spots.

It had two small slits for a nose and massive fanged mouth underneath, revealing dozens of jagged teeth. It ran toward them chaotically swinging a large spiked club in a wide arc.

The three dove out of the way so the club cracked into a tree, leaving a massive dent and sending shards of bark everywhere.

"Ow!" Theo yelled as wood splinters stung his face and a piece of wood went into his left eye. He rubbed and blinked it out. With the magical ring on his finger, it was already healing quickly, but his vision was slightly blurred.

Mizu leaped up first, throwing both her daggers with precise aim. One of them penetrated an inch, and the other clattered harmlessly off the thick hide.

Theo dropped to the ground and, despite fuzzy vision, aimed his crossbow, releasing a bolt toward the giant troll. The bolt sank a couple of inches into its massive torso, looking like a tiny pin in a pincushion.

Basil darted toward the troll, thrusting upward into its stomach with the short sword, then pulling it out quickly and doing the same with the long sword. Unfortunately, with the troll's wild movements, the long sword missed the opening and clattered against the thick hide, cracking the top off the blade and causing the hilt to vibrate.

Intense pain shot through Basil's arm, all the way up to his shoulder. "Aaah!" He dropped the long sword and rolled away.

The troll looked around at them as if confused, then turned and continued running through the woods in the direction it had been heading before. The three looked at each other perplexed.

"Is it afraid of us?" Basil asked.

Mizu held up her finger. "Quiet! Listen."

The crashing and stomping of the troll resonated through the forest. They all wondered, what could cause a troll of that magnitude to run past them so quickly? Then, from where the troll had come, the trio made out the sound of many small creatures scrambling through the underbrush.

Crashing through the bushes came dozens of racoon-like creatures running toward them on two feet. A few of them were carrying small tools or had straps over their shoulders with little bags or tools attached. Their gray-brown furry bodies had long noses with sharp teeth, and they stood about two feet tall, with little outfits that almost made them look cute.

The first ones paused when they saw the three, then they continued running into the clearing.

"Mikons!" Mizu shouted. "Don't let them bite you."

"What's a mikon?" Basil spun around with his short sword at the ready.

Theo rubbed his eyes and stumbled back a step.

"These things!" Mizu dashed toward a tree with Lorien at her heels.

The first ones reached Basil and climbed up his leg. He whirled and created a wind spiral, but it blew the approaching ones, not the three that were already climbing up his pants. He swiped at them anxiously, knocking one off into the wind

spiral, but one of them managed to sneak its face under his shirt and bite into his side.

"Aaah!" Basil knocked it in the head with his fist, but it was too late. He became woozy and the world turned blurry. He fell to the forest floor.

Theo was next. He had no chance with his eyes in their fuzzy state. The mikons surrounded him, and one of them nipped him through his pant leg. He dropped to the ground a moment later.

Mizu dashed in a zigzag pattern, dozens of mikons following close behind. She leaped and spun, throwing a knife that dropped one mikon to the ground. Reaching the nearest tree, she ran up the trunk with two well-placed steps, grabbed the lowest branch, and swung up, landing gracefully with both feet and getting a view of the scene below.

Lorien was nowhere to be seen, and dozens of mikons were scrambling up the tree behind her while a few stayed near Basil and Theo. She leaped up again to the next branch, and then the next. She could outrun a few mikons in the trees, certainly. But then she heard a scream and turned to look.

Lorien was surrounded by four of them out in the open, hackles raised. The cat hissed and swiped, scratching one of them and sending it reeling. But two more mikons joined the others, surrounding the large cat on every side.

She couldn't watch. Not Lorien! She took aim and threw a knife, dropping the one directly behind the cat which looked ready to attack. Could she save the cat? Her eyes darted around, and then she realized, too late, that one of the mikons was an awfully good tree climber. As the mikon bit into her leg, she had a brief moment to wonder how badly it would hurt, falling from such a great height, and then the world went black.

✳ ✳ ✳

"Psst! Basil!" Theo's eyes darted around. They were in a poorly lit cave at the bottom of a pit, tied to the floor with strong, thin ropes and wooden stakes. The click-clack of tiny claws drifted in from above. The two humans, the elf, and the large cat were all lying on the ground, tied down. The others were all asleep.

"Basil! Wake up!" Theo whispered urgently. "Mizu! Can you hear me?"

Silence. They slept deeply. He took a deep breath in thought. *The healing ring must be what woke me. I wonder how long I slept?*

He scanned the area for ideas. The pit was empty of items. In the low light it appeared that some rope was piled up on the edge of the pit, a good fifteen feet above them. He closed his eyes. *Could there be an animal nearby?* He sensed right away— thirty yards to the left was the forest, with plenty of animals. But the squirrels he beckoned had no desire to come inside. He searched further.

There! Not too far away, two magpies were sitting on a branch. *Come lend some help, would you?* Theo pleaded with them gently. They cocked their heads and stayed, as if asking, *Why?*

We could really use your help, little friends. Theo tried to remain calm. *Would these simple creatures take a risk for them?*

After a moment, they flapped off the branch, drifting into the cave. They fluttered down the passageway and down the pit, landing on Theo, who sighed in relief.

There it is. Thank you, my friends. Now, just break these ropes, please.

The magpies pecked at the ropes on Theo, nipping bits off a little at a time. The first rope snapped, then the second. Theo lifted his left arm and yanked at the rope on his right. Amazing. He couldn't just snap it. However small they appeared, the ropes were quite strong. But with two snapped, the rest loosened, and Theo squirmed and wiggled his way out.

Would you mind breaking the ropes on my friends, as well? The magpies got to work on Mizu as Theo crawled over to Basil, placing his hand with healing ring on his head.

A moment later Basil's eyes opened wide. Theo put his finger over his lips and whispered, "Shh! Don't make a sound."

Basil's eyes returned to a relaxed state. "Where are we?" he whispered back.

"The mikons' cave, I guess." Theo shrugged. "We'll have to ask Mizu what they want with us. I'll have the birds free you next."

Basil nodded, and Theo crawled over to Mizu. A scuffling noise came from above and he froze. Were they coming to check on them? He stayed still with wide eyes for a moment. When the sound passed, he crawled the rest of the way to Mizu, putting his hand on her head.

She opened her eyes frantically and took some ragged breaths before calming down. Without a word, she gave a slight nod to Theo and glanced around the pit. Theo went over to Lorien and put his hand on the giant cat, waking it from its slumber.

Basil sat up and rubbed his arms where the ropes had been. "Mizu, what do they want with us?" His whisper echoed in the darkness.

"They want us to become like them. A single bite usually does it. It takes a week for the transformation to happen. I'm assuming we'll be fine—with Theo's ring. My people have a potion which can bring someone back to elf form within the first few weeks. But after that, it's permanent. They're not awful creatures for most of the month, but when the moon is full, they go on the hunt to gather more."

"Can they bite all creatures to change them?"

Mizu shook her head. "Oh no. Only those of us on two legs. Goblins are the most common, I think because they're stupid, so easy to catch. Lorien here, I don't know why they bit him."

Basil stifled a yawn. "How do we get out of here without alerting them?"

Theo glanced at the magpies. Any help there? *Can you pass us some rope? It's just up there.* He pointed to a pile of rope at the wall's upper edge.

The birds fluttered up and tried grabbing at the rope. But they scuffled and pulled to no avail.

Theo scrunched up his face. "I think it's tied to something. They can't get the rope. Or maybe it's not even rope. It's hard to tell in this low light."

"Shhh!" Mizu suddenly jumped over and grabbed Theo's arm. "They're coming. Have the birds hide."

The three of them quickly lay down on the ground where they'd been, and the birds hopped into the corner. Two mikons walked into the chamber and over to the edge with torches that flickered and lit up the room unevenly. They spoke in high-pitched gurgling noises to each other.

Theo's heart was beating loudly in his ears. Would they notice the snapped ropes? Were they in similar enough spots not to cause an alarm?

Thankfully, the creatures glanced down at the bottom of the pit with barely a look before continuing on their way. The friends breathed in relief. That was close.

Theo whispered, "I don't know what's up there, but the magpies aren't having much luck getting us rope. Any other ideas?"

Mizu studied the top of the pit, nearly four times her height. She suddenly dashed toward the wall and leaped toward it, pivoting off and leaping a full body height above herself, grasping for a handhold in the wall.

No luck. She gracefully dropped to the ground, scanning the walls for other possible places to grab.

Basil stared at the walls with pursed lips. He took a deep breath and air swirled around him. He lifted an inch above the ground, then another, until he was a good two feet off the ground. Then his eyes grew wide, and he toppled forward and rolled onto the ground with a thump.

They all stood breathless, listening for any noises from above. When nothing changed, Theo gestured them over. "I have an idea."

"What is it?" Basil was breathing raggedly.

"I think you can do it, Basil. You're getting better and better, and one day I'm sure you'll be able to lift into the air like that dark wizard. But maybe you should start with someone lighter." He gestured to Mizu, who nodded approvingly.

"Of course!" Basil patted his shoulder. "Let's do this. Are you ready?"

Mizu took a deep breath and bent her knees. "I am ready."

Basil focused with his fingers pointed toward Mizu. He took a deep breath, then lifted his hands abruptly and a gust of wind swept Mizu up a good four feet. She started to drop, but Basil swept his arms in circles like a choir director. The air turned into a funnel, and Mizu dropped only two feet before lifting again. Slowly, she was lifted by the whirlwind up the pit.

She was almost at the top when they realized just how much noise the wind was making. They heard high-pitched shouts from down the cave.

"Hurry, Basil!" Theo whispered.

"I am!" Basil whispered back angrily. "Look. She's there."

Mizu reached the edge and twisted her body so that she could grasp it. Once her hands were on the rocky floor, she scrambled up the rest of the way, and Basil let the wind die down. Her eyes darted around as tiny footsteps came click-clacking toward the pit.

What they'd seen from below was a system of pulleys and ropes, which would allow raising and lowering people of their size—or even the size of a troll—into the pit. There was a shelving system to the left, so Mizu dashed to it and scrunched down, making herself as invisible as possible.

Basil and Theo darted back to their spots and lay down. Theo asked Lorien to do the same, and the large cat obliged. Torchlight flickered into the chamber and dozens of mikons ran in, peering over the edge and gurgling in their high-pitched language to each other. They shouted and gestured wildly, then ran around the pit toward the open air.

A moment later, Mizu's head appeared. She whispered down to them: "There's a pulley system here that will lift you. But it'll be slow and loud. Can you climb ropes?"

They spoke at the same time:

"Yes"

"No."

Basil and Theo looked at each other. Basil frowned. "Theo, we don't have time! I'll help you with my wind."

Theo sighed. "Throw the rope down."

The thin rope dropped down, and Theo shook his head, then grasped it. Sure enough, he was terrible at climbing, even with Mizu trying to lift from the top. But as Basil had promised, a gentle whirlwind formed, giving him the necessary boost to get up the rope quickly. Theo grabbed Mizu's outstretched hand and her eyes darted.

"Hurry! I hear them coming back!"

Basil picked up Lorien and placed him on the rope. The large black cat instantly knew what to do and climbed up rapidly. However, some of the rope was ripped where the cat's claws had grabbed on, and when Basil started climbing, he felt it tear. He concentrated and a whirlwind formed underneath him. He was buoyed up, and using the rope hand over hand, he rose to the top swiftly.

Just as Basil landed on the floor, Theo called, "They're here!"

They turned to see dozens of mikons clattering down the hall toward them, blocking the passage that led outside.

Basil shouted, "Run toward them!" He pushed his hands forward and a huge gust of wind blew through, pushing the small creatures to the left and right.

The friends ran down the tunnel, past the creatures who were still tumbling to the sides. The passageway was wide, but even so, a mikon regained its bearings and very nearly grabbed Theo's foot as he ran past. Basil was running right behind Theo and dashed toward the creature, kicking it out of the way. He felt faster than ever.

Suddenly Basil had an idea. "Keep running. I'll hold them off."

Theo, Mizu, and Lorien dashed down the passage to the outdoors with Basil right behind them. The mikons regained their legs and ran after them. Basil turned and whipped the wind toward them again, barreling toward the closest one and kicking it.

The mikon went flying and Basil leaped toward the next closest one, kicking it into another. He *was* faster. Much faster. The wind pushed and pulled, speeding up his every movement. He leaped toward another mikon, kicking it and swooping down to grab another, throwing it into two more.

It was incredible! He sped back and forth between them, the mikons barely able to keep themselves upright. Basil dashed after them and continued to kick and throw the small creatures, till finally they turned and fled back down the tunnel.

Basil stood panting, watching the two dozen creatures run out of his grasp. They stopped and turned to look at him. He waited, breathing heavily. One of them took a tentative step toward Basil and he roared, "YAAAAAH!" A gust of wind shoved the mikon back into the others.

That was the tipping point. The mikons all turned and fled back into their cave. Basil smiled and gave a little chuckle, then turned and ran back toward his friends. Although they were well into the woods, he grew curious. How quickly could he catch up to them with his newfound super speed?

He dashed into the woods, faster than he'd ever run before. It wasn't long before he heard them crashing through the trees and bushes. He called out, "It's ok! I'm back. They've retreated."

Theo and Mizu stopped, panting, and looked at Basil. Theo's eyes grew wide. "How did you get here so fast?"

Basil smirked. "Turns out the wind helps in more ways than we knew."

"Ah. Of course! You're faster." Theo's eyes glistened.

They took a moment to look around. Theo pulled on an arm sleeve. "So . . . does anyone know where our horses are?"

They searched the area, but the effort felt futile. There was no way they would find their original path without going back to the mikon cave, which they definitely didn't want to do.

Suddenly Theo lit up. "I have an idea."

Basil and Mizu stared at him curiously as he gazed into the air, then looked at them and grinned. "Someone's coming who can lend a hand."

Thump. Thump. Thump. A large creature approached. Basil's hand instinctively fluttered to his side where his sword normally was. Then he stood calmly at the ready.

An enormous dark-brown bear poked its nose through the nearby bush. Its shoulder height was well above Basil, the tallest there.

Theo proudly opened his arm toward the bear. "Meet Zoomy. She's *very* fast. She got here from a mile away."

"Wow." Basil puzzled as he looked at Theo. "Wait. Does that mean you can sense that far now? That's incredible. And it also means our horses are farther than that."

Theo nodded. "But that's no problem for Zoomy. She can smell *super* far. I bet she can smell stuff twenty miles away. Ok Zoomy, where are the horses?"

The giant bear sniffed the air, then gave a little grunt, "Rwooeer."

Theo laughed.

Basil looked at him curiously. "What is it?"

Theo looked at him with a smirk. "I'm not the only one here who thinks you're starting to stink."

Basil's eyes grew wide, and he sniffed his armpit, then recoiled and shrugged.

"Let's hop on." Theo walked over, and the bear knelt onto the ground, letting him clamber up. Basil followed, with Mizu close behind. With the three on top, the bear turned and headed into the woods, Lorien loping behind. The forest felt peaceful and safe atop the enormous bear. Even a troll would probably stay away, they surmised.

The horses were only a twenty-minute walk away. When they entered the clearing, they instantly knew something was wrong. Only two horses were standing.

"I don't sense Butterfly anywhere." Theo frowned. "I wonder if she ran off . . ." His voice trailed off and he furrowed his brow. "Oh no!"

He dismounted and ran behind a bush. Butterfly lay dead on the forest floor, with a large branch on top of her. "Butterfly!" Theo choked.

Basil came up behind him and put his hand on his shoulder. "Looks like it happened when the troll hit that tree with its club." He pointed to the dent in the tree. "Sorry, Theo."

"My poor Butterfly! The ring won't heal her now. She served me well all these years. She was never meant for adventure like this." His eyes were downcast.

"Yeah. That was a good horse." Basil shook his head slowly. "But . . . maybe you have a new friend who can give you a ride?"

Theo looked at the bear and grew a wistful smile. The bear gazed into his eyes, waiting patiently. "What do you say, Zoomy? Are you interested in sticking with us for a while?"

The bear let out a happy growl. "Rwoooooor."

Basil laughed. "I take that as a yes. And, Zoomy . . . welcome to the party!"

The bear looked at him curiously, and Theo gave a little smile. "Zoomy thinks you're funny, however stinky."

They spent the next half hour getting themselves back on track to find Amber. Basil left his broken long sword but was happy to find his enchanted short sword in the grass nearby.

"This long sword isn't really working for me anyway. Too slow." He gave it a little kick.

Theo decided to leave his saddle behind and mounted the saddlebags as best he could onto the giant bear, cutting off the strap from the saddle and using the reins as straps.

Mizu mounted Buttercup but also leaped off regularly to inspect the ground and climb trees for a better view.

Theo had asked Zoomy to smell out another human or giant ants. But despite the bear's ability to sense a lot of creatures within a dozen miles—including two-legged ones like goblins and trolls—it apparently couldn't sense other humans, from what Theo could tell.

So as the group walked along the cliff, they looked carefully for signs of Amber. They felt they were close to where she had fallen.

After an hour of scouring the area, Mizu called out, "Here! Dead monster ants. Killed by a blade."

They gathered around the three giant dead ants. Definitely killed by Amber.

Basil quickly found Amber's trail. "She survived!" He smiled. "I knew she'd figure out how to take care of herself. Looks like she headed this way."

They came upon a tiny creek with a blood-encrusted scrap of clothing. Basil held it up.

Theo wrinkled his nose. "Looks like she has a pretty bloody wound. She could sure use the power of the ring."

They continued on, finally getting to the river and then the natural hot spring, where her trail ended.

Basil pointed at a giant paw print. "This was a large creature. It has the paws of a cat, but it's enormous. And look here—a gigantic bird print. It looks like her prints interacted with them somehow. But it's impossible to tell what happened.

See, the creature chased her to this tree, and you can tell from the tree's shape that Amber used it to imprison the creature. But I don't see her prints leave the area. Do you, Mizu? I can't tell if the creatures ate her or if she somehow got away."

"Is there no sign of her leaving?" Theo wrung his hands together.

"Not exactly." Basil stroked his chin thoughtfully.

Mizu peered at the tracks closely, then stood. "I know what this is." She pointed to the paw print. "Not a cat. It's a griffin. She ran into a griffin. They can be tamed and ridden. If the griffin had eaten her, there'd be scraps of clothing and blood. Also, see here? Both of their tracks are interacting calmly, then neither of them leave this spot. What makes the most sense is she rode it out."

"Really?" Theo looked skeptical. "Although . . . she did have the amulet."

Basil turned to Theo. "Can't you use your powers somehow to find out? Like, ask an animal or something?"

"Not really." Theo looked down and shook his head. "Other forest creatures don't remember details like that. Well, I guess they do, actually, but not if it happened a while ago and not if they thought it was insignificant."

"Hmm." Basil frowned and put his fists on his hips, looking at the tracks.

Theo scratched his arm, then pulled his sleeve down. "Well, I do know one thing."

"What's that?"

"If she's riding a griffin with the amulet, that means she's safe. And so . . ." He gave a sly grin. "Since at least one of us stinks . . ." He glanced at the hot spring suggestively.

Basil gave him a mischievous smirk. "Sure. Why not, Butterballs?"

192

Chapter 14

The Griffin Nest

THREE GRIFFINS WITH GLOWING RED EYES crouched and growled at Amber and the good griffin. Two of them circled toward her left. She instinctively stepped closer to her friendly griffin and reached into her pouch for the amulet, making sure it didn't have any tangles.

She calculated her options. Could she get the necklace around even a single griffin's head without being torn to shreds? A glance around the large cave didn't raise her hopes. It would be easier if she could confront a griffin in a more-controlled environment instead of the wide-open cavern.

Like in one of the back tunnels.

She gauged her chances of making it to one of the three smaller openings at the back. The griffins were partially blocking two of them.

If they're like other animals, slow movements are the way to go so they don't give chase.

She took a slow step toward the opening on the far right, behind the tables. The other griffins growled and watched her, and one of them took a step toward her.

She took another step, a little faster than the last one. Then another and another.

The two griffins kept pace with her, then slowed as they approached the friendly griffin. Amber took a few more steps.

Halfway there.

The griffins that had been moving stopped, but the third one now had a clear line toward her and turned, growling. She took a few more steps, somewhat hurriedly but as calmly as she could. The griffin took a menacing step closer, and she began visualizing what she'd do.

She was almost at the opening when the third griffin suddenly pounced toward her.

She dashed inside the small tunnel, turned, and held the chain with two hands, prepared to toss it like a large hoop. As the griffin approached—its open beak toward her—she waited till the last possible moment, then flung the chain and rolled back to her right.

The rock floor of the tunnel bruised her already banged-up body, but she ignored the pain and sprang to her feet. The griffin stood looking somewhat puzzled, the amulet sitting perfectly around its neck.

"It's ok," Amber said calmly as she walked toward it. "You had an evil spell cast on you. We need this amulet back though. Your friends are still enchanted."

The griffin recoiled and squawked, then turned back to the room where the three other griffins were growling at each other. It gave a little gurgle sound, and the first griffin gurgled back, not taking its eyes off the other two. It sided with the first griffin, facing off two against two.

Amber walked back toward the griffins, thinking of a plan.

A loud crash came from the entranceway, and all heads turned. A short, stocky man with a huge brown beard, a large bulbous nose, and leather armor stood with an axe and shield. Even from a distance, she guessed him to be shorter than she was.

He banged his axe against the shield again and shouted. "Agishom! Bashilea!"

The griffins looked at one another. The two under the spell turned toward him. In the blink of an eye, they leaped at him, front claws outstretched in attack. Simultaneously, the short man rolled out of the way while the two other griffins leaped to his protection.

The four griffins collided and attacked one another, clawing and snapping their beaks. Some claws made contact as the growls turned into loud caws and shrieks.

Amber yelled, "We need to get that necklace onto them!"

The short man whipped his head around to look at her. She pointed at the griffin that wore the necklace. "The necklace! It will break their spell. We have to get it onto them!"

He gave a slight nod, then proceeded to amaze Amber by dropping his axe and shield and leaping into the battle. He dodged and then jumped on the back of the griffin with the amulet. Somehow, in the midst of the griffins jumping and clawing at each other, the man managed to stay on and say something in its ear.

At once the griffin spread its wings and leaped high, barreling into the other one, bowling it over and pinning it down. In one fluid movement, the stocky man pulled the chain off the one he was on and leaped onto the other.

He tried putting the chain around its head, but the griffin flailed wildly. He tried again, then grabbed its beak with his strong hands and forced the necklace over its head. As soon as the necklace fell below the griffin's ears it calmed down and looked around.

"Heeshoway." The man gently pet its head. Then he pulled the necklace off and looked toward the last one. The two other griffins were having a fierce battle, tearing at each other with their beaks, and one of them was bleeding. Amber couldn't tell them apart anymore.

The man turned to the other two griffins, pointed to the two battling, and said, "Anshin! Anshin sonk!"

The two griffins leaped toward the other two and instantly pinned down one of them. It flailed and scratched at them, but they held it while the man ran over and put the necklace over its head.

And just like that, the cavern was calm.

All four griffins stood up and looked at the man, who grinned at them. "Heeshoway angalla." He gestured and the fourth griffin lowered its head for him to take the necklace off. "Shweep." He had them go to the back of the cave.

As the griffins turned and walked to their straw beds, he turned to Amber and smiled. "I be thanking you."

"Um. You're welcome."

The man had a low gravelly voice with a thick accent and talked with a twinkle in his eyes. "A spell they have been under for two months now. With our knowledge, we knew not how to break the spell. How do you be coming here helping us?"

"Well . . ." Amber looked shyly down at her feet. "That's sort of a long story."

The sound of scuffling feet came from the cave entrance, and they both turned to look. Six other short, stocky men came barreling into the room. When they saw the griffins at the back, calm and licking their wounds on the straw beds, they turned to Amber and the man in the center of the cavern.

"Howk am snoovle?" One of them pointed toward Amber.

The man Amber had been talking to gestured grandly. "Her name I do not know, but she be bringing this." He held up the amulet on its long, thin chain. "And it be breaking the evil enchantment."

The other one spoke haltingly. "But who . . . she?"

All the short men turned and looked at her expectantly.

She looked at them awkwardly. "Um . . . hi . . . my name is Amber."

"Welcome, Amber," said the first stocky man, "to Kindlemere . . . kingdom of dwarves."

Chapter 15

People of Earth and Sky

AFTER SOME INTRODUCTIONS, the dwarves led Amber out of the cave and down a trail. The first dwarf turned out to be a leader, although Amber didn't understand his role exactly. But the other dwarves treated him as the one in charge.

"Kish be my name," he said gruffly, "And in charge of all griffins I am. I hope you be fine with us using the necklace a bit more. Three more griffin nests we be needing to take care of."

"Of course," Amber replied, thinking, I just want to make sure I get it back. "So, Kish, where is your kingdom? I don't see it anywhere."

"Well, enemies in the skies there be." Kish pointed up and gave a nasty look upward as he walked. "So we be staying hidden."

"Enemies in the skies?"

"Yes. Evil elves—graft elves. Always hindering us they are. Awful vermin." Kish spat on the ground. "A large fortress they have, in the tallest trees many mountains from here. Also flying creatures and floating warships. The ships be dangerous, always hiding in the clouds. We took one over once but knew not how to control it . . . float all over it did and didn't do us much good at all."

"How do they fly?"

"Dracos are their steeds." When the dwarf saw the look of confusion on Amber's face, he said, "Small dragons of sorts, smaller than griffins. They'd lose in a fight, but quick they be, so we never catch 'em."

They wound down the rocky ridge trail, then headed toward dense trees. As Amber approached the trees, she felt a sense of safety and her energy revitalize. *It's amazing how much I've come to appreciate and rely on my powers.*

"Our kingdom be most famous among dwarves for our flying." Kish paused to say something in their native tongue to another dwarf and gestured for him to go ahead. "In fact, we be the messengers between the different kingdoms."

"How many kingdoms are there?" Amber asked.

"The ones we talk with . . . three others. But around the world be many more. Even across the great seas."

They walked into the shelter of the huge, densely packed trees, and the world around them grew much darker. The trail continued winding downward through the trees, then they approached the foot of a large cliff. When they rounded a bend, Amber gasped.

Before them, built into the wall of the cliff and obscured by the towering trees around them, were two massive doors, making an archway at least twenty-five feet high. There were two dwarves in full armor standing guard, and the doors were wide open, revealing a perfectly smooth walkway into the cave.

Amber stared wide-eyed at the workmanship of the giant doors—they were at least a foot thick and able to withstand any attack she could imagine.

Kish, Amber, and three other dwarves walked into the grand hallway, then rounded a corner and continued on. Amber looked around for a light source.

Kish saw her gaze. "You wonder how we have light? An old dwarf practice it is, many centuries at this point—two rare metals combined, plus a little dwarf magic." He turned and winked at her. "See those in the ceiling?"

Glowing spots lined the great hallway in places where she'd expect to see torches in wall sconces. She realized the torches she'd seen in the griffin's nest were the same.

They continued farther down toward a great light and entered a massive room—the largest Amber had ever seen. It was hundreds of feet tall with staircases up and down the walls, leading to many other entrances. They had come out of one of many smaller entrances, she realized, as the only option was to go down two long flights of stairs to reach the bottom.

At the bottom, countless dwarves were in a flurry of activity: displaying workmanship of one sort or another, buying and selling food, eating and talking around tables at cafes. It was a huge market square with a central area much like a town center—and all the noisiness and busyness she'd seen at the market in Lugo, although she'd only seen that in passing.

The dwarves varied in size, ranging from much shorter than Amber to some just a bit taller. Kish seemed to be somewhere right in the middle, about half a head shorter than her. All the men had large beards and big protruding noses, while the women seemed like perfect matches, with plump cheeks and just as stocky.

The smells wafting through the large chamber made Amber feel instantly hungry. Smells she recognized, like roasting meat mixed with spices, captivated her imagination. She sorely remembered she'd only eaten a few root vegetables over the last two days.

The colors and lights were vivid and festive, and the whole chamber was filled with the constant chatter of voices and activity, people going about their daily life together. In the center of the large room was a stage, surrounded by many chairs.

Some dwarf children passed them in the lanes between stalls, shouting happily. She smiled as they turned the corner, then realized Kish was speaking to her.

"And it helps when we least expect it," Kish said, pointing. "These landings be helpful if we bring in our griffins."

Amber turned to look. Scattered throughout the room were taller podiums where a griffin could easily land without knocking into anything, and there were stairs leading down from the podiums.

Just then, another dwarf ran up to Kish and spoke in their language. Amber waited patiently and watched Kish give instruction to the dwarf and then hand him the amulet.

He turned back to Amber and saw her expression of concern. "Be not worried. All will be fine. We must care for other griffins. Forty-two there be in our care, and all of them under the spell. So far, with your help, four be freed. But the rest remain in need. When we finish, you will be given this spell-breaking chain once again. On my word." Kish placed his hand over his heart.

"Of course," Amber said meekly. "Please use it."

"Enough about us," he said. "About you I would know more. Who you are, why you be in our parts, riding one of our griffins, and how this necklace of great power comes into your possession?"

Amber proceeded to tell Kish of her adventures as they made their way into the market. She walked past a stand that had fantastic smelling meat on skewers and looked at it wistfully.

Kish saw her and interrupted her storytelling. "Would you be liking a bite of one o' these?" Amber nodded and Kish tossed the woman behind the counter a small copper coin, then took one and handed it to Amber. She bit into it and felt a tremendous sense of satisfaction through her whole body. Not only was it the first real food she'd had in days, it was delicious. And exotic. She'd never had flavors like that before.

"Wonderful," she said.

"But of course." Kish beamed. "A dwarf specialty it is. Peanut satay is what we call it."

"Oh! Peanut butter! That's what we were told Crodor the Ancient likes."

"Is that so?" Kish scratched his beard. "Hmm. Very interesting. And some of this . . . peanut butter. Do you be having any of it?"

"Yes. We have some. It's with my horse."

Kish laughed a deep stomach-laugh that made it natural for Amber to smile. "Well, are you not the most prepared human child ever!" He clapped his hands happily. "Come on! Much more I will show you."

As they walked past the other dwarves, their eyes watched her, and she felt conspicuous. She stood taller than most of them and was very skinny in comparison.

At a courtyard table outside a pub, two dwarves who were having a loud conversation over beers suddenly stopped talking and looked curiously at Amber. Then one shouted out, "Honchi bon shay, Kish?"

"Human shom," Kish shouted over the din of the square.

So others can hear as well, Amber thought. Smart. He's introducing me without making it formal.

Kish spoke in their language loudly for a few seconds, then laughed. The two dwarves looked satisfied with Kish's answer and nodded with admiring grins, watching Amber as they walked past.

Kish turned to Amber. "I said you be bringing a way to break the spell on the griffins."

Amber smiled back at the dwarves. Better to make the best impression possible.

Kish pointed to an exit past some buildings at the back that were filled with large barrels. "This way."

They walked through a hallway, then came to a split and took the left, kept walking, took a right at the next one, and then came to a door with something written in the same diamond-shaped language as the other signs.

On the large door, there was a huge golden ring. Kish used it to knock three times loudly. He smiled at her, then stood up straight, watching. The other three dwarves with them stood similarly in silence.

After a few minutes, the door creaked open, and a dwarf dressed in fine clothing poked his head out. "Bakya?"

Kish spoke to him briefly and with authority in his voice, never dropping his gaze.

Amber watched them curiously.

The finely dressed dwarf glanced at Amber, then mumbled something and went inside, not shutting the door all the way. He returned a moment later with a big smile and gestured for them to come in.

Amber followed Kish past the door to another long corridor. This one was more elegant, with a beautiful orange-red carpet covering the floor, and tapestries lining the walls.

They trailed behind the finely dressed dwarf down a hall, then left to an entranceway with four dwarf guards stationed in full armor. Their hands rested on the handles of axes.

Amber suddenly felt small. Is this a king I'm about to meet? Am I ready for that? Do I need to behave a certain way? Her stomach did flips. But she had no time to prepare as they entered a large room with multiple seats and tables.

At first glance, there were just over a dozen dwarves in the room. A dwarf sat at one of the large tables, different papers sprawled over it. Amber instinctively knew the dwarf to be their king.

It wasn't that he was wearing a big crown. The actual crown on his head was barely a strip of ornate metal with only a few gems in it. It wasn't even his clothing that gave it away, since most of the dwarves in the room were wearing finer clothing than the dwarves she'd seen in the common area. It was more the way he carried himself and the way everyone in the room deferred to him.

He looked to be older than most of the dwarves she'd seen, with gray taking over half of his beard and hair. An intricate gold necklace hung down to his chest, and he wore three rings, each with different emblems.

He looked up at them and said, "Bakya bo hon, Kish?"

Kish gave a short bow and proceeded to make a long speech in their language. At one point he gestured toward Amber, and the king's eyebrows raised. He looked over at her and nodded, then turned back to Kish.

Kish began gesturing with his hands, and Amber imagined him explaining how he put the necklace over the griffin's head. He kept talking for another few minutes, then finished by saying, "And Amber here, if we be including her, then the language of humans we must speak."

"Of course." The king gave a tight-lipped smile and turned to Amber with a regal nod. "Welcome to the kingdom of Kindlemere. We be having much appreciation for your arrival with this disenchanting necklace. We be a people who rely on our griffins, and it be difficult indeed to have them fighting with us these last months. Causing trouble they have been, not only with us, but much farther away."

Amber stood quietly. Her stomach gurgled and groaned. I shouldn't have eaten all that food on an empty stomach, she worried. She was so nervous, she felt somewhat nauseous.

The king went on, "Much there is for us to do now. A warm welcome to the dwarf kingdom I give you, and Kish be caring for your every need. Whatever you need, ask and we'll provide it. Indebted to you we are."

Amber stood for a moment in awkward silence. What do I say now? What would my parents tell me to say? They always tell me to be polite to elders, but this is way more important than that. A king! Should I be bowing? Or saying more of my story? Say something, Amber! At least say something!

Amber cleared her throat, "Yes. Of course. It's my pleasure. We're all in this together against the evil wizards who caused this."

Then she burped.

She didn't mean to. She didn't even know it was coming, or she'd have stifled it. But eating that meat after two days of eating practically nothing made it suddenly gurgle up. The dwarves all laughed, and her face turned beet red.

The king guffawed with the others. "Kish already been taking care of your food, has he?" Their laughter thundered throughout the room.

"Yes." She shrunk down. How could she have done that? What should she say now? "Thank you."

The king quieted down, and the room fell silent. Scratching his well-manicured beard, he looked at Amber and sat back. "Evil wizards, you say? What more can you be telling us?"

"Yes, evil wizards," Amber said. She looked down at the ground, then gathered courage and looked back up at the king. "We believe they cast a spell over the whole land, all the way to the great sea, where I'm from. I'm working with the wizard Sage, and we're trying to see if there's a way to break the spell. We're on our way to find the dragon Crodor the Ancient to free him from the spell. And there's a massive army of goblins and giants heading toward the city of Lugo, as we speak. So we're in a rush to figure all of this out."

The king nodded. "Familiar this sounds. In fact, it be similar to stories my father told me of another war when he was king, two hundred years ago."

His father? she thought. That means this king is very old indeed!

She nodded. "Yes, we think it's very similar."

One of the dwarves started speaking in their language, and another interrupted. An argument broke out, different dwarves debating in their language. Amber watched silently, trying to gauge what they might be discussing. The king listened to the argument for a little while, then interrupted and asked Kish a question.

Kish cleared his throat nervously and spoke slowly, as if he were choosing his words carefully. Another dwarf pointed at him and spoke in a hostile tone. Amber had the distinct feeling that this dwarf didn't like Kish at all.

Kish held his palm up and spoke calmly, gathering courage, then he patted Amber on the shoulder. "So you see, at the very least, we must be helping her."

The other dwarf stared at him icily. "I be not disagreeing with that, but one and done. We can't be getting involved in another war where we lose our friends. Not again."

"What then?" Kish asked confidently. "Let's say the goblins be destroying the human city. Then what? They be coming our way next, I guarantee it."

The king lifted his hand, and the room went silent. "Enough. We can be discussing these things at another time. For now, let us welcome the first human who be coming into our homes in many a decade and helping in a grand way, nonetheless."

One of the dwarves near the king said something in their language and everyone laughed. Amber didn't have any idea what it was, but smiled along with them, hoping she wasn't doing something else embarrassing.

The king lifted his hand and gave a slight nod toward Amber. "Kish be taking care of you now." He turned to the dwarves next to him and began speaking in their own language again.

Kish smiled at Amber as they turned. "That went well. We be going now." He walked Amber out the door, with the three dwarves from earlier trailing behind them. "What be your greatest needs?"

"Food, provisions, safety, and passage to Crodor the Ancient," Amber said without a pause.

"Done," he said. "First, we give you a proper feast! Your belch, though notable, was not quite at the dwarven level." He had a big grin as he walked alongside her. "By the time you've tried our most succulent specialties, your belching be far grander than ever before."

Chapter 16

To the Clouds

AMBER LICKED HER LIPS IN DELIGHT. "That was possibly the best meal I've ever eaten!" She leaned back in her chair happily and patted her belly.

Kish grinned. "A few things we do right here in Kindlemere. Food be one of them! And now." He stood up from the restaurant table. "Time it be to show you another of our specialties."

With no further explanation, Kish led her toward one of the many exits from the common space. As they walked, Amber felt the courage to pry.

"What was that argument about, in the room with the king?"

"Ah, that." Kish brushed his hands, as if clearing away a bad thought. "Think nothing of it. Some of my kindred be scared of losing our kind in a war. And some may be . . . how shall I say? . . . jealous of me."

He stopped and gave her a serious look. "Not all dwarves be of the same mind. Some are not pure-hearted. They say one thing and mean another. Their words are blown about like leaves in the wind. But this one . . ." He put his thumb to his chest. "When I give my word, I always . . . *always* stay true. If you ever be needing help, you let me know."

He stared at her intently, then he smiled. "Come along! I have much to be showing you."

They wound through a passageway and approached the sound of banging. The sound grew louder, then they walked past a room with six blacksmiths working on various projects. They all had strange-looking cloths sticking out of their ears.

As they passed, Kish lifted his voice to a shout. "We at Kindlemere be renowned for our workmanship on many levels. Our ability to create works not only of great beauty but also to create methods that combine certain metals and magic from the earth to give our creations . . . special properties."

They walked through the passageway to the next room where the walls and shelves were lined with weapons, armor, and equipment. Kish walked in, then gestured for Amber to follow. He went over to a wall with armor, considered some options, then pulled one off and held it up.

"This one be about right." The armor looked similar to the chain mail Amber had seen on the soldiers in Lugo, only the links were extremely tiny in comparison. It was a dull silver, which didn't seem to reflect light like regular metal. "Here." He held it out to Amber. "Try this on."

She was surprised how light it was. It was more like a cloth jacket, not something made of metal. She took off her cloak, then put the armor on top of her ragged shirt. It was much too wide and long in the belly, and the arms were too short. But she loved the feel of it.

Kish grabbed the flap at the side. "It's sized for a dwarf. But we'll make one for you. Come."

The two walked back to the first room with the blacksmiths. Kish tapped one of the blacksmith's shoulder and spoke to him, gesturing toward Amber. The blacksmith put his hammer down and walked over to Amber, then looked at the armor and walked around her. He held his hand over the length of the arm where the sleeve ended and noted that it was nearly a full hand width too short. He also grabbed the front and eyeball-measured how much he'd have to remove.

"Hake," he said nodding.

Kish gave him a thumbs-up. "Akawn." He turned toward Amber. "Pass him the armor. He be refitting it today."

She took it off and handed it to the other dwarf. Kish waved and turned to leave. He spoke loudly over the dwarves' pounding. "We be wearing this armor between two layers of clothing, so the skin doesn't chafe. It also be invisible to attackers. Speaking of clothing, how be your clothes?"

"Ok, I suppose." She looked down. Her shirt was ripped with holes from all the battles and climbing she'd been doing— plus it was missing the entire bottom six inches from the makeshift bandages she'd made from it. Her pants were completely torn and full of holes. And her boots were ripping open. The only item of clothing she had that looked perfect was the enchanted cape from Sage. She thought of how ridiculous she must have sounded saying that her clothes were okay.

"Well . . . I suppose I could use new clothing."

Kish shook his head. "And yer boots?"

She didn't want to press the dwarves' hospitality, but her boots were definitely in need of repair. "Maybe?"

"Good. Good." Kish grinned. "With me you come."

She followed him through more passageways into a room filled with various footwear. Amber couldn't believe how many different styles of boots and shoes there were to pick from. She admired the many designs, trying to imagine herself wearing them. At one point she realized she wasn't just thinking about how functional the boot would be, but also what it would look like. It felt good to be able to think in that way, even in the midst of the turmoil happening in the world.

Finally, she decided. "These." She held a tall boot, with a rugged leather-like material and a built-in sheath for a knife. Plus, it looked sleek and beautiful, a dark brown with a dark buckle near the top.

Kish grabbed the other boot, and they walked to the next room where cobblers were busy at work. He spoke to them, and one of them measured Amber's foot size as well as her calf.

"Ready by tomorrow these will be." Kish held his belt buckle and stood proudly. "Which means you'll be staying here one night. Also, these boots be having a special property, which makes your feet feel light and springy. An excellent feature for long travel it is—it be helping to go the extra mile."

Amber smiled. She was starting to enjoy all the surprises Kish was giving her.

They spent the rest of the day going around the dwarf kingdom, gathering more supplies and hearing more stories about dwarves and their ways. Amber was impressed by the size of the underground kingdom. Some of the rooms were enormous, and the city was full of thousands of dwarves, from what she could tell.

At one point they went by an infirmary where a kind dwarf gave her proper stitches for her injury. By the end of the day, they replaced her clothing. The new pants were brown and lightweight, yet as sturdy as strong leather. They were very comfortable with many pockets, and Amber marveled again at the dwarves' great ingenuity. The green shirt matched her previous one, but had two pockets, which she instantly slid her hands into.

They also gave her a backpack with dozens of pockets and compartments, completely filled with important items like bandages, dried meats and nuts, a water flask, and a blanket that seemed seriously thin and folded up into a tight little roll yet did a great job of keeping a person warm.

One of the items they gave her—called a lamp—confused her at first, because it looked like a small rod with a button on it. When the button was pressed, it opened the front of the rod to reveal a glowing rock within, which shed a small amount of light. It wasn't as powerful as an oil lamp with fire, but she was impressed by it, nonetheless.

Finally, they gave her a coil of rope, which at first seemed so thin she wouldn't have thought it useful, but they explained that it was built to hold a thousand pounds. She thankfully added it to her new pack.

By the end of the day, Amber was exhausted and slept soundly in the bed they provided. The next morning she awoke feeling rested and ready to tackle the day. After a big breakfast of sausages and eggs, Kish handed her the boots and chain-mail armor that they'd picked out. Everything fit perfectly.

In the midst of their preparations, they heard a commotion. Kish walked out to the main courtyard, Amber close behind. A dwarf was being supported by another down the stairs, holding his side. When he saw Kish, they made their way over to him, as a small crowd gathered around in interest.

Sticking out of the dwarf's side was an elegant arrow with dark fletching. The dwarves spoke hastily in their language and looked like they would head straight to the infirmary, but Kish pressed them with a few questions before they went on. The dwarf who was uninjured handed the amulet to Kish, then they continued inside.

Kish frowned and stood with folded arms for a moment, lost in thought. The crowd dispersed. He looked up at Amber and handed her the amulet nonchalantly. "Come with me." He turned toward a passageway they hadn't taken yet. The dwarf was quiet, for the first time since Amber had met him.

They passed through a doorway into a room—like a little library—with five other dwarves sitting at tables and having conversations. The room went quiet when they entered.

"Hawkawn." Kish said seriously, and they all went back to quiet conversation.

"Here. Sit." He gestured to a small table with some rolled up papers.

When they were both seated, he folded his hands and looked Amber in the eyes. "The attack be the evil graft elves. They be knowing we have our griffins back, and their floating ships are watching. This be a harder effort than we might have hoped."

He unrolled a map and pointed at a mountain. "Here we be. The dragon lives in this mountain over here." He pointed to a mountain five mountains over. "Far less than an hour it would take on a griffin to fly there, but the graft elves be here." He pointed directly between them. "So, you see, we be having a challenge on our hands."

"We must be flying around the elves. But me thinks they be on high alert. We never know when a cloud passing by be one of their evil floating ships, watching, ever watching." He glanced up, as if elves were in the room with them. "The griffins' homes are no secret, so they be ever prepared."

He winked at her. "If evil elves be watching, we'll be needing to care for your safety. So come with you I will—me and some of my men. We'll bring you to Crodor, we will."

Amber smiled. She felt a warmth spread over her body. "Wonderful! Yes. That would be perfect."

"Then it be settled." Kish rolled up the map. "With you we will travel. Just say the word for when."

Amber thought barely a moment. All she could think about was the fact that her friends may be in trouble. She wanted to see them badly. "As soon as possible."

Kish nodded. In a matter of moments, preparations were underway. Amber was impressed at how quickly organized the dwarves were. They were by far the most ordered group she'd ever come across.

In twenty minutes, she was standing in a room with five dwarves including Kish, who were all packing gear and weapons. They each had a long dagger, similar to hers, as well as a larger weapon like an axe or spear, and a crossbow with three quivers of bolts. It got her thinking about her bow. Soon, she thought. If all goes well, I'll have my bow again soon.

The six of them made their way through winding corridors, up some stairs, and around corners until they emerged at large doors that were opened a tiny crack, with daylight coming in.

They walked outside, and two dwarves greeted them. Amber looked around confused. This felt so similar to the doors she'd used to enter the kingdom, but they were clearly in a different spot—perhaps on the other side of the mountain. There was a trail much like the one she'd used to arrive at the dwarf kingdom. They followed it underneath humongous trees, where it wound its way until it emerged at some craggy rocks.

They climbed up the rocks for a bit, then came across a path, which led up and up the mountain to another griffin nest. This one was larger than the first one, with eight griffins inside. Two dwarves were waiting there.

The five dwarves went in and immediately began taking saddles off racks and placing them on the griffins. Kish turned to Amber. "See that griffin there—with speckles on its feathers?" He pointed to a smaller griffin in the corner. "That be the one you shall ride. The saddle for him be over here. His name be Bolt."

Amber walked over to the wall and looked at the saddle. It had a lot of similarities to the saddles she used on Buttercup, but also some key differences. The seat of the saddle was the same, only a little wider. There was a pommel and horn to hold on to, much like hers, and stirrups for her feet. The stirrups were interesting, though, because they had an extra buckle to keep feet in. On a horse, that would have seemed dangerous— but on a flying griffin, it made a lot of sense. There were two built-in quivers to hold crossbow bolts and a holster on the front right to hold a crossbow or axe.

The saddle itself was a beautiful brown leather with intricate etchings. Hers had images of flowers, trees, and a large owl. Amber looked back at Bolt. He did have some characteristics of an owl. His eyes were a little larger than the others, and his feathers had a certain splotchiness to them that made him more camouflaged, like a bird.

Amber lifted the saddle and was surprised at how light it was. Next to the saddle was something curious. It was like a strong helmet, much too large for her, with a strap and large-looking glasses to cover the eyes. She instantly smiled—every time she'd flown before, she'd wondered about using glasses to prevent her eyes tearing from the wind.

Kish walked over. "Another gift for you have we." He held out a much smaller set for Amber. "These be a proper helmet and goggles."

Amber put the goggles over her eyes. She was impressed that it mostly didn't block her view. Her peripheral vision suffered slightly on the sides, but she could see straight ahead clearly. The helmet fit well, and she gave Kish a thumbs-up.

With a little help, she attached the saddle to Bolt, then walked in front of him so they could see eye to eye. She put her hand on his head—something she liked to do with any horses she rode. It gave her a sense that they knew each other better and would respect each other.

Pleased that her griffin had a name she understood, she wondered if he was fast, like a bolt of lightning. But then it struck her that it probably meant something different in the dwarf language. She called out to Kish, "What does Bolt mean?"

He was sitting on his griffin watching her. "Owl!" he called back with a grin.

The first dwarves had already mounted and flown out of the cave. They circled, waiting for the others. Amber and Kish were the last. As Amber mounted, Kish gestured for her to follow the others, then he patiently watched as she leaned, and the griffin moved toward the cave entrance.

She gave a slight kick, and Bolt leaped into the sky—at which point Amber suddenly realized she hadn't asked Kish how to steer! Bolt didn't seem to mind. He began flying around with the others, but Amber's heart leaped into her throat

Her mind raced. I didn't even strap in. And I don't know the first thing about how to control a griffin without reins. I need to let Kish know—but how?

It was too late. Kish was leading the group forward, and they formed a V-formation toward the mountains, northwest.

Amber's griffin fell in perfectly. She tried leaning and applying pressure with her legs, as she'd done with Blazey, and the griffin somewhat moved with her.

Ok, I can do this, she thought. It's a bit different but nothing unusual. I wonder if they use their hands for steering? She looked around at the other dwarves. Their arms were completely free. Some were holding on, but others were inspecting crossbows or sitting back.

Maybe they keep their arms free so they can use their crossbows. I'll have to watch them. In the meantime, I need to figure out these feet straps.

She didn't want to risk leaning down to look at the straps, and they weren't an obvious system to her by feel, so she did her best without looking. They felt sort of snug. Probably ok.

As Amber felt more comfortable, she was able to enjoy the view. Never had she been able to see so clearly while flying. The goggles helped enormously. The mountains stretched as far as she could see in every direction. Many of them were capped with snow, even in the middle of summer. Some were incredibly craggy and jagged. One in particular looked as if it was tilted.

Meanwhile, the dwarves stayed clear of any clouds.

Amber thought she saw some movement by the tilted mountain. She peered more closely and realized there were tiny shapes flying from it, staying low. She watched curiously for a bit, then a thought gave her a start: Are those the graft elves?

She looked around. The other dwarves seemed oblivious. She wanted to give them a signal but couldn't figure out a way to communicate. She dug in her heels, and thankfully, Bolt took a couple of extra flaps to pick up speed, helping her fly next to another dwarf.

The dwarf looked over at her. She waved her arms and pointed down toward the moving shapes. The dwarf looked down and nodded to her, then maneuvered to the front and held his left hand up. He pointed to his eyes and pointed toward the moving shapes.

All the dwarves slowed down and looked. One of them pulled out a small spyglass and held it carefully with both his hands, as he peered down. Amber wondered what signal he'd given his griffin, because it stopped flapping completely and went into a glide for more stability.

The dwarf watched for half a minute, then put the spyglass back in a sleeve on the saddle, turned to the others, and began gesturing. Amber tried to guess what he was saying in their hand language, but it was much too fast for her to follow.

She tried to move her griffin closer to Kish. It clumsily obliged, still unsure of what Amber was trying to get it to do. She shouted, "What is it?"

Kish shouted back over the wind. "Graft elves. At least eight of them."

Amber nodded. They didn't seem surprised or upset but picked up speed again, heading in the same direction. The dwarf with the spyglass kept it to the side, pulling it out from time to time. She looked back and didn't see them anywhere, but then realized that they were much closer. When Kish said dracos were faster than griffins, he wasn't kidding.

She did some mental math. *If they can travel that great distance in a few minutes, they'll be on us very shortly.* Her heart throbbed madly. *If the dracos are faster than griffins, why are we fleeing?*

A cloud drifted in front of them, and Kish held up his fist. The griffins slowed and he shouted, "Insha hockoway!"

He sped forward, then veered left to avoid the cloud. The cloud drifted to their left, blocking them off.

Kish turned in a circle. He saw Amber's confusion and shouted, "It be a trap."

He lifted two fingers up and swirled his hand in a circle, then pointed. The griffins diverted into two groups, flying in opposing circles. Amber's griffin flapped awkwardly to the side, as if it wanted to join. But without Amber's guidance, it didn't know which group to follow.

The dracos approached—eight miniature dragons flapping on the wind with small figures all in black riding them.

The elves released a flurry of arrows from their short bows toward the dwarves. In return, the dwarves sent a volley of crossbow bolts toward the elves. Both sides had no successful hits at their distance, but the gap between them was closing quickly.

And then the cloud dissipated.

Lurking behind the haze was an incredible warship. It was a solid eighty feet long from stern to bow, made of a sleek white wood that blended in with the cloud itself. It had three masts and full sails, as well as sails along the sides. It looked much like a ship Amber would have expected to find on the sea—not up in the air. Except it was elegant through and through, a work of incredible craftsmanship, with ornate carvings lining the walls.

It would have been a sight to behold. Except the ship started firing on them.

Enormous arrows—a solid four feet long each—flew at toward the dwarves. The griffins dodged, but now the attack was coming from both sides, and the elves on dracos fired another volley of arrows.

The dwarves were trapped.

Amber watched in horror as an arrow punctured the side of a griffin, causing it to falter for a moment in its flight path. Thankfully, none of the enormous arrows from the ballistae on the ship landed.

Kish let out a shout and suddenly all the griffins changed into a V-formation and rose up into the air, heading over the ship. Amber's griffin followed clumsily.

I wish I'd had a lesson on how to guide these things! She realized her griffin was completely exposing itself to the elves on the dracos.

The dracos quickly pursued them, but it was clear the griffins would reach the ship first. To what end? Amber wondered.

The first of the dwarves breached the ship, and a net with six weights flew down onto the deck, capturing a darkly dressed elf under its weight. The next dwarves did the same. By the time Amber rose high enough to see for herself, three elves were caught in nets, but a fourth was turning a ballista toward the retreating dwarves.

"Watch out!" Amber shouted, instinctively urging her griffin to lift higher.

An enormous arrow flew through the air and impaled the under-wing of one of the griffins. A loud eagle's scream pierced the air, and the griffin tucked its wing in as the arrow exited the other side. The dwarf lowered his head, and the two of them barreled down and out of the fighting area.

"I hope they'll be ok," Amber whispered to no one.

She flew up higher over the elves on the ship, then instinctively looked behind, just in time to realize the dracos were almost caught up. Her breathing stopped. How can I get Bolt to get out of harm's reach?

She kicked, then pulled on the saddle horn. The griffin moved a little to the left, then right, confused. She rose up above the highest sail, moving erratically. And then an arrow sunk soundly into Bolt's left haunch. He screamed and jerked wildly to the left and flew sideways for a moment, avoiding other arrows.

Before Amber could even think of what to do next, she felt herself lifting out of the saddle. The poor job she'd done strapping in suddenly created a life-or-death moment. In an instant, she was plummeting.

Desperate, she tried grasping at something—anything.

She gauged her options in the blink of an eye. There was no way she'd grab onto a sail. No way she'd be able to land somewhere safe. She'd either die by hitting the ship's deck head-on, or by missing and falling the enormous height to the world far below.

Suddenly a searing pain shot through her shoulders. She grabbed them, only to realize she was grasping the clawed lizard feet of a draco. She'd been caught!

The draco flew in a circle down to the ship below. She immediately realized that between the protective cape and the dwarven armor, she wouldn't have serious injuries. So as the draco dropped, her breathing calmed, and she quickly assessed her possibilities.

The dwarves were out of sight, and the clouds were closing in around the ship. Bolt flapped away uncomfortably and disappeared into the clouds. The elves on the ship below— blurs of black, scrambled—freeing the caught ones from nets and gathering in an open space.

There was no helping it now. Amber was caught by the evil graft elves.

Chapter 17

The First Attack

"IS THE ARMY READY TO MARCH?" The White Queen sat on a throne of glass, spinning a white wand nimbly in between her fingers.

"Yes, my queen." The gruff-looking human bowed deeply. He looked weary, as if he'd been up all night, for many nights in a row. His bushy brown beard was scraggly, partially covering his colorful red-and-yellow shirt.

"Then we leave today—before they're prepared to defend themselves."

"If I may?"

"Of course." She shook her head impatiently.

"As we send them out, it will take at least a week for seven thousand goblins with their war machines to get to Lugo. How about we send a smaller troop ahead of them? We can send five hundred goblins easily, and they'll be there in a matter of days. The smaller army will help us determine how prepared they are. You did let that human elementalist go. I'm sure he's warned them, and they've most certainly taken steps to be ready for us."

"Yes, yes, I know." She rolled her fingers across the arm of her throne. "You're right, as always, Farsworth. Yes, let's do that. Send five hundred. Let's see if we can defeat them, even with the smaller number. And see how prepared they are. What have we got ready at this point?"

"We have seven thousand goblins. Three tribes. Thankfully, Lucio's spell remains strong, even though he isn't here to enforce it."

He swallowed and cleared his throat uncomfortably as they both thought of how the powerful wizard had been killed by the very phoenix that he'd been enchanting.

Someone was out there trying to stop them. Someone with power.

"There's one hobgoblin for every fifty goblins," he said, "which, of course, is plenty. I've also drummed up a group of ogres—almost a hundred, actually. They're pretty powerful in their own right."

The queen was silent. "Is that all?"

"All, my queen? You expect more? We have the wizards, as you know."

"No. No. More. Can't we have more creatures? Don't we have griffins? Hippogriffs? Dragons? There must be some sort of flying creatures we can employ."

"Well, there are the gargoyles, although they're mostly good for keeping watch. I suppose we don't have good attacking creatures that fly. But we could. I have my hippogriff, but that was before all of this. Caster has a new hippogriff. I'll ask him where he got it and see if he can get some more. As for dragons . . . I know Lucio's spell went far and wide. And he was supposed to target the dragons. I think the red dragon to the west is enchanted—and a blue one to the south. There could be others to the south. I can check if you'd like."

"Yes, a dragon! That sounds perfect. After you send out this . . . troop . . . I want you to fly over and see if you can get help from these dragons."

The gruff man bowed. "Of course, my queen."

He left the room and immediately mounted his hippogriff, lifting into the air and flying over to the amassing goblin army. Every day it grew in number, ready to be sent out for destruction. He landed next to a large tent that was far more impressive than the ones around it.

He dismounted and entered. A large goblin king sat on a wooden throne, surrounded by dozens of goblins and hobgoblins.

Farsworth bowed. "Your highness. I bring news from the White Queen."

The goblin's voice was harsh and clumsy. "Out with it!"

"She says it's time to attack. We will send the army at once. We'll also send five hundred brave warriors ahead to the largest human city—to test the city defenses and see how prepared they are. We may find victory with this small group, but either way, it will help us know what they're prepared for."

"Yes. Yes. We do this." The goblin king stood and raised a scepter. "Time for blood! Army will destroy the human cities!"

A cheer went up among the goblins surrounding him.

"We leave now. Get the weapons of war. You!" He pointed to a menacing-looking hobgoblin with a jagged sword and black armor. "You lead a smaller group ahead to tear the city down. You take a thousand goblins!"

"Um, five hundred your highness," Farsworth said politely, as he stood next to him.

The goblin king looked at him with an evil grin. "We goblins don't count too well. Ha ha ha!"

Farsworth sighed and walked out of the room. Regardless of the number, a thousand could probably still travel fast—faster than seven thousand with all the larger war machines, anyway. Soon enough they would see how prepared the humans really were.

$$* * *$$

Two days later, around eight hundred goblins—led by the hobgoblin with the jagged sword and a dozen other hobgoblins—approached the gates of Ballmore. In order to move quickly, they hadn't brought the largest of the war machines, but they still had two ballistae, enormous crossbow-like weapons on wheels.

A thin, old human wizard with a long angular nose and neatly trimmed white beard accompanied them. He carried himself confidently, dressed in black and dark blues with a dark-blue cape. He had a wand tucked into his belt on one side and a scepter on the other.

The city of Ballmore was half deserted, and the remaining people were ill prepared for an army of that size. As they drew near, the humans shot arrows toward the goblins, which were blocked mostly by the goblins' shields. The lead hobgoblin protected the wizard as he approached the walls.

When the old wizard was three hundred yards away, he lifted his arms, then lowered them abruptly. The ground shook, then cracked underneath the wall, causing it to cave in.

The goblins roared and ran in for the attack. Half of them had crossbows and stayed back, firing randomly behind the walls. The other half ran in with clubs, scimitars, and axes. In less than an hour, Ballmore was in flames and a pile of rubble. The remaining survivors fled as fast as they could through the mountain pass toward Lugo.

The goblins continued through the pass, having lost only a couple dozen in that first attack and thirsty to conquer the bigger city. The pass was narrow, and they had to travel two or three wide at most, which slowed them down. But they were still only two days from the enormous walls of Lugo.

✳ ✳ ✳

Ryder awoke with a start. A solider gently shook his shoulder. "The goblins are approaching. You're needed on the wall."

It was nighttime, but the moon provided enough light to see his surroundings. He shook himself awake and quickly dressed, putting on the chain-mail armor he'd been given and strapping on a sword. This is it. The battle I've been preparing for. He'd only had two days to strengthen the city walls and prepare a trench surrounding the city, but hopefully it would be enough to hold the goblin army back.

From the wall, he looked out over the plains at the eight hundred goblins running toward the walls. He turned to the captain next to him. "This isn't the whole army. There are thousands of goblins and even giants. This is a smaller group."

"Well, we'll just show them what we're all about then, shall we?" The captain turned to the soldiers on the wall. "Ready the ballistae. At my signal."

The goblins drew closer, somehow crossing the trenches without a problem. It looked as if the trenches were filled in where they crossed. As they came into range, the captain raised his hand, then dropped it. A dozen ballistae filled with rocks released at once, sending a barrage of rocks onto the first of the goblins. Some had the sense to raise shields; others were knocked out or injured.

"Reload! And continue firing!"

The goblins slowed under the attack but continued forward. Nearing, they formed a protective huddle around a tall hobgoblin and a human with a dark-blue cape. They drew close enough for bows, and the captain ordered archers to send a barrage of arrows down, which were mostly blocked by shields, although some did connect and drop goblins.

Under the protection of shields, the human raised his hands, and the earth began to shake.

Ryder suddenly understood. An elementalist! Like me! This must be the one the queen was talking about.

He focused on the earth. An unnatural rending was happening under the city wall to his right. He ran closer to the shaking and focused, trying to make the earth calm itself.

Instantly he felt the tension. The earth wanted badly to continue shaking but also began calming itself under Ryder's direction. Unfortunately, the other wizard was clearly more powerful, so the shaking continued.

Ryder watched in horror as the city wall weakened and some of the large stone blocks slipped loose.

He decided to focus on keeping the wall intact, rather than stop the earth from shaking. The stone blocks rejoined themselves. But the shaking turned into a full crack in the earth, a chasm that broke open beneath the wall.

It was all Ryder could do to keep the wall from collapsing—he focused with all his strength. The chasm grew and turned into a perfect opening, then widened even more. The evil wizard had decided to ignore the wall and simply create a way in underneath it.

The goblins roared and ran toward the opening. Ryder couldn't stop his focus, protecting the city wall—if he stopped, the whole wall would crumble in that spot. He only hoped the soldiers would be able to handle the goblins.

Before the goblins arrived at the opening under the wall, nine Zylin monks calmly walked through the gap and watched them. The soldiers lining the walls watched in fascination.

As hundreds of goblins rushed toward them, the monks crouched in a fighting position as one, just as Ryder had seen them do each night when they were traveling together. The first of the goblins got into range, and instantly the monks became a flurry of activity. They moved almost as if in a dance.

Goblins tried attacking with their clumsy weapons but couldn't connect. Instead, they whirled around uselessly and accidentally hit each other. At one point, three goblins closed in on a monk, but the monk leaped ten feet into the air, causing the goblins to collide.

One monk ended up facing over twenty goblins on his own. Swirling his hands, he created a circle of dark a good thirty feet around himself—an impenetrable darkness. The sound of goblins yelling and crashing into each other followed.

When the darkness lifted, the monk stood in the center untouched, the goblins lying at his feet.

Another monk was much more offensive—attacking goblins left and right with ease, dropping them as she cut through them like butter, using only her body.

It looked as if the monks would hold off the hundreds of goblins, but then the lanky wizard approached and raised his scepter. A fireball spurted from its tip, headed right toward the center of the monks, growing as it flew through the air. By the time it reached the monks, it was easily twenty feet across.

One of the monks yelled, "Heb!"

Six monks in the vicinity all stood with legs wide and raised their hands together. In that moment, a shimmering yellow glow appeared in front of them, directly in the path of the enormous fireball. The ball of flames hit the shimmering shield and died out instantly.

The monks returned to their battle techniques from before, each with their individual flair and approach. Ryder was exhausted from holding up the castle wall, but with the evil wizard distracted, he took the opportunity to raise up the earth. Slowly, the earth gathered itself, crumpling and rolling underneath the wall to support it.

The wizard on the field shot another fireball toward the monks, and again they all stopped their attacks to gather and stand in unison, creating a shimmering wall to block it. One of the monks immediately leaped into the air toward the wizard, landing briefly on the head of a goblin, stepping on the shoulder of another before it could react, and leaping again.

The wizard shot a fireball toward the leaping monk, which the monk avoided by doing a cartwheel to the left. Then she leaped again toward the wizard, blocking three goblin attacks with her hand movements.

The wizard shot another fireball, then sheathed the scepter, pulling out a wand.

The monk dropped to the ground to avoid the fiery blaze, which scorched into a handful of goblins. She then leaped up toward the wizard—and at twenty feet away, pushed both hands forward. A blaze of light flashed toward the wizard, blinding him. The wizard lifted his free hand to his eyes, but the monk approached quickly, shouting something as the wizard waved his wand.

A protective bubble appeared around him, causing the monk to bounce off. The monk looked around, surprised, and the enormous hobgoblin with black armor and a jagged sword rounded in for the attack.

The sword might have connected except for the monk's extraordinary reflexes. She bent backward, belly exposed to the air, till her hands touched the ground. She kicked, sending the sword flying from the hobgoblin's hands.

The creature immediately shouted a few words in his guttural language. The word went out among all the goblins, and they turned—tripping and scrambling over goblin bodies, back across the walkway that had been created over the ditch.

The monks stood as one and watched, letting them go.

The large hobgoblin scooped up his sword and grabbed the old wizard over his shoulder, then turned and ran. The attacking monk stopped her action and stood calmly as goblins ran past. The goblins gathered some of their wounded who were in good enough shape to move, then ran out of the range of the ballistae.

Ryder felt like he couldn't do any more work to repair the hole under the wall and mustered the last of his energy to finish strengthening it. He then slumped against the turret and watched the evil army retreat.

There were at most three hundred goblins left from their original eight hundred. A cry of joy went up along the wall. The people knew they were safe. Soldiers came alongside Ryder and patted him on the back.

A few moments later, the General approached, smiling. "Well done! Between you and the Zylin, those goblins and wizards were a snap!" He frowned when Ryder looked up weakly. "Are you ok?"

"Yes," Ryder said faintly. "That other wizard was much stronger than me. He'd have succeeded in taking down the wall if the monks hadn't been here."

"Well, they were. And we've succeeded. Well done, lad."

Ryder shook his head wearily. "But this was a tiny group. There are thousands more. Plus at least two giants. And more wizards. I think this was just a test—to see what kind of defenses we have. We're going to need more."

"I'll send out scouts immediately. And, yes, you're right. We need better defenses. We mustn't forget our foe has magic. It will take all we can to defend against them. We do have some magic of our own . . . not like yours, but we'll come up with some ideas. If we've got a few days, that might be enough time."

"Will it be enough?"

"Perhaps not. We do have the wildcard of three kids with powers who set out looking to bring back a dragon to help." He gave Ryder a knowing look. "But who knows how that's going. In the meantime, we'll work with what we can."

Ryder struggled to his feet. "Whatever I can do to help."

He thought of Amber and the boys. How were they doing? Would they find the dragon? And if so, would it help?

He sighed. They needed help—and inspiration. He put his hand in his pocket and felt the enchanted rock. There had to be something more strategic he could come up with. He didn't want to rely on the rock—but he could sure use some ideas.

He held the rock for a moment. Instantly he saw ways to strengthen the walls from rending the earth beneath. The blocks were stacked like bricks, but if he created round pillars of thick stone at key intervals throughout and slightly changed the bricks to have sharper edges, more closely packed together, it could withstand much greater stress.

Thicker walls were less important than straighter and tighter designs. And there were places the ground was softer. He could make it dense and powerful by lifting the bedrock, able to hold the wall much more stably.

He looked out over the plain at the trench he'd created—the one the evil wizard had filled in so easily. It needed spikes made from trees. And the trench should be much deeper. There were still many innocent people fleeing to Lugo for safety, so there would have to be a bridge that could be removed. The evil wizard would overcome it, but he couldn't be everywhere at the same time. They would do what they could to make it that much harder to surpass.

He let go of the enchanted stone. Although he felt new insight about their defenses, he also got to thinking about why they were fighting in the first place. Maybe the queen had good reasons for the fight? She hadn't explained herself well enough for Ryder to understand, but she obviously had a lot of experience and knowledge. She must have some other motivation. He shrugged the thought away and focused.

There was a lot to be done and a short amount of time to do it. He'd have a good breakfast, then get straight to work. No matter how much it would tire him out, he'd make that city as impenetrable as possible. The evil was coming.

Chapter 18

The Hidden City

AS AMBER AND HER LIZARD CAPTOR SOARED over the deck of the elves' floating warship, she found herself calmly admiring the ship's construction. Its rigging matched other ships for the sea, with three masts and sails, and a boom on the middle mast, which was taller than the others.

It also had two extra sails on the left and right sides, sticking out like extended fish gills. There was a crow's nest and even a helm, yet how it could be steered up in the sky seemed a mystery.

The draco flapped above the ship and lowered Amber gently to the deck. She rolled, then stood warily, staring at the three elves in front of her. The draco landed a few feet away, and a small rider dismounted. Three more dracos came in behind them.

Amber stared at the large lizards. Seeing them up close, she noticed more details. She hadn't seen dragons before, except once in the distance and in pictures, but she imagined these looked like a cross between a dragon and a lizard. They were green and scaly, but the scales were very fine and smooth, not like what she'd heard of dragon scales. They had lizard-like heads but flaring nostrils and wider mouths with many teeth.

Two short horns protruded from their heads, just behind their tiny ears, little bumps with holes. The eyes were large like a lizard, yet a bit bat-like, leathery and wide. They had a ridge along their backs, starting between their eyes and trailing down to their tails.

The approaching elf was completely silver—his long hair glistened even with no light shining off it, and his skin was a similar silvery-white color. His thin body stood nearly a foot shorter than Amber, under four feet she guessed. His head had long pointy ears and large almond-shaped eyes with dark-black pupils. He walked gracefully like a cat, dressed in tight-fitting black clothing, with a long black cape that billowed behind him as he walked.

Amber gulped. She took her helmet and goggles off, so the elf could see she wasn't a dwarf. Maybe he'll be nice to me if he sees I'm a human, she hoped.

The elf cocked his head and looked at her strangely, then said haltingly, "Hello . . . human. Am I speaking rightly?"

"Yes." Remember, be polite, she told herself. Give a good impression, and maybe you can get out of this safely. "My name is Amber. What's your name?"

The elf continued to watch her without speaking, his eyebrows crinkled. "I am a sky elf." He put his hand to his chest. "What . . . why you being with the dwarves?" Three other elves slowly walked up behind him, looking at her curiously. They all had the same pale silver skin, white hair, and dark leather outfits. It would be impossible to tell them apart in a crowd.

Amber spoke slowly, to make sure the elves would understand her. "I was lost in the mountains and ran into a griffin. When I got on it, it took me to the dwarves, and they took care of me. I'm trying to go to the dragon—Crodor the Ancient—to break an evil spell on it."

The elf looked at her quizzically.

"Do you understand what I'm saying?"

A female elf said, "You . . . go to dragon?" She pointed behind her to their right.

"Yes," Amber said. "An evil spell made the dragon act badly. I can help fix it." She was trying her best to speak in short words and speak even slower than before.

The elves continued to look at her with curious expressions, then one said, "You come with us." He gestured with his hand.

Amber followed the silver elf into the fog along the deck, the other elves falling in silently behind. They passed a few elves as they went, all different shades of white or silver. The elf at the helm of the ship was a silvery-orange, and Amber stared at him as they walked past.

They climbed a short ladder, then came upon a small door, so Amber instinctively lowered her head to go through. Inside was a perfectly laid-out captain's chamber, much like she'd seen on sea vessels only more compact. Three more elves were in the chamber and stood when the others arrived. All of them were a similar height and stature, with pale silvery-white skin, except for one who had hints of gold.

The elves began speaking to each other in a language quite different than the dwarves. Amber suddenly had a thought: How many languages are out there? Do all the different races speak their own languages? She'd never thought of it before with pixies. Do the pixies have their own language too?

After a bit, they looked at Amber, and the one who was white with a hint of gold spoke: "We very much want to know your reason for being here. What is this about the dragon?"

"Yes," She spoke with great animation and as slowly as possible since the earlier ones didn't seem to understand her very well. "The dragon, Crodor the Ancient, has a magic spell on him, causing him to attack and hurt others. We need to break the spell." She gestured as if snapping a branch. "So he can help us fight a goblin army, that is coming to attack one of our biggest human cities."

She paused and looked at the elf, then continued. "We save dragon from spell. We get dragon to help against goblins."

The elf nodded. "I see. You save humans from goblins by getting dragon's help." He paused. "But why you with dwarves?"

"The dwarves are helping me. I broke the spell on their griffins, so they want to help me."

The elf cocked his head, "You have magic? You be a mage?"

"Me? No, no, no." Amber shook her head. "But I know a wizard who helped us." She almost reached for her amulet, then thought better of it. If the elves weren't to be trusted, then it would be foolish to show them her most powerful tool. "So now I can break the spell too."

"Hmm." The elf spoke a few words in his language to the one next to him, and the other responded. Then he turned back to her. "We can break spell. Our mages break spell like easy." He looked proudly at Amber with his head high. "We elves not need humans to break spell."

"Of course." She hadn't thought that the elves would have their own wizards. And that would explain why they were flying on their dracos, even if the dracos had been enchanted.

"I need to go help my people," Amber said. "I need to go. Can you let me go?" She looked at the elf with big, pleading eyes.

The elf nodded. "Yes, yes, we do not kill you. We put you in prison."

Amber sighed. At least I won't die—yet. But how will I help Lugo in a prison cell?

The elves spoke among themselves again, then two of them walked up to her and gestured for her to follow. They walked out the chamber onto the deck again.

Suddenly a yell came from behind, and they twirled around. The dwarves were attacking! Amber's heart leaped with joy. This was it! Her chance to escape. The dwarves crested the boat, firing crossbow bolts and sending nets onto unsuspecting elves. The elves scattered, some to dracos, others to the large ballistae on either side.

Only one elf was left guarding her, standing to her left. She elbowed him in the stomach and ran down the deck. Bolts flew. One elf shrieked, a bolt protruding from his leg. Amber continued to run, heading to the prow of the boat, hoping the dwarves would see her.

She heard shouting behind her. The elves were a flurry of motion, and she couldn't make out who was doing what. The dwarves were circling above.

She felt hope welling up. She jumped and waved. "Over here! Kish!" A griffin flew toward her.

But then she felt a sharp pain in her side. A female elf stood next to her. Amber stared at her dazed. The elf kicked her in the stomach again, and Amber crumpled to the deck.

The elf nudged her slightly. When Amber didn't move, she whistled. A draco with an elf rider landed next to them.

The elf lifted Amber to her feet, then guided her onto the draco. As she settled onto its back, it turned its head around and looked at her with eyes narrowed. Her mind raced. What could she possibly do to get out of the situation? No plants were nearby to ask for help, and she certainly wouldn't try escaping once they were in flight.

The elves had minimal versions of saddles, small leathery-like seats, and stirrups for their feet, and there seemed to be no real place for a second person. The elf she sat behind reached back and took her hand, then pulled it around his waist. Amber took the cue and reached around with both arms, holding on.

The elf was skinny but strong and sturdy. He gave a slight squeeze with his legs, and they took off instantly. Amber tried to gauge how the elf was steering, because the draco flew quickly and maneuvered with ease.

The dwarves on their griffins continued to attack the ship. Did they see her? One of them split off in pursuit. But the draco was already in the lead and two more dracos joined it.

All the dwarves suddenly stopped their attack on the ship and pursued Amber. But the griffins' wings beat like giant snails compared to the dracos, who were able to move instantly in any direction.

As Amber feared, the dwarves couldn't catch up quickly enough, and the elves shot ahead into the open air. Even with Amber weighing the draco down, it was incredibly fast. The gap between them grew larger, until the dwarves became specks behind them.

Amber sighed. No great rescue would save her this time. At least she wasn't in a prison—yet. They passed a mountain and headed toward a tall, narrow mountain capped with snow and covered with a lush old forest. The closer they got, Amber realized that some of the trees weren't exactly trees but tree-looking towers.

She felt torn between wanting to escape from the elves and her curiosity to see what their home was like from the inside. Was it like Mizu's home? She imagined everything Mizu had told them, of cities in the trees. Were these elves somehow connected to Mizu's people?

They flew past a tall tower that peeked up above the tree line, then dropped straight down. Amber ducked her head, thinking they'd hit some branches, but they flew right past and under the tree canopy. Her breath caught in her throat.

There was an entire city hiding underneath the tree cover. Houses looked like they were growing out of the trees, interspersed up and down every side. The trees themselves were enormous—far larger than any she'd ever seen. She knew you could tell how old a tree was by the number of rings . . . but these must be hundreds or even thousands of years old.

Her body tingled—her elemental power with plants amplified and felt stronger than ever. She could sense age-old trees as far as her senses would allow, and the trees were almost . . . happy. She couldn't explain it. But this forest felt at peace compared to the wild land she'd been in two days before.

The houses were connected by rope bridges and walkways built into the gigantic branches. Everything looked and felt like it was created by someone with elemental power, not constructed with a hammer and nails. The wood and designs all felt organic and natural. Was this what the old tree in her dream was talking about?

And the elves! They were everywhere. Most of them were white-silver like the first ones she'd met, but there were others who were completely different colors—shades of blue like Mizu, red, green, yellow. Amber wondered if there was a color that elves weren't. But most were quite pale and dressed darkly, like the first ones.

The forest grew dim below the tree line, yet every window had a glowing orange light inside. The lights pierced through the trees as far as the eye could see and gave the entire city a mystical quality.

The dracos flew past what Amber assumed was the elf equivalent of a castle. It had large archways and a handful of elves stationed outside with long spears and sharp black uniforms. The dracos slowed and landed gently on the large platform in front. She and the elves dismounted.

When the guards saw her, they stood up a little straighter and watched carefully. She was about a half a head taller than the tallest of them and dressed very differently.

The dracos flew off, and Amber wondered again how the elves communicated with them since she hadn't seen the elves using any signals. An elf touched her arm and gestured to the entryway, so she walked toward the large arch. Guards nodded at the elves behind her, and she suddenly felt incredibly nervous.

What do they want with me? Are they still going to put me in prison? Hold your head high, Amber, she told herself. Show them you're strong.

She entered the hall of the large building and marveled at how much space there was inside a tower that far up a tree. She walked into a room that was elegant through and through, in a natural sort of way. There was no gold or metallic ornamentation like the dwarf kingdom, but the wood was ornate and intricate with embellished shapes and patterns on every surface.

And the floor! The sheer amount of time that must have been spent decorating the mosaic-patterned floor was awe inspiring. She tried to determine a shape out of the patterns, but it was hard to imagine from her vantage point.

They walked across the hall and toward a staircase at the back. The elves who accompanied her spoke with some other elves for a few minutes, then left Amber and went back outside. Two new elves looked her over carefully. Their eyes paused on her dagger and stiletto, as well as her pack. They also looked curiously at her cloak, as if seeing the magic built into it.

Amber felt exposed and awkward, wondering if she would have to part with any of her things—and just after being fully equipped!

But the elves did nothing. They stood and waited, watching her, so she stood watching them.

"Um . . . nice place you have here," she said awkwardly. The elves didn't bat an eyelash but continued to stare at her.

That was stupid of me! she thought. What would Theo say? He's always saying the right thing to make everyone feel relaxed.

She tried again: "Who are we waiting to see?"

Again the elves did nothing. I get it, she thought. They probably aren't supposed to talk to me. Or maybe they just don't speak my language.

She scanned the room again. Now that it was clear she had time to look around, she appreciated the tapestries lining the walls. They were filled with elaborate artwork and various scenes of elves engaging with one another and other creatures. There were a few with dragons, and Amber wondered if they had a history with Crodor the Ancient.

She wandered around the room looking more closely at the tapestries. The elf guards didn't stop her. The artwork seemed to tell snippets of their history. There were some pictures of elves in flight on dracos. But one tapestry stood out: human wizards and two large armies in battle.

Could this be the Great War from two centuries ago? If so, maybe these elves have some advice or knowledge they can pass on to us humans about the prophecy.

Except . . . I might be part-elf. I hadn't thought of that. I'll make sure to play that card if it comes up, if it seems like they're going to throw me in prison or something. Surely, they'll have mercy on someone who is part elf?

She made her way around the great hall, examining every tapestry with great detail. The two elf guards remained standing in their same spot. She took her pack off and sat on the floor cross-legged. Taking a deep breath, she felt the trees with her powers. She felt a stronger connection to the trees than ever. Perhaps if she stayed there long enough, she could talk to them during the day.

She kept an eye on the elves at the door but focused her attention on the forest around her. The elf city seemed to go on as far as her senses allowed—or at least their dwellings among the trees. She mused: How many people live here? Probably thousands. It feels even bigger than the dwarf kingdom. I wonder how it compares to Lugo?

She considered the tree she sat in, sensing it was ancient and almost at peace, as if it were happy with having elves living in it. She sensed that there was work done to carve and build around the tree, but also that there was a lot of cooperation. Perhaps the elves who built these more impressive buildings had her elemental power or similar.

One of the elves walked over to her, interrupting her thoughts. She immediately stood and gathered her pack. The elf gestured, and she followed him up the staircase.

It was narrow and wound around, with the occasional window to the forest outside. They walked up the tree for a few minutes, till she started to feel a slight burn in her thighs. Then they came to a doorway.

The elf opened the door, leading to a gorgeous room overlooking the entire city with ornate artwork on every wall. Five older elves sat at a large table, watching her calmly. Behind them stood two soldiers and an archway with a view to the tree city below. A younger elf stood next to them.

The younger elf immediately stood out to Amber, because his skin and hair was red-brown, like leaves that have turned color in the autumn. He wore the same tight black outfits the soldiers did, while the older elves wore more loose-fitting clothing and much lighter colors—whites, browns, and silvers—to match their skin and surroundings.

One of the older elves beckoned Amber over. She walked to the table and stood before the five elves.

Don't be the first to speak, Amber told herself, waiting nervously. Hold your head high. Show respect and wait for them to speak first.

The elves waited a moment longer than she would have liked, but finally the one who gestured to her spoke: "And so you come here at last, Amber, the half-elf."

Chapter 19

The Emerald Lake

MIZU PEERED AT THE CRAGGY mountain and frowned. She dismounted Buttercup and pulled out her map. The dragon's mountain should be right there. But nothing looked familiar. And where was the large lake she remembered? Were they even in the right spot?

Basil dismounted Storm, and Theo slid off Zoomy's back, scratching the large bear behind the ears.

"Is this it?" Basil peered over Mizu's shoulder.

"I don't think so. There's no lake." She pointed at the map in frustration.

"Are you sure your map is accurate?"

"Yes! Of course." She frowned at him.

Basil shook his head. "Well, this isn't working. You've been staring at that map all day now, and we're no further along. We're just wandering through the woods, completely lost."

Mizu's eyes flared. "The map is accurate. I can find the dragon. It's not just for your puny human issues I'm looking, you know."

"Puny?" Basil stood, fists on hips. "Are you saying finding Amber—who could be in danger—is puny? Or the army of goblins approaching Lugo?"

"No. No. I didn't mean that. Just that I'm not only looking for those reasons." Mizu pointed at him. "But your whining isn't helping."

"Whining?" Basil looked indignant. "Hey, I'm just trying to help. We need to find the dragon quickly."

"I know!" Mizu whipped the map away and huffed off to a large rock. She climbed it and looked around.

"Look. You don't have to be mean about it. All I'm saying is, let's find the right mountain."

"I'm not being mean!" Mizu's eyes flashed. "Just give me a minute!"

Basil shot Theo a bewildered expression, and Theo shrugged.

Zoomy wandered over to some bushes and expertly chomped into clusters of berries, pulling them off in large bites. The two boys waited. It was a pleasant day, with a few fluffy clouds in the sky, but it was hard to appreciate it at the moment.

Theo finally broke the silence. "You're looking for a lake, right? I can find a bird to fly around and point us to it."

Mizu instantly lightened up. "Oh. That would be great. Would you?"

"Of course! Look above you." A large golden eagle was circling lower toward them. "I'll call her Scout, because she's going to help us find the way." Theo gave her a smile, then looked away sheepishly as she smiled back.

The eagle swooped down, then flew high into the air. It rose up the mountain they were on, then turned toward the one they'd been looking at. It passed over to the mountain far to their right.

"Found it!" Theo pointed. "It's that way. No need to climb a mountain at all. Looks like we were just one mountain away."

Basil glared at Mizu. "See how quick it was when you mentioned the lake? We can help, you know. It's not just about you and your elf mission."

Mizu frowned at him silently. Why did he have to rub it in?

They mounted their steeds and made their way through the forest, climbing up a ravine, then down again till they saw a gorgeous body of water below. The lake glistened in the sunlight, a rich green-blue, like a gem nestled in between tall mountains on each side.

It was enormous, almost three miles across, and the far side had some unnatural looking structures, perhaps docks. Maybe even ships. The side they were on was lined with pebble beaches and rocks all around.

"That's it!" Mizu sighed in relief. "Just as I remember. The dragon should be on the big craggy mountain past that far shore to the left."

They sped up, eagerly riding down the mountain. Finally their destination was close at hand.

They were a few minutes away when Basil stopped Storm. "A boat!" He pulled his spyglass out of the side bag and peered through it. "It's an elf! I think. He's on a small boat near those cliffs to the right over there."

"Really?" Mizu lit up. "Can I see?"

"Sure." Basil handed her the spyglass, and she squinted through it.

"Yes. That's an elvish craft. I think he's fishing, or . . . wait. What was that?"

The water rippled in a big rolling wave, coming from the cliff area.

"Here, let me see." Basil took the spyglass and scanned the sea. The water rippled again, then a fin emerged. Was it a giant fish? But then another bump emerged behind it. They weren't fins at all, but the spines of one long creature.

"A sea serpent!" he shouted. "Headed right for that elf!"

He jammed the spyglass back into his side bag and kicked Storm down the mountain. "We've got to warn them!"

"Basil! Wait for me!" Mizu fumbled with Buttercup's reins, still not used to riding horses.

Basil called out as he rode. "Come to shore! A sea creature is coming!"

The elf in the boat looked up curiously at the faint sound.

Theo stayed on Zoomy fixed in one spot, fretting. "Oh no. Oh no."

Mizu kicked Buttercup after Storm. "Basil, wait! I can help!"

Basil had a singular focus on getting down the steep mountain quickly and safely, and his horse's hooves drowned out Mizu.

The elf stood in his boat and put his hand above his eyes to block the sun, peering at the small dot of a rider hurtling down the mountainside—and completely oblivious to the large creature making its way toward him under the water.

Mizu tried catching up, to no avail. She fumed with frustration. "Basil! Don't distract him. He's watching you instead of the water!"

Basil arrived at the shore, waving and pointing to the water. Finally, the elf realized what was going on and turned, just in time to see a large serpent-like creature leaping out of the water to attack.

The serpent was enormous, its head nearly as large as the entire boat. Its lizard-like body was covered in blue-green scales, with vibrant red fins and two long, protruding horns. Its underside was smooth like a snake, and its gaping mouth was full of razor-sharp teeth.

The elf nimbly darted to the side, just out of reach from the dangerous teeth, but the large body of the creature crashed into the tiny boat, splintering it into pieces. The elf went flying into the water. His head popped up a moment later, and he splashed frantically as the serpent submerged. The water became eerily calm, and the elf turned wildly in every direction.

Mizu rode Buttercup a few feet into the water, and in one fluid motion stripped off an outer layer of clothing and dove in, swimming at an incredible speed toward the other elf.

Theo remained on the mountainside thinking through his options. Basil turned toward him. "Theo! Get down here and help! Bring that bear and that crossbow of yours!"

Snapping out of his thoughts, Theo urged Zoomy forward. The bear proved her name and lumbered down the mountain, deftly dodging trees, logs, and holes faster than the horses.

Mizu emerged from the water like a dolphin leaping out of the waves. She swam at a speed and an elegance unmatched by any other elf or human.

Basil watched in awe as it dawned on him. Mizu was a water elementalist!

The next moment, the sea creature's head surfaced a small distance from the elf, then opened its gaping mouth in a

251

deadly attack. Mizu leaped out of the water and swung her right arm upward.

Just as the serpent was about to connect, the water around the elf churned and lifted, flinging the elf into the air toward Mizu. The serpent's teeth scraped along the elf's side and down his leg, instead of swallowing the elf whole. The large head disappeared below the waves, followed by the lumps of the serpent's huge body.

Mizu dove under the water. Under the surface, she could see the serpent turn and snake its body around for another attack. It spotted the elf splashing desperately and zipped forward.

But Mizu got to his side first. As the serpent leaped for its next attack a whirlpool formed, pushing it to their left so that it barely missed.

Swimming with the elf in her arms, she kept a fast pace toward the shore. She swam like a fish, moving back and forth rather than using her arms. The water propelled her forward almost as fast as the serpent could swim.

But the serpent turned and sped after them again—and it was faster.

As they neared the shore Mizu glanced behind her. The serpent was closing in. It would catch up to them in seconds.

She focused all her energy to propel them faster while also pushing the serpent away.

With a shout of triumph, Mizu shot out of the water, hanging onto the elf, with the serpent right at their heels. She was headed toward the shallows, hopefully too shallow for the giant creature. But the serpent emerged from the water in pursuit, snapping as it soared through the air.

Theo and Basil watched in horror as the serpent bit into the elf's leg.

"Get that crossbow!" Basil shouted, pulling off his bow and stringing an arrow. Theo fumbled for the crossbow and slid off the bear's back. Zoomy growled and lowered her head.

Thankfully, the serpent wasn't able to sink a solid grip as Mizu pulled away, awkwardly holding the elf over her shoulder. She staggered to the pebble beach with the serpent darting through the shallows after them.

She took five heavy steps and rolled onto the pebbles with the elf in tow. A wall of water appeared between her and the beast, blocking the view. The serpent popped its head through the water-wall, deciding whether to attack. As soon as it showed its face, Basil and Theo fired their weapons. The arrow and bolt bounced off its scales harmlessly. But Zoomy took the opportunity to pounce.

The fierce bear leaped into the water and grasped the serpent's neck, tearing in with her huge claws. The serpent lunged and gashed the bear's side.

Theo fumbled as he tried reloading his crossbow and dropped the bolt. He bent to pick it up and tried again, his fingers slippery like butter.

The bear and serpent tussled in the water, and the blood from both pooled around them. They turned and moved so quickly that Basil and Theo couldn't get more shots in, though Basil kept aiming. Zoomy growled fiercely, and the serpent hissed in reply.

Mizu was focused on the elf, watching his eyes begin to glaze over. "Don't die! Where are you from?" She glanced down at his injured leg and side, a bloody mess.

"Nocea . . ." He pointed raggedly and closed his eyes, going limp.

"Theo!" Mizu's eyes flashed as she looked up. "Put down that crossbow and get over here with that healing ring!"

Theo shook his head as if waking up and ran over. He put his hand on the elf's leg, and the blood stopped gushing.

Zoomy ripped into the serpent again before the serpent gave one last hiss, then wriggled free and slipped back into the lake. The bear stood on her hind legs, peering into the rippling waves.

Mizu waited in desperation as the elf's wounds closed ever so slowly. She turned to Theo. "Can you make the ring heal quicker?"

"This is it." Theo grimaced. "You never know, though. Remember how it healed Lorien? It might still work."

Mizu wrung her hands, watching the muscles knit themselves slowly back into place. The elf's breathing slowed, then stopped altogether.

"No!" Mizu beat on his chest. "No! Come on, Theo!"

Theo frowned, but the ring only had one speed, and the wounds were too deep and serious. They kept at it for another minute, then Mizu stood and stormed away.

She picked up a rock and threw it into the lake, where the water suddenly lifted up, twirled a moment with the rock floating at the tip, then whipped the rock far into the depths of the lake.

She watched the lake in silence, then shouted. "Nooo! It didn't have to be this way! Basil! Why do you always have to barge in! The elf didn't even *see* the serpent till it was too late because of you! And Theo— why are you always stuck *thinking* instead of actually *doing* anything useful?"

She scowled and picked up another rock, throwing it far into the lake, using the lake once again to send it flying even farther.

"Well," Basil began, "it would have been nice to know you had powers with *water* before we got into a fight with a water creature. I'm sure I would've done something different had I known that."

Mizu stared at him angrily, then huffed and went over to a large rock. She sat down and buried her face in her hands. Her shoulders shook as she silently cried.

Theo stood and gave Basil a sideways look. "Nice job, Squiggles."

Basil shrugged his shoulders and cocked his head. They walked over to Mizu and sat next to her on either side. The three sat in silence, till Mizu's crying slowed and stopped. They sat like that for a while, till the lake was calm and glistening like a perfect emerald again.

A large flock of birds flew over the mountain toward them. At first, it seemed like a normal flock of birds, but they kept coming and coming till there were thousands of them. Tens of thousands. The birds didn't seem amazing or different—they were small, dark starlings, not much bigger than the small songbirds all around the forest.

But as they swooped down over the lake catching flying insects, something beautiful happened. Though there were thousands upon thousands of birds, they moved together in perfect unison—a murmuration. Somehow, miraculously, they were almost right upon each other yet never collided. They swirled around and around, the shape condensing and expanding majestically, sometimes becoming so dense that it was impossible to see through. And then spreading out to reveal the sky.

The pulsing wonder of the birds was awe inspiring. They continued to swarm above the lake for a good half hour in a mesmerizing dance. Then, just as they had arrived, they flew off as one, back the way they'd come.

After a moment more of silence, Theo said, "You know, we could learn a thing or two from those birds. The way they work together. It would mean no more secrets between us." He glanced at Mizu. "And also all of us sticking to one plan, not doing our own thing."

He stood and looked at them. "We're three amazing people here, and when we find Amber, that's four. A lot of people are counting on us working together. I'm the last person I thought would be out here on an adventure battling sea serpents . . . but I'll tell you what, I'm glad to be here with you two. And I'm hopeful. I think we really can do it. I mean, we've dealt with a phoenix and a powerful wizard. We've traveled across the country and dealt with goblins, trolls, and a sea serpent. We can do this, but we have to do it together."

Basil stood and grasped Theo's hand. "You're right, Theo. And I'm sorry for being harsh with you, Mizu. We know where the lake is now. We can find the dragon, right?"

"Not yet." Mizu stood with them. "I'm sorry, too, for not telling you about my powers. I wasn't sure about you. I know you saved my life, but . . . well, it takes a long time for me to warm up to people. Especially humans. And I agree. We need to work together. But first . . . we need to bring that elf back to his home. I don't think it's too far from here."

"Is it really that important to bring the elf back?" Basil asked. "More than finding the dragon?"

"Well, there's something else. And I won't keep it from you." Mizu sighed. "My aunt lives here. Part of my mission has been to find the dragon, but also part of it has been to connect with my aunt again and give her messages from my family."

Theo patted Zoomy behind the ears absently. "Wonderful! You see how great it is to *not* keep secrets? Now that we know, we'll go with you. Right, Basil?"

Basil frowned. "Amber is possibly flying on a griffin to find the dragon right now. An army of goblins, giants, and wizards is heading toward Lugo. And you want to check in on family? Really?"

"It's important." Mizu looked him in the eyes. "I'm not holding back now. Can you trust me?"

He looked at Theo, who was nodding, then back at the blue elf. "You know where it is?"

She shrugged. "I'll find it. My map is obviously lacking. But it can't be far. Not with an elf right here."

Theo smiled. "Besides, how many humans get a chance to see an elven city, right Basil?"

Basil looked at the mountain in the distance that was most likely home to the dragon. Then he looked back at Theo and Mizu and pursed his lips. "Let's make it quick."

Chapter 20

Scepters and Prophecies

THE GOLDEN-HUED ELF STOOD SHORTER than Amber but somehow looked tall and elegant.

"My name is Gratian. Azarel, here, will explain many things to you." The older elf gestured to the young red elf standing next to him. He spoke in the same sing-songy, lilting way as Mizu. "However, we have a few questions for you, before we send you back to find Crodor."

Amber's mind raced, but she kept quiet.

Gratian tossed her something small, and Amber instinctively caught it. It was a seed. "What kind of plant is this?"

She looked at him quizzically, but he stared at her calmly, waiting. Does he know of my gift? she wondered. Probably. They somehow seem to know everything else about me.

She eyed the seed, tempted to make it grow, but wondered if this was some sort of test. She sensed the seed, picturing and imagining what it would do if she asked it to grow. With a start, she realized she knew exactly what kind of plant it was. However tiny it was, she suddenly understood all its possibility.

"This is a seed from the very tree we are standing in right now," Amber said confidently, looking the elf in the eyes. He stared back and his gold, almond-shaped eyes seemed to smile for a moment, glistening and speaking volumes of acceptance to her without a word being spoken.

"Well done." He turned to the other elves at the table. "Yes, she's the one we've been waiting for. We may proceed."

Another elf at the table with bright silver robes matching her hair and skin spoke next. "Amber, we are the Conclave of Nocea. We have seen many things over the ages, including the rise and fall of many human civilizations. But in these last centuries, there has been a great evil stirring among us, a power we elves have not been able to discern on our own."

She stood elegantly and gestured to a tapestry on the wall behind Amber that depicted many elves with weapons facing a human wizard. "The last Great War was very difficult on our race, and elves were scattered—our numbers diminished across the continent. Our great city here is the last of its kind, protected by the mountains and by its great distance to the other civilizations. All our other cousins live in much smaller homes, mere villages compared to what they once were."

She walked to the tapestry and gazed at it. "Sadly, the difficulties we have faced are far from over. We have great insight among us about what is to come, and we know that the only way for us to succeed is to join with other races. The battles of old only paused the effort. We still don't understand what the fighting was all about. But now, those who would kill us are growing in power, gathering scepters, preparing themselves for great evil."

"The scepters from the prophecy?" Amber blurted, then wondered if she should have spoken.

The elf gave a slight nod. "One of our people gave a great prophecy long ago that spoke of evil ones using the scepters of old for ill. However, they are far from their goal, since we have three here." She lifted a scepter that had been hidden in her robes, and Amber felt a tingle of power emanating from it.

She couldn't place why she felt power, or what it was exactly. The scepter itself was beautiful—ornately carved of wood and intricately patterned as if created by interweaving vines. At the tip was a bulbous pattern and an embedded smooth silver stone.

"Each scepter has its own power, and each in its own right is formidable. Together, they can do more than apart. Most of our home here was created using scepters." She gazed around at the intricate designs around the walls, doors, and archway. "And, of course, at the hands of those with powers like yours."

She smiled, and Amber felt herself growing warm. Was that embarrassment she felt—or pride? Or both, perhaps? The woman stared at Amber a moment. "What questions do you have?"

Amber's mind raced with dozens of thoughts. "Well, how do you know about me?"

Gratian stood and said, "That is partly thanks to a friend of yours named Sage."

"The wizard! He was here?"

"Indeed. A few weeks ago. He told us a great many things and helped us know how to prepare. However, I believe it will not be easy this time."

"This time?" Amber twirled her hair nervously.

"Yes. Compared to the Great War, where we had more elves, mages, and scepters. Times have changed. We are scattered and wield much less power than before. You humans have nearly no mages in this part of the world. We have no idea yet how great the evil is. So far, a single army seems like nothing compared to the destruction that caught us unaware two centuries ago."

"However . . ." He gazed out the large window and folded his arms. "Darius, one of our mages of old, had a prophecy that seemed centuries in the making. He spoke that the end of the evil was not yet ours to celebrate. And so, we have been watchful for many years, for this time to arise again."

Turning to Amber, he added, "And we are prepared— even if all human cities fall, our city is protected far greater than before."

"All human cities?" Amber asked. "You'd let the human cities fall?"

"They aren't our concern," Gratian said, almost with pity in his voice. "If they couldn't learn from the last war, it doesn't fall on us to protect them. We will be busy enough protecting ourselves, you see." He explained it as if to a child, and Amber suddenly felt patronized.

"But it's been so long! That was eight generations ago. How can you expect us to remember?"

Gratian shrugged. "As I said, it is not our main concern. In fact, there are still among us today some elves who were there at the time of the Great War."

She fumed at him. "That's exactly what I'm saying! Can't you have some pity on the humans who live such shorter lives than you? Can't you see we need your help?"

The elves all nodded. At least they understood that. But Amber could see she wasn't getting through to them. So she switched gears. "But you do intend to help me?"

"Yes, of course," the woman said. "We have reason to believe you may be one of the youths from the prophecy, and we want to support your efforts. One person can cripple a giant by attacking the tendon above its heel. Some wars are won not through big battles, but through a smaller number who work together. Which brings us to Azarel."

She gestured at the young elf standing next to her. "We have reason to believe that Azarel should join your efforts, wherever they lead you, if you will have him."

Azarel turned to her with anger in his eyes. "But mother!" She raised a hand, and he instantly quieted.

"Azarel has power over flames, and I believe your party only has three of the elements covered at this point?"

Amber nodded. She looked over the red elf again. It would certainly help to have more powers with their mission, but Azarel seemed to be fuming inside. His mother went on. "If you require help, do let us know. We want you to succeed." She waited a moment.

Amber said, "I'd like to get back to my friends, the dwarves."

The elf looked disgusted. "What do you have to do with those filthy people? They can't possibly be of service to you."

"Yes," Amber said quickly. "They helped me when I was all alone. They were taking me to the dragon. They were even going to help me break the spell on him."

"They didn't seem to teach you the basics of flying, now did they?" she asked bitterly. "You fell off the griffin almost immediately, from what my people say."

"Well, I guess that's true." She didn't like where the conversation was going but didn't know what to say.

"Indeed. Trust them for a moment, and they will backstab you the next. Know this, child, we have many centuries of dealing with dwarves. Some dwarves may seem pleasant, but they are never unified. There is always at least one among them who will kill you for their own purpose."

Amber gulped and thought of Kish's comment. Not all the dwarves were to be trusted. But *he'd* made her a promise. "I trust at least one," she said.

The elf turned to the others and said a few words in their language, at which point they all murmured in agreement. Then she turned back to Amber. "Enough. What you choose to do and how you choose to move forward is not up to us. But we will not help you reconnect with them. That is up to you to figure out. Azarel is our contribution to your mission. If you need more, he will help you."

She gestured, and one of the guards approached Amber to escort her down the stairway. And with no further ado the conversation was over.

Walking down the narrow stairs, Amber quietly thought about their exchange. These elves seem very powerful, yet stuck in their ways, with no room for other species, especially dwarves. Although I guess they're helping me.

They arrived in the great hall below, and Amber was surprised to see Azarel casually standing there. He stood almost a full head shorter than her, and his color was striking, different than the other elves she'd seen. She wondered if colors had anything to do with their gifts.

"Hi." He gave her a terse nod. "I'm supposed to ask you if you need anything." He seemed like a bundle of unhappy energy, his eyes flashing with scorn. Amber hoped his mood would change—if he was to be a traveling companion, it would be a much nicer trip if he could be cheerful.

"The dwarves have given me all the supplies I need," Amber said, ignoring Azarel's scowl when she mentioned the dwarves. "I'd like to get a look around here, though. This place is amazing!"

Azarel's posture lightened. "Oh, yes, it is. I can show you."

He gestured, and she followed him onto the landing. What Amber hadn't noticed earlier, since she'd flown in on a draco, were the rope footbridges that connected to the large landing. There were two, as well as an outside staircase that wound around the tree.

Azarel walked on the rope footbridge easily without swaying, with footing almost like a cat. Amber felt incredibly clumsy in comparison, making the bridge rock and move with each step. Even with all her ragged shaking, Azarel didn't miss a single step as he walked ahead of her, lightly, as if expecting the bridge to move randomly in any direction.

They arrived on the other end, and she stepped on another landing. The walkway ringed an entire great tree and had rope walkways running in every direction—a hub of bridges.

Azarel started walking down another rope bridge and spoke casually. "We don't get visitors here, so I'm not sure what you care about—"

"All of it," Amber said. "How old is this place?"

"Ah. Well, our history goes back thousands of years. I'm no historian myself, so can't tell you much."

Is that all? Amber wondered in frustration. Do you really have nothing more to say? What's wrong with you? Can't you see I know nothing?

But she just followed behind in silence, thinking of another tactic. He was obviously still upset about his sudden responsibility. Maybe she needed to be more specific.

"Tell me about what's happened since the Great War."

"Well." Azarel paused and gave her a polite but I'm-trying-to-be-patient look. "Our city was unaffected, but the other elves around the land were attacked, so we went to their aid. We lost many elves in those years. Thankfully, our mages were able to restore order quickly, and we took it upon ourselves to be prepared for the next uprising. Watch yourself here." Azarel pointed to a gap in the rope bridge walkways.

"Who are the mages?" Amber asked.

"I suppose you would call them wizards," Azarel said. "And you've met five of them. There are twelve in all, each with their own strengths. Some are quite powerful," he said grandly, as if trying to impress her.

"Do tell." Amber was happy he was saying anything at all.

"Some mages know the ancient magic, and of course we wield three of the scepters, as you've been told already. Then there are others with the magic to foretell the future—like knowing you were going to arrive here. And finally there are those with magic like ours, over the elements."

Amber nodded as Azarel crossed another bridge, leading her from bridge to bridge downward into trees. They passed elves occasionally who all gave Amber interesting looks but didn't interrupt as they continued.

"What do these scepters do?" Amber asked.

"They have power kind of like ours. You need to be a mage to use them, but they drain energy differently than other types of spells. That one you saw has power to create and craft, so all our buildings and equipment are of the utmost quality. We have another that has the power to sway minds."

Amber interrupted. "Like the spell of enchantment over the creatures we've been encountering?"

Azarel paused. "Perhaps. I do know that some time ago our dracos were affected by a spell causing them to turn on us, and our mages were able to release them quite easily."

Hmm, Amber thought. That would be very useful indeed over the goblins, trolls, and other creatures we've been running into. Although I don't know if it would keep evil creatures from being evil. But I wonder if they'd be working together against us if the spell were broken.

Azarel continued, "One of the scepters can call up frost and ice. I'd think that would be formidable in a battle, although I've only heard of it."

So far, the buildings they'd walked past were all public places, from what Amber could gather. There were places to eat, craftsmen and tailors, one she guessed was a hospital, and another dedicated to caring for animals.

The next one they approached was in a less-trafficked area and felt more like a home. Amber admired the beautiful design of the doors and windows, and how the home felt like a natural growth out of the tree, like all the buildings there.

"We're starting to come to houses," Azarel said. "I'm going to take you to my place. I need to gather some belongings since I'll be journeying with you." He stopped abruptly and turned to her. "When are you planning on heading out?"

Amber was startled. Just a few hours ago she'd been worried about being thrown into prison, and now she had the chance to see her friends and find the dragon yet again. "As soon as possible."

She thought of her friends—of Basil and Theo especially—but even the short time she'd spent with Mizu made her think of her fondly. I hope they're near Crodor.

Amber felt distraught. Were they even there yet? How could she find her friends in that massive mountainous forest? Azarel saw her expression and seemed about to say something, then closed his mouth.

She looked down but still couldn't see the ground from where she stood. There were too many branches and leaves blocking it. She was suddenly curious. "How far down is it?"

"That's a funny question," Azarel said. "I don't know. Quite a ways. Why?"

"No reason. Just wondering."

Azarel looked at her curiously for a moment. "How old are you?"

Amber was startled. "Why do you ask?"

"Just wondering," he said, then smirked. "You're taller than all of us, so I can't tell."

"Hmm," Amber said. "Well, I'm twelve."

His smirk grew. "Younger than me. I'm fifteen. Look, you're young. And I got thrown into this against my will. I'm supposed to help you, but don't take offense if I have different ideas from you. My whole life I've been raised to sit on the Conclave—and I'm a leader of young and old alike. I'll help you ... *my* way. And you're not the leader. We'll work together."

He stared at Amber till she instinctively grew awkward and looked down. Then he turned and said, "This way."

They stepped on a wide branch with no railings. Although it was high above the hidden ground, the branch was easy to walk on and felt safe. They continued making their way through branches, foot bridges, and walkways until they reached a house built into the side of a tree quite a ways from the first buildings.

Azarel's house was small, but inside it felt even more spacious than Amber's house back in Seabrook. Looking around, she tried to guess what his family was like. This home had a dining table that emerged directly from the tree. Amber imagined it was created by someone with her elemental gift; she felt inspired by the beauty and craftsmanship.

I could do things like that, she thought. All I've thought about using my gift for is stuff to help us survive and navigate.

But this is beautiful!

She was surprised at the house's simplicity, since Azarel's mother was someone of such significance.

"I imagined you'd live in a place more like a palace, what with your mother having such an important role."

"That's what's wrong with you humans." Azarel frowned and shook his head. "That's why you don't live well. This home has been in my family for many centuries. We wouldn't dream of living anywhere else." He turned and went through a door into a small bedroom.

Amber stood and thought about what Azarel had said. We certainly don't have any sense like he's talking about. I have no idea who my great-grandparents were—obviously, since it turns out I'm part elf! It's like we humans have no sense of permanence.

Her thoughts were interrupted by an elf calling from outside. "Azarel! Quickly!"

Azarel emerged from his bedroom, and they looked outside. A silver elf was hovering on a draco. "Azarel! More humans are here! Fantana has asked for you to come immediately."

He looked at Amber. "Both of you."

Chapter 21

Mages and Wizards

AMBER AND AZAREL raced along the winding branches and walkways toward the buildings where she'd first arrived. The elf on the draco hovered next to them briefly, then sped ahead, deftly weaving in and out of branches without hesitation.

Amber tried not to watch—keeping track of where she was stepping was more important—but the intricate way the dracos were flown was impressive. "How do they do that?" she wondered aloud.

"Who? Do what?" Azarel waited impatiently for her.

"The elves on the dracos. How do they control them without any equipment?"

"Oh," Azarel said. "Not all elves can fly them. They control dracos with their minds. I think it's like our powers—but I wouldn't know, since I can't do it."

271

"Ah!" Amber said, breathing heavily as she scrambled next to him. "Now I get it. So is it a common thing for your people?"

"Not really. There are only thirty or so. It's not uncommon for elves to have connections with animals though. What powers are most common with you humans?"

Amber paused. "I don't know."

They came around a large tree and saw the landing. They rushed inside, but there were only the two guards at the doorway and one other elf waiting.

"Where are they?" Amber asked. Azarel shrugged.

He spoke in his language with the elf, then turned back to Amber. "They're being brought here. It sounds like there are two young humans. Do you know about them?"

Amber's heart leaped. "Yes! It must be my friends. Are they with an elf as well?"

Azarel spoke with the elf again. "Yes. And with some horses, a large cat, and a bear."

"A bear?"

Azarel thought about it. "Maybe I have the wrong word? A large hairy creature with big claws and teeth." He held his arms up bear-like and showed his teeth.

Amber smiled. Maybe he's warming up to me? "Yes, you have the right word." But where did the bear come from? Theo. Most definitely Theo.

She waited for what felt like a small eternity.

Finally Amber heard Theo talking. It sounded like he was asking questions about the buildings. Amber smiled. Unquestionably Theo, always chatting away.

Theo rounded the corner, saw Amber, and stopped with his jaw open.

Basil bumped into him and said, "Hey! Why'd you stop?" Then he looked up and saw Amber and his jaw dropped as well. "Amber!"

Both boys ran to her at the same time and gave her a big hug. She started crying. She had no idea how relieved she'd be to see them. Basil stepped back and looked at her with a big grin.

Theo stepped back as well, then said, "Well, I thought you'd be happier to see us!"

Amber laughed and wiped her eyes. "I didn't know if I'd ever see you again!"

"Us either." Basil patted her shoulders. "Boy, it sure is good to see you. And you look great!"

Amber looked down at her brand-new clothing from head to foot, the best the dwarves had to offer. And they didn't even see the hidden armor she wore underneath! She smiled. "We have a lot to catch up on!"

"We sure do!" Basil hugged her again.

"Where's Mizu?" Amber asked.

"Oh, she went to speak with her aunt or something or other," Basil said. "She'll join us in a bit, I'm sure. So how'd you survive the fall off that cliff?"

As she began telling them her story, she realized just how much she'd been through. "And how about you? I heard you came with a bear?"

Theo grinned. "Yeah. I call her Zoomy. She's been a *huge* help."

"Zoomy?"

"She's a lot faster than I thought a bear could go," Theo admitted. "Faster than the horses, even."

Amber smiled. "Tell me everything. Starting with the giant ants. How'd you get away from them?"

After Basil told the story with animation and dancing around with hand gestures, the trio had to decide their next steps.

"I could use a break." Basil sighed. "But when I think about that huge army headed toward Lugo—sheesh it might even be there already—there's no time to lose."

"Yeah, you're right." Amber nodded. "I was about to head out with Azarel when you showed up. I was hoping to find the dwarves again. They have griffins that could get us there today. But who knows where the dwarves are?"

At the mention of the dwarves, Azarel blew a *pfff* sound. Basil and Theo looked over, and Basil held out his hand. "The name's Basil, and this is Theo."

Azarel looked at him and his hand oddly.

"You're supposed to shake it," Amber said. "Don't you elves do that?"

"No, we do not." Azarel slowly put his hand out and Basil grasped it. The red elf cocked his head in interest. "I like it. It shows that you've connected with the other person. Interesting."

Amber twirled a strand of hair thoughtfully. "Azarel is joining us, and he has power over fire. Now that we know Mizu has power over water, that gives our little group five elemental powers."

"Five!" Theo whistled. "The prophecy really *is* true! No elementalists have been around for ages, and suddenly there are five of us, each with a different power. That means there's one left. And also . . . that there are dark powers trying to devastate the land. Something we're responsible to stop."

Basil wiped a long curl away from his eyes. "So we'd better get moving, huh?"

"Well, Azarel and I were going to leave shortly, but you *can't* leave without a quick tour! Azarel still hasn't packed, and Mizu's off and about. Let's leave as soon as they're ready."

Basil and Theo grinned at each other.

"Azarel, why don't you pack, and I'll show them just a few things, if that's ok?" Amber said.

Azarel hesitated. "Yes, that makes sense." He turned to the elf who'd escorted Theo and Basil. "Haltro. Guide them and keep an eye on things."

The silver elf behind them nodded, and Azarel dashed down a swinging footbridge. Basil watched him with raised eyebrows. "He's not one for many words, is he?"

"Not that I've seen yet," Amber said. "He also gets pretty upset when I mention the dwarves. They *all* do. And they don't care much about humans, either. So let's be careful not to bother anyone." She glanced at the silver elf standing behind them.

Amber told them more of her first impressions of the elves' city and took them on a footbridge for a different view. Soon after, they saw a blue elf walking with a white elf toward them, and they waited. Sure enough, the elf in the front was Mizu.

Mizu walked up with a large smile. "Amber! So good to see you!"

Amber opened her arms to hug her, and Mizu looked at her puzzled. Amber grinned and wrapped her arms around the small blue elf. She hadn't thought about it, but if elves didn't do handshakes, maybe they also didn't hug? She had a lot to learn.

At first Mizu stood stiffly, but then she lifted her arms and returned the hug.

"I missed you," Amber said. "I didn't know if I'd see you again."

They stood back from each other, and Mizu looked her in the eyes. "Destiny didn't allow it. I'm certain there's a very good reason for our being apart."

Amber looked at her puzzled. "A *reason* for us to be apart? Like this is all meant to be, somehow?"

Mizu shrugged, then turned to the slightly taller woman behind her. The woman was striking in her beauty. She was pure white, from head to toe, in her clothing as well as her entire body. The only thing not white were her almond-shaped brown eyes. "This is my aunt, Rubía."

Rubía nodded, and Amber and the others nodded back. That must be how they greet, Amber realized. Just nodding. No contact with others.

"Welcome to our city," Rubía said. "I assume you are the children Sage spoke of."

"You know Sage?" Theo's eyes lit up.

"Yes. He was here not long ago," Rubía said.

"Where was he headed? Did he say anything?" Basil asked.

"Not enough," Rubía said. "But he did tell us about you elementalists—and of your efforts. I am very pleased indeed that you are traveling with Mizu." She folded her hands pleasantly.

"Tell us," Theo said, "if you're related, then how come you don't look like each other?"

"But we do!" Mizu furrowed her brow. "Look at our eyes."

The three humans looked from one elf to the other and shook their heads. The color was entirely different, and they weren't sure what they were looking for. All the elves' eyes looked the same to them, compared to human eyes, like large slanted almonds.

Rubía turned to Mizu. "Before you leave, I want to give you this." She pulled a small, ornately shaped silver ring from a hidden pocket in her shirt. It looked like many leaves wrapped around each other.

She handed it to Mizu with both hands. "It gives you great leaps and landings, like a grasshopper. I would advise to wear it only now and then, so that you don't grow too accustomed to it or wear down its magic. That way, it will be far more effective."

With two hands, Mizu took the ring, nodding her head respectfully. She was about to put it into a pocket when Rubía said, "Please, try it out now, so you know what to expect. It does take some time to get used to it."

Mizu put the ring on and gave a slight smile, which quickly turned into a huge grin as she gave a tiny bounce. She suddenly leaped high into the air toward some branches, partly landing on them and springing to another branch far across the open space on a different great tree. She grabbed the branch and turned, then leaped back to the group, landing perfectly like a cat.

"I think I've got the hang of it." Mizu walked over to Lorien and petted him on the head.

"Wow! That was awesome!" Theo marveled at the distance she'd just crossed. "I'm sure that'll come in handy."

"Thank you." Mizu bowed to her aunt, then removed the ring and put it into a pocket.

"Of course." Rubía gracefully lifted her hands with palms open. "It belonged to your grandmother. It is fitting that you take it. Your dad would be proud if he saw you now."

Mizu's smile disappeared, and she pursed her lips. She stood quietly and nodded.

There was an awkward silence where everyone stood around looking at one another. Theo broke the silence. "So did you always live here?"

Rubía turned. "My parents were from Lorcaster, but during the Great War they were displaced and moved here. My brother and I were very young at the time." She looked at Mizu when she said that. "We endured a lot of hardship in those days and lost many friends."

She paused, then turned back to Theo. "Part of my heart is in Lorcaster. I do like to visit. But this is my home." She smiled, then looked firm. "Children, you must depart. This isn't the time for a lovely visit. The evils that have been stirred up are on the move. Sage has told us some of what he knows, but there is much more to know. I plan on heading west to seek the council of the sea elves."

"One last thing." She pulled a small pale brown stick from her side. It looked smooth, well-worn, and somehow beautiful, even though very simple. "Mizu, I want you to consider what I said about the mages. It's in your blood." She offered it to Mizu with two hands, nodding her head. Mizu took it with both hands and nodded back, then turned toward the stairs.

Amber wondered about the way the elves said goodbye without saying goodbye at all. Somehow nodding at each other seemed to be enough. Before following, she waved and called, "Thanks for everything!"

She found herself thinking of the stick. That has to be a wand. Which would mean Mizu must know something about how to use it, otherwise why would her aunt have given it to her. I wonder if Mizu would know anything about the purple scepter we took from that other wizard. I think Basil must have it—we'll have to remember to ask her later.

She found herself getting excited. More people on the journey. More magical helps. More knowledge. They were sure to find Crodor and save Lugo! She just knew it.

Chapter 22

Thousands of Goblins

A MAN IN CHAIN MAIL PEERED through a long spyglass at the top of the city wall at Lugo. A crossbow was leaning against the wall next to him. He squinted, and without removing his gaze, called to the captain waiting below.

"I count another two to three hundred people arriving from the southwest. Within the hour, I'd guess."

"Thank you." The captain stood with folded arms and a thoughtful expression, then mounted a large horse and quickly made his way to the center of the city to the military complex and the General's planning room.

The room was bustling with activity, people coming in and out. Five other captains were present, along with two Zylin monks, Ryder, Chandler, four royal officials, a young scribe, and the General himself. There were five different discussions going on at once, with the General listening patiently to two royal officials.

As the captain walked over to the General, one of the royal officials was finishing his argument: "And the king says you *must* protect him in his vacation house to the south. It's absolutely necessary."

The General laughed in disbelief. "More important than protecting the city? You can tell the king I'll send another five soldiers, but that's all. We have much more formidable things to deal with here." He turned to the captain who'd just arrived. "What's the word from the walls?"

The captain saluted stiffly. "Within the next two hours, there are close to a thousand people arriving from all directions. Every town and village appear to be coming here for safety."

The General turned to another captain. "Rogers. When will the goblins arrive?"

"Tomorrow, most likely, at their current rate. We also have more news on the army itself."

"Tell us, then." The General's eyes grew intense, and the room quieted.

"Close to seven thousand goblins are counted, including hobgoblins for every fifty or so. We think there are three goblin kingdoms working together. There are also two enormous giants and around a hundred ogres. They have various war machines, catapults, and ballistae. No idea how many wizards or other allies they have."

The General turned to Chandler. "What say you, then? What do all your books advise us to do in such a situation?"

The entire room quieted and turned its gaze to the thin, well-dressed man with glasses awkwardly clutching a large book.

"Yes. Yes." Chandler cleared his throat and gained some composure. "Just remember a war isn't fought on the day of the battle. It's all the activity that leads up to it. The battle is the tactics, and that's important, but war is fought well before blood is shed. One must look at all the resources and issues at play and work from there."

"You're not saying anything new." The General pointed his finger at him and shook his head sternly. "Give some proper advice or none at all."

Chandler smoothed his shirt and took a breath. "It's like this. War between people always has a reason. What's the reason for this war? There must be one. The best way to end a war is not bloodshed. It's negotiation. That costs both sides the least. If we can get to the heart of why this is happening, and who is responsible, we may get further along."

He turned to Ryder, and so did the General. Ryder fumbled with a small metal figurine he'd been holding as part of the battle planning. He cleared his throat. "Their leader is Laticia, Queen of Westerlye to the south. A wizard with great power, the little I saw of it. She has at least two other wizards on her side. She said they're coming to take down our civilization in order to build another one. And that it's part of a plan to gain great magical power, somehow. They don't want goblins running the world, but they seem intent on shaking ours up."

The General turned to Chandler. "How does one negotiate with that?"

Chandler nodded slowly. "Indeed. Not your normal negotiation situation. But there are nine more steps to war before actually fighting the battle." He opened the book and skimmed the pages for a moment. "According to this, one of the greatest generals of all time has laid them out. We have to consider our resources, our tactics, our environment, timing, our position, how to use spies, and more. The most important thing, from what I'm reading, is we need to hide our greatest strengths from them. The element of surprise is key. If we can trick them into thinking our strengths are our weaknesses, we'll have the upper edge."

He looked at the General's furrowed brow and continued. "Here's an example. They know about the Zylin monks now. And so far, they're our greatest strength. According to this tactic, we'd pretend that there's a place of weakness in our defenses, but then have the monks there in disguise and take them by surprise. Much like a strategy game, you must take the offense, even if in a defensive situation."

"Yes. This makes sense." The General looked at the map of the city sprawled on the table. "We need more than the monks. We do have more strengths. He turned to look around the room. "You each have a job. Our number one goal is to protect Lugo and all these people streaming in. Whatever you can devise in the next day to protect the city and gain the upper hand against these goblins and wizards, bring the information here. We need to write it all down and plan it."

He gazed at people individually, ensuring they understood. "This will be an enormous effort, but our entire kingdom is at stake. Not just our city." He looked at one of the captains, who stood out from the others, his insignia wasn't a griffin but a shield with crossed swords behind it.

"Captain Wilkins, how many soldiers can we get from Orendale by tomorrow."

The captain shook his head and frowned. "I can't get any here in that kind of time frame." The General looked annoyed, and Wilkins continued. "If I send a pigeon with the message right now, and the king agrees and sends men, he'd only be able to send a hundred at most with horses fast enough to get here in that kind of time. And you know what the king is like. He wants to support Lugo but not at the risk of losing his own protection."

The General tapped his fingers on the table for a moment. "We do have men arriving. They're not trained soldiers. But they can lend a hand." He turned to a young man next to him. "Start writing this down. Any person within the city walls of Lugo must help with the war effort. Nobody is going to be a victim here."

The young man scrawled some words down, and the General continued. "Everyone's duty is clear. Find not only what you can do to help but consider what other resources we have. And as Chandler here pointed out, some of them may not be in the form of a person. Consider our environment and other strengths we have."

One of the royal officials raised his hand slightly. "There's an apothecary from the islands who has a stand in the market—he can brew magical potions. I'm not sure how much he could do with such short notice, but I know he brewed a healing potion once that was quite effective. I'm certain he has other types of potions as well."

"Good. Good. Magical help will be much appreciated, especially since our foes have magic on their side." He looked at Ryder with a piercing gaze. "Your powers were necessary to prevent the break in our wall against that wizard. We need those other three wizards—your friends. We must do the best we can without them. Let's hope they get here soon. We need them. More than they may know."

Chapter 23

The Dragon's Den

WHEN AZAREL RETURNED with a small backpack, the five young adventurers made their way down the stairs to a lower landing and then down a hidden staircase inside the tree where a door led to the floor of the forest.

After the last of them emerged onto the ground, the elf who had escorted them nodded to Azarel and shut the door on the side of the enormous tree.

Theo peered at the large tree curiously. The door was practically invisible to the eye unless you looked quite closely. The elves' city was all but invisible, and they were directly beneath the busiest part with the largest buildings.

Not too far away, they found their horses, and Amber gave Buttercup a big hug. "Hello, old friend." The horse flipped its tail happily, and she felt a tear well up.

She was startled by a grumbling sound behind her and turned to see an enormous dark bear walk up to Theo and nuzzle his face. "Zoomy! Good to see you too!" Theo grinned ear to ear, and she found herself smiling along with him.

They loaded the heavier items onto the two horses.

"So . . ." Basil began, "three riding animals and five of us. What's the plan?"

But Azarel set out on foot with a serious expression on his face, and the others began walking behind him, leading the animals. He didn't speak a word and walked far ahead of them, not looking back.

"Wonder if he's always like this." Basil looked skeptically at Amber.

She shrugged. "Hard to say. I'm hoping he'll loosen up. I don't think he knew till today that he was going to join our mission, and he was definitely reluctant about it."

"Ah. Not the most ideal companion." He looked at Theo. "Hey, bud, maybe you can break the ice with our new friend?" He motioned toward Azarel.

Theo nodded and trotted up to Azarel, then began walking next to him and talking.

Basil turned to Amber. "Well, if Theo can't open him up, no one can!"

The walk through the woods felt pleasant with all the friends reunited. Amber showed Basil some of her new gear from the dwarves. Mizu joined the conversation and asked lots of questions about the dwarves, so Amber told them many more details about their kingdom. She wondered whether the elves in Mizu's home were as bitter toward the dwarves as the graft elves in Nocea.

They journeyed like that for a couple of hours, and Amber smiled when she heard Theo laughing and joking. It would seem Theo really could crack through Azarel's walls.

Azarel led the way the entire time, directing them to camp near a small brook.

"So do you know exactly where we're going?" Basil asked, as they set up bedding and made a ring of rocks for a fire.

"Yes, indeed," Azarel said. "I've been there before. We'll arrive tomorrow, midday."

When it came time to start a fire, Azarel watched with a smirk as Basil gathered wood and moss, preparing each piece of wood by slicing larger ones with a hatchet, lining up smaller branches together, and topping it with moss.

Basil pulled out a flint and steel and began scraping them to get a spark onto the moss. But Azarel held up his hand. "You may not realize it, but I can do this much faster."

Basil looked at him curiously but said nothing. Azarel stepped over, lifted his hand and focused. A tiny flame appeared on the moss, followed by a greater flame and then a full fire, all in a few seconds.

"Nice work!" Basil patted him on the back, and the elf flinched. "We'll be asking you for help with fire next time around."

"Of course." Azarel responded with a smug look on his face and moved away from Basil.

They sat around the fire and relaxed. Azarel caused the fire to form little floating figures that danced. Basil then flung his fingers toward the fire, and a perfect ring of fire floated up and around the figures before dissipating.

"Very nice." Azarel cocked his head. "Perhaps we should practice working together."

Basil shrugged. "Sure. Wouldn't hurt."

The conversation that evening revolved around everyone's hometown. Mizu picked up where she left off, asking Amber about what life on the sea was like—the weather, the patterns, and the types of sea creatures.

"It's a lot of work, but we love it," Amber said. "I miss being on the sea. When you're out there, the rest of the world is gone, and you're just... there, in that moment, with the people you're with. I don't know how to explain it. Part of you needs to stay alert so you don't die from certain weather conditions or other things, like catching an enormous fish that might tip your boat. But part of you is the most relaxed you've ever been, because you aren't around anything else. Just waves and birds and fish."

Theo pulled out the Castles game and started teaching Azarel how to play. Azarel was a quick student, and within half an hour Theo looked stumped.

Theo did win in the end, after frequent long pauses. As he made his last move, he said, "You've picked up some of the nuances of this game much faster than the rest of us."

"There's a reason for that." Azarel formed a small dragon in the light of the fire. "We elves have a similar game, and I was using some of the tricks I know from that one. Interesting how I can use one game's strategy and improve upon another one."

Theo nodded. "Let's play again!"

The five companions relaxed around the fire until it grew late.

The next morning they headed out early to find Crodor.

Theo, as usual, was the first to consider their plan. "We'll get there in a couple of hours, if Azarel's time is accurate. Have we thought through what's next? The amulet probably won't fit over a dragon's head. It's too small."

"Not only that," Azarel turned to look at him sternly, "dragons are extremely smart. Smarter even than all of us. You won't outsmart the beast, for sure. You'll have to find another tactic."

Basil frowned. "Do we even know if the dragon is enchanted? What if the amulet doesn't do anything?"

"That's a sobering thought." Theo fiddled with his fingers nervously. "If the dragon isn't enchanted, would it listen to us? Although, remember that pixie Lila told us he is enchanted. Mizu, you were coming to find the dragon. What do you think?"

Mizu thought for a moment. "I have a speech I've practiced for many, many weeks. If Crodor isn't spellbound, then I have the things to say. But if he's not himself, we'll need to break the spell before I say a thing."

"Hey, Basil," Amber said. "Don't you think maybe we should tell our elf friends about that scepter?"

Azarel turned abruptly and gaped at them. Basil shrugged. "I suppose. Yeah, we have a scepter. We got it off a wizard who was using it on Blazey. I've got it right here." He patted his saddlebag.

"May I see it?" Azarel asked. Mizu also looked extremely interested.

Basil pulled out the scepter. It was blackened from when Blazey had burned up the evil wizard, but otherwise it looked intact. Basil rubbed off some of the char. "Do you know anything about how to use these?"

Azarel shook his head. "Not exactly. May I see?"

Basil handed it to him. Azarel looked it over and held it up a moment, then turned to Mizu. "Can you use this?"

Mizu shrugged, then put her hand out. Azarel handed her the scepter, and Mizu closed her eyes. She stood silently for a moment. "Yes, it is magical. It has great power, but I cannot tell what exactly it does. You said a mage wielded it to control the phoenix?'

"That's right," Basil said. "He held it out and told the phoenix to burn down the next village on the coast. Blazey looked like he understood, and we figure he would have done it if we hadn't broken the spell."

"I wonder if this is how they've enchanted everything? Maybe combined with some other sort of magic." Mizu mused. "May I try it out on one of your animals?"

Amber looked at Buttercup suddenly protective. "How about Theo finds us a bird or something?"

"Good idea, Amber!" Theo said. "A moment later a robin came fluttering over and landed on his shoulder.

Mizu furrowed her brow and pointed the scepter at the small bird. "I command you to fly circles around us." The stone glowed a slight purple and the tiny bird instantly leaped off Theo's shoulder and circled the group.

"I can use this. But I don't fully fathom all its power yet. I think it could be used on you or me, but smarter creatures would be much more difficult. It's definitely quite the powerful scepter. You said the wizard used it to enchant the phoenix?"

"Yes." Amber looked at the scepter with a frown. "We think it may have been behind all sorts of enchantments. Like the goblins . . . and maybe even the dragon."

Mizu stared at the charred scepter curiously and handed it back to Basil. "Let's try the amulet."

"Of course!" Amber pulled the amulet from her side pouch. Watching the bird carefully as it continued to fly in circles, she tossed it in a perfect loop, and the robin flew directly through. It flittered back to Theo's shoulder and looked around, as if getting its bearings.

"Yep, that's it." Theo petted the bird gently. "What did you do to use the scepter?"

"I drew on mana much like my elemental power. I'm guessing only mages would be able to use it."

"I wonder if any of us could." Basil rubbed the scepter, exposing more of the dull silver beneath the black. "Since we all have mana inside us."

Mizu shrugged her shoulders, "Perhaps. I'd be happy to teach you."

"I like that idea." Basil put the scepter back in the saddlebag. "But not today. Won't be able to use it on a dragon yet, that's for sure."

They continued on their journey through the forest in good spirits. Simply being reunited with each other made the trip fun.

But as they began hiking up a mountain with thick trees, Theo picked up where he'd left off. "So, we need to think of a plan. Remember what Sage said—we should be thinking four moves ahead."

Basil shrugged. "You and Azarel are best at the game. What do you two think?"

Theo paused. "We now have lots of magical powers here. Plus, a whole bunch of magical items . . . the most important thing is the amulet. Get that around Crodor's head first—no matter what."

Azarel nodded in agreement. "If Crodor is under the evil spell, then that's the most important. Nothing else will work until the spell is broken. But even if we free him, we still need plans for what to do. What if he fights? We wouldn't stand a chance against a dragon. Crodor is fierce and powerful, wise and cunning. We will not overpower or outsmart him."

Mizu chimed in. "As I've already said, I volunteer to speak. I've been planning this conversation for almost a month now." Everyone nodded and looked relieved.

Theo looked thoughtful. "We should have a backup plan."

They discussed a number of different ideas and tried to think of some ways their powers could work together. As they'd discovered around the campfire the night before, wind with fire could be powerful together, until they realized Crodor was a fire-breathing dragon and probably resistant to fire.

Theo suddenly lit up. "Azarel, with your power with fire, can you be burned?"

Azarel looked thoughtful for a moment. "Normal fires do not affect me. A dragon's flame, I cannot tell. But even if I'm safe from dragon flames—I'm not safe from teeth."

"I know. But if we do need to distract the dragon . . ." Theo looked at Azarel suggestively.

The red elf cocked his head, then pointed at some rocks ahead. "This is where it gets rougher. Crodor is an hour from here."

This is it, isn't it? Amber thought. Azarel was as serious as always. She wondered if all the graft elves were like that. Mizu was so lighthearted by comparison.

"Here you must leave your horses," he said. "We will go up. Crodor lives somewhere in those crags." He gestured to the pointy rock faces that jutted up in multiple places above them. "I suggest you leave the bear as well."

The companions tied their horses to trees, removing saddles and saddlebags, and Theo asked Zoomy to stay nearby. After lunch they gathered whatever they might need for the rest of the trek. Amber wore the backpack the dwarves had given her already stock full of many excellent and helpful items. She also made sure she had her bow and a full quiver, not that she'd need them against a dragon, but she felt naked without them.

She laughed when she came across the jar of peanut butter. Whether it was true or not about Crodor the Ancient's fondness for it, it couldn't hurt. She removed some food from her pack and made room for the large jar.

They followed a deer trail that wound around the mountain through dense trees and increasingly steeper rocks. Then they rounded a corner and came to an impassible waterfall. The trail seemed to go right through it. During the autumn when there was less water, it would most surely have been easier to cross than now—in early summer with the water raging. There was no way they'd be able to pass.

Azarel turned and gestured to go back, but Mizu walked past him toward the waterfall.

"I've got this one," she said with a knowing smile. She walked right up to the intense cascading water and lifted her hands. The waterfall obediently lifted itself off the cliff face—as if a roof had been perfectly placed over it—revealing the trail underneath with water cascading past it.

Azarel gave a nod. "Nicely done." He was the first to walk underneath and didn't even look up but strode through confidently.

When everyone had passed through, they set off on foot up the craggy rocks. Occasionally it felt a bit dangerous but still climbable. There were many sections where they had to use both hands and feet, and one section was very steep, requiring all their concentration.

Amber felt clumsy next to the elves, Basil, and Lorien—but as she climbed, she grew more confident in her abilities. Poor Theo, though, straggled behind and looked miserable. At one point, he leaned against the cliff wall resting, rubbing his forehead as he looked at the steep drop.

He thought achingly of Mizu's jumping ring. Would she loan it to him?

Amber turned to him and noticed he looked tired. "Theo, want to use a rope?" If the dwarves' rope was as strong as they said, it would lift Theo no problem.

Theo looked up with a grateful expression on his face. "That would be great."

"Basil!" Amber called up ahead of her. "Tie this around your waist."

She tossed the rope to Basil. It was going to fall short, but Basil gave a little flip of his hand and the rope lifted just a little higher into his fingers. Amber smiled. It was so easy to forget that everyone she was with had special powers.

Basil tied the rope around his waist and then tossed down the other end to Theo, who tied it around his waist as well. Suddenly the climb went much faster, and they reached a flat section where everyone paused and drank some water.

From their resting spot, the views were enjoyable. Dense trees lay in every direction, and mountains went on and on as far as the eye could see. Some were snowcapped, others shorter, and many very craggy like the one they were on.

The humans had no idea where the elves lived—but was that a dense cloud hiding a floating ship?

"Azarel, I've been meaning to ask." Amber pointed at the cloud. "How do the floating ships work? Is that one there?"

The red elf glanced up nonchalantly. "Yes, that's one. They float with magic, of course. And blackwood tree."

"What's that?" She looked around curiously. "Is there any here? Why that tree?"

"It's good for both the sea and sky, and easier to enchant. I'm not aware myself of how it works. I'm sure with your gifts you'll find the same if you try to build a ship."

Theo perked up. "Do you think one of us could ever enchant stuff like that?"

"Of course." Azarel looked over impatiently. "You all have the power to be mages. It just takes practice and choosing your focus. Mizu, for example, has chosen the illusion realm with her wand. You could learn more than one realm over a lifetime, but it's usually better to stay focused."

Theo looked thoughtful and fiddled with his shirtsleeve as he watched the cloud. "I wonder if we'll all learn spells. If it's best to focus on one area, we should think about it carefully. Have you picked one yet?"

"Not me." Azarel shook his head. "I can barely create fire from nothing yet. That's my focus. If I have a spark, it's much easier for me. But they say I should be able to create fire from pure air. I have a feeling it may take years before I'm interested in other types of magic."

Theo almost finished the water in his waterskin, then stopped. What if they didn't come across more in a while. But he suddenly had a thought and turned toward Mizu. "So, what all can you do with water?"

"What do you mean?" Mizu asked.

"Like, can you make the water in my waterskin expand to fill it up?"

"Of course not. But I could get you some more from the ground over there."

"Where?" Theo looked at the grassy area. There was no water source in sight.

"Right over there." She pointed at a spot where some plants and a small tree were growing. "It's in the ground."

"Show me."

Mizu concentrated. A thin line of water bubbled out of the ground, and then rose up, like an upside-down rope. "Open your water skin."

Theo opened it, and the water from the earth flowed up and into it, filling it perfectly. He smiled at her with eyes sparkling. "Fantastic."

Basil watched with a big grin on his face. He playfully twirled his fingers and a small whirlwind carried some of the water through the air toward him. He opened his mouth and tried catching it. Some landed in his mouth, and some splattered across the rest of his face. Theo laughed, and the rest of the group laughed with him.

Basil chuckled and shrugged his shoulders. "It's a work in progress."

Amber thought with a start, Maybe the prophecy is about us using our powers together. On their own, they're pretty amazing, and combining two together even more so. But all of them—what if we can figure out how they all work together? While they continued to climb, she thought about possibilities.

It wasn't long, though, before Azarel called back, "Quiet now. I think we're near. Try to walk as silently as possible."

They climbed the rest of the way to the top of the cliff in silence. Below them lay the dragon's entrance, visible from the craggy rocks. The cave entrance was large enough for a dragon to go in and out—and well disguised from above, with an overhanging shelf blocking the entrance.

That would also keep rain and snow out, Amber thought. It seemed like a perfect spot to live if you were a reclusive old dragon.

They quietly climbed down the rocks and neared the cave entrance. There were massive taloned footprints the size of a pony in the dirt. Crodor was enormous.

That's when every doubt Amber could imagine came crashing into her mind. What on earth are we thinking? This dragon is going to eat us alive! How are we possibly going to get the amulet around its neck? It's going to find us before we even have a chance. Our powers won't help at all. We're doomed!

Panic welled up inside her. But then a memory flashed. She was with her dad and scared of circling sharks out on the great sea. He'd said, "Take a deep breath. Now ask yourself, What's the worst possible thing that could happen? Picture it clearly in your head. How bad is it? Ok. So, now let's look at what's before you. Can you face it?"

Somehow, visualizing the worst possible outcome made Amber relax and feel better. She looked around. Basil seemed fine, but Theo looked even more panicked than her. She moved over to him and whispered, "Take a deep breath and think about what's the worst that could happen. It helped me."

He looked at her and forced a smile. He looked pale and almost green, like he was going to throw up.

The five travelers walked quietly through the large opening into the cave. Basil pulled out his short sword, but it wasn't glowing. They walked further into the large passageway, which grew darker and darker. Amber reached into a side pocket and touched the amulet. Still there.

She straightened her backpack and adjusted her enchanted protective cape. It gave her a tiny comfort knowing she was wearing something fireproof. She pulled out one of the dwarves' special lantern sticks from her backpack. The light bounced down the passageway and ended in darkness, not less than a hundred steps down.

Ahead lay only darkness . . . and the pungent smell of reptile.

They walked more slowly, each one not wanting to be first. If Crodor was in there, what would they do? Their plan was feeling incredibly weak now. After a few minutes of painstakingly slow walking, Mizu stood up straight, turned to Amber and silently held out her hand. Amber gave her the light stick, and Mizu led the way, walking briskly.

The others followed behind, trying to keep up without making any sounds. But the three humans constantly scuffed the cave floor as they walked. At each sound, they cringed.

A few more minutes down the passageway and around a corner, a light appeared in the distance. They crept toward it. As it grew brighter, Amber held the amulet more tightly.

They entered an enormous room with tall ceilings and glowing lamps on the walls. But what stood out the most was the mounds of treasure. More treasure than any person could ever imagine seeing in their lifetime. More treasure than Amber's entire village could have spent in a hundred years.

There were gold and silver coins, jewels, chests full to the brim and others overflowing. One whole section of the room was full of armor and weapons—some enormous, like for giants, and some tiny for beings even smaller than elves. There were glasses and goblets and sculptures and statues. Large and small, from jewelry to a ten-foot figure.

Amber's mind raced. What is a dragon doing with all this? How could he spend it? What use is it here? If humans somehow got their hands on all this treasure, what would happen? Would we all be better for it? Where did he get it? He must have stolen it. And if he stole it, who's to say we couldn't steal some of it back?

She shook her head. She wasn't going to steal anything. She wondered where the thought had come from—so unlike her usual self.

"He's not here." Mizu's words broke the silence. "Not yet."

"Is this the only entrance?" Basil asked.

"I doubt it," Mizu said. "But I'm guessing we found the front door. Why?"

"Well . . ." Basil looked around, "if Crodor is enchanted, and as large as I think he is, we're going to have a hard time getting the amulet around his neck. But I wonder if the power is only in the amulet or is it in the necklace as well."

Amber's eyes lit up, "Of course! Sage said it's in the amulet, and I'm thinking the necklace is just a way to surround something with it. We could try changing what it's on. Like using this." She pulled out the dwarven rope from her pack.

Basil nodded. "It's a risk, and if it doesn't work, we'll have to be ready with another plan. But it makes sense to me."

"I wish Sage were here," Theo said. "Am I the only one who feels like this is the most-likely-to-kill-us plan we've had yet?"

"Yeah, but Sage isn't here," Basil replied. "And unless you've got a better idea . . ." He waited for Theo to shake his head. "Azarel? Anyone?"

After a moment, Basil went on: "The dragon might come back at any minute, so we need to take our best plan and commit to it."

He paused grandly. "I'm starting to agree with Mizu that this isn't a coincidence—the five of us with different elemental powers. How many people have you seen out there with elemental powers? I've never been one to think about destiny, but I'm encouraged to think we five have a lot going for us."

The others nodded, and they all got to work quickly. Amber unloosed the chain from the amulet and fastened it around the dwarven rope, attaching the tips of the chain to the two ends of the rope. Using sword hilts, they tacked it into cracks to completely encircle the entrance to the treasure room, so the dragon would have to walk through it in order to enter. At least, if he came through that entrance.

Amber stepped back admiring their handiwork. It was a bit obvious. Hopefully, Crodor wouldn't notice. But would the rope carry the enchantment of the chain?

"Is that going to work?" Theo rubbed his hands nervously.

The others looked around awkwardly.

"You know . . ." His face tensed. "This may not be very strategic. We should figure out some backup plans. Like now."

But at that very moment, a loud thump sounded at the end of the tunnel, followed by the sound of large feet padding down the passageway.

They quieted.

A massive body was walking toward them.

The smell of death filled the room, and terror filled their hearts.

They froze in their tracks and looked around anxiously.

Ready or not, Crodor the Ancient was about to arrive.

Chapter 24

The Great Tower

DOZENS OF PIXIES HID in tree hollows, beneath rocks, and inside hollowed-out logs. Two imps flitted from tree to tree, creeping through the area searching for them.

Flurry—dressed in a ragged and impractical blue-and-white outfit from a happier time—mind-spoke to Wix, who sat next to her in the tree hole: *I can't do anything unless we get them close to the ground.*

I know! he responded impatiently. *I'm not stupid.*

They waited for what felt like an eternity. The imps continued to circle nearby.

Wix mind-spoke to the area: *Are there any pixies out here who have ideas? They know we're here. We have to do something.*

As if on cue, the happy shriek of an imp echoed through the woods, and they all heard a pixie mind-speak: *Nooo!*

Then there was silence.

A moment later, a pixie across the clearing spoke: *It killed someone. Hiding behind a rock. They're going to find us all! We have to flee!* He sounded hysterical, even in mind-speak.

No! Wix mind-spoke forcefully. *As soon as we fly, they'll know where we are. We can't. We need a better plan—or we're all dead. And so close to the tower . . .*

He saw Flurry's desperate eyes darting around. He calmed himself and mind-spoke with a tranquility and strength that he didn't actually feel but projected for the sake of his friend: *We need to know what powers we have among us. Flurry here has power with earth. If we can get them near the ground, she can attack. Remember they're resistant to our direct spells, and we can't fool them with illusions if we're flying. I'm good with animals. Does anyone else here have powers or ideas?*

There was a moment of silence, then a young voice mind-spoke: *I can make illusions. But I'll need to know where.*

Ok, anyone else? Wix stared directly into Flurry's eyes as they waited. Flurry stared back numbly, glad Wix was taking charge but feeling exhausted from the pain and death they continued to go through.

Over the last month, she'd seen the death of dozens of pixies. And although they'd had some victories, no matter where they went, the imps continued to follow. She wondered how many of her home tribe were still alive, scattered across the land.

She and Wix had stuck together, thankfully, and survived many imp attacks. Each one felt worse than the one before, the closer they got to the tower. If there weren't imps constantly chasing them, they'd have arrived at the tower weeks ago.

Even in that moment, it was less than a day's travel away. But they had to be careful about keeping its location secret, and they couldn't travel since flying meant certain death from the imps.

Ok, Wix said, that's two—plus we have the forest creatures on our side. It might be enough. Can you see that rock down there, next to the mushrooms and mossy area?

Yes, I see it.

That's where we'll pretend to be, and Flurry can get close enough to attack.

Wait! a pixie sounded urgent. *That's where I am!*

Well, Wix mind-spoke in a matter-of-fact tone, *you'll want to move.*

They waited till the imps passed, then Wix nodded and Flurry climbed out of the hole and down the tree trunk. In the last month, she'd climbed and walked more than she had her entire life.

Her fingers were rough, and her arms were full of scrapes and bruises. She climbed down as quickly as possible and darted next to the area Wix had mentioned, then caused the ground next to it to create a natural-looking protective covey, large enough for three pixies.

The pixie who'd been hiding in their decoy spot ran over to her—and a moment later, another pixie came from further away. That must be the one with the illusion power, Flurry thought.

Suddenly an imp came hurtling toward the pixie who was running along the forest floor. *Change of plans!* Flurry mind-shouted to her. *Imps are coming.*

The pixie glanced behind her and saw both imps coming after her at an impossible speed. She leaped and flew with all her strength toward Flurry, the imps hot on her tail.

Just another moment... Flurry stood prepared.

The pixie shot toward her, then dropped to the ground and created the illusion that she was still flying. It wasn't the best illusion—if you looked closely—but in the heat of the moment, it was enough to draw in the imps.

The imps caught up to her illusion, right in front of Flurry's hiding spot. She raised her hands and a large rock shot out of the ground in front of the imps. They both collided with it and dropped to the forest floor. Flurry instantly twirled her hands, and the ground swallowed them up like quicksand.

And just like that, it was over. Flurry mind-spoke to the entire area. *That did it. The imps are gone.*

A cheer went up among the pixies as they emerged from their hiding spots and flew over. Flurry fluttered over to the pixie who'd created the illusion. "Nice work. That was some quick thinking on your part. My name's Flurry."

"Jade." She nodded. She was a teenager, just like Flurry, and just as ragged looking.

"Let's stick together," Flurry said. "We make a good team."

"Definitely," Jade said.

Wix arrived and took charge. "Gather around. How many of us are there here?" He counted each head as the pixies arrived. "Twenty-seven. A good-sized group. No elders, though." He frowned. "We need to get to the tower, but we also need to be sure there aren't any imps after us. Or that wizard."

A pixie covered in dirt and grime who had been hiding under leaves spoke up: "How can we be sure? Every time we fly, and the imps are nearby, they find us."

"Yes, that's right. We should send a decoy group to draw them away, while the other group goes to the tower."

"And split up again?" Flurry looked aghast. "Every time we split up we lose people. Come on, Wix. Think about it!"

"I am thinking!" Wix stamped his foot. "Can't you tell?"

"I don't want to split up anymore! We need to stick together."

"Well, what's *your* brilliant idea then?" Wix crossed his arms in a huff. "How do you suggest we get to the tower without attracting imps along the way. Do you want to walk the whole way?"

Flurry folded her arms and frowned. "No. Of course not. That would take days instead of hours. But there's got to be another solution than splitting up." She looked at him with pleading eyes.

Wix looked into her eyes and softened. "I don't want to split up either, but what other choice do we have?"

The dirty pixie spoke again. "We have no idea how many more imps are out there. There could be none. There could be twenty. Even a hundred! Until we know that, we're going to have to make a lot of guesses. The safest thing is to guess that there's a hundred. I've just been buried in dirt. Not something I ever thought would happen. Look around. There aren't any elders here. The old ways aren't keeping us alive. I say, forget about flying and instead play it safe. Walking for a few days is a small price to pay to get us there safely. And closer to the ground is better with the powers we've got here."

He waved his hand toward Flurry and Jade. "As soon as we get to the tower, we'll know exactly how many imps we're dealing with—and how many pixies are still out there. We'll be able to help in every way."

"I agree." Flurry stepped toward Wix. "I don't want to walk, but it's safe. And . . . ." She turned to Jade. "It will give us time to figure out some more strategies against the imps."

"Alright." Wix took charge again. "Then it's settled. We'll walk to the tower. If this is our plan, we're sticking to it.

Nobody can fly. We can't risk it. I don't know what good scouts will be on foot, but it's a good practice and will give us at least a minute warning if we run into imps. Two scouts to lead us, two trailing behind. Let's go."

Wix directed the group to move out, and Flurry stood watching him. In the midst of his activity, he sensed her and turned. When they made eye contact, she smiled and mouthed the words, "Thank you."

He smiled back and mind-spoke: *Come on, anxious warrior. Let's get to that tower and save some friends!*

✳ ✳ ✳

As expected, a three-day hike to the tower was extremely tiresome for the twenty-seven pixies. Their feet were sore, and their bodies ached.

But they all survived, even though the scouts noticed an imp at one point. On foot, they were able to stay completely hidden, and the imp went on its way.

Only one pixie in the group had been to the tower before. But when they entered the protective ring surrounding it, they felt a huge burden lift. Safe at last!

The power surrounding the tower was palpable. Flurry felt like she could create another rock tower next to it—the mana coursed through her and felt intoxicating.

The tower itself was a tall gray pinnacle jutting up majestically near the coast, a good eighty yards above the land. There were cliffs somewhat nearby, and rocky terrain surrounding it, but also plenty of forest. If not for the illusion spells protecting it, it would have stood out grandly.

The pinnacle was rough and looked easy to climb, with lots of ledges and grooves.

"We did it!" Wix flew up and around it, circling to the top and back. The other pixies excitedly followed suit. It felt good to fly again! When they'd settled down, he grew serious. "Now, what's first?"

The pixie who'd been to the tower once before spoke up: "Our powers are amplified here, as we all feel, but more important are all the magical items." She fluttered to the base of the tower into a small crack and disappeared. The other pixies followed.

Inside the tower was a spacious feeling cavern, large enough to fit a couple hundred pixies. It was a comfortable space with a mossy floor that felt delightful to step on, especially after a three-day hike. Colorful tapestries and artwork covered the walls.

A magical light filled the room as soon as they entered, revealing a handful of objects lining the walls, as well as an entire wall with over a hundred holes burrowed in a perfect grid, each with small living quarters for up to four pixies.

The magical objects were a wonder to see—dozens of items with different enchantments. The pixies would have been lost figuring out what each did if it wasn't for a scroll on a table next to a large mirror.

The pixie who'd been there before unrolled the scroll and spoke: "This lists the different objects that are here and gives simple instructions how to use them. You can get better at using them with practice, but the built-in magic, amplified by the power of the great tower, means any of us could use them. Most of them need to be used within the tower."

"This mirror here . . ." She gestured to the simple-looking mirror hanging on the wall next to her, "has the power to show you anything you ask it." She turned to the mirror. "Show me how many imps are still attacking pixies."

The mirror changed from a normal reflection to looking like clouds, then revealed two dozen imps, all flying and searching for pixies throughout the land.

"That one there," the pixie said, pointing to one in the corner. "Show me where it is on a map in relation to us."

The image in the mirror focused on that one imp and zoomed out, continuing to zoom out till it mapped the imp's location and theirs. A dark dot representing the imp was over fifty miles from the tower.

"Show me on the map how many pixies are still left in the area, and where they are in relation to the imps."

The map zoomed out more, a couple hundred miles across, and showed hundreds and hundreds of small bright dots representing pixies. Some of the pixies were on their own, but most were in small groups, much like theirs had been. The two dozen dark dots representing imps were also spread out, with one or two near every group of pixies.

A few pixies cheered when they saw how many were still alive. Flurry breathed a sigh of relief. With everyone scattered, it was so hard to know who had survived.

Another pixie, the one who'd been filthy three days earlier, was reading over the scroll and grinned. "Hey! This looks like it'll help!"

He walked over to a yellow hat with little feathers sticking out all over and put it on. It looked ridiculous on him, especially in his current tattered state.

He mind-spoke, and it went out to all the pixies in the two-hundred-mile radius.

We made it to the Tower! Twenty-seven of us! Take heart, there are hundreds and hundreds of you out there still alive, and only two dozen imps. We're all young and new to the tower, but we'll figure out how to help you.

Flurry felt tears well up. It was so hard to believe they were safe at last. Their troubles were ended! She took a look at the list of items on the scroll as it was passed around. There was a blanket with the power to heal. An apron that when worn could make a delicious feast with the snap of a finger. A wand that could create illusions near and far. A bowl that would fill itself with any food when you asked it. A branch that when shaken over things helped them grow in whatever way desired.

She was particularly interested in whatever items could help them battle against the imps:

A necklace that could create a protective barrier up to thirty feet in diameter.

A rod that when pointed at someone and given the word "stop" would freeze the person in place. That could be super useful!

A wand that could make others fall asleep.

But would these items work against the imps who seem resistant to magic? There was only one way to find out.

Pixies were going to items and using them. The sound of happiness echoed throughout the chamber. One injured pixie was now completely healed. A big feast was sitting on a long table nearby.

The sound of music started up. Flurry smiled but then had a serious thought and stood before the mirror. "Show me the wizards who are making all this happen. Who's attacking us?"

A dozen pixies gathered around to watch as the mirror clouded over, then showed five people all busy in their own way. She recognized the wizard with a red cape from his attacks earlier. He looked like he was actually quite nearby! Probably looking for them.

There was no sign of the evil dark wizard who'd also attacked them over a month earlier. She wondered what had happened to him. There was an older woman all in white, an old thin man, a gruff-looking man with a big beard, and a blue-tinted elf.

"Show me what they're doing, where they are on a map."

The mirror first showed the wizard with the red cape. looking through some trees next to a hippogriff near the coast. According to the map, he was only three miles away. The woman in white was sitting on a throne over three hundred miles to their east, talking to someone. The gruff-looking man was even further away, flying far south searching for something. The elf was in the same area as the queen, and the lanky wizard looked like he was near the human city of Lugo.

It was hard to know what to do about all of them. Why are they attacking? What can be done about them? "Show us our best hope for stopping these wizards."

The mirror clouded over, then showed a scene in a dark cave. "Amber!" Flurry's eyes went wide. Amber, two humans and two elves were scrambling around in a large treasure-filled cavern. But what on earth are they doing? And does she need help?

She kept her gaze on the mirror and continued her train of thinking out loud. "If we use the power of the tower, will we reveal ourselves?"

The pixies all stopped. "I don't think so, but that's a good question. We need to be careful."

Flurry rubbed her chin thoughtfully. "There are five wizards after us. Are they after the power of the tower? I bet they are. One of them is so close! We need to be careful using powers and going in and out of the tower. We need to lead him away and be extra careful when going in and out."

"This can help with that!" A pixie held up a hoop. "It creates a hole to another place, anywhere you want. It can last a couple minutes but can be closed when you want."

The pixies around her admired the hoop. "Perfect!" Flurry held up the scroll. "Let's make sure we know all the powers at our disposal before we head out. Remember, the imps are invulnerable to direct attacks of magic, so we'll have to be creative and think of ways to attack them indirectly."

The scroll continued to get passed around, and pixies tried a few different things. One asked the mirror, "Show me the pixies in the most danger."

Flurry admired the brilliance of that question. Better to save those first. With the hoop and the dozens of other enchanted objects, the pixies began saving their friends and bringing everyone to the tower.

Soon enough they would all be safe. But they still didn't have an answer to the most pressing question: why were these wizards after them in the first place?

Chapter 25

Crodor the Ancient

THE ANCIENT DRAGON WALKED down the passageway toward the treasure room. The five youths and large cat scrambled and hid as silently as they could.

Mizu stayed near the entrance, just out of sight behind an ornate statue of a person with a wolf head. The others crouched behind rocks, not looking, ears tuned to every click-clack of the dragon's claws on the rocks.

As the enormous lizard got closer, a wave of heat washed into the room. With it came a reptile smell that stung their noses and a wash of terror that filled their bodies.

Amber's mind raced. All she could think of was fleeing—but she was frozen in place. Sweat trickled down her brow. What if the rope didn't work with the amulet? They had no backup plan. None at all.

Theo began shaking uncontrollably, and Basil darted his eyes toward him with his finger up to his lips. Theo took a deep breath through his nose and closed his eyes. The shaking stopped in his legs, but he looked like a wreck.

The smell of death and roasted meat permeated the cavern as the sound of the footsteps neared.

Then the dragon stopped.

None of them dared to look, but he was clearly still in the passageway, not yet through the ring of the amulet.

And then a deep voice sounding much like an elderly human broke the silence. "I smell you. Humans and elves, working together. Thieves! You will be delicious tonight. No bother hiding."

Amber's heart thumped so loudly she imagined Crodor could hear it from across the giant room. "An elf. There's an elf right over here. I smell you." The sound of licking lips filled the cave.

Amber peeked around the side of the rock she was hiding behind. Just as she suspected, the dragon was huge—everything she had imagined but worse.

Gigantic in every respect and bright red with scales that shimmered in the dim light revealing colorful tinges of blue.

He was like a draco only fifty times larger. Every part of him was spiky and dangerous, from the horns on his head and teeth to his claws and the spines along the top of his back, and his pointy barbed tail.

His scales looked thick and impenetrable and were spiky as well—some parts more than others. His breath smelled of blood and death. Some cow or deer or some other unlucky creature. And his eyes were large and yellow, slitted like a cat.

Amber quickly darted her head back, not daring to reveal herself. The sound of Crodor's enormous foot stepped closer.

He should have crossed the threshold. Another step. He was closer still. Was he inside the cavern?

A quick peek revealed the fearsome dragon's head peering into the cavern.

He opened his mouth, and the stench grew powerful. "I smell you. And I shall now devour you."

Mizu suddenly popped out from behind the statue. "Greetings, Crodor. I bring you glad tidings from the elves."

The dragon instantly shot flames toward her, and she darted behind the statue. Amber frantically craned her neck toward the cave entrance where the amulet was tied. The bottom of the rope had a break in it—it had ripped when the dragon had stepped on it. The dragon was still enchanted!

They would have to act quickly. Amber called out, "Basil! The rope got ripped."

The dragon was halfway toward Mizu and swiveled his enormous head to look at the others. Basil and Azarel darted out of their hiding places. Basil put on a burst of speed toward the cave entrance.

Azarel shouted and waved his arms. "Hey, beast! Try your flames on me!"

The dragon spat fire, a large funnel of flame, heating the entire room uncomfortably, and engulfing Azarel. But the flame did a fork where it approached him and moved around, not touching him at all.

The flames died down, and Azarel shouted, "Is that all you've got?"

The dragon looked confused for a moment. Then instead of blowing flames again, he paused. In that moment, Basil almost reached the ripped rope. The dragon's eyes darted toward Basil, then back to Azarel. Though his eyes glowed red with the enchantment, they were intelligent and calculating.

He turned toward Basil and bolted toward him, much more quickly than would have seemed possible for a creature of that size.

Basil was crouched down, focused intently on tying the snapped rope together. Come on . . . just one more twist. The dragon was nearly upon him when he suddenly leaped up and ran down the passage away from the chamber like a blur.

Crodor breathed a blast of flame that filled the entire tunnel. Amber held her breath.

Basil heard the rush of fire and swept air through the tunnel from the outside. The flame blasted into the right wall behind him. Even so, he flew forward from the rush of fire and fell to the ground, rolling on the bumpy rock floor.

He felt singed but not burned. The smell of burning boots reached his nostrils, and he quickly leaped back to his feet to continue his escape.

The dragon roared and chased after him. In that same moment, his head crossed through the ring of the amulet and he stopped.

Silence.

In some ways, the horror grew worse every second that the silence continued. Did the spell work? Was Crodor freed from the enchantment?

The dragon backed into the chamber again, turned around, and gazed at the two elves in front of him.

Mizu breathed deeply and walked fully into view, approaching the enormous dragon. Azarel immediately walked with her, staying close in case another fire blast came.

But it didn't. Crodor cocked his head slightly, then spoke in the same deep voice but sounding much friendlier. "Who are you, then?"

"It is I, Mizu, granddaughter of Farlier, from the wood elves of Lorcaster. I have come seeking your advice in a grave matter."

"Farlier?" Crodor mused, "I haven't heard from him for many years. Such a long time ago. There were more dragons in these parts then."

There was a moment of silence, and the others peeked over and around their rocks. Basil slowly walked back into the chamber to hear the conversation.

The dragon showed even more detail in the light. Blood dripped from his massive teeth, and there were tendrils of smoke coming from his large, flaring nostrils. His scales were shades of red and orange, and bumpy all over. His underbelly was completely different, orange-yellow and smoother scales—probably more comfortable for lying on—and with pieces of treasure stuck in between his many scales.

Crodor's voice rumbled and filled the chamber. "Was I under some sort of enchantment? I feel as if I've just awoken from a long slumber."

"Yes." Mizu stood boldly and held her hands out. "Thanks to our human friends, the spell is broken."

"A spell? It would take a powerful wizard to enchant me. I have great resistance to magic."

"Some of the people here killed that wizard. And they brought the means to free you. We are on your side."

"Hmm . . ." The dragon looked skeptical.

"We come seeking your advice."

"Any descendent of Farlier is worthy of asking one question of me. And of course, I will refrain from eating your tiny bodies."

Mizu paused and looked around the large cave. "You can come out now."

The others reluctantly emerged from their hiding spots. As Basil entered the chamber, he partially pulled his sword from its sheath and showed it to Theo and Amber, as if to say— no more glowing here.

Theo was the last to stand next to Mizu, and he nearly tripped on the way, out of nervousness. He tugged on his sleeves and moved from foot to foot. All five stood in a row before the gigantic red dragon.

"What sort of advice are you seeking?" Crodor asked Mizu.

"We are facing some difficult times, with many creatures coming under enchantment. Not just you. We seek your wisdom and years of experience to know how to proceed. You were a great ally to our people back in the wizard wars nearly two hundred years ago."

"Indeed." Crodor smiled with a smug expression. "But times have changed."

The dragon showed them his enormous teeth. Was it a grin? Or was he trying to appear menacing? Either way, it wasn't a pleasant sight.

"I'd normally have eaten you by now. How lucky for you. So tell me more about this spell I was under."

"The wizard that some of us killed was casting the spell on a phoenix. We believe he was only one of many, affecting creatures all across the land."

"Why are they doing such things?" Crodor asked.

Mizu looked over at Amber and gestured for her to speak. Amber cleared her throat. "We think they have a master plan to destroy the human cities for some reason. We don't know a lot about them, but we do know they've gathered an army of goblins that's probably marching on one of our largest cities right now."

Crodor shrugged. "Humans. They come and go over time. It makes no difference to me."

"But," Amber started, then paused. She didn't know what to say. She tried imagining the world from a dragon's perspective, but realized she knew nothing, so she asked, "What *do* you care about?"

"Hmm," Crodor mused. "That's a very interesting question, indeed. Besides my treasure, I assume." He gazed at a large golden statue. "Well, I suppose I do want the land to be relatively peaceful, so I can hunt in peace. Wars aren't good for anyone."

"Are there other dragons like you?" Amber asked.

"Of course," Crodor said. "There are many of us. Everywhere you go, there are dragons who truly rule the land. Across the great sea there are even more—far more. We allow people like yourselves to set up your cities, but we know who the real rulers are."

Amber reached into her pack. "We also heard from a fairy that you might like peanut butter, and so we brought you some."

At that, Crodor lifted his eyebrows and took interest in Amber. "Peanut butter? Really? I haven't had peanut butter for many years."

He lifted his front leg to step toward her, then paused. "What do you want in return?"

Dozens of thoughts ran through Amber's mind in a flash of a moment. We could trade the peanut butter for his help with the goblin army. She thought four moves ahead, like playing Castles. A little taste of food would be incentive to help, especially if he loved it. But then what if the army was a threat to him? He wouldn't stick around just because he had a little taste of something delicious.

319

He might offer them a ride back to Lugo, and they might be able to convince him to help on the way. But that probably wouldn't work either. This dragon was used to doing things his way. He wouldn't be easy to convince—of that she was certain. *We need his help with the goblins, but there's no way he'll do that for a jar of peanut butter. It isn't even worth asking.*

Think Amber! What would Old Mr. Thompson do? As she thought about it, she instantly knew.

She forced a smile. "This? It's a free gift. We don't require anything in return. Although we could certainly use your help with this goblin war."

"Goblins?" Crodor said with a look of distaste. "What wretched creatures. I'd like to rid the world of them, honestly."

He walked closer to Amber, and despite his somewhat friendly voice, she cringed when he got close enough to touch. He reached out his huge claw, and she put the jar in it.

The five were surprised when the dragon managed to carefully unscrew the lid with his enormous talons. He dabbed the tip of his tongue into the jar. His eyes softened and he smiled—then licked again and sighed.

"This is excellent. Where did it come from?"

"Lugo. The city under attack," Amber said.

"Really?" Crodor raised his scaly eyebrows. "This city, there must be more peanut butter there, wouldn't you think?"

"Oh, yes! If you come with us and help protect them, we'll give you as much peanut butter as we can!"

"Lovely." Crodor tossed the jar into his mouth and sucked on it, rolling the jar around, then gently spat it out without breaking it. The jar rolled in a small circle, and the five stared in shock that the jar was completely clean. How an enormous creature could suck such a sticky substance out of a tiny jar was beyond them.

He revealed enormous blood-covered teeth. Was that his version of a smile? "Then it's settled. I will take you to this city, prevent its demise, and receive more peanut butter for my efforts."

Amber grinned and looked at Basil and Theo. They were smiling as well. It was all Amber could have expected and more. Now they just had to hope the army hadn't gotten there yet.

"Lugo is an hour away, if I give you a ride." Crodor bared all his teeth again.

Theo gulped audibly.

Basil put his fists on his hips. "That sounds great! I just hope we're not too late!"

Amber's eyes darted to him. "But what about our horses. We can't just leave them tied to a tree."

"True . . ." Basil flipped a curl of hair out of his eyes and scratched his head.

"I'll take them." Azarel said calmly.

"Really?" Amber glanced at Theo, as if asking his advice. "You're not going to join us in our battle?"

Azarel shook his head. "Look, I'm new to your little group and all, but when I'm committed to something, I do it fully. Yes, I will join the battle. If we really are five of the six in the prophecy, it's important we work together. However . . . I have some ideas of my own. And the first is, why not see if we can get some elves to help?"

"Wonderful!" Amber's eyes lightened. "That's a great idea! Do you think they'll actually help protect humans? It didn't seem like they were excited about that when I talked to them."

"They won't want to. But as I told you before, I've been raised to be a Conclave member. Which means I have authority over a great many elves." He gave a sly smile. "And perhaps I can convince a mage to join. Having a mage on our side would be a good idea, if there are many on the other side as well."

Amber found herself grinning. Who'd have thought Azarel would be such a help? He was so quiet and pushy. Then she had a thought. Kish and the dwarves! They would most certainly help, if Azarel could be convinced to send them a message from her. But he hated the dwarves—would he do it?

Chapter 26

The Second Wizard War

SOON AFTER THEIR DISCUSSION with Crodor, the five youths were on his spiky back, hanging on for dear life.

There was no great place to hold on, but he flew gently, with minimal flapping, as if he'd given rides before. The horses jumped and neighed as the dragon glided in, and Zoomy ran into the woods. Theo tried to calm them, but when the giant dragon landed, they were skittish and pulled at their reins.

After they calmed down, Amber walked up to her golden horse and gave a hug. "I don't know if I'll ever see you again, Buttercup. You've been a wonderful traveling companion. I'll come back for you if I can."

She loaded the saddle and gear onto the horse, gave it one last pat, and turned to the others. Theo was saying goodbye to Zoomy, and Basil was done saying goodbye to Storm.

Azarel saw Amber's look. "I'll make sure the animals are treated well."

"Listen, this is a pretty important moment." Amber tugged on a strand of long hair that had fallen into her face. "So, if you can convince the dwarves to help—"

"Seriously?" Azarel looked disgusted.

"We need to put our differences aside, Azarel. This is a big deal." She stood before him meekly.

"Hmm." The elf folded his arms.

She held out a piece of paper.

"What is it?"

"This is a note for the dwarves. They may not be your favorite people—but, please, we need all the help we can get. Deliver it to a griffin nest. It will get to the right person."

With pursed lips, he reluctantly put the note in his pocket. "I will do this for you. Although I do not like it, I do agree we need many allies with a goblin army of that size."

With that, the four companions climbed on Crodor again, and he lifted into the sky. Amber still had her dwarf helmet and goggles, and wore them happily, enjoying the fact that the wind in her face felt nice, not a hindrance.

Despite the bedding they had placed on the dragon's spiney back, they were still uncomfortable. And Amber was worried about a longer flight—especially after falling off a griffin with a full saddle.

The higher they went, the further each flap propelled them past the ground below. They passed mountains quickly and smoothly.

At one point, they saw a floating elf warship. It was different from the one Amber had seen before, and she thought back to her first encounter with the elves. She'd been so frightened of them. This time she smiled and gave a wave.

Theo waved with her. "Seems like a nice way to travel!" he shouted.

"Yes. I'd like to get on one again when all this is over."

It was difficult to hear each other without shouting in the wind, so for the rest of the trip they watched the land below in silence. Before long, they passed the mountains and were over the plains again, seeing what looked like the city of Lugo and a large army nearby.

They were just in time.

Thousands of goblins and hobgoblins had set up encampments in the distance, and hundreds were wandering around inspecting the land near the city. They looked like they could attack at any minute, but the city was peaceful for now.

"There has got to be way more than five thousand!" Basil shouted over the wind.

"Yes, more than the last time I saw them." Amber surveyed the masses of goblins and their war machines.

As they flew closer to the city, they saw that the people of Lugo had done a decent job of preparing for the army, with trenches and large spikes surrounding the entire city. The walls looked stronger than before, and they wondered if more stones had been added since they had been there a mere two weeks earlier.

Soldiers lined the entire top perimeter of the wall while catapults and other war machines, mostly on the southeast, sat strategically positioned, scattered throughout the inside. The normally bustling docks at the giant river were empty— everyone hunkered behind the protective walls.

The army was directly to the southeast, with some spreading as far as the mighty river that ran by Lugo from the south and up past the west side of the city. The attack would most likely come from the east.

Crodor glided over Lugo, causing the people to shout and scramble. Soldiers on the walls pointed their crossbows toward the encroaching beast. The four youths suddenly realized how dangerous their idea was—what if the soldiers shot at them before they had a chance to explain?

But the soldiers waited to fire. Crodor settled into an open space near the center of the city just as the General who they'd met earlier came riding over on an enormous white horse, followed by a dozen other armed men on horses. When he saw the youths, he smiled and gestured with his hand for the men to lower their weapons.

He dismounted at the same time the youths slid off the dragon. "Well!" He had his hands open as he greeted them warmly. "Your timing is wonderful. And I see you've brought a new friend!" He glanced at Crodor a little nervously.

Crodor spoke in his ancient low voice: "I am not here so much to help you, as to get rid of some goblins and eat some more of that delicious peanut butter." He licked his lips.

The General glanced at Amber and winked. She beamed. He turned back to the dragon. "Of course. When we send these goblins running, you can empty our reserves of all the peanut butter you'd like."

"Has there been any fighting yet?" Basil asked.

"Yes." The General gazed toward the wall. "They sent a group of eight hundred goblins with a wizard a few days ago. It was a fierce battle, but we defeated them. In large part, thanks to your friend."

"Our friend?" Amber, Basil, and Theo looked at each other.

He gestured and one of the soldiers at the back rode forward and dismounted. It wasn't a soldier at all.

"Ryder!" Amber ran to give him a big hug. "*You* helped defeat the goblins?"

Ryder laughed. "While you've been out and about on your grand adventures, I've had quite the adventures of my own. But, yes, my powers with earth have proven to be quite helpful indeed. That and some amazing warrior monks I enlisted."

"Aha!" Amber's eyes lit up, and she gazed at Ryder. "You're the sixth one from the prophecy!"

"Oh, yeah!" Theo came over and patted Ryder on the back. "Of course! That makes all six of the elements!"

"Prophecy?"

"We have a *lot* to catch up on!" Amber squeezed his arm.

Basil turned to the General. "How long has the goblin army been there?"

"They just arrived today. They look like they might attack at any moment, but I wonder from what I've been told of goblins if they'll wait till night. They don't do as well in the sun—you probably noticed all their tents and canopies."

"Yes, that makes sense." Basil's eyes wandered in thought. "Any idea of what all we're facing?"

"The army is gigantic—even bigger than we'd imagined. There are roughly seventy-five hundred goblins and hobgoblins, at least a hundred ogres, two giants, and I imagine wizards and other beasts."

"So, there *are* evil wizards leading these goblins. We figured." Basil patted his sword hilt thoughtfully.

"How can we possibly handle an army of this magnitude?" Theo shook his head. "Even with Crodor."

The General had a steely gaze. "We are fighting for our home. That gives us an edge." He turned toward the wall. "We've had many ideas, and now that you're a part of the plans, we can come up with some new strategies. I'm certain your powers will be of incredible value. And the dragon may just be the game changer."

Crodor spoke in his deep voice: "I'm glad you recognize what I bring. No army, no matter how big, has ever been much trouble for me. I can help before they attack. I will fly above the army and give them a little taste of dragon."

"Excellent." The General nodded. "I'm certain you will make all the difference. See what damage you can do before they get here."

Amber strode in front of the dragon as he was about to fly away. "Just be aware, there are wizards. It's not just a bunch of goblins."

"Indeed." Crodor crouched and launched into the air with wide wings, flying out of the city and toward the army.

They turned and walked toward the wall. The General gestured to the people bustling around them. "When you left two weeks ago, we took action on a great many things. We sent our fastest messengers to get help, one of which is Ryder, who was able to bring Zylin monks."

"What's that?" Amber asked.

"Think of them as warrior-mages," the General said. "Those who know the art of fighting as well as magical gifts. We have nine led by Pax, who is very experienced. They have powers, different than your elemental powers or what you'd think from a wizard—quite effective in their own right."

They wound down cobblestone streets, passing people who were all quite busy-looking. Everyone from civilians to soldiers who noticed the General would stop and salute before continuing.

"As I was saying, we also have an apothecary here who has concocted a potion of strength and protection. It lasts many hours. We've made hundreds of vials. When the attack begins, those on the front lines will be instructed to take a drink, which should give us a considerable edge."

"We've also built many war machines and have been training our soldiers. I think you'll find we have a great deal in our favor. Now, shall we look through a spyglass to see how our dragon friend is doing?"

"Yes!" The youths said in unison. They made their way to the top of the city wall and peered through spyglasses. The dragon was flying over the goblin encampment breathing fire in long jets, setting tents ablaze and goblins running.

"So far so good!" Basil gave a thumbs-up as he looked through his spyglass. "Wait. There's something wrong. He's flying slower—he's not attacking anymore. He's turned back."

The dragon glided over the land toward the city, barely moving his wings at all. As he drew nearer, they could see a look of anger on his face. He made imperceptible movements with his wings and glided to a stop in front of the walls. Something was obviously wrong—he continued to hold the same position with his wings out, even though he'd landed.

Amber suddenly understood. "That's what the dark wizard did to me! Remember? It was a spell that kept me from moving. Theo, your ring is what helped me. You need to get down there!"

"What's the nearest way?" Theo scanned the wall for an opening.

"Not close." The General frowned.

Amber grew excited. "Basil! What about your powers? You raised yourselves out of that pit, right?"

"Yep! I can do it. I'll create a wind funnel to lower you." Basil patted Theo on the back.

Theo looked at him uncomfortably. "Are you sure? You've only just started getting the hang of it. It's a long way down."

"Yes, I've got you, buddy. It's easier to lower someone than to raise them. You can trust me."

Theo breathed deeply through his nose. "Let's do it, then."

Basil created a whirlwind around him, which lifted him gently over the wall and down to the ground below without a single issue. "Told you! I'm getting better!" Basil called down.

Theo gave a thumbs-up, then ran over to the dragon that was awkwardly splayed out on the ground. A minute of Theo's magical ring, and the dragon's wings relaxed, then he stood and stretched. Theo climbed up, and the two lifted into the air and inside the city walls, landing on a nearby street that was barely wide enough for the dragon's enormous body.

The group ran over to him. He looked fierce. "A wizard's spell took hold of me. When I felt it, I barely had time to change course to head to safety. If I hadn't, I would have fallen right there at their mercy. How are you kids planning on dealing with wizards with this kind of power?"

"We've done it before," said Basil with his fists on his hips. "The three of us and a phoenix worked together and took on a powerful wizard—the one who enchanted you in the first place. But it didn't just happen by one of us attacking him. We planned ahead and worked together. You'll just have to work with us."

Theo and Amber nodded in agreement.

Ryder watched Amber with renewed admiration. The young girl who'd left her sleepy town less than two months earlier was full of wisdom and life experiences he hadn't imagined possible.

"What's your plan, then?" The dragon stared at Basil with his dangerous-looking slitted eyes.

"Um . . . Theo?"

Theo cleared his throat. "Besides the army and our dragon friend, we have five elemental powers represented here. Maybe all six, if Azarel can make it back in time. We have special wizard-like monks, plus special potions. That seems like a lot . . . but if I were playing Castles, I'd want to know more about what we're dealing with here. Besides what we see, do any of you know more about these wizards?"

"I do." Ryder stepped forward, and everyone turned to him. "There are at least three of them. I don't know what they're capable of, but the one I faced the other day has power over the earth, like me. He also has a scepter that shoots fireballs, and a wand that protects him from attacks."

"How do you know about the other two?" Amber asked.

"I snuck into their castle."

"Really? And you made it out alive?"

"Well . . ." Ryder fumbled for words. He had a strange feeling of guilt because of how easy it had been to get away. "They did discover me, but they let me live."

"Why?"

"I don't exactly know. They wanted me to join their side, and, of course, I said no. And they said to think about it. I just walked right out."

"That's weird. I don't get it." Amber scratched her head.

"I don't either. Why would they let me go? Maybe there's more to them than meets the eye. They also gave me this." He held up the pale blue enchanted stone. "It helps me have more insight and awareness. Like, as I hold it right now, I'm noticing a lot more. I can tell that the spell still hasn't completely worn off of Crodor. And I can sense some kind of magic in Basil's backpack. A wand? Or a scepter perhaps?"

"Yes. That's right." Basil patted his backpack. The General eyed it with interest. "We have the scepter the evil wizard used to enchant the creatures. Do you think we should use it, Theo?"

"No. I don't think so." Theo scratched his arm. "None of us has practice with it. It takes mana and effort to learn how to use it properly. Ryder, anything else you notice by holding that stone? Can I try?"

"Sure." Ryder passed it to Theo, whose eyes instantly lit up.

"Wow. This is pretty amazing. Ok. I have an idea. Just like in Castles."

"Tell me more." The General was suddenly interested.

Theo mentioned a number of different ideas, with the General listening attentively. Then he looked uncomfortable and turned toward the dragon. "I hate to say this, but I think I should ride Crodor, at least to start. That way, if they try that spell again, I'll be right there."

He handed the stone back to Ryder. "Thanks. Makes me wonder why they'd give you a stone with such power. It's going to help us against them."

"I've thought the same thing many times." Ryder put it back in his pocket. "I wonder if I should trust using it, but then every time I have, it's helped in some way. So . . ." He shrugged.

The General cleared his throat. "Let's continue this conversation in the planning room with our captains and Pax." He motioned for them to follow. "We need everyone to work together and be a part of these discussions."

✳ ✳ ✳

The planning room was perfectly designed for discussing the attack. A map showed the city and surrounding area, and there were small pebbles of different colors and metal figurines representing the various creatures and soldiers.

The General pulled out distinct rocks for the five youths and the monks. Then, he opened a drawer in the table and took out a figurine for the dragon.

"Kept this one handy, just in case." He winked at the kids.

333

Chandler was sitting in the corner, reading a book next to a tall stack of different-sized books and scrolls. When they saw him, Theo shouted, "Chandler!" He glanced up and gave a little wave of the hand, then went back to reading.

Amber shook her head in disbelief. It was as if he'd expected them to return. Or perhaps didn't care. Or maybe he was just stuck in his book.

Over the next few hours, they discussed strategies and made plans. Nobody in the room had ever been in a large-scale war before. The last war of that size was nearly two hundred years earlier.

The General knew a thing or two about smaller battles. But Chandler had many ideas from reading books. Wars were still a thing around the world, and some of the principles he found were instantly received as truth.

At different times during the planning, he'd suddenly spout out a sentence: "The most ideal situation is to outsmart the opponent without having to engage in physical combat."

"We must appear weak where we are strongest—and strong where we are weakest."

"Our plans must be as dark as night, unpredictable and striking like a thunderbolt."

Some of them took turns holding Ryder's enchanted stone, each one contributing ideas. When the stone was offered to Amber, she held up her hand. "No thanks." Something didn't sit well with her about it.

People brought in food and water at one point, and the group continued to plan past dusk. As the sky darkened, the tension in the room grew thicker. The goblins might attack at any minute.

As if on cue, a young man came running into the room to the General. "Sir!" He breathed raggedly.

"Yes?" The General was peering at the stones on the map with furrowed brow. "What's the word?"

"The goblins are on the move, almost in range of the catapults, sir," the young man continued. "And they are starting to spread out, to surround the city."

"Our time of planning is over." He gazed at the people in the room slowly. "Whatever happens—however our best plans might fail—working together we have a chance. Everyone in this room is critical for our success. You know your spots. Let's get out there and defeat some evil."

Everyone hurried to their assigned spots. Even at dusk, the summer air was muggy and warm. Once outside, Theo walked up to the dragon. "Well, Crodor, looks like it's time for you to cause some trouble."

"Indeed," Crodor said with a toothy grin. "Climb aboard!"

Theo took a deep breath and climbed up the spiky scales, holding on in the best spot possible.

Crodor craned his neck around. "Ready?"

Was the dragon grinning? Teeth were everywhere, and smoke was starting to come out. He nodded, and the dragon launched himself into the air toward the approaching goblins.

By the time the others arrived at the wall, the giants had torn up the spikes in a few spots where the goblins could get through. The city ballistae and catapults were in full swing, sending rocks and flaming balls into the thick of the goblins. But there were only a dozen catapults, and the goblins were many.

Unfortunately, the goblins had ballistae and catapults of their own and began hurtling dangerous rocks over the city walls. Some buildings were impacted, sending rocks and debris dangerously in every direction. People scattered for cover, and a few were hit.

One of the captains shouted, "Aim for their catapults! Destroy them first, if possible."

Crodor flew straight toward a giant and breathed fire. The green ogre-like giant swung its club and missed. The fire didn't appear to do any real damage, only blackened its already dark-and-dirty skin. Theo held on for dear life, glad the club missed, wondering why he volunteered for such a crazy mission.

At the top of the wall, Ryder scanned the dark crowd for the earth elementalist. It was impossible to see in the dim light. The goblins had gotten past the ditch easily, which meant the wizard must not be far behind.

The archers shot arrows and bolts into the goblins as they got nearer, dropping dozens. But the goblins had their own archers with crossbows and returned the volley.

Arrows and rocks flew in both directions, wounding and killing goblins and humans alike.

Amber raised the hood of her magical protective cape and focused on slowing down the goblins in an area with thick grass. The grass coiled around their legs, tripping some.

Next to her was a Zylin monk, who shoved his hands forward as if attacking someone with his palms. A warm light grew over the goblins.

The goblins recoiled for a moment, then continued, now more visible. The monks were spread out along the top of the wall, sending out magical light over the approaching horde in every direction. The light only went a few hundred feet, but it helped enormously to see the closest ones.

The monk next to Amber had a grim look on his face. "Those giants will be deadly if they get to the walls."

Amber glanced over. The giants were their biggest and most-immediate threat, for sure. Looming a good forty feet, they were taller than the wall and incredibly muscular. They held huge spiky clubs built from trees and their roots. If they reached the wall, they could knock it over like toy bricks.

Thankfully, Crodor was blocking them from getting any further. The dragon continued to swoop low and breathe flames onto the giants, although it only seemed to slow them down—not seriously injure them.

"Let's see if I can help!" Basil focused and twirled his hands, and a small dust devil formed around one of the enormous green beasts, which turned into a larger vortex until it resembled a small tornado. It didn't pick up the giant but forced it back a step. The giant howled in rage.

Even with the giants kept at bay, the goblins were a force to contend with. The first wave reached the walls, putting up ladders and climbing to the top of the wall.

A hobgoblin with two swords emerged on the wall and killed two soldiers. A Zylin monk sprinted toward it and dodged its sword, attacking with the palm of his hand and sending the hobgoblin flying backward over the wall.

Goblins began popping over the edge, all down the wall. One emerged in front of Amber, but the monk near her dodged and kicked it off. Another took its place, and the monk twirled, grabbing its arm and throwing it down the ladder, knocking down the entire ladder with all the goblins.

But the goblins kept coming. Amber focused on the grass below the ground where the nearest ladder was resting. It grew around the legs, then pulled the ladder off the wall—sending goblins tumbling to the ground.

With one of the giants held off by Basil's tornado, Crodor attacked the other more fiercely. The giant swung its club—the trunk of a colossal tree with spikes formed by the roots—but the dragon held back a moment to dodge, then dove in, claws extended, and latched on.

Poor Theo! In the heat of battle, Crodor had forgotten about his rider, and Theo slid off. Basil quickly shifted his focus, creating another whirlwind to slow Theo's descent.

"Theo!" Amber yelled, then turned to the Zylin monk nearby. "Can you help him?"

The monk instantly leaped off the city wall. He landed on the ground in between startled goblins, then leaped again like a grasshopper toward Theo.

At the fifth bounce, he reached Theo, scooping him up and bounding back. He deftly dodged some arrows shot at him and leaped again toward one of the goblin ladders. He scrambled up the ladder, over a goblin, and kicked it down in the process, finally reaching safety at the top of the city wall.

He put Theo down next to Amber. He looked green but unharmed.

"Are you ok?" Amber put her hand on his shoulder.

"Yes . . . Probably . . . Because of the ring."

"Take a rest." Amber patted him and turned back to the battle.

But just then Theo saw a flaming rock land behind the wall into a building and injure someone badly. He struggled to his feet and wobbled down the steps to heal the man. As he went, he saw more and more injured. He just hoped the dragon would be ok without him and got to work healing others as quickly as he could.

The giants were enormous—with long pointed ears and enormously muscular necks and torsos. But Crodor wasn't much smaller. The dragon gripped a giant's body and bit at it, aiming for its neck. His claws only scratched the surface, but his teeth created a large gash in the giant's chest.

The giant tried to rip the large lizard off, but Crodor's scaly protection and fierce energy prevented it. After a brief tussle, the dragon managed to scramble up and get a good bite to the neck. The giant grasped the wound with a thundering yell and toppled to the ground, crushing fifteen goblins beneath it.

With a triumphant roar, Crodor rode the giant down to the ground and stood on it for a moment, ensuring it wouldn't move. Then he took to the air again, swooping over the goblins and breathing fire. Goblins scrambled and fled. He flew along the wall where the fighting was fiercest, scattering goblins.

A cheer went up from the city wall. The dragon was really winning the battle! It felt as if they were going to hold off the entire army, but then a group of flying shapes came swooping in from the darkness toward the city. They came into the light, and Amber's heart dropped.

Dozens of griffins, hippogriffs, and other flying creatures were joining the attack—some with riders.

But the creature in the lead was the most worrisome—a gigantic blue dragon.

Chapter 27

The Trouble with Wizards

CRODOR TURNED toward the giant blue dragon and shouted, "Avelon! What are you doing with them?" But the dragon ignored his words and flew at him with a fire in his eyes.

Crodor flew up to draw the attack away from the city and shouted again, "Avelon! Wake up! What did they do to you?"

The blue dragon attacked with outstretched claws, and Crodor dodged and barreled into him, then flew higher. He grappled, not ripping with his teeth and claws. At least for the moment. Amber wondered what they could do to free Avelon from the evil spell. It seemed impossible in the middle of a battle, even with the amulet and the scepter.

With Crodor pulled off, the goblins resumed their attack. The griffins swooped in, attacking the soldiers on the walls. One of the griffins was shot by an arrow and fell to the ground.

Amber felt sorry for it. They're under a spell. They wouldn't be attacking at all otherwise! But the people of Lugo had to protect themselves.

The griffins had powerful beaks and claws, and soldiers scrambled. Those with shields went to the front of the wall to form protective barriers.

Then the earth began to shake, and a huge crack formed thirty yards from the wall, running toward the city. The crack grew wider, right underneath and past the wall!

Stones dropped, then more, until the integrity of the wall was lost, and it sagged above the ever-widening gap. Then a large stretch of wall slowly collapsed into the growing chasm, sending dust and debris flying.

When the dust settled, the devastation became visible. The deep crack in the earth was now twenty yards across and hundreds of yards long, going well into the city.

Behind the goblins, an old human stood ominously, gesturing with his arms like an orchestra conductor while eight hobgoblins protected him. Rocks grew up from the depths as the earth elementalist made sweeping motions. Then, as he lowered his arms toward the earth, the entire wall shuddered all the way around the city.

Would this one wizard make the entire city wall fall?

In that same moment, a dozen spears hurtled through the sky and into soldiers. They turned to see a woman all in white riding a white pegasus—and watched in horror as she reached into a side bag and threw pebble-like specks toward the soldiers on the wall.

The specks grew into spears and penetrated the people mercilessly.

Is that my power? Amber wondered. Power over plants? I would never have thought to do that.

Amber focused on the spears with her own powers, trying to stop the next attack. Some of the spears grew bushy and leafy, landing harmlessly on the soldiers. However, she wasn't able to change many, and in the next wave two of them hit soldiers.

What else can I do to help? she wondered. Carrying a side bag of seeds into a battle suddenly seemed like a great idea. Next time. If there is a next time.

Meanwhile, not far from her, Ryder ran as fast as he could to the broken wall. A deep chasm hundreds of feet deep was now right where the wall used to be—an impossible task to repair. But he had to try.

As soon as he was close enough, he focused and drew from within himself, magically repairing the wall. The fissure had done considerable damage, but he felt stronger than ever in the heat of the battle.

The stones of the wall stacked upon themselves again, working their way up and across. But the gap was enormous. Was it too big a task for him?

He felt a stirring below, at the bottom of the crack in the earth. Stones, boulders, and dirt were shifting and magically filling in the gap. The wizard was lifting it up so the goblins could just waltz right in! The gap in the wall was still huge, so he intensified his focus. But how could he work against a more powerful wizard?

On the other side of the wall, Basil continued to hold the second giant in place. It was all he could do to prevent the giant from breaking free and reaching the city.

"Can anyone help with this giant?" He looked around desperately, feeling strained. A Zylin monk fought next to him, preventing all goblins from reaching Basil by throwing the creatures into each other and off the wall.

The monk pointed into the sky and twirled his hand. Two female monks somehow "heard" him and came running over. The monk gestured again without words and pointed at the giant, then turned to Basil. "You must help us, and we can do it."

"Will do!" Basil refocused his energy, ensuring the tornado was strong.

The monk turned to two nearby soldiers and pointed at Basil. "Protect the lad. He needs to focus." Then he leaped from the wall, and the two other monks leaped from their spots as well.

One of them landed on a goblin's head and bounded off again. Another landed between two goblins and did a quick spin-kick causing a goblin's sword to stab into the other. Then she ran up its body and leaped again. The third monk blocked an arrow and redirected a spear attack before continuing on.

They all continued leaping and bounding toward the giant and arrived at a similar time, with goblins sloppily shooting bolts after them. Unfortunately, Basil's tornado surrounding it turned out to be impenetrable.

Basil saw the predicament and eased up on the wind. The monks leaped up, grabbing hold of the skins the giant wore, and clambered up its body. But as soon as the giant broke free from the whirlwind, it lumbered toward the wall, shaking one of the monks off its back and swiping at another, forcing her to jump away for a moment.

One monk managed to stay on the beast and continued climbing higher for an attack. The giant came close to the wall, and Basil created another whirlwind to slow it down. But the monk who was still on the giant struggled to stay there and get a good attack because the giant's muscular chest didn't have places to hold on.

She punched the giant in its side with both hands, then leaped back to the wall and landed with a roll. The giant held its side and grimaced. It was a big blow, even against such a massive giant. But not enough. The giant pushed forward and swung its enormous club.

The huge spiky club connected with the wall and shattered stones in every direction, creating a large dent.

The monk leaped toward the giant again. She dove into it with both fists pounding into its chest.

Thwack! The giant staggered back for a moment. Two catapults on the wall sent flaming balls into its chest. It looked down, swiped away the remaining fire, then lumbered forward and swung again.

The Zylin monk sent out a magical flare of light that blinded the giant—but that didn't change the course of the club. With a horrible cracking sound, the enormous club broke completely through the wall, sending rocks flying in all directions and causing the soldiers on top to go flying.

The Zylin monk leaped high out of the way, and Basil rolled quickly to his right, unscathed by the attack.

But the damage was done. The surrounding goblins cheered and began pouring into the city walls. Now there were two holes in the wall in different sections—and although this one was much smaller than the one with the chasm, it was worse because goblins had ground to cross on.

As the goblins poured in, archers directed a volley of arrows at them, which dropped some, but many continued into the city.

Dozens of soldiers quaffed their potions and drew swords, plowing into the goblins and holding them from entering further.

The nearby Zylin monk leaped down to help, and the other two came running over. They were formidable and kept the goblins from pushing into the city, but there were hundreds behind them.

Meanwhile, at the other much-larger gap in the wall, Ryder focused on repairing it while the attacking wizard simultaneously filled the earth underneath. Goblins stood prepared to enter as soon as they had ground to walk on— which would be soon.

A fireball flew from the wizard directly toward Ryder. He stopped what he was doing and ran out of the way. A nearby Zylin monk leaped and held his hands up. As the fireball came near, he rotated his body around and moved his hands as if catching the fireball from a distance. The fireball flew around him and changed course, flying straight into the goblins below.

Another fireball flew, followed by another, and Ryder continued to run to safety. As he ran, stones lifted to block his path, and he tripped. Rolling, he felt the castle wall caving in underneath him, swallowing him whole.

He panicked and scrambled away, instinctively causing the earth to reverse its movement and grow strong beneath him again. Stones broke from the wall and flew toward him. They flew from multiple directions all at once. He dodged and rolled, with no time to think of a counterattack.

A rock flew into his arm with huge force.

"Enough!" he shouted, wincing at the big blow.

He lifted his hands and the stones around him immediately formed a protective shell that blocked the other flying rocks. He breathed in relief, but then the shell began to tighten and enclose him further. Wide-eyed, he created an opening and dashed free as it collapsed into a pile of rubble behind him.

His mind raced as more rocks flew at him. He had to figure something out! But with a wizard so utterly powerful, what could he do?

$$* * *$$

In between the two gaps in the wall, Amber was completely focused on preventing the white wizard on her flying horse from sending her deadly barrage of spears into people. The wizard was powerful, but Amber somehow knew when the spears were coming and was able to ask them to continue their quick growth into harmless, fluffy trees.

When archers tried to shoot the flying wizard down, the arrows bounced off a protective field. She flew down the wall, then back again toward Amber. When she got closer, Amber was able to prevent more of the attacks.

The white wizard was quick, but Amber felt herself gaining in speed as she learned the woman's patterns. Then suddenly the woman turned to stare at Amber. Even from that distance, Amber felt the gaze pierce through her. The wizard somehow knew.

The woman shouted, "Formido!" and suddenly everyone within hearing range, including Amber, felt deep, intense terror well up from within. Everyone was already crouched or hiding, and now they cried out and trembled. Amber cringed and hid behind the battlements.

The wizard flew toward Amber and threw dozens of seeds at her. Amber realized she couldn't stop all of them at once, so she caused the spears strewn about from earlier attacks to grow quickly into a blocking tree, then turned and squatted under her protective cape.

The spears were intense, but only two made it past her makeshift tree wall and bounced off her enchanted cape. It still

hurt, though, and Amber winced. She definitely would have some bruises.

The woman grabbed another handful of seeds and flew even closer.

Amber stiffened. The seeds in the woman's side bag! She saw them in her mind's eye. She felt them.

Despite the terrible fear she felt, she mustered the courage to cause the seeds to grow all at once. The bag bulged and took on weight, causing the flying horse to flap awkwardly. The wizard unloosed the bag, letting it fall to the ground, then threw her last handful of seeds at Amber.

Amber had just enough time to add a few more branches to the blocking tree and turn again with her cape against the oncoming rush of spears.

Like before, the tree blocked many of the spears, but this time four more landed solidly on her. If she hadn't been wearing that protective cape and special dwarven armor, she surely would have died.

As it was, she got the wind knocked out of her. The pain was intense, and the deep fear she felt made her want to disappear. There was no hope in taking on a wizard that powerful. Only the hope for survival. She lay down for a minute to catch her breath. At least she'd prevented the woman from continuing her horrible attack.

$$* * *$$

To Amber's left, the battle of the earth elementalists was fierce. The chasm was nearly filled in, and Ryder was hiding from an ongoing fireball attack, which prevented him from being much help. It looked like the goblins were going to overtake the city! Desperation filled the hearts of the humans on the city walls. But then, a whistle pierced the air.

Just over thirty elves on dracos came into view, flying toward them from the mountains. As they came into range, the elves fired arrows into the goblins and swooped toward the spots where the wall was cracked and the battling most fierce.

The elves had fantastic aim. Dozens of goblins dropped to the ground. One elf rode behind another with a scepter, which sent out a cone of cold that enveloped three goblins, freezing them in their tracks.

Under the hobgoblins' leadership, the goblins fell back into a protective formation, raised shields, and fired their crossbows at the elves in return. The elves flew around them, finding the occasional opening to shoot through and pick off another goblin.

Hippogriffs and griffins shifted from circling over the wall to engaging with the flying elves. The battle was fierce and chaotic, with volleys of arrows spewing in all directions as the soaring creatures flew circles around each other.

A surge sounded. At the crack in the wall near Basil, a hundred ogres came hurtling along the ranks of the much-shorter goblins, heading straight through the guarding soldiers like they were children.

The ogres were twice the height of the men, green, and well-armed with clubs, axes, maces, and spiked balls on chains that cracked into the tiny humans like one might swat a fly.

Four of the monks pulled themselves away from the other fighting and gathered to focus on the ogres. It was dazzling to watch. Fighting with all their might, the monks moved out of the way, sometimes dodging completely and sometimes using the force of the blow back on the attacking ogre or on to another one. They also leaped to match the height of the ogres and moved so quickly that the ogres couldn't connect any blows.

Occasionally a monk would use a force field to prevent an attack—and a few times used blinding light, which slowed down and confused the ogres. They managed to keep the ogres from advancing further into the city, but with a hundred of the creatures, the battle was intense.

Basil couldn't lend a hand. He was too focused on keeping the giant at bay with a tornado. The giant blinked, regaining its sight. With the dragons tied up, and all the attacks they'd tried so far, it felt like this was the only option. His mind raced. He thought of all the other battles he'd had that week. The giant ants. The mikons. The serpent. Each one he'd learned something new. And one thing he'd learned was his first idea was often not the best.

He needed Theo's ideas! But a quick glance showed he was all alone. He would have to come up with his own plan of attack. And he would have to do it soon. He wasn't sure how much longer he could keep up a tornado of that size.

✳ ✳ ✳

On the other side of the wall, the earth elementalist focused again on lifting the earth inside the giant crack, giving Ryder a moment to escape the ongoing barrage of attacks. He crept behind a battlement and sat down, hiding from view, sweating and dirty. He let his breathing calm for a moment and tried to come up with ideas.

A guttural cheer rose from the goblins and Ryder peeked over the gap in the battlement. The ground had risen enough that the first of the goblins entered the city. He panicked. He wasn't going to be able to stop them from entering. He was too slow.

Then, his face lit up. Could he create a crack in the earth of his own? How had that wizard done it?

350

Then he pictured it—there was a big rock formation underneath that met with another one. He could cause them to rub against each other, opening the earth. But would it be in the right spot? Or make their situation worse?

He stood up from his hiding spot, but the opposing wizard spotted him and shot another fireball. With no more monks to protect him, Ryder ducked behind the wall and kept his head down, hoping he wouldn't be too badly burned.

But the fireball fizzled out before it reached him. He glanced up in surprise. Above him flapped a draco with two elves on it. One was silvery white and the other red.

The white elf lit an arrow and sent it into the thick of the goblins pouring into the city. The red elf lifted his hands, and the fiery arrow grew into a large fireball, engulfing the goblins.

Azarel! And just in time.

Another fireball came from the opposing wizard, but Azarel raised his hands, forcing it to squelch into nothing before it could hit Ryder.

The battle raged below him. Goblins surged through the gap in the city wall as soldiers armed with potions of strength protected their home with a vengeance.

It's now or never, Ryder thought. He closed his eyes and felt the earth beneath. There it was. The fissure the other wizard had used to create the big crack in the earth.

If he rubbed the two huge rock plates together, they'd do more damage to the city walls, but the fault-line continued into the field on the other side of the wall, in the middle of the goblins. It wouldn't help with the city wall issue, but it would definitely slow down more goblins from arriving.

Ryder focused, ignoring the fireballs being shot at him, each one fizzling out with Azarel's effort. The earth rumbled and shook. Goblins were thrown to the ground.

Then the earth split, creating a gap much like the first one, only farther from the city walls. Goblins tumbled into the new chasm. The gap grew till it was a solid fifteen yards across.

The goblin army was now split.

However, plenty were still on the side of the city and continued to pour in, barely held at bay by the potion-strengthened soldiers and Zylin monks.

* * *

A few hundred yards along the top of the wall, Amber lay dazed in her protective tree-cage. After a couple of minutes, the fear subsided, and she pushed herself up to a sitting position to look around groggily. Something inside felt like it was damaged from the spears, like a kidney or other organ.

She tried to get to her feet, her eyes crying from the pain. She stayed still and looked around for ideas.

And then, in the distance, a small group of flying creatures came toward the battle. They slowly came into focus.

Kish! It's griffins with riders!

Her heart leaped with joy. Maybe, just maybe, it would be enough to change the tide. The griffins came more fully into view, and behind them something even more exciting: three floating warships!

The elvish ships were blown by an unnatural wind straight above the goblins. Elves scrambled along the decks excitedly. A sparkling dust fell from the ships onto the goblins on the front line. Everywhere the dust landed, the goblins grew confused and stared at one another dumbly.

Some of the ogres were affected as well, and stood amongst themselves awkwardly, dangling their weapons like they didn't know what they were holding.

The dwarves were also effective in their first attack. They swooped low and let loose a volley of crossbow bolts aimed at the taller hobgoblins. Their aim was true, and nearly a dozen of the hobgoblins fell to the ground. The goblins who lost their leaders scrambled away.

The dwarves weaved in and out, dodging the goblins' volley of crossbow bolts as they flew over the horde. One dwarf raised a scepter. A crackling energy gathered around it like lightning, and dark clouds formed over the goblin army. The scepter crackled more, then lightning flashed from the clouds down to the scepter and then further down to the goblins, sending half a dozen of them flying.

In her achiness Amber breathed a sigh of relief. This was going to change the tide of the battle!

She let herself lay back down. Her vision was starting to get blurry. She needed to get to Theo, but the idea of standing seemed like too much.

Maybe I can just rest here for a few minutes, she thought.

Suddenly, the woman dressed all in white was standing above her with an evil smile.

Amber's mind reeled, confused. The white wizard? What's she doing here?

The woman lifted Amber from under her arms and draped her over the pegasus. Then she climbed on and the two of them lifted into the air.

Before Amber blacked out, her mind filled with confusion. This isn't right. This isn't how it's supposed to end. The dwarves and elves are just arriving to save the day. And we're the six from the prophecy. We have to win.

And then the world went dark.

Chapter 28

Ancient Enemies

MIZU STOOD WAITING at a small building as the sound of battle raged on the wall. Finally, one of the captains arrived with a Zylin monk and three other soldiers. They entered the building and went through a hallway to a musty room in the back.

There they lit torches and opened an old wooden door with rusted hinges, which revealed a tunnel and stairs leading downward. Cobwebs were everywhere, and the torches served more than light, burning anything the group might walk into.

The stairs were long and repetitive. Mizu realized she was counting steps, a habit from her youth when she climbed the five-level spiral staircase in the great old tree. She decided to keep counting—it would be nice to know in case she had to return the same way.

At 375, they arrived at a smooth tunnel, which eventually led to actual caves with offshoot passages and twisty catacombs.

The main tunnel was always obvious, though, and they continued in it until they came to a key intersection with two definitive options and a sign. The captain brushed the dust off the sign and read it, then continued through the left passageway.

They walked single file, with the captain in the lead giving advice on obstacles, like "Watch your head here" or "Careful with the big rock in the path."

After a few more minutes, they came to more stairs leading up, then exited through a hidden doorway set in large rocks near the river and emerged into the refreshing warm night air.

The battle raged between them and the city. Down the river, further south, were goblin-like shapes, somewhat visible in the moonlight. The other direction, a small lake with the docks of the city were far downstream to their right.

"Are you ready?" The captain's eyes darted around anxiously.

"Yes." Mizu walked to the river. It was a good eighty yards across. She could control water, but would she be able to do as much as they were asking of her?

She concentrated and the water slowed. A mound of water grew like an enormous bubble. If she could create a dam and release it all at once toward the army, she could flood them. At least, that was the plan.

But Mizu felt another power trying to block her efforts. At first, she was confused. Was there something odd about this river? Then realization sunk in. "There's another mage hindering me. We need to do something."

The Zylin monk shoved her hands into the air, and the darkness of night brightened magically upstream from them. There, a mere 250 yards away, were around fifty goblins and an elf watching them closely. The elf looked quite similar to Mizu, with blue skin and a blue outfit. He had a wand tucked in his belt and a serious look on his face.

As he lifted his arm, a shape emerged from the water. It grew into a creature with arms and a head made entirely of water, till it was a good sixty yards high. It sucked water out of the dam Mizu had been creating, growing taller still.

Then it turned toward Mizu and her five companions, raised a massive water arm, and smashed it toward them.

"Hold your ground!" Mizu shouted, raising her hands protectively. The water parted around them, leaving them completely dry, while flooding the entire countryside, including the tunnel they'd come through.

This wizard is stronger than me, Mizu realized with fear. Their whole plan depended on her sneak attack from the other side of the fighting. But how could she stop a wizard with this kind of power? Her mind raced as she thought of options.

The captain was saying something, but it didn't sink in. He stood in front of her, then crouched down to look her in the eyes and held her shoulders. "What should we do?"

"That mage is too powerful. I can't do the water attack with him there."

The captain stood. "This would be a good time to drink those potions."

The soldiers obediently pulled the small vials out and drank. They instantly looked refreshed and energized. Mizu watched them, wondering why she hadn't thought to take a potion with her. Then she had second thoughts: Would it hinder my magic? I bet it would.

The ring! I do have a little extra magic. She put it on and smiled. She felt as light as a feather.

The captain pulled out his sword. "We face a wizard and dozens of goblins, but remember, we fight for our homes and our families. They fight for evil. This is our fight to win. Mizu—keep us safe from that wizard's attacks."

And at that, he turned and ran toward the goblins, the other four running after him. Mizu took up the rear, watching the water for another attack.

Sure enough, the water regrouped itself, and another wave came pouring down toward them. It was challenging to prevent the attack while she was running, but the lightness of her feet helped. She created a bubble of air around them—a water-free zone that kept completely dry.

The water flooded the land, slowing down the soldiers' run. Mizu leaped ten yards into the air and twirled her hands, causing the water in their path to clear away. A crossbow bolt went flying, just missing her.

That was close! she thought. I'll have to be careful leaping till the goblins are occupied.

The goblins drew swords and axes, then ran head-on toward them with a raging war cry. The first goblins fell instantly, with the soldiers feeling extra strength from the potions. The Zylin monk was a flurry of action, avoiding attacks and redirecting them from one goblin to another.

But the elven wizard pulled out his wand and caused the grass around their feet to grow and twine, slowing them down.

Mizu felt the wand in her belt and wondered if she should do anything with it. She only knew two illusion spells—one could disguise her to look like something else. The other was shooting out a spray of color—not terribly useful in the heat of battle.

She ran and leaped toward the other elf, then suddenly began moving very slowly, even in midair. What happened? A desperate glance saw him pointing his wand at her. It was a hopeless attack.

Then, as she looked at the wizard more closely, her heart dropped. "Dad?"

The elf lowered his wand and frowned.

Mizu slowly landed next to him and turned. Both elves stared into the other's eyes as the goblins and four humans battled fiercely nearby. They watched each other for a few moments, as if time stood still.

The wizard broke the silence. "Mizu."

A million thoughts raced through her mind. A thousand unanswered questions. Which one to ask first? She folded her arms. "Why?"

"Nobody understood." He held his hands out, speaking in elvish. "I tried explaining to your mother a dozen times. And the elders. This work we're doing—it can really change things for the better."

"What work?"

"You were too young to understand when I left. But look at you now. The work we're doing is going to bring peace and prosperity to this world. This war is like growing pains. It'll be over soon, and then we can take the next step."

"What could possibly be so important to leave your family behind?" Mizu's eyes flared.

"It's an ancient magic. I've seen the spell, Mizu. It's been done before. At that time, it brought the greatest abundance and peace in all our history. But it requires sacrifice."

"You seriously think leaving your five-year-old daughter and the rest of the family behind and joining a goblin war that's killing innocent people is somehow going to help this world?"

Her cheeks flushed red-purple.

Her dad remained calm. "I know it's hard to understand. I didn't at first. But the White Queen convinced me over time. It all makes perfect sense."

"Listen to you! You're just as messed up as Mom says you are. You're talking nonsense and telling me it's all logical. What happened to you?"

She stepped closer and wagged a finger at him. "You abandoned me. And after ten years, the first time I see you is out here on the battlefield trying to kill me! You don't belong in my life. You're a horrible person and I never want to see you again!"

He frowned and nodded. "I deserve that. But I hope I can convince you one day to understand." He looked around at the nearby fighting. The goblins were down to their last dozen, ringed in a protective circle with a hobgoblin directing them. Only one human soldier lay on the ground, for the dozens of fallen goblins.

He sighed. "I'm going to leave now. I don't want to hurt you. Please think about what I'm saying. The more you learn, the more you'll understand. Look into *Arellium Mardicum*. You might be surprised."

Turning toward the remaining goblins, he lifted his wand and said a few words. The humans suddenly fell to the ground as if blown by a big wind—while the goblins were blown in the opposite direction. He gave a signal to the hobgoblin, and they retreated upriver.

"I'm glad you're alive, Mizu, and following the way of the mage. I hope to see you again in better circumstances." And with that, he turned and disappeared into the dark night.

Mizu stood fuming. She wanted to pursue him, to say something more. But her feet remained planted on the ground.

The monk and three soldiers rose to their feet and looked around in the darkness, spotting her.

"Are you ok?" The captain was splattered with goblin blood and looked tired.

"Yes. I'm fine." She watched the darkness where her dad had disappeared.

"Shall we continue with our plan?"

She looked out over the battle. The fighting was still fierce. She had no time to dwell on her feelings. She needed to help her friends.

✳ ✳ ✳

Basil watched the giant with pursed lips. It was one thing to do some tricks with air—another entirely to hold back a forty-foot giant from demolishing a city wall. But what else could he do?

He watched the dwarf with the scepter send lightning bolts into hobgoblins. Then, as if reading his mind, the dwarf circled the giant and the large tornado holding it back.

The scepter glowed and crackled again, and a bolt of lightning struck the giant directly in the chest. The giant reeled back, stunned.

Basil felt his chest tighten. If there was ever an open opportunity, this was it. He took a deep breath and leaped off the city wall, using the air to slow his descent. He landed and sprang into action, sprinting toward the giant with his short sword drawn.

The sword glowed bright orange, and goblins ran toward him to attack. But Basil had an intense focus. The goblins were blown back, pushed by a tremendous gust of wind, and Basil had an open channel to get to the giant.

Propelled by the wind, he ran faster than humanly possible and, in a matter of seconds, arrived at the giant without a scratch.

A large rock with a good vantage point was nearby, so he scrambled up, breathing heavily as the giant blinked its eyes back into focus. The giant noticed him and let out a fierce low-pitched growl, eyes glowing intense red.

Hundreds of surrounding goblins stepped back, watching. The sounds of battle diminished in their vicinity. Time felt like it slowed down.

Basil took a deep breath. No time to wait. The giant was still recovering from the lightning. Now or never.

"Yaaaah!" Basil leaped off the rock and dashed forward. The giant took a step forward and swung its enormous club. Basil leaped high into the air, far above the club and toward the giant's now-exposed side. He landed on the side of its boot, and with a single bound went flying into the air again, landing on the skins around the giant's waist.

The giant dropped its club and smashed down at Basil with its free hand. Anticipating the blow, Basil leaped into the air and was brushed by the huge hand. He went flying into the air but didn't land on the ground. Instead, he hovered in front of the giant, his glowing short sword at the ready.

Time slowed further. Basil watched the giant's body, anticipating its next move. The creature swung at him again with its clumsy fist, and Basil lifted up to the right, grabbing onto the giant's knuckle as it swept past. Then, using the momentum from the giant's arm, he allowed himself to be tossed high into the air.

The giant squinted at him, a little speck disappearing into the darkness outside of the monks' magical light. Basil peaked, focused in, and dove headfirst toward the giant's chest—with his glowing sword leading the way, like a shooting star on its way to the ground.

Before the giant had time to react, Basil hurtled into its chest, plunging his short sword all the way in, straight into the heart.

Time stopped. Every eye for hundreds of yards watched as the giant looked down at the tiny prick of a sword sticking out of its chest, a young lad hanging from it. It stared at Basil in shock, then its eyes glazed over, and it toppled backward.

Goblins who had been watching in stunned silence suddenly scrambled to get out of the way. Many of them weren't fast enough and were crushed.

Basil stayed on the giant's chest holding his sword. He pulled it out just as the giant landed.

When the dust settled, Basil realized what had happened. He looked down at the giant in awe and gave an astonished chuckle. Did he really just slay a giant?

The dwarf with the scepter swooped by and landed his griffin next to him on top of the giant's chest. Basil shook his head to clear his thoughts. There still was much to do.

He spoke quickly. "We have a water wizard by the river over there! You can use your lightning with the water. We need to work with her."

The dwarf spoke no words but nodded and put his gloved hand out. Basil took the hand and was pulled up behind him. The griffin instantly took to the sky again and flew toward the river. Basil instinctively urged the wind to change course to get there more quickly.

He scanned the glistening water in the dark. Where was Mizu? She had to be there somewhere. He saw goblins further to the south. Then he spotted her. There was some magical monk-light as well as a few people.

They circled once, then landed next to Mizu.

Basil waved her over. "This dwarf can create lightning. Can you create a sea of water to douse the goblin army?"

"Yes." Mizu set her jaw. "I'll do it. It'll take me a couple of minutes."

She turned toward the water and began creating another water dam, like the one she'd created before. Basil patted the dwarf, and they took to the skies again. As they flew above the army, he marveled at how the fighting seemed so small from above, although thousands of goblins and over half of the ogres remained.

Flames lit up the sky—some caused by fireballs from a standoff between Azarel and the other wizard at a large opening in the wall. Others were from fire above them, a duel between two dragons in the sky.

Mizu concentrated and poured all her energy into the mounting pillar of water. It was a critical moment, but she felt more capable than ever. The pillar kept growing till it was eighty yards tall, then all at once it was released onto the plains.

The initial wall of water surged into the goblins, causing the closest ones to lose their footing and fall. The remaining water flowed over the vast plain, dousing half the army with a few inches.

Basil shouted at the dwarf, "Now! Strike lightning now!"

The dwarf's scepter crackled, then a bolt of lightning struck down right in the center of the goblin army. Hundreds of goblins standing in the water near the lightning fell to the ground. Even goblins hundreds of feet away were visibly jolted by the electricity. They looked around with wild eyes.

Some of them turned and ran back the way they'd come, knocking into the braver ones on their way. The dwarf holding the scepter was growing visibly fatigued and switched the scepter to his other arm.

The other dwarves and elves flew around Basil's griffin, protecting them from the other flying creatures. Two griffins fought in the air nearby—the dwarf on one of them hanging on for dear life. Another dwarf shot a crossbow bolt into the attacking griffin, and it dropped to the ground.

Mizu continued to make the river flow onto the battlefield, and another crackling sound began. More goblins turned and fled. A second bolt of lightning hit the water, sending a shock through the goblins.

Again, all the goblins within a few hundred feet dropped to the ground, and the ones further out tensed up.

Even the goblins on the far side of the battlefield realized something was going on. The fighting remained fierce for a moment, then slowed down as the goblins stopped to watch the thousands of their cohort on the south side run around in confusion.

The dwarf sent another bolt of lightning in a different section, knocking down a hundred goblins and shocking hundreds more.

The soldiers on the wall cheered. The lightning attack was powerful, but with thousands of goblins far from the water, would it be enough to stop the entire army?

$$* * *$$

With a queue of injured people that continued to grow, Theo stayed focused on healing for close to an hour. The other doctors of the city had set up a spot safe from stray arrows and other projectiles, but close enough so people could be dragged or carried to them quickly.

Every injury he saw was serious—they were giving him the worst: huge gashes, torn limbs, battered bodies. Over the course of an hour, the ring was taking longer and longer to heal than it used to, as it slowly started to use up its power.

Theo threw up, then pushed through. It was a hot night and bugs circled the bodies of those laying there. He instinctively used his powers to keep the bugs off himself.

His mind began to wander. Is this really what I should be doing? I know my ring can heal, but I have my own powers. And from the feel of it, the ring will lose all its power completely in another hour if I keep doing this. If I were playing Castles right now, I'd let a few soldier pieces die and take the offense.

As if waking from a dream, he pulled himself away, then stood and looked around, analyzing his situation afresh. As usual, he was playing it safe while his friends were out there doing the dangerous work.

A wounded woman hobbled past him, and his heart ached, wanting so badly to help her. He tore his gaze away. It hurt to let her pass by. But if he could prevent even more injuries from happening, that was the better path.

Shouting and clashing metal came from the wall. The general hum of thousands of goblins could still be heard on the other side. People ran wildly through the city streets, trying to help in whatever way they could.

There was a bright flash and a crackle of thunder, then a cheer went up from the wall. Theo walked up the stairs cautiously. A mass of rocks came flying and battered the buildings to his left. He clenched his jaw and kept on till he got a view from the top, then quickly took in the entire battle.

He calculated how far the water could go. This was probably it—covering about half the goblin army to his right.

Another attack of large rocks came flying over the wall from his left. The goblins on that side were still attacking.

The elvish warships were circling above the goblins. Their dust attack had apparently run out, and although effective, it wasn't enough to stop the entire horde.

Were there any large numbers of animals around he could work with? He took a deep breath and sensed the area. No big flocks of birds, besides some crows scavenging. There were some horses, of course, and other domesticated animals. He sensed the dracos and griffins flying above the fight.

And then he realized . . . the insects!

There were millions of insects everywhere. He focused on the ones nearby, and they obediently lifted and hovered in front of him, waiting for his command. He gave a little smile.

It was his turn now.

He closed his eyes, sensing the insects as far as he could, all the way down to the river. Then he asked them to work as one and attack.

Swarms of bugs arose from seemingly nowhere and surrounded thousands of goblins, getting into eyes and biting at every piece of exposed skin. Even the ogres slowed down their attack as bugs blinded them.

Theo poured all his energy into asking every bug he could find to attack.

Bees awoke from their slumber and dive-bombed victims. Spiders crawled out from under rocks and up legs, looking for a place to bite. Mosquitos and flies and no-see-ums swarmed and bit mercilessly.

Goblins dropped swords, stumbled, bumped into each other, slapped at skin, rubbed eyes. The wizard stopped his fireball attack and slapped at his neck, then turned and disappeared.

A few bugs would have stopped the fight for a moment, but millions of bugs proved to be the final thing needed. Against this new attack the goblins turned and retreated.

The entire city of Lugo cheered. Theo blinked in shock. His last-minute idea seemed like it would tip the tide to win the battle. He waited for a counterattack, but none came. They had really done it. At least for now. Thousands of goblins lay on the ground, and the rest were retreating into the darkness.

Theo looked up. The two dragons continued to grapple above and covered the moon for a moment, their silhouettes revealing a fierce encounter. He felt thankful for Crodor but worried for the dragon's safety.

Then he turned his gaze to his friends. Where was Amber? His mind raced anxiously, a hundred bad possibilities playing out.

He went to the section of the wall where he'd last seen her and walked up to the captain there. "Have you seen Amber?"

The soldier grimly gazed over the dark battlefield at the retreating goblins. "Taken. That white wizard on a pegasus took her. We could do nothing. The wizard had a protective field around her, and our arrows bounced off uselessly. I'm sorry." He continued to stare across the field.

Theo panicked. He searched the area mentally for animals. Hundreds of crows were pecking at the dead bodies, and he called to them. They lifted and hovered attentively.

Find Amber! Go search the goblin camp. He pictured what she looked like, then sent them off. The crows cawed and fluttered into the darkness.

Theo pulled on his sleeve and watched them disappear. Oh, Amber, where are you?

Chapter 29

A Two-Hundred-Year Grudge

AMBER AWOKE WITH A START, confused. Where am I?

She lay on a mat on an intricate carpet inside a large, deluxe tent. To her left was a plush bed with four posts and a canopy draped over it. Next to it sat a few ornate chests and an exquisitely crafted wardrobe. Two human soldiers wearing black leather armor and black capes stood at the entrance, resting their hands on long jagged swords. To her right, her backpack and weapons were lying nearby on an ornate shelf.

Her entire body ached, and she felt like her insides were on fire. She tried to remember the last thing she'd seen. The white wizard taking her. She blinked away the confusion she felt, and struggled to sit up, managing to get onto one elbow.

"That was some creative fighting out there," a woman's voice said behind her.

With great effort, Amber turned and looked at the woman who sat at an elaborately designed wooden table. She wore an elegant, flowing white outfit, matching her pale skin and pure white hair. Her eyes were entirely black and seemed to reach into Amber's soul. She looked ghost-like.

Amber tried to guess the woman's age—was the hair white from age? Perhaps. But she had very few wrinkles, like someone in her forties.

Amber felt confused looking at her. At the same time, every wound she had from the battle was on fire.

"You must feel terrible." The woman smirked. "Let me help with that so you can focus." She lifted a wand and said, "Restorivo."

Amber's body felt warm and tingly, and the pain subsided. Healing coursed through her body, removing the bruises even faster than Theo's ring. She breathed deeply and stood. "Why did you take me?"

"For two hundred years we've waited for the right moment. And then what causes me the most trouble? A human girl." The woman spoke in a regal sort of way, like Amber imagined a queen would talk. She had a strong accent, but Amber had no idea from where.

The woman shook her head. "Not that it really matters. We only lost some goblins and giants." She laughed. "Which is probably better for all of us, am I right?" She gave Amber a knowing look. "But still, you certainly are an annoyance."

Amber kept silent, staring at her while trying to figure out what to say.

"I suppose it does make our endeavor a bit more interesting—having a real foe. Kind of like last time."

"Last time?" Amber pulled on her hair, confused. She felt her energy returning, and with it, her attention.

"Pish-posh. You know perfectly well what I'm talking about. I've read your mind, you know." She wagged her finger.

Amber blinked. Remember not to think about too much.

"A good idea." The woman straightened her robes. "And one that sometimes works. But it does take years of practice, and I'm certain you haven't had that!" She gave a little laugh.

She's talking about the Wizard War from two hundred years ago! Was she there? Amber wondered.

"I knew you'd figure it out. You are a smart one, after all." The woman smirked again.

"But how . . ." Amber began, then stopped. She has magic beyond my understanding. That's how.

"Indeed. And now, forgive me for not introducing myself properly. I am Laticia of Westerlye. Queen of the South. I have gathered many wizards and friends for a great plan to improve this world of ours. But for some reason, many have worked against me and continue to do so." She gave a knowing look. "Perhaps not knowing why."

"What do you mean?" Amber asked. "You're the one who brought the goblin army to attack a city!"

"A mere step toward the best scenario for all," she said casually. "The goblins need fighting to feel important. Otherwise, it's not even worth the trouble." She yawned, as if bored. "Such simple, expendable creatures. The real interest lies in their orbs, and of course reclaiming what was unrightfully stolen from us long ago."

I wonder if she's talking about the scepters, Amber thought. Then caught herself. Try not to think.

"The scepters are indeed important to us, yes." The queen twirled a wand between her fingers with great dexterity— never once taking her eyes off Amber. "Although the goblins' earth orbs will prove most critical to our success."

Leaning forward, she pointed her wand at Amber's face. "Now that's the *real* reason we had to get them out of their caves, honestly. But no matter. The fact is, these are wonderful opportunities, you see. Two more of the scepters have appeared today, and now we know where they are. How lovely for us." She sat back in her chair.

"Why are you telling me all this?" Amber asked.

"Because . . . I'm hoping you'll join us."

"Why would I do that?"

"Because you, my dear, whether you know it or not, could play an important role in our plans."

"But why would I join you? I don't understand what you're going to do."

"We . . . are going to rule the world."

Amber shook her head. She wanted to think and figure out what was going on but didn't dare open her mind any more than she already had.

"I'm not interested. I just want peace back in our land."

"What is peace? It's an illusion," Laticia said. "You could rule with us—however you desire. That would be your choice. The peace you had before was full of pain, suffering, and injustice. With the power we could gain, you could easily bring much more comfort and satisfaction to all those you love."

Amber instantly remembered all the loved ones who had suffered or died in her twelve years. There were many, even from her small town. She thought of how Ryder had lost his mom when he was even younger than her. Whatever power this woman was talking about, it was certainly intriguing.

"But I won't be part of any killing. What you're doing is wrong! Why are you causing creatures to turn on us?"

"It's a necessary step to gaining total control. The people do need to know their place—better to let them learn it through some simple fighting with goblins than force it upon them later."

"This is madness," Amber said. She wondered what sort of wisdom Old Mr. Thompson would say right now.

"It is madness not to join us. But no matter. And now, I have some questions for you."

"Like what?" Amber tried guarding her thoughts.

"How many of you are there—you children with powers? Do you have all the elements yet?"

"All the elements?" Amber instantly knew the queen was referring to the prophecy. She'd been thinking that very thing earlier—all six of the elemental powers represented in herself and her five friends.

The queen smiled. "Wonderful. Is that Ryder fellow part of your little group, I assume?"

Amber struggled to block all thoughts from her mind. It seemed like an impossible task. At the mention of Ryder's name, a dozen images of him came up.

Laticia smirked. "Alright, next question. How did you survive my attacks?"

Amber tried not to think of her enchanted cape but couldn't help herself. Laticia pointed her wand at her again. "Revilium."

She removed Amber's cape. "A nice enchantment . . . protection, even from fire." She set the cape on the table, then reached into Amber's side pocket and took out the amulet and white pixie stone.

She lifted the small white stone on a string. "This is a nice little pixie enchantment to find things. Very nice. And this one . . ." She held up the amulet. "obviously breaks our spells of enchantment. I see how you've gotten this far, now."

She glanced back at Amber and removed the necklace with pendant. Amber winced when the necklace was removed, as if her connection to her family left with it. "What's this, then?"

She inspected the small pendant with a picture of a sun on it, then gave a sharp intake of breath and turned to Amber with a start. "How did you come to carry this?"

Amber's brow furrowed as she tried thinking of other things to block the queen's mind-reading ability. She thought of the fight they'd just been in. She wondered how her friends were doing since she'd passed out while the fight was still raging.

"No," the queen looked serious. "I'm asking you a question. Where did you get this pendant?"

Amber gritted her teeth. It was working! She just had to keep thinking of her friends. But could she keep it up? The pendant seemed so important to the White Queen, which made Amber wonder why. Before she knew it, a brief thought about her dad mentioning Majestic Rose ran through her mind.

"Ah ha! Majestic Rose! I knew it. Are you a descendant of hers? Ah, yes, of course you are. And so, history repeats itself. It is truly a pleasure to meet you, Amber." The queen's mood lightened slightly. "I should have known the most formidable enemy to meet me in all these years would be her descendant."

The queen suddenly grew serious, and her eyes went cold, striking fear into Amber's heart. "I'm afraid I can't allow you to leave now. We're going to need much more time to acquaint ourselves with one another. But first, let's take care of those powers of yours."

She walked over to a chest and pulled out small metal handcuffs, then gestured for Amber to put her hands out. Amber's mind raced, thinking of how she could possibly escape. She backed away, but immediately sensed a large person directly behind her and stopped.

The queen drew closer, and Amber checked over her shoulder. Nobody there. Why did she feel like someone was right behind her? As the cuffs touched her wrists, she tried thinking of other options. No brilliant ideas were forthcoming. She felt the cold steel cuffs clamp onto her wrists. Her face went pale as the power drained from her. It was as if she never had the ability to communicate with plants.

As her energy faded her mind traced all the ways she'd taken her power for granted: Four years old and knowing peace amidst the deep forest, while other kids saw more of the dangers—she'd met the pixies then, the first in her village. Eight years old, she was already giving advice to the farmers to improve their crops tenfold—and everyone trusted her more than their own experience. At ten, the garden she grew at home flourished no matter what pests attacked. Over the last month, her powers had saved her from a fall off a cliff, protected her from a griffin, and helped her take on the White Queen. And then there were her new conversations with the trees while she dreamed—they'd only just begun. And it was all gone.

Her heart seized up. Like she was close to death, but somehow still alive. She felt tears welling up in her eyes and closed them. Breathing deeply, she firmed herself and stared at Laticia. Be strong, she thought.

The White Queen patted her shoulder. "Don't be sad, my dear. Look, as a sign of good faith, ask me any question and I'll answer it."

She waited till her heart calmed down. A few big questions ran through her mind. Each one she discarded. Don't ask why she's doing the war, she already said why, and it made no sense. Maybe ask about the scepters? No, too obscure. How about something to do with the phoenix? That's what got me into all of this in the first place.

She cleared her throat. "I want to know why you sent a phoenix to burn my village."

The queen raised her eyebrows. "That's a good question, indeed. Impressive. And you assume I'm the one who sent the phoenix, which is not entirely wrong, since I did send Lucio on that errand."

She paused and Amber thought of the dark wizard they'd encountered a month earlier.

The queen stopped twirling her wand. "Are you the one who killed him?" Her gaze was penetrating.

Amber tried to clear her mind, but with the handcuffs and the tiredness from an incredibly long day, she couldn't help but remember the wizard burning up in flames. It had been the most significant day of her life, working together with her friends and the phoenix.

The queen tapped the wand on the table lightly in thought. "I see. You are more powerful than even I had assumed. That is not a small feat."

Amber puzzled. "Powerful? But I have no power compared to you."

"Power isn't just about waving wands and controlling elements. It's about people. That's where you're most dangerous, little child." She waved her hand, as if passing the thought. "Anyway, enough of that. I promised an answer to a question, and you shall get it. We needed to send the pixies off, so they'd expose their secret tower to us. Very boring. And now I have a question for you: how do you know about the prophecy—which prophecies are you aware of?"

Amber wondered if it was worth trying to block her mind at all. She sighed. This wizard was obviously going to get the information from her one way or another. "Sage," she said. "Plus, we found it in a library."

"Ah ha!" Laticia drummed her fingers on the table. "The grumpy old man strikes again! How did he find you?"

"Um . . . We found him, actually."

"Hmmpf." The queen shook her head and gave a tight smile. "The wizard would have wanted to be found, obviously. He's a mastermind far greater than you know. Not someone I would trust, if I were you."

Amber's mind raced. Sage? A mastermind not to be trusted? It sounded ridiculous . . . and yet. This woman was being completely open, and obviously could have killed her at any moment but was politely sitting at the table in conversation. Was there more going on than Sage had mentioned? What did the White Queen mean when she said there's more than one prophecy? What more was going on that Sage didn't tell them?

"Enough." The White Queen stood. "You have more questions than you started with. That's good. We'll have plenty of time to get to know one another. Let's pick up this conversation tomorrow. I need to attend to many things."

She snapped her fingers, and one of the soldiers guided Amber out of the tent into the dark night. Even in Amber's tiredness, she had the wherewithal to look around. They were in the middle of the goblin camp that had dingy tents all around, nothing like the queen's regal one.

But far more than goblins surrounded them. Creatures of all sorts moved about—griffins; small dragon-like kobolds; short, furry humanoid creatures; an enormous lion sleeping at the side of the tent; and many more creatures just out of sight.

The soldier called, and a large ogre lumbered over behind them as they walked Amber past many tents toward a rocky hill with trees and a small cave. The soldier gestured, and she reluctantly walked inside. The ogre rolled a large rock over the opening, leaving only a small crack for air. She faintly heard the human and ogre exchange some muffled words.

Amber stumbled on a rock and fell, unable to catch herself because of the handcuffs. The cave was dark and uneven. She tried sensing the trees she knew were nearby but felt nothing. How could she let this happen? Trapped and all her powers blocked. She was empty and lifeless. The mana that always felt like a light within her was completely snuffed out.

She lay on the cave floor feeling the weight of the situation as it sunk in. Not only did she have no idea how her friends were doing, but she was stuck, maybe forever. The darkness and cold seeped into her bones, and she shivered. Was this the end? Was the prophecy really about her—or someone else?

In silence, she listened to the loud noises of the camp. It sounded like more goblins were arriving, and she wondered if that meant Lugo had won. At first, she felt encouraged, but then wondered what difference it would make for her.

There had to be something she could do. She reached out her sense to the nearby trees again. Nothing. She looked around. It was just a shallow cave with nothing else in it.

"Can you hear me?" she called through the crack of air.

Silence. She called again. "Hello. Are you there?"

A low, guttural voice sounded on the other side. "I not talk to girl prisoner. Go sleep."

Amber's mind raced. *The ogre is my guard. Do I know anything about ogres?* Her heart dropped. *Ogres are simple creatures, like goblins. Who could reason with that?*

If the goblins were returning, that meant her friends had somehow figured out a way to turn the war. But how long before they'd realize she was gone?

What will the White Queen do with me? She ran her finger along the rugged cave wall, scraping it uncomfortably. It felt good to still feel things. She clenched her jaw till it hurt, then released. Getting down on her knees, she felt along the base of the cave till her fingers felt raw.

The White Queen must be crazy. How can anyone seem so normal in a conversation about killing people in war? And she can mess with minds. She could read my mind, for sure. She also made me think someone was behind me. What if she's messing with me right now, somehow?

She lay down on the cold cave floor. There was an uncomfortable lump under her right hip, but she ignored it.

If I'm really one of the six in the prophecy, I'll get out of this. But am I? She imagined Sage. The peculiar wizard had got her thinking she was important. Am I too young and naïve? What if all this time I've been wrong? If I were playing Castles, this would be the move before I lost. But in Castles, when you lose, you just reset the board and try again. Not in real life. Not this time. No way to start again.

She thought of her family back in Seabrook, and the time she'd tried so hard to win the archery contest. She'd practiced for hours—every day for weeks—and her brother Patrick still won. He was just naturally so good at it, where she had to work hard. Her fingers had bled, and she'd poured in every extra ounce of strength to win, but it still wasn't enough. Was she always destined to lose, no matter how hard she tried?

She felt a chill run through her body. How could it be so cold here and so warm outside? She wished for her enchanted cape—not for its magical properties but for its warmth.

A slight scraping noise came from the entrance. She quieted and focused. With her part-elf eyes, she picked up a bird darting through the crack above the large stone.

She sat up. "Hello, little bird. What brings you here?"

The bird stood on the large rock and looked around. She walked closer and saw it was a crow. "Did Theo send you?" She hoped desperately. The crow didn't make a sound, but after a moment it turned and went back the way it came.

"Wait!" Amber called. "Tell Theo where I am! Are you a friend?" She suddenly had a chilling thought. "Or are you from the White Queen, checking on me?" The thought of the queen having not only an ogre and countless other nasty creatures guarding her but also crows to check on her cut to the heart.

She stood in the darkness. A tear ran down her cheek. Then another. She went to the back of the cave and sat down hugging her knees.

"Theo, I hope that bird was a friend of yours." She called into the darkness. "I'm ready for one of your bright ideas."

Before she drifted off to sleep, her resolve firmed. Even if it wasn't a bird from Theo, she wasn't dead—she was a prisoner. And even prisoners can have hope, as long as the sun rises the next day.

Chapter 30

A Stealthy Plan

THEO STOOD WAITING ON THE WALL for what felt like an eternity. Most of the goblins had retreated, but there were many—like those inside the city walls—who kept attacking, oblivious to the rest of the army.

Even worse were the ogres who cared not one bit that the goblins had gone. Barely held back by the warrior monks and the bug attack, they continued to press further into the city.

The crows had been gone for twenty minutes, long enough to get to the goblin camp. But Theo couldn't sense them from that great distance. Any other animals that could help?

He sensed a griffin nearby who had an open mind. He beckoned it gently. The dwarf riding it yelled in surprise as the griffin changed course and glided to Theo. As it landed, the dwarf yelled angrily at it in his native tongue.

Theo walked up calmly. "I called her over. We need to do a stealth mission to rescue our friend Amber."

"Amber the human?" The dwarf was suddenly interested.

"Yes. She was taken by the wizards. We need to rescue her, if possible. But we can't be seen."

With a serious expression, the dwarf offered his hand to Theo who mounted the griffin behind him, then they took to the skies.

"Kish be my name. What be your plan?"

"I'm Theo—and I don't have a plan yet. But I have other friends. This way." He pointed toward Ryder on the far side of the wall.

Ryder was busy rebuilding the wall while he listened to Azarel. Below them, the last of the goblins were trapped on their side of the crack, battling soldiers.

The griffin swooped down and landed next to them.

Theo was in a panic. "Amber's been taken by a wizard! We have to save her."

Ryder whirled to look at the goblin camp, a distant dark mass of moving shapes and flames. "Bring the others here. We need a plan."

Theo jumped up behind Kish and flew toward the river. His stomach twisted painfully. Oh Amber! Please be ok.

✳ ✳ ✳

Soon after, the five elementalists stood looking at the goblin camp, lost in thought. The sounds of battle rang out below them, but they felt distant compared to their main focus.

Basil spoke first. "You sent crows, but we can't just wait around for them to come back. She could be in serious danger. Why would the white wizard take her?"

"I agree," Ryder said. "We should go to the goblin camp to find her."

"But they'll kill us, for sure." Theo wrung his hands.

Azarel spoke calmly. "They've just fled a battle where many have died and there's chaos. If there's any time we thought to go there, now would be it. We have allies here with flying creatures. We could be there in moments."

"Aye." Kish stood behind them, stroking a short sword strapped to his side. "In the darkness me thinks you could be slipping right in. If ye wear cloaks to disguise yourselves, how would they know it's you?"

"He's right," Mizu said. "Let's get some cloaks and see if we can get close enough to find her. If we're disguised, in the dark, we have a chance. And if your crows have found her, they'll tell you, right?"

"Yes, yes." Theo fiddled with his fingers anxiously. "But what if they find out we're there? We'll be trapped just like her. Those wizards are powerful—and surrounded by an army. How would we get out?"

Kish patted Theo's shoulder. "We can circle the skies nearby. Send us a signal, and we'll come for you."

Basil patted Theo's other shoulder. "The dwarf is right. We have to act now, Theo. Most of us can use our powers to alert them to pick us up. We can't plan four moves ahead on this one . . . We just need to get over there and do this." He glanced at Mizu, who nodded slowly. "No rushing in. But we can't take our time either. We'll work together. All five of us."

Theo took a deep breath. "You're right, Basil. Everyone get a ride and a cloak. We'll leave at once."

✳ ✳ ✳

The flight took only fifteen minutes with the dwarves manning the griffins. Azarel and Mizu were hesitant to ride with dwarves, but Theo pleaded with them. "Look, the elves and dracos are all busy right now, helping take care of the remaining goblins. You'll just have to set aside your differences for now. Amber is more important."

Azarel was particularly unhappy about riding behind a dwarf, but he swallowed hard and agreed. "Just this once. For Amber's sake."

Thousands of goblins were crossing the fields and pouring into their camp, so the group stayed high, out of sight and out of crossbow range. They were surprised to see another large flying shape in the dark ahead of them—an enemy griffin above the camp.

Theo focused. How many more were there? He instantly sensed dozens of flying creatures, not just griffins, also hippogriffs and gargoyles. Below he sensed hundreds of crows flying around the camp. He tried to perceive if any had found Amber. The crows were smarter than other birds, but their minds constantly wandered. He wondered if they even remembered the mission he'd given them.

Persuading the crows to refocus their search, he had Kish circle over the enormous camp, blending in with the other flying creatures.

After the third loop, Kish called over his shoulder. "The south side of the camp be the best for us to land, by my estimation. Less activity. Pull up your hood."

Theo waved and pointed to the group to follow. All the riders pulled hoods over their heads. In the darkness, the dwarves could have passed for small goblins.

When they landed just outside the camp, the five dismounted. Basil turned to the dwarves. "If you have to leave this spot, remember our most obvious signals—a flame that reaches high, a whirlwind, or Theo will just find you and call your steeds over." He turned to the others. "Let's do this. Theo, which way?"

Theo focused on the hundreds of crows again. Each one was treating what they saw as important, making it hard for Theo to know if any of them had seen Amber. He did sense that the crows in the center of the camp were completely surrounded by goblins, whereas on the camp's east side there was more variety. Probably a better chance.

Pointing northeast, he said, "I don't know for sure, but this seems like a better direction than the rest."

Basil stood, fists on his hips. "Now remember, we're not going to sulk around. We have to act like we belong here in case we're spotted, so walk with purpose and with heads held high. But keep your hoods down. If we need to, I think we can hide pretty easily—but let's try to stick together no matter what."

He looked at Theo who was biting his lip. "You've got this, Theo. We'll find her. Let's go."

They walked through the camp, passing occasional goblins and other smaller creatures, like lizard-ish kobolds.

Basil strode up next to Theo. "Any luck?"

"Maybe . . . one crow seems to have come across something different than the others. I think it's someone trapped in a cave."

He altered their course slightly toward a hill on the edge of the camp. As the crow circled him, Theo asked it to go back to the cave, and they followed it.

A giant ogre stood by a rocky hill looking bored.

Theo stopped the group behind a tent and whispered, "There's a cave behind those rocks with a person in it. I'm guessing this ogre is guarding it."

"I can find out pretty quickly," Ryder said, crouching to the ground and putting his hands down. With all the movement around them, he couldn't feel any vibrations from a person inside a cave, but he could sense the way the rocks were formed.

"That large rock can be rolled aside to get to a cave. We need to get that ogre out of the way."

Theo sent the crow over, and it landed on the giant rock, then disappeared into a crack and reappeared a moment later. Theo smiled. "It must be her. There's someone in there—a human."

They watched the ogre for a minute. Basil scratched his head. "How do we get it to move away from there without drawing attention to us?"

Theo looked around the area and sensed the animals nearby. There were griffins, hippogriffs, even a pegasus, but the enchantment blocked his connection. However, there were other animals, a couple of dogs in particular, that he connected with.

Azarel spoke first. "There's no one around. We could attack it, perhaps. I think fire might draw too much attention. But if anyone has other ideas, let's hear them."

"There are a couple of dogs I can ask to come over." Theo shrugged. "Maybe they can distract it for whatever else we try."

"A distraction. Excellent idea." Mizu was smiling and pulled her wand out. "I'm pretty new to this, but I can create an illusion. I have to work with something—like I could make a dog look like something else. It will only be as realistic as something I've seen for myself."

"Another ogre?" Basil shrugged.

"No. They might want to talk to each other. I can't make it sound like anything, just looks."

Basil tapped his foot. "We're on the right track. But it's not complete. How do we make sure no one else around finds out?"

Theo's eyes lit up. "Hey, you can create clouds, right?"

"Sure," Basil said. "I just have to squeeze the air till they appear. Depends on how humid it is. But it feels pretty muggy tonight. I bet I can make some nice clouds."

"Okay, then I've got a plan."

* * *

Fog drifted in and filled the entire area. To make it more natural, Basil made it as widespread as possible. The fog grew thicker, till the ogre leaning against the boulder was hard to spot.

Then Theo called a dog over. It was tall, lanky, and had long gray fur. Mizu raised her wand and whispered, "Impostro!" A flickering image of Amber suddenly replaced the dog. It looked like Amber from head to toe. The image sputtered and revealed the dog behind, then grew strong.

"This is as good as I can do for now," she said with an apologetic shrug. "I'm new to these things . . . but hopefully in the dark fog, it will work."

The dog, looking like Amber, loped over to the ogre. The ogre suddenly straightened up and gaped at the illusion in surprise. "Gorfal!" it yelled and grabbed at her. She danced back, then turned and ran into the dark. The ogre quickly pursued her, clomping along noisily.

"Quick!" Ryder called and dashed to the boulder. He put his hands on it, and the rock slowly rolled away to reveal a small cave. He peered inside, heart thumping. There, at the back of the cave, barely visible in the dark fog, was a small person lying on the cave floor.

He ran to get a better look. Azarel came behind with a small fire in his hand, revealing what they'd all hoped.

Dirty and with a tear-streaked face, Amber woke up, looking around groggily.

Ryder grinned and scooped her up, giving her a big hug.

She pushed him away and squinted in the dark. "Is it really you, Ryder? She's not messing with me, is she?"

"Yes, it's me, Dreamer. It's really me. All of us. We're all here."

She looked up at the others cramming into the cave with big smiles and her eyes brightened. She turned back to Ryder and gave him a hug back.

Ryder beamed. "Let's get you out of here before that ogre comes back. I'm sure it'll sound an alarm soon now that you're rescued."

Amber's eyes glistened. "I'm not dreaming. You found me." She turned to Theo. "Was it the crows?"

Theo smiled sheepishly. "Yep! They led us right to you."

"I knew it!" Amber smiled with new strength. "I knew you'd come up with some crazy idea." She stood on shaky legs.

When Basil saw her shackles, he pointed. "What are those?"

"They block my powers. I don't feel any connection to the plants at all."

"Wow. How do we get those off?" He looked at them carefully, then guided her out of the cave and into the brush behind the hill. When they were concealed by trees, they stopped to examine the handcuffs.

"Looks like we'll need a key to get them off." Ryder said with a frown.

"Let me try asking these nearby ants to help," Theo said. "Don't move, Amber. This might tickle."

Amber gave a little laugh as dozens of ants crawled up her pant leg and down her arms. They crawled around into the key holes. Theo grew puzzled. "I don't know if I can do this. Ants aren't prone to figuring out puzzles. Although they do work well together. I think there are three pins. I don't think it should be impossible, but it might take me a while."

"We don't have a while," Ryder said. "That ogre is probably already coming back and pretty soon this whole camp is going to be after us. We need to go. Now."

"Well, set off the signal, then," Theo said impatiently. "I can work on this while we're flying."

"Wait!" Amber said. "My things!"

"What do you mean?"

"I can't leave without my things. She took my backpack, weapons, and all of my enchanted items. My cape. The amulet. The rock. And my necklace. At the very least I have to have the necklace. It's important."

"No way. Too dangerous." Ryder shook his head. "The whole camp is going to be after us soon. We can't go back in there."

Amber looked at him with pleading eyes. "It's what landed me in this cave, instead of staying out there. It's been in the family for generations, and apparently my great-great-aunt or something was important to the White Queen way back during the Wizard War. She recognized it and that's when her attitude changed toward me and she said I had to be put in prison. It must be important."

Ryder continued shaking his head. "We just can't risk it. Is it really worth it?"

Basil jumped in. "Well, whatever we decide, let's do it quickly. I still haven't heard that ogre get back yet. But I wouldn't press our luck."

Ryder sighed, then looked at the others who were waiting expectantly. "Well, this will put all our lives in danger. I hope it's as important as you think."

"Thank you, Ryder," Amber said with relief. "I . . . I just don't want to lose everything."

"Come on, silly," Ryder said, tussling her already messy hair. "You won't lose everything. You've got us!" He turned to leave, then paused. "Where are we going? And we'd better figure out a disguise for you, since you don't have a hood."

"I can help with that." Mizu raised her eyebrows a few times playfully.

Her spell turned Amber into a goblin—tallish but quite realistic looking. In the dark and fog, they hoped it would be enough.

"How long will this last?" Amber admired her stocky green arms still in handcuffs.

Mizu tapped her wand on her other hand. "It should last ten or fifteen minutes. I think."

"Let's go." Ryder tapped his foot several times.

One of Amber's handcuffs suddenly opened up. "Got it!" Theo grinned and followed behind Amber the goblin. "Just have to get the other one now."

The six friends walked quietly and quickly, Amber leading the way toward the first tents. The fog started to thin, so Basil concentrated, causing it to thicken again.

They saw a light ahead and continued toward it, passing by a campfire with four goblins sitting around it. The group walked forward, only giving sideways glances to remain less obvious.

Amber suddenly stopped. "No. I don't think this is right. All these tents are starting to look the same. I need to find the queen's tent. Basil, I know we need this fog and all, but can you perhaps thin it and fly up a bit to see if you can spot it. It's larger, cleaner and with fancier doors than all the other tents. It's probably close by."

Basil frowned and turned to Ryder, who looked unhappy. "Is there another way? Maybe you can remember more."

"Just be quick." She glanced around nervously. "It's important, Basil."

Basil took a deep breath and circled his hands a few times. A small whirlwind formed underneath him, lifting him above the tent. The fog thinned around him. He spun around, then floated gently down to the ground again.

"Ok. It's straight that way. You weren't far off track. Looks like only a few minutes from here."

The fog thickened again as they set off in the right direction toward the center of camp. They passed more goblins, all talking loudly to each other in their guttural language as they poured into the camp from the battle.

In a few moments, Amber and the group walked directly toward dozens of goblins heading in the other direction. One of them saw Amber and raised a hand, saying, "Coshlaw."

Theo stifled a laugh. Amber reminded herself to ask him later what was so funny. For now, she raised her hand in return but dared not speak. The cuff dangled off the hand she raised, so she lowered it quickly.

Luckily, the goblins continued on their way. But Amber's goblin disguise started to flicker. "Mizu, I think the goblin disguise is wearing off. Can you do it again?"

"Yes, but this kind of magic is hard for me. It's sapping my mana more than manipulating water. Let's hope this is the last time we need it." She cast the spell again, and the goblin disguise solidified.

"Let's walk quickly, then." Amber strode purposefully toward the queen's tent.

Theo was close behind her. "Wait, Amber. Hold your hand still while you walk. I think I can get the other hand free if you stop swinging your arm."

"Hey, what was so funny back there?" Amber turned with raised goblin eyebrows.

"Oh. I thought he said coleslaw. Seems like a funny way to greet each other!"

The four humans laughed, breaking the tension in the air. The two elves looked at each other with puzzled expressions and followed behind.

Basil punched Theo in the arm playfully. "Leave it to you, Butterballs, to get us all laughing in the middle of a dangerous mission!"

They made their way toward the White Queen's tent.

Just outside of it, Amber's second handcuff finally fell off. Her goblin eyes lit up. "I feel like myself again! I feel all my power. It's still there. Thank you, Theo!"

"You bet!" He smiled and kicked the handcuffs to the side.

"Not so fast," Ryder said, scooping them up and putting them in his pocket. "We may find these handy later."

They came up to the large, elegant tent with ornate trim around the doors and a triangular flag at the top depicting a lion's head. There were dozens of goblins mulling about in front, two hobgoblins standing guard at the front entrance, and an enormous golden lion sleeping at the side. A human in full armor strode through the goblins toward the entrance. The hobgoblins nodded as he strode past them into the tent.

"This way," Amber whispered, walking them to the backside of the tent. "Careful to not think about stuff. She can read minds."

Ryder suddenly stopped. "Last time I tried sneaking up on her, she knew I was there. We can't go inside. Theo, can you find an animal to do it for us? How about that lion?"

Theo focused. "No, the lion is under a spell. But there are still plenty of crows around." He gazed into the distance, then three crows fluttered in from different directions. They flew around the tent a few times, then hovered in front of him.

"There's no other entrance. That's it. Maybe we can lift it up from the bottom?"

No one had any other ideas, so they quietly lifted the back wall of the tent a tiny crack. Amber and Theo peered inside.

The tent was exactly as Amber had left it, with her things sitting on the table. The queen was standing near the entrance, talking to the human. It was the perfect time to act.

She gestured to Theo, and he lifted the flap slightly more. The crows landed and walked into the tent, then fluttered up to the table, grabbing the different items in their beaks. The cape, backpack, and weapons were far too big, but they were able to lift the amulet, the small pixie rock, and the necklace.

At one point they were worried the queen would turn and notice. She grew loud and forceful. But a quick look showed her pointing at the human assertively, completely wrapped up in her conversation.

The five crows carried the items back and landed at the flap. They snuck back under and dropped each of the items in front of Amber. She put the necklace around her neck and the stone and amulet into pockets. Would the crows be able to bring anything else back on a second trip?

Suddenly there was shouting on the other side of the tent. Their eyes grew wide. They couldn't make out the words, but it sounded like someone was upset. Was Amber's escape finally alerted?

They moved away from the tent and huddled together. Basil was urgent. "What do we do? Should we give the signal here? So near the wizard?"

"No." Amber shook her head. "She's too powerful. We need some distance."

"Let's run for it." Ryder put his hand nervously on the hilt of his short sword. "Let's get as far as we can and send the signal. Look, it's almost morning. They'll spot us for sure, even with Basil's fog."

Suddenly they heard a voice cry out nearby. "There!"

They all turned to look. A human in armor had just rounded the tent and was pointing at them. They instantly took off, Ryder in the lead, running as quickly as they could in between goblin tents.

The man ran behind them in pursuit, and Basil sent a whirlwind, causing him to fly back and roll onto the ground.

"This way!" Ryder called, turning at a tent to avoid a dozen goblins coming back from the battle.

They ran with all their hearts, weaving in and out of tents. At one point, Ryder knocked into a tent and fell into it. Basil gave him an arm and a slight wind to help him get up quickly. A goblin had been lying down inside and yelled in alarm.

They continued on their way, the sound of pursuit growing louder behind them. They rounded a corner and ran straight into twenty goblins. The goblins stared at them in surprise and they bumped shoulders and ran around and through as quickly as possible.

"Rowkawr?" one of them called.

A goblin at the rear of the group stood in the way of Ryder, who lowered his shoulder and shoved him to the side. The group sped past them as the goblins pulled out weapons and took up pursuit.

Ryder looked over his shoulder. The goblins were right behind them, running furiously. "Someone give a signal!"

They passed another fire with goblins sitting at it, and Azarel waved his hand. The fire exploded, scorching the goblins and sending a huge flame high into the air.

Theo shook his head as they ran past. "Well, our rides may know where we are, but now so do all the bad guys."

They kept on, then suddenly Theo called, "Watch out! The lion!"

Everyone stopped and turned to look. The lion leaped toward Mizu. She dove to the left as Basil created a whirlwind to knock it slightly off course. The lion landed and lunged toward Mizu again. She rolled onto her feet, then leaped twenty feet into the air over the nearby tent.

The lion looked around confused, then turned and pounced toward Azarel. He dodged to the side, but his arm was slightly swiped by a claw.

Basil kept trying to make whirlwinds to hold it in place. "It's moving too quickly for me to stop it with wind!"

"We need to get the amulet around its neck!" Theo's eyes darted.

Amber pulled the amulet and chain out of her pocket. How could she possibly get it around its neck without getting killed?

"Toss it!" Basil yelled. Amber obediently threw it toward the lion and Basil focused all his might causing it to hover and open up into a perfect ring right in front of Azarel.

The lion turned and pounced toward Azarel again, jumping right through the enchanted amulet. Azarel tried dodging but instead fell to the ground under the huge weight of the enormous cat. The lion's giant claws ripped into him as it landed, then it stood and looked at Theo.

Azarel clutched his chest and yelled in pain.

Theo stared at the cat, then it turned and ran back the way it came. A moment later they heard the sound of goblins yelling as the cat ripped into them.

"That should hold them off for a minute." Theo ran toward Azarel and put his healing ring on his chest.

Azarel instantly relaxed, sinking to the ground. The wound was deep and would have killed him.

"I need time to heal this!" Theo called. "It's going to take three or four minutes. But we also need to keep moving."

Ryder picked Azarel up in his arms. "Good thing elves are so light." He laughed. "Run alongside me, Theo."

Six goblins suddenly emerged from the darkness behind them, swords and clubs raised. A knife landed in the throat of one of them from above. Mizu landed next to them. "Come on, then. Let's take care of these ones and move out."

Basil drew his glowing orange sword and darted toward them with inhuman speed, dodging the first blow and plunging his sword into a goblin's side before speeding toward the next.

Ryder and Theo trotted in the direction they were going before, Amber close behind. "The amulet!" she suddenly cried. "We left it on the lion!"

"Too late now," Theo called back. "Let it go, Amber. You got your necklace. That was most important, right?"

A goblin staggered toward Mizu, and she threw a knife, dropping it to the ground. Basil blocked a blow from another one and killed it quickly. Mizu ran over in large bounds and removed her throwing knives, wiping them off, and sheathing them before leaping after the others.

Basil battled the last one easily with his superhuman speed and then ran after Mizu. The sound of dozens more goblins in pursuit rang out behind them.

Then they saw five flying shapes heading where their signal had been, behind them.

"Everyone, come here!" Basil yelled. He sent a whirlwind up into the air, spinning as loudly and as fast as possible. The flying shapes changed course to their current location. Five griffins flapped down toward them.

Ryder brought Azarel to a griffin. "Theo, stay with him. Everyone else, mount up." They all clambered onto their steeds and lifted into the air. They watched the tents get smaller as they rose. They were going to make it!

But then, in the dawn light, a white shape appeared flying toward them from the center of the encampment. A woman, all in white, riding a pegasus.

Chapter 31

The Elementalists

WITH LONG, POWERFUL FLAPS, the five griffins with eleven riders flew away from the goblin camp. But it quickly became apparent that the griffins wouldn't outpace the pegasus.

"We need to get to Lugo!" Ryder yelled back to the others. The dwarf riders focused on the lights of the city in the distance.

Azarel startled awake, sitting between Theo and a dwarf. "What's going on?"

"You took a big blow. My ring is healing you. The white wizard is pursuing us, so we're trying to figure out what to do next." Theo kept his hand on Azarel's chest as they rode to finish the healing process.

Azarel reached into his side pouch and pulled out a flint and steel. He twisted to see the pursuing pegasus and struck a spark, instantly turning it into a fireball that floated in his hand. He then shot the fireball at the white horse.

At first the flame looked like it would connect but then fizzled out. Azarel's shoulders slumped. "Her powers are too great! Anyone else?"

Basil swiveled around backward and lifted his arms. A huge wind suddenly picked up from the south and blew into the pegasus, shoving it to the side like it would be blown off course. But an invisible force field came into being that blocked the massive wind from hitting the creature.

"Keep trying!" Ryder shouted. "Anything to slow it down. We need to reach the city!"

Out of nowhere, they all started feeling confused. Which way is Lugo? Is there just the pegasus or are there other flying creatures attacking from the sides? The griffins started veering off in different directions.

Amber was exhausted but grew alert when she felt warmth on her chest and all the others acting like they were under attack. "What's happening?" she shouted. "Keep flying toward the city!"

Some of the griffins swooped low—others went high. She glanced at the warm medallion around her neck. Her mind raced with possibilities.

"It's an illusion!" Amber cried. "Listen to me! Everyone, gather at the ground. We've got to stop flying and take her on. We're not going to get away by flying all over the place! We have to work together!"

Thankfully, the dwarves heard and guided their griffins to the ground. They landed and gathered in a circle, still fending off invisible foes.

"Whatever you're seeing, it's not real!" Amber called. "Her spell didn't affect me, and I don't see them. Ignore what you're seeing and focus on the wizard. She's our only real target."

The others struggled. It felt like dark flying creatures were about to attack on every side, but the friends listened to Amber, and sure enough, nothing actually touched them. The illusions flickered and became semi-translucent, like darting shadows. Only two dwarves continued to swipe at them.

"We need a plan. And fast!" Theo shouted.

But it was hard to think. The dark illusions continued to badger them, making it hard to focus. Soon enough, the pegasus landed on the field in front of them, and Laticia, the White Queen of Westerlye, dismounted with an evil grin.

"You think your paltry magic is enough to face me?" She shook her head and smirked. "I have two hundred years of experience, my dear children. Why would you even *think* of attacking me? Why not join me instead?"

It seemed so ridiculous to Amber, yet she looked around and saw the others pause—as if they were considering it! It must be a spell.

"Ignore her! There's nothing to join!" she shouted. "We can do this—we're the children of the prophecy."

The others shook their heads, like waking from a dream. Basil created a whirlwind on a collision course toward the queen. Azarel pulled out his flint and steel for another fireball. Meanwhile, Ryder felt the rocks below them and rippled the earth, creating a shock that would send her falling.

But she created a protective shield around herself, which blocked every attack. She walked toward them boldly. "It's not too late, children. I forgive your lack of knowledge. But this is your last chance. Join me or die."

Theo searched the area for responsive animals. A family of ferrets hid in a nearby tree, but what good could they do? The griffins were the only obvious choice for a powerful attack.

Their dwarf riders—still confused by the illusion attacks—stood on the ground with swords and axes swiping at the empty air.

The griffins rose as one and sped toward the wizard. But a massive thorn wall appeared in front of the queen, rising up from the ground a solid twenty-five feet. The griffins plunged into it and screeched wildly as the thorns ripped into their flesh. Theo fell to the ground, feeling their horrific pain.

Amber focused intently. The thorns parted, then formed a pathway to the wizard. She asked them to entwine the queen, but they resisted. She was far too formidable!

The wizard raised her wand—she glowed white, emanating authority. They were uncertain what sort of spell she'd cast, but whatever it was, it felt daunting even before it reached them.

Ryder in particular was awed by the White Queen's power. It was incredible. He shook his head. One day, if he survived this, he wanted to have power like that.

Basil put his hand on Theo's shoulder. "If you have a plan, now's the time."

Theo gritted his teeth. "Ryder, do you still have those handcuffs?"

Ryder nodded. "In my pocket."

"Ok. I've got an idea. Everyone hit her with all you've got. And. Ryder, toss those cuffs here."

All the kids focused the full extent of their powers on the wizard. Flames zoomed toward her. A water jet emerged from the ground and surrounded her. A small tornado spun in her direction. The earth erupted beneath her. And thorns entwined all around.

"You have no idea who you're attacking. That was your last chance!" Her protective force field blocked their attacks, and her eyes flared brilliantly. Then a shockwave emanated from her over the countryside and jarred them.

Instant terror filled their hearts, piercing them to their bones, and they fell to the ground. Everyone felt like running and hiding, crawling under a rock, disappearing forever. A stabbing sensation pierced their hearts and steadily grew into an even deeper pain.

"Nobody defies the White Queen and lives!" she shouted, the power pouring from her body in all directions.

All six youths writhed on the ground, as did the dwarves. The pain was odd—it felt very real yet didn't damage them physically. It was in their heads—an illusion of sorts—but nonetheless they suffered.

The White Queen shook her head in distaste. "You dare attack the most powerful wizard in all the world? My power now is a tiny sliver compared to what is to come. You foolish youths. Once I master the scepters at the pixie's tower, the whole world will bow down to me. You had the chance to join me. What a waste! Now . . . you must pay for your mistake."

The wizard was so focused, she didn't notice two ferrets leap from a nearby tree to grab the handcuffs from Theo. He held them loosely in his hand as he lay on the ground, struggling. His whole body throbbed as the pain streaked from his heart in all directions.

When the ferrets grabbed the cuffs, Theo nodded at them weakly. "We need you, my little friends."

The queen's voice boomed across the field: "Very soon your bodies will shut down, and soon after, death. Amber, you will come with me. The rest of you, it is a pity to have to kill you. Especially you, Ryder."

Ryder peered at her feebly. Why did she continue to single him out? What was it she saw in him?

The ferrets bounded across the field, handcuffs in their mouths, scrambling easily through the thornbushes and over the shaking ground.

The queen laughed evilly. Her power sent small rocks tumbling toward the youths. "Goodbye, young elementalists."

The ferrets dodged rocks as they rolled past and reached the queen. They quickly crawled up her legs and latched the cuffs onto her wrists.

Suddenly there was utter and complete silence.

The power emanating from her dimmed. She looked around confused, then noticed the cuffs on her hands.

At first, her eyes were furious. Then she laughed. It started as a little chuckle, then grew to a loud, sinister laugh that sent chills through their bodies. "You children are truly more resourceful than I'd thought. Know that I'll never underestimate you again. You win this time. You'd better be more prepared for the next encounter." She laughed again, then dashed toward her pegasus. She leaped on it in one graceful bound without using her hands and lifted into the air, heading back to the goblin camp.

They lay watching her in stunned silence. Was that really the end? They struggled to their feet. A dull energy coursed through their bodies. The memory of the pain. But they felt completely fine—and in some ways, even better than before.

Basil was the first to cheer. "Hooray! Theo, you did it! I knew you'd come up with something!" He ran over and gave his friend a hug.

Theo smiled. "Who'd have thought it would be so easy?"

"Easy?" Ryder shook his head and patted them on the backs. "Without those cuffs, we'd have surely died."

"It was all six of us that made the difference." Amber stood quietly, and they all turned to look at her serious expression.

"It's the prophecy. On our own, we couldn't do it. But together, we took on the most powerful wizard in the world."

She shook her head and gazed at the lights of Lugo in the early dawn. "I learned some of the queen's plan tonight. This fight was only one part of it. I don't understand what they're up to yet—but we have to stop it. I have a terrible feeling that we've won the battle, but the war has just begun."

The others looked at her in silence. "This could get far worse. I believe we need to stick together. I, for one, am planning on working against them. So, who's with me? Are you committed to seeing this through and making sure these wizards aren't successful?"

Basil and Ryder stepped toward her at once and said, "Yes." They turned to each other and nodded approvingly.

Theo stepped forward next. "Of course. Who'd have thought I'd get this far. Yes, I'm with you."

Azarel was next. "I am with you, as I committed back in Nocea. When I say yes, I mean yes." He gazed at the dwarves lying behind him and scrunched up his nose. "Even if it means riding with dwarves."

They all turned toward Mizu. She stood quietly a moment. "I was planning on heading home, to bring an update to my people." Amber's shoulders dropped, and Mizu continued. "However, I do believe fate has brought us together. I too commit to being a member of the six."

Kish walked toward them from further away. "I know ye not be speaking to me, lassie. But when ye be needing me in the future, ye'll be having my axe arm with you."

Amber smiled toward him. The elves' warning about dwarves and their lack of trustworthiness echoed in her mind. If only they could meet Kish. Trustworthy through and through.

The sun suddenly peeked at them from over the goblin camp, brightening the world around them. Amber realized some of the griffins were still stuck in thorns and asked the thornbush to loosen and let them go. Theo would have to heal them from the worst of the damage.

Amber sighed. "I'm so thankful for you friends. I thought I was captured forever back there. And there's a lot to think about, but honestly, right now, all I want is sleep."

Theo smiled. "Sounds like a plan. Let's get out of here before that wizard comes back!"

Azarel turned to Theo. "Speaking of the enemy, what's coleslaw?"

The humans laughed. Theo smirked. "I'll tell you on the way back. Let's ride together."

The friends headed back to the city. As they passed by thousands of dead goblins and two dead giants, the enormity of what they'd accomplished sunk in.

The triangular flags with griffins flapped in the breeze on the tall pinnacles of Lugo's castle. The sun beamed, creating a gorgeous sunrise that made their return feel almost magical.

A cheer went up from the city wall as they flew over, then landed in the courtyard inside.

A moment later, the General strode in with a huge smile as they wearily dismounted. "I take it all went well?"

Basil stood proudly with head held high. "We took on the most powerful wizard ever and won!"

"She's dead?"

"No. No. But we stopped her for now."

"I see." He turned to a few soldiers nearby. "Everyone is to continue their posts until all signs of the army are gone."

The soldiers stood at attention and said in unison, "Yes, General!"

"As for you . . ." The General turned to the youths. "I want to hear all about what you've learned, but . . ." He glanced at Amber's weary expression. "You look like you could use some rest first. Let's meet this afternoon in the planning room. You can get some sleep in the army barracks."

"Thank you, General," Theo said. "I could use some sleep, for sure."

Basil elbowed Theo in the ribs, "Hey. Wouldn't you say, that was the longest day of your life?"

They thought about it a moment. The day had started by freeing Crodor the Ancient from the enchantment. So much had transpired it was hard to remember all of it.

As Amber's mind traced back, she grew curious. "How did the dragons end up? They're obviously not fighting in the sky anymore."

The General shrugged. "From what I gather Crodor drew the blue one away. I assume it was to get it far from the fight."

"I hope he's ok."

The General smirked. "I'm certain we'll find out soon enough, when he comes back for his peanut butter reward."

The youths laughed. There was a lot left to sort out. First and foremost, the goblin army was still there across the plain.

But Basil's mind was elsewhere. "So . . . about that peanut butter reward—are you planning on giving it *all* to the dragon, or could you perhaps spare a bit for the *other* giant slayer?"

The General chuckled. "We may need to encourage more peanut farmers when this is all said and done. Yes, I'm certain we can spare some extra."

Amber gazed at him wearily and smiled. She hadn't seen Basil take down the giant, but she was sure he'd tell the story soon enough, complete with lots of embellishments.

Chapter 32

The Green Scepter

AMBER BLINKED HERSELF AWAKE. She was lying in a bed in a narrow room with twenty other bunk beds. Where was she? She sat up and looked to see if anyone else was in the room, but it was entirely empty.

She tried not to panic and remember what happened. In a flood, the entire day's events returned, all the way from recruiting the ancient dragon to taking on goblins at the city wall, imprisonment in a cave, and confronting the White Queen on the plain.

Where are the others? she wondered, then remembered the General's words. The planning room!

She dressed quickly and rushed out the door into the blinding afternoon light.

She'd slept a long time!

She looked around to get her bearings, then walked quickly over to the building where they'd planned their attack on the goblins the day before. Two soldiers stood guard outside and nodded at her as she approached the door and went inside.

The planning room was full of people—the General, soldiers, captains, monks, dwarves, elves, and all her friends. Some were standing and talking in groups, and many were seated around a large circular table.

Theo noticed her first. "You're up!" He stood. "Come! Come join us!"

She relaxed and took the seat he offered at the table. Next to Theo sat Chandler, Basil, and Ryder. Mizu and Azarel were at the other end of the table with Gratian and another older elf. Kish sat with another dwarf next to them. The General and two captains were at another side of the table. Other captains, some of the monks, and a few other dwarves stood around them.

The whole room grew quiet as she sat down.

"We were just comparing notes on the battle," Basil said cheerily. "I was so focused on stopping that giant, I didn't get to see much else."

"Can't wait to hear your side of the story, Amber," Mizu said. "Seems we all played a pretty important role. Are you ready to tell us what happened to you?"

Everyone's eyes turned toward her. "Well ... As you know, I was kidnapped by their leader." She tried remembering the details of their conversation, and everyone in the room hung on her every word. Chandler was good at asking her questions, probing for every detail. When she finally finished, there was silence in the room.

The General spoke first. "Thank you for your courage yesterday. We have no idea how to fight in a war against wizards, but you proved that age isn't the most important factor."

"There's more going on here than we know," Basil said. "Multiple prophecies. An ancient enemy. This would be a good time to have Sage back. You elves seem to know a thing or two about prophecies and such. Care to fill us in?"

"Yes. I do have more insight." Gratian sighed somberly. Amber recognized him from the older elves she'd met when she first arrived in Nocea. "The evil queen was our foe at the last Wizard War. It was all we could do to prevent her from succeeding in her evil plan, and we lost a great many elves in the process, including my uncle and my best friend." He looked sad.

"What were they trying to do?" Basil asked.

"Back then they had goblin orbs of great power. Goblin orbs use earth magic. They can be used to enlarge the effects of a spell, and then they shatter. They used the orbs to control the goblins and cast a great spell that killed many. They had a number of scepters. Each scepter is powerful on its own, but combined they are a far greater danger. But they didn't have all the scepters, because we had three, including the Green."

"What's that?" Theo perked up.

"It's a most precious scepter with a powerful green gemstone. It gives the person holding it power to see through time quite clearly, many minutes in advance—and for some, even prophetic visions much further out. It's a glimpse into the possible future. Anyone who holds it is nearly invincible, because they'll always know what's about to happen and act beforehand. It also gives the power to cast different types of spells—to connect with the hidden realm of spirits."

"Is that how you stopped the wizards back then?" Amber asked.

"It was using the Green, yes. But it was many things. A lot of people giving their lives."

"Where is the Green now?" Theo asked.

Gratian shook his head sadly. "We don't know. It was a time of chaos. One of our greatest mages of all time, Darius, wielded it to give a great many prophecies. He was particularly gifted at using the scepter to see far into the future, and his efforts nearly turned the course of the war. However, he died—we don't know how—and the scepter disappeared. Some say the evil wizards found it, and some say the dwarves took it." He glanced at the dwarves around the table with a vicious glare. The dwarves fidgeted nervously and glanced away.

The gold-tinted elf gazed at the ceiling for a moment in thought. "As I was saying, we aren't entirely certain what the wizards were trying to do, but we do know they marched a great goblin army, much like they appear to be doing here. We believe they had intended to gather many scepters together and that would somehow grant them the power they needed to perform a greater spell. We never knew exactly where they were headed."

"The Great Tower." Amber breathed. "She mentioned that was why they caused the phoenix to burn the field in my town. To scare the pixies away and reveal their tower. It sounds like it's an abundant source of mana."

"Ah!" Chandler smiled smugly. "That would prove my theory to be correct! An epicenter of mana. Perhaps the spell they want to cast relies on the location."

"Yes, that makes sense." The elf cocked his head. "We do have mention of such things in our lore, but no elf has seen this tower in my lifetime, and some wonder if it was an ancient thing that no longer exists."

"An ancient magical place! How come we've lost track of these things?" Theo scratched his scraggly hair.

"You humans lose your knowledge so quickly. Back in those days, you had many more mages. In fact, you had schools for mages, like we elves do." Gratian sighed. "You die so quickly that you seem to forget instantly. I do know the last great wars ended with the destruction of all your schools, as well as the death of a great many human mages. Only a few survived in all the land."

"Do you know anything about the other wizards who are involved?" Theo asked.

The elf slowly held up his fingers. "Along with the white queen, I believe at least one of the other mages we fought last night was present during the wars back in those days."

"There's at least one new one," Mizu looked down at the table somberly.

Gratian turned to her. "Tell us."

"My father, Maliko of Lorcaster. He turned to their side ten years ago." She spoke with her eyes downcast.

Amber's heart went out to Mizu. Her experience with elves so far was that they generally didn't express a lot of emotion, but she could see the elf's pain and sorrow clearly. "So sorry, Mizu."

The elves gave looks to each other—as if to say, we'll discuss this privately.

Theo broke the awkward moment. "So, what happened to the Green scepter? If it was so powerful, how did it go missing?"

Kish cleared his throat. "We may be knowing a thing or two about the Green."

The elves turned to him with icy stares as he continued gruffly. "Our people be having a story or two of it. The details may be rough, but this we do know. An elf did hold it during the great wars. And that elf did more in the battle than any other. The dwarves of those days be impressed by how he would stand in the one safe spot during an attack or tell his people when to fight and when to hide. He saved many."

He shifted in his seat. "But a crippling fear overtook them all, something even the Green couldn't stop, and the elf be killed. Before the evil wizards be taking it for themselves, one of our own be claiming it. That be how us dwarves survived the worst of the attacks at the end."

Gratian's eyes flashed. "Where is it now?"

"That I not be knowing." Kish shook his head. "Our stories say Fallon the Great took it across the sea to build treaties with other tribes and seek greater power still. We never heard since what came of it."

"Indeed," Gratian replied stiffly. "This is yet another example of why we elves never trust you dwarves. And why we've never worked together since those days. Your thirst for treasure outweighs your morals."

There was an awkward silence. Kish opened and closed his mouth a couple of times. "But . . ."

Gratian waited with cocked head. Then he gave a slight scoffing laugh. "I thought so."

Amber suddenly stood. "No!" All eyes turned on her, and she instantly felt tiny. Her cheeks turned red.

She blinked a few times and straightened. "I've met the dwarves. And I've met the elves. You're both good. Kish saved me and cared for me. And you elves guided my mission. And you both came to fight with us when we called on you."

As the room remained silent, she gathered courage. "I don't know about your past, but that was a long time ago, and different people. Not the people I see before me today."

Gratian raised his eyebrows. "This spoken from a human, and a young one at that. What would you know of the patterns we've seen in these people throughout the ages?"

Kish cleared his throat. "She's right."

Everyone turned to look at him, and he turned to the elf with pleading eyes. "You be speaking of different dwarves from a different age. But let's be talking about you and me. We be fighting together yesterday. That be what matters—and the greater good."

The elf looked thoughtful. "Indeed."

"If what the lassie says be true, the war be far from over. We can't be letting our differences keep us from working together." The dwarf smiled feebly—his normal bold bravado gone.

Dozens of people in the room held their breaths. Gratian glanced at the elves next to him, then stood. "What you say rings with truth. We shall never forget what you dwarves are like. But perhaps it is time to let go of this grudge we've held against one another for so long."

Kish stood, and the two stared at each other for a moment. Gratian gave a slight nod and smiled. Kish grinned and gave a little laugh. The tension in the room relaxed, as an unseen burden suddenly lifted.

Amber felt tears well up. She'd spent time with both people and knew there was plenty of good in both.

After that, there was a lightness in the room. They spent the rest of the afternoon talking with one another around the tables. Each person's stories sounded more unbelievable than the last. Basil, as usual, talked with great detail and energy, jumping up and down with grand hand gestures. The way he described his attack on the giant, he may as well have been a bolt of lightning, zipping through the air and striking straight to the heart. Although he really could somewhat fly, and his speed was indeed incredible.

Amber was delighted to hear that while she slept, Crodor had visited the peanut butter maker in good spirits and with very few injuries and made off with dozens of jars back to his home. He'd battled the blue dragon all through the night, until it suddenly stopped and flew away in the morning, soon after they'd returned back to the city.

The General listened to many of the stories, then focused on planning the city's defenses with the captains and monks. The uncertainty of the future was obvious. They may not have the help from the elementalists the next time—they would need to be as prepared as possible for anything.

After a couple of hours, it was clear the youths, elves, and dwarves weren't needed in the room anymore. Basil turned to Amber. "Well, what's next? You said we need to keep working on things, but what should we do?"

"I don't know. Without Sage guiding us, it's hard to say."

Theo nodded. "I'm with you, but can it be something less dangerous this time? Like no more large, scary creatures?"

Basil laughed. "Come on, fancy pants. You know that'll never happen."

"I can always hope, right?" Theo shrugged. "But with our current track record, I bet it will be."

Basil ran his hands through his long curls. "Well, we don't have a lot to go on. Unless anyone has ideas. Maybe we should stay here and help with the city's defenses? Or perhaps we can keep trying to find creatures to release from the spell?"

An old familiar voice came from the doorway. "That won't be necessary."

They turned and saw a short wizard wearing a billowy yellow shirt and leaning on a long staff.

"Sage!" Amber jumped to her feet. "Finally!"

"Yes. Yes." Sage waved at her dismissively. "Of course. Of course."

The room grew quiet. Even those who didn't know the wizard could sense he was somehow important.

"Many things I have learned. And many things are left to do." He gazed around the room slowly and grandly. "I fear you will be needed for an even greater challenge than what you have faced so far. In fact, I believe it will be the only possible way of preventing the worst from happening."

Everyone in the room was silent, waiting expectantly on his next words. The old wizard gave a quirky smile, then pointed. "You must go to the sea. Travel deep into the sea. And you must find the Kraken."

"I knew it!" Theo pointed at the wizard energetically.

Basil elbowed him and raised his eyebrows playfully. "Told you so."

Theo looked around at the five others and sighed. "Ok. You know I'm in. But maybe before we go off looking for the next most dangerous creature I could ever imagine, perhaps we could . . . I don't know . . . hang out and read a few books?"

Epilogue

A GRUFF-LOOKING MIDDLE-AGED MAN approached Laticia. "We found another one, over in Burmere." He played with a golden scepter, running his thick fingers over the orange gem in its top.

"That makes five," the pale queen responded. "Excellent. We're much closer now. What does this one do?"

The man lifted the scepter and peered at it curiously. "Not sure, really. I think it can heal things, from what they were using it for. Haven't tried it, though."

"Like wounds?"

"Yeah, and also stuff. Like rips and cracks. Not sure. You'll have to do your thing to figure it out."

"Of course I will." She waved him off and turned to a piece of parchment in front of her.

He stared down at his hands. "I see you didn't win the battle against Lugo."

"A minor setback." She gave him a cold look. "But all still lines up according to our greater plan. It brought out the six young elementalists that I've been waiting for all these years. One young girl has brought them together, along with exposing two scepters. She's playing directly into our hands."

"Wonderful."

"Yes. Pity she didn't take my offer."

"You talked with her?"

"Of course. It was child's play removing her from the battle."

"What's our next plan? Do you want more goblins?"

"No need. Now that we have two of their orbs, and we've exposed the six, the goblins' primary purpose is through. Let's disperse them across the land to attack everyone they come across. That way they won't be a burden to us, but also keep the elementalists thinking they're still a threat. They'll continue trying to fulfill their prophecy."

"Yes, my queen," the man said with another bow. "And what about all the other creatures we've been gathering?"

"Well, we can't lose them all, now can we?" She tapped on the table in thought. "Send them back to the castle. I don't know that we'll need more than our flying steeds to get around at this point, but you never know."

"And our next plan of attack—or are we waiting?"

"A bit of both. We'll need to find that tower. It sounds like Caster has had a setback—apparently the pixies are suddenly powerful foes again, which means they've probably reached their tower. I'd hoped they wouldn't, but perhaps we can use that to find them more easily. I may send you to help him. But eventually we'll need to get to the sea. The elementalists may be headed that way."

He fumbled with the scepter, then peered at her thoughtfully. "To find the Green?"

"Yes. The girl revealed that they have Sage on their side, who knows a thing or two. But I'm not worried about that old-timer. We're not going to lose this time. No, this time we're prepared."

She laughed evilly. "They've got a suggestion stone. Not only can we turn their minds from afar, we can find them anywhere whenever they use it. And we have time—I'm certain they won't leave for many months. And by then, we'll be ready. They won't surprise me again. You can count on that."

About the Authors

Ephie (dad) has been writing his whole life. Inspired by his sixth-grade teacher to write a story every week, he enrolled in the writing program at his undergrad and has been writing ever since. He loves the outdoors, music, and opportunities to tell stories. He lives in beautiful Bozeman, Montana, where he works in software development and is active in various community groups.

Celia (daughter) is an avid book lover and packs a novel with her wherever she goes. She developed the book series idea at age nine inspired by a 3rd grade writing assignment. She was born in Vancouver, Canada where her first two syllable word was "hockey"! She, along with her brother, is being raised in the mountains of Montana, where she enjoys art projects, performance art, and her dragon figurine collection.

Acknowledgments

First and foremost, we are indebted to you, our readers. You are what drives us to keep creating! We love hearing from you, and plenty of the ideas in this book have come about because of suggestions from our readers.

This book was produced amidst home isolation during a global pandemic, which makes us so thankful for those who reached out in one form or another to encourage our efforts. We are so appreciative of the support of Michelle Risho, who knows and loves us both so well. We also appreciate Joshua Risho's ideas and inspirations.

Like book 1, this book was produced with a crowdfunding platform, which allowed us to work with the editor and artists of our choice. That goes a long way to encouraging us, and we are so grateful for all you folks who supported us that way. It really helps get over the initial hump.

In particular, we'd like to give a special thanks Sally Laing-Malcolmson, Jordan Campbell, Rebecca Holman, Jonathan Cole, Jason Moore and Frank Beaty.

A few folks went above and beyond supporting us, and we wanted to say a huge thanks to Ray & Susie Risho, Patti & Ron Harwood, Jeff & Melissa Pernell, and Ivan & Angie Ting.

We are grateful for the amazing creativity of our cover artist, Stephan Martiniere, who took an idea and went further with it. Nice work!

It has been such a pleasure to work with our inside illustrator, Olena Bushana. She's not only a great artist who can read our minds, she has an amazing attitude, even when we have to go back to the drawing board ten times! (Sorry, Olena.)

And this book would not be anywhere near the quality it is without the developmental/line editing of Ann Castro. Unlike many editors, Ann doesn't just notice that missing comma, she lets us know when a scene is going long or is missing that extra oomph. We rewrote entire chapters at her encouragement. Thank you, Ann.

We appreciate you readers so much. This book exists because of you! Please do reach out to us! We are always eager to hear from you.

Author's Note

We were able to publish this book in the way we wanted by self-publishing. During crowdfunding, people were given the option to pick character names as a way of backing the project. For *Crodor the Ancient*, our new and better name is Gratian the elf.

Thanks for reading! Please add a short review on Amazon or Goodreads, and let us know what you thought.

To keep up with our progress on the next books in the series, visit theelementalists.net. Coming soon: Book 3 of *The Elementalists series – Secret of the Kraken*.

Till the next adventure!
Ephie & Celia Risho

Don't miss the next exciting adventure in
THE ELEMENTALISTS Series

SECRET OF THE KRAKEN

Chapter 1 - The Map of the Dwarf

THE SUN SHONE THROUGH THE WINDOW, warming Amber's back as she sat at a table, focused on her project. The smell of salt water and fish hung in the air, but she didn't notice. She held up an intricate wooden figurine of a castle with an emblem of a griffin and smiled.

"Alright, Theo, I think I've got it. Come take a look."

Theo sat up on the worn yellow couch nearby where he'd been reading a dwarven history book. "Alright! This is so exciting." He stood, sending a black-and-white cat to the ground unhappily, and peered at the small castle.

"May I?" He held his hand out and Amber handed him the piece. It was beautiful—a work of art. "And you're sure it's going to stay on the board, even if it's tilted?"

"Watch." Amber placed the castle onto the square of a checkered board. Each checkered spot had a perfectly placed magnet at its center and one inside each figurine. The castle stuck exactly where Amber put it. She tilted the board sideways, and the castle stayed put.

"Huzzah!" Theo clapped his hands. "That will definitely work on a sea voyage. Oh, Amber, thank you! This is great! And it folds up?"

"Of course." She folded the board, and it snapped shut with magnets holding it in place.

Theo gazed with respect at the board and the thirty-two pieces sitting next to it. Each piece was intricate and beautiful, looking as if it had been crafted naturally from the tree. And every board square had a different pattern—many so detailed, they were like works of art themselves.

"You say you saw patterns like this in Nocea? I vaguely remember that, but I guess I had a lot of other things on my mind."

"Yes. The elves inspired me."

"Well, that was the last thing for me. We can get on that ship now." Theo winked at her.

She laughed. "Well, the captain did say the worst of winter is over. But we still don't know exactly where to go. Do you really think we should?"

Theo straightened his sleeves, then dusted off his frilly white shirt. "No. Of course not. It does feel weird just sitting around though. I was getting used to working under pressure. It's been seven months since Sage got us rolling on this new adventure—and here we are killing time."

Amber shrugged. "I'm learning a lot, though." She looked at some ornate chairs she'd made that would be picked up shortly, a project for some nobleman or other.

"Easy for you to say. I guess I'm learning a lot about dwarves, but I haven't had anyone come for animal help in almost a week!"

"Well. You never know when someone will just . . . show up."

As if on cue, a blast of cold blew into the room as the door opened. Basil walked in, shut the door, and brushed snow off his cloak before draping it on a coat rack. "Good news!" He smiled and clomped inside.

"Hey, blockhead! Take those big snowy boots off." Theo pointed at the snow Basil was tracking inside. "The rest of us are wearing socks."

Basil continued smiling as he took his boots off. "Mizu found something."

"Seriously?" Amber stood so abruptly she knocked her knee on the table and winced.

"Yeah." Basil kicked his boots to the side of the door and walked in. "It's an old, rusted tube with dwarf writing on it. We tried opening it, but it was sealed shut."

"Where are the others now?" Theo peered out the dingy window to the snow-filled street.

"We just landed at the docks, and I ran right over. I'm sure they'll be here soon."

"Here they come!" Theo shouted. Ryder, Azarel, and Mizu hurried through the deep, falling snow down the narrow street.

Theo almost turned but paused. Was someone following after them? He waited at the window a moment as his friends arrived at their small rental house. Behind them, a tall man with a hood obscuring most of his face trudged through the snow.

The man walked with his head down headed straight toward them, but then glanced up and saw Theo watching him. He quickly pulled his hood down further and changed course.

The door banged open, bringing in a gust of wind that chilled the room. "We've got something!" Ryder grinned and held up a leather tube with metal ends, dark with rust and grime. "How are your dwarf reading skills?"

Theo laughed. "Still not great. But enough to get an idea."

Ryder handed him the tube, and Theo peered at the sides. Faint dwarven writing was imprinted on the leather. "Well, I'm positive this word is map." He pointed at the last word. "I do know that word, but it's awfully faint and scratched up."

"This has got to be it!" Ryder beamed.

"You couldn't open it?" Theo gave one of the ends a little twist.

"No. Completely sealed shut. And we don't want to damage whatever's inside. A map! That would be super helpful."

Azarel quietly walked over and held his hand out. "Perhaps I can try."

Theo gave him the tube. Azarel held the end and focused, causing the metal to glow slightly.

"Careful!" Ryder said. "We don't want to burn whatever's inside."

Azarel gave him an annoyed look and focused more, then tried twisting it. Nothing happened, so he flipped it and tried the other side. Again, the metal glowed. He twisted it harder. "It moved!" Azarel looked up at Ryder with a smug smile and gave it another try. This time they all heard the tiny scraping sound as it opened slightly. A few more attempts and the cap loosened more.

Azarel walked over to the table—as the others gathered around, holding their breaths. He twisted the tube a few more times, and the cap came off gently, revealing a rolled parchment. He carefully turned the tube upside down and unrolled the map onto the table ever so slowly, making sure not to damage it. The paper was old but thick, and still had life left in it.

They gasped. It was a map with dwarven writing and markings scattered all over it. Eight different dwarven cities were prominently marked, from far north all the way south past the great sea and many islands.

They stared at it quietly for a while, then Basil asked, "Do you think it belonged to Fallon the Great?"

"Maybe." Theo peered at the writing. "I thought I was learning enough of the language to help with this stuff, but I can't understand half of this."

Then his eyes twinkled with excitement. "Ah. Here we go. We know from Kish that Fallon was uniting all the dwarven kingdoms for a long ways, and this map looks like it's showing at least that much. And these other highlighted spots are definitely places of interest. I can't make out why."

He pointed to a spot with larger words. "But this place over here . . . Well, this proves Sage right, once again. Fallon the Great wasn't just uniting the dwarf kingdoms. This spot is where he was headed when he disappeared. I don't know a lot of dwarven words, but this one I made sure to learn—the alleged lair of the Kraken."

There was a slight scraping sound by the window and Theo whipped his head to look. There was no one there, but something seemed odd about the way the snow was falling.

"What is it?" Basil turned.

"I think someone is following us."

"What?" Basil dashed to the door and opened it, peering around to see what was in front of the window without getting his socked feet in the snow. "There are tracks in the snow. Someone was there at the window watching us. If I didn't know better, I'd say they're still there. But that's not possible."

"What do you mean?" Theo asked.

"The snow is falling weird there. Almost as if someone is standing there invisible—" Basil suddenly dashed out into the snow toward the window.

The tracks by the window abruptly moved, and new tracks appeared running down the street. Basil focused his power over the air and used his super speed to gain on the moving tracks. The tracks zigzagged but Basil was much quicker, closing the gap between them.

He was about ready to jump on the invisible person when he stubbed his toe on a rock.

"Ow!" He paused and held his toe a moment, then limped and ran after the tracks again. The tracks ran around a corner. Basil dashed and suddenly felt his entire body lock up. His eyes grew wide, and he fell solidly into a foot of snow like a felled tree.

He had the sense to use the last of his energy to twist his body so he'd fall looking up the street. A cloaked person stood twenty feet away with an arm pointed toward him. Another cloaked person suddenly appeared out of thin air next to the other one. They watched Basil for a moment, then turned and ran down the street together.

Still unable to move, Basil lay deep in the snow as thick flakes continued to fall and cover him. He sighed when he heard the sound of footsteps running toward him.

Ryder propped him up and looked him over. "Are you ok?"

Basil croaked words out without moving his lips. "Two o' the' . . ."

"Two of what?"

"They 'ent that 'ay."

"What?" Ryder looked around, confused.

"Two 'en in cloaks." Basil grew frustrated.

"Two men?"

"Yech!"

Ryder crouched down and put his hand through a foot of snow onto the ground. The snow made it difficult to sense vibrations. He could sense that most people in the small port town were in their homes or down at the docks—but he also felt the vibrations of two people running a few hundred yards away.

"Yes. I sense them. But I can't leave you here. They're too far away for me anyway. Come on." He reached under Basil's armpits and lifted. "Ugh. You're heavy! Can you help at all?"

"Ngo. Can't ngoove."

"Can't move. I get it. Ok." Ryder crouched lower and tried again. He struggled until Azarel showed up, and the two of them managed to get Basil onto Ryder's shoulders. They slowly walked through the deep snow till they saw Amber watching them through the window.

The door opened and Amber's eyes grew wide, then twitched to gaze at the street behind them. She held a bow and notched arrow in her other hand. She stared at them a moment. "Is he ok? Where's Mizu?"

"Not with us." Ryder twisted to fit Basil through the door without banging his head and set him down on the couch. "Theo, can you use your ring to help him?"

Theo stood up from the table and absentmindedly placed his hand on Basil, keeping one eye on the map in thought. "What was it? What happened?"

Basil felt his tongue come unglued and breathed a sigh of relief. "An invisible man. And another one who froze me. They were definitely watching us from the window. Has anyone sensed they were being followed before?"

Everyone shook their heads. Theo looked back toward the window. "There was someone following you back from the docks. I saw him and thought he looked a bit different than the rest of the town. I couldn't place it, but maybe it was his clothing. Like a different style jacket and cloak. Not from around here."

Ryder went to the window to stand watch. "Do you think they want the map?"

"That makes sense." Theo moved his hand down Basil's body, loosening it a little at a time. "Since they suddenly showed up and took an interest in us—right when we found it. Did Sage give anyone clues about it?"

None of them had more insight, so they went back to the map to study it again, taking turns watching out the window. Theo pulled out a dictionary of dwarven words and studied the map, flipping back and forth between the two. After half an hour, Mizu showed up. The small, blue elf shook inches of snow off her cloak and hung it up.

"What did you find?" Azarel held his hands up and warmed the air around Mizu.

She gave a silent nod of thanks. "I followed their tracks. They went through the town, then merged with the tracks at the docks. They were very clearly trying to disguise where they were headed. I followed some of the tracks at the docks. I tried three different sets, and ... well ... It's too hard to know. Maybe they got on a boat. I lost them."

"Thanks for trying."

She peered over Theo's shoulder. "Any new things from the map?"

Theo smiled. "Yes. I think I know what it's about."

"Really?" Basil looked at the parchment curiously.

"This map most definitely belonged to Fallon the Great, or at least one of his crew members. It shows notes from their previous journeys as well—where they were planning to go before meeting the Kraken. This southern dwarf city, here, is called Luxorio. It's close to what Fallon surmised was the Kraken's lair. And it's clear they had plans to stop at different islands and spots on the way."

"What are the different notes?"

Theo furrowed his brow. "It's not entirely clear to me. These ones with words are definitely dwarf cities. As for the other notes, I need help reading them. But one thing is certain, this small island is where they thought the Kraken could be found."

"Wow." Basil gazed out the window. "Do you think we should go straight there?"

Theo shook his head. "I don't think so. I'll need to find a dwarf library. My little dictionary can only help so much. My guess is these other islands and stops are all significant for some reason or other."

They all stared at the map. Ryder pulled out his enchanted rock and grew thoughtful. "Well, without Sage here, we can't know what to do with this map, since this is his mission and all. Rather than guessing what to do next, let's do something useful. The enemy is still sending goblins everywhere, and we can do something to stop it. The people of Arendon need our help. Lugo's army, however much it's growing, isn't big enough to protect everyone yet."

He gained energy. "You've all been cooped up here in this quiet town for months now. I'm the only one getting around the countryside, and I see it. Things aren't safe anymore. I say we get to the source of the issue. The six of us should head to the enemy fortress to sneak attack the other wizards."

Basil shook his head. "We left Lugo when Sage said our work there was done, remember? He said this is more important."

Ryder frowned. "But Sage isn't here! I'm holding the rock, and I can see that. It's a weak plan to make any assumptions based on an old dwarf map found at the bottom of the sea."

"Is it?" Basil stood and put his fists on his hips. "Or is it exactly what Sage was hoping we'd find?"

Ryder stood and folded his arms. Basil had grown a few inches over the last months, and they almost stood eye to eye. They stared at each other a moment, then Ryder turned. "Here, Theo, take the rock. See if you can figure out more."

Theo reached his hand out and took it, then his eyes brightened. "Let's go through what we know. Sage thinks the Green scepter is what we need to actually defeat the wizards. That spell he cast, to lead us to it, led us here, to the great sea, right? Now we've finally found this map. This has to be what will lead us to the Green. Think about it. The scepter was last seen with Fallon the Great, and he was on a journey to the Kraken. I think we should head south toward the first dwarven city on the map. Kirkengold. It's only a few weeks away."

Ryder took the stone back and thought for a moment. "You make a good point—*if* the Green will actually help us defeat those wizards. But why bother going to dwarf cities at all? You say the Kraken's location is marked on the map. Why not go straight there? Isn't that what Sage thought we should do in the first place?"

"Sort of." Theo shook his head. "If the Kraken really does have the scepter, from what I've read about the creature, it won't just give it to us. I think there are clues on this map that we need to figure out. And look. Kirkengold is practically on the way. Let's go there first and see what more we can learn."

The others nodded, and Ryder shrugged, putting the stone back in his pocket. "I can live with that. First, the dwarf city, and then the Kraken."

"Kirkengold." Basil studied the island on the map for a few moments. "Well, friends, it's been a long time coming—and Sage and Kish may not be here to help anymore. But it's finally time to pack our bags and find some sunken treasure."

Made in the USA
Monee, IL
08 April 2024